i

LABYRINTH

LABYRINTH

THOMAS WISEMAN

JONATHAN CAPE
LONDON

First published 1991
© Thomas Wiseman 1991
Jonathan Cape, 20 Vauxhall Bridge Road, London SW1V 2SA

Thomas Wiseman has asserted his right
under the Copyright, Designs and Patents Act, 1988
to be identified as the author of this work

A CIP catalogue record for this book
is available from the British Library

ISBN 0–224–03091–4

Printed in Great Britain by
Mackays of Chatham PLC, Chatham, Kent

AUTHOR'S NOTE

Purity is a notion for monks and fakirs ... As for me, I have dirtied my hands ... I have plunged them in the shit, and in blood ... Do you imagine that one can govern innocently?

Hoederer in *Les Mains Sales* by Jean-Paul Sartre

The terrain of the political thriller is that grey area of public life where things are done that cannot be seen to be done. From time to time we get a look into this world, by virtue of a Watergate, an 'Irangate', leaks and scandals, kidnappings and assassinations, and then we discover a little, a very little, of what is done by those who govern us, when they believe themselves unseen. The author of the political thriller becomes a conscientious collector of such material and learns about the systems, the methodologies, the double-standards, the dirty tricks of the game. He is greatly helped when someone like Alexandre de Marenches, former head of French foreign intelligence, in retirement speaks freely, and lets us in on the 'secrets of princes'. From these and other sources he may stumble upon, the author of the political thriller draws his material. But he is not a journalist, he is not after documentary evidence *per se*. The novelist deals in what sounds right to his ear. He borrows from real life what he can, pieces together the rest. So he creates a fiction which in this context might be described as a way of being imaginative with the truth, as opposed to economical. But it *is* fiction (however close it may come to the 'truth') and the reader of this book should not be tempted to think that the man who in my story serves as Vice-president of the United States under Reagan, and very badly wants to be President, is meant to depict the Vice-president who became President. In any case, he is only a minor (if pivotal) character in my tale. If I have ventured into those areas where things can't be seen to be done, part of my purpose has been to show the sorts of things that *are* done, but that is not to say that these particular events happened.

T.W.

ONE

I⟨T WAS THE⟩ year the American tourists had stopped coming to France, because of all the terrorist scares; a Friday in mid-November. Heller was waiting by the baggage carousel, watching a green metal trunk going round and round unclaimed, while other baggage tumbling out of the chute was quickly gathered up and carried away. People were jumpy, there was a mood of free-floating anxiety that the presence of all those gendarmes with submachine-guns and bullet-proof vests increased rather than alleviated.

Those passengers still waiting for their bags were uneasily watching the green metal trunk: dented, rusting in parts, with a brand new combination number padlock that seemed too expensive for such a battered old trunk. The many labels on this trunk were covered with indecipherable writing. Where the hell was the owner? Why wasn't he claiming it?

OK, so this was the *psychose* that they talked about in France as undermining the nation's fundamental sense of security. There had been carnage in the streets of Paris, a bomb had gone off outside a popular department store, leaving eight dead, many others maimed; another device had been found in the metro and removed just in time – could have caused appalling havoc had it gone off in the confined space of a packed subway train carriage. A bomb had exploded in the Pub Renault on the Champs-Elysées, killing two. Another in the Préfecture de police. In a café at La

I

Défense. No place was safe and everybody was a target. That was the message these terrorists wanted to get across, and they were succeeding. They were succeeding.

Heller could feel the apprehension coming from the other passengers watching that damned trunk go round. They were mesmerised by it. He was beginning to feel uneasy himself. The feeling of something wrong was very quickly passed on from person to person.

'How you Fred?'

The flat voice of Bill Gibson. It would probably have sounded as flat if the setting of their unexpected encounter had been the middle of the Sahara desert. Life's peculiar coincidences, the twists and turns of fate never held any surprise for Bill. He was an old hand at arranging fate's twists and turns, so why should he be surprised by them? A large round – yes, rounder than ever, Heller noted – sombre-faced man in a big overcoat, a good Crombie coat but now showing long-term signs of wear and tear, as Bill was himself.

'Bill! What you doing here?'

'Waiting for my bag! What's it look as though I'm doing?'

'What brings you to Paris?'

'I have this project . . .'

'Yes?'

Heller remembered some of Bill's projects of long ago. Bill loved creating impenetrable mazes, they were his own special form of creativity, expressing the tortuousness of the man, his tricky, devious and elegant mind; yes, his ploys and stratagems had had elegance, he had been one of the best in his field. Heller had learned from him.

He remembered the first of Bill's seminars he'd attended – when was that? Back in the fifties. Bill had enunciated the basis of his credo. That camouflage – i.e. deception – was the first biological rule of survival in nature. It was Bill's rationale for much of what he did. Heller remembered Bill's introducing him to the sayings of Sun Tzu, who all those centuries ago had set out the principles of their trade: that you need not conquer foreign lands

2

to lord over men, you conquered their souls, you mastered their psychology. Once you knew his psyche, you had the man. And once you had the man, his territory fell to you as well. It wasn't necessary to fight conventional battles and win victories by force of arms. The victory could be won secretly by other means.

'So what's it you're up to, Bill?' Heller asked.

'Well, I'll tell you,' Bill murmured confidentially. 'My project is to eat my way across France. Plan to sample the fare at a dozen or so three-star rest'rants from Paris, down through the centre, and then along the Côte d'Azur . . .'

'That's quite a project. You need to go into training in preparation for something like that.'

'Oh, I already got started – had to go out of the country for a few days on business, but I got started on Paris.'

'Any discoveries?'

'Lucas-Carton.'

'Grandiose eating, that. With prices to match.'

'What the hell! Can't take it with you. What did the fellow say? I have more provisions for the road than I have road left to take. What have I got: four, maybe five years? At the most. Can't expect more at my time of life, amount I've drunk. And the other things, and the other things. Huh? Try the duck liver millefeuille. An insidious taste . . .' He gave his sardonic chuckle. 'Covert stuff. Creeps up on your taste buds before you notice. Those mean little slivers of celery? And apple. I'd give him twelve out of twenty. Gault and Millau give 19.5 but they're more generous than me and better motivated I guess.'

And that was all it amounted to, the airport meeting, Heller told the special prosecutor: nothing else was talked about, except that Heller had made some reference to Charles Decourten's recent appointment as Minister of National Safety in the Chirac government, and Bill had said he didn't think that Charles was 'up to it'. Bill had never been known for his hagiolatry of politicians and public figures; a rather substantial number of them, in his view, 'were not up to it', so it came as no great surprise that Charles Decourten should be found lacking too. 'Charles . . . well,

3

I've known him a hell of a long time, like you have, maybe even longer than you, and Charles ... he's a lightweight, that's what he is and that's what he's always been ...'

After the pronouncement of this verdict, Bill's bags had arrived, and he'd gone off, saying something about, 'May run into each other someplace – at one of those rest'rants, huh?' Heller had considered this unlikely. But that same day, waiting to see Charles Decourten at the Ministère de la Sûreté Nationale, early for his appointment, he had seen Bill leaving and they had exchanged a few words. Bill had mentioned nothing at the airport about having an appointment to see Charles. Which of course fitted with Bill's almost fetishistic secretiveness in matters large and small. It was strange that a busy minister in the French government should have found the time to see Bill, who had been put out to grass by the powers that be at Langley seven years ago. And then, on the Sunday evening Heller had run into Bill for the third time, on this occasion at La Coupole.

'Are you following me, or am I following you?' Heller had asked him, stopping at his table. And after chatting a couple of minutes Heller had said, 'Don't want to keep running into each other. Let's have dinner one evening instead. When are you free?'

'I'm free Tuesday,' Bill had said after consulting a typed itinerary that he took out of his pocket.

'Tuesday's good for me, too. Where d'you want to go?'

'Let's make it Lipp. They're keeping a table for me.'

'Nine o'clock?'

'Make it quarter to. Nine's when they start to get frantic.'

Heller sat on the terrace of the Brasserie Lipp, under the old sign with the fading gold-leaf lettering inscribed on black glass. It was half past eight. Being early gave him a chance to check out a place, establish where the fire exits were, what the 'feel' of the room was, who was there ...

To look at, Fred Heller was a man of undeniable presence,

4

though a little dated perhaps, past his prime – one of the best and the brightest of the America of twenty years ago was the impression he gave. He was tall and still quite good-looking in a conventional sort of way. His formerly fair hair if now mostly grey was handsomely grey, short, and well cut. The haircut of a certain class. The suit he wore was dark blue and sober. The tie was blue with orange stripes. The shoes were handmade in Jermyn Street, London. It might have been concluded from his appearance that he was in one of the liberal professions, an expert of some sort, a person possessing special skills – exactly what these were it would have been harder to say. To Fred Heller there were aspects of the State Department that weren't in accord with the sobriety of his manner, the conventionality of his suit, the correctness of his haircut, his air of liberality: the fact, for instance, that he had with him in Paris two handarms, a Smith & Wesson 357 magnum revolver and a 9mm Browning automatic.

He was not, however, armed at present, as he sat sipping white wine. He brought a gun only if he had reason to expect trouble. To resort to the use of arms was hardly appropriate for a special adviser to the Secretary of State, though at times it could be considered a continuation of diplomacy by other means.

Bill Gibson arrived, lumberingly, a few minutes late and sat down. Heller found himself looking at an ordnance map of broken capillaries, with dense conglomerations around the jowls, the nose, the cheekbones, the whole face the vivid red of madder root. Bill said he'd have a vodka martini.

Having given his order, he heaved himself to his feet, with some effort.

'Have our drinks inside,' he said. 'Keep an eye on 'em. See they don't give my table away. You can't trust the French!' It was said kiddingly, but meant.

Lipp was filling up fast; already some of the less than charismatic personalities extruded by the revolving door were being offered second-best tables upstairs. Others were given the option of a table in the bar section, still well within earshot of the renowned Lipp buzz, which reaches its climax at around nine and then continues to convey an unrelenting sense of expectancy for the rest of the evening.

Bill Gibson and Fred Heller were installed in Lipp's inner room, beyond the long zinc bar, where the buzz, for those with the ear for such distinctions, was reputed to have a more exclusive pitch, due to the fact that this was where Lipp's most notable customers were seated.

Heller accepted a menu from the head-waiter, and while glancing down it, asked:

'So, is it working out, Bill?'

'What are you talking about? What is in your devious little mind, Heller? Hah-hah!' Alcohol-propelled, Bill's resentments tended to surface in the form of teasing insults.

'Just had the feeling, knowing you, that you must be up to something. And then when I saw you at the Ministry, coming out of Charles's office, I said ah-huh!' It was a feeble attempt to flatter the old guy.

'I'm here as a private citizen,' Bill snapped back. 'Nothing else.' His irascibility, his little outbursts of rudeness, had always been characteristic of him, and now he could claim for himself the additional privileges and excuses that went with age.

'I heard that you do a little freelancing from time to time, to keep your hand in.'

The menu, limited though it was, appeared to be presenting Bill with a problem of choice. Perhaps Lipp's rather basic dishes didn't inspire him in his current phase of gastronomic awareness.

'There ... things I know ... that I've learned, remember I learned a thing or two in the course of my fifty years in this trade, and there some individuals, some pretty high-placed individuals, I can tell you, who do me the honour of seeking my opinions on matters that they know I have knowledge of, see ...'

There was a strong sense of grievance coming through from Bill as he spoke.

In this square rear room, wherever you were seated you saw yourself reflected in mirrors within mirrors, and Bill's flushed-red, resentful face getting smaller and smaller as it disappeared towards the confused vanishing point said something about the way people faded into the background, however much they had held the centre stage at one time. There were some you thought it could never happen to, they had been so intensely involved in the major action, as Bill had been, but it had happened to him, too. He was out of things now, and he minded, he minded like hell!

The atmosphere at Lipp was very lively today, with the buzz of the in-people mounting steadily. Heller looked around to see who all these people were. They were packed in tight on the worn brown leather banquettes. Left side of the room: mother and daughter eating together ... next to them a group of Middle Easterners, could be Lebanese. Then a swarthy man, fiftyish, with a young attractive girl. Oh a most delectable girl. To whom the swarthy individual was not at all entitled, in Heller's instant judgment. His eye moved on: a table with four men dining together. They looked like Israelis. Members of an air crew? A cultured homosexual with his mother. A husband and wife, middle-aged, with a dog, which they fed surreptitiously under the table, in defiance of the explicit instruction on the wall prohibiting this. And right next to Heller, an American couple, man and woman, who seemed to have recently met, and whose conversation occasionally overlapped with the one that Heller was seeking to have with Bill Gibson. 'It's real funny,' the American woman was saying, 'how late in life these things come to you ... not just the physical thing ... ' And the man was saying, 'I know what you mean, Betsy. But it's narrowing it down ... '

Something in this room is not right, Heller thought. What the hell is it?

The waiter had come to take their order at last, and Bill misanthropically settled on the sole, nothing to start. He wasn't too hungry. But to bring the wine straight away, he said. The Chablis.

'What did Charles have to say?' Heller asked, by way of attempting conversation.

'Oh Charles, you know Charles,' Bill shook his head enigmatically. 'What he have to say to you?'

'We just chatted about ... this and that. It was mostly social. He seems in good form. The post suits him.'

'Sure it suits him. Question is does he suit it. Hah-hah!'

'You don't think so?'

'Who am I to say? I'm out of it now. I don't know anything about these things any more. I'm an old fogy ... nobody pays any attention to me. People say I'm an alarmist because I say to them we're already fighting the Third World War only we don't know it.'

The delectable girl with the swarthy man – whom Heller had dubbed 'the Greek' in his private identity parade – was looking around the room, as Heller was doing himself, and occasionally their roaming eyes met, and she smiled faintly at him, as if commiserating with him on his choice of dinner companion, and he returned the commiseration. 'The Greek' was expatiating on something, with tremendous explanatory gestures, hand going to heart, to forehead, to cheeks, to stomach. Hairs from his chest protruded through his voile shirt. He seemed most unworthy of this lovely girl with her short blonde hair, her big jacket with padded shoulders, broad lapels, collar turned up as if a wind were blowing ... She seemed curious about Heller. She was trying to work out who he was, just as he was trying to figure out who she was, and what she was doing with this 'Greek'.

Bill was rambling ... 'equally democracy can be defeated without being beaten in an all-out shooting war, that's not what it's about today ... there other ways ...'

'Conquer a man's soul and you have the man, and his territory falls to you?' Heller said, loosely quoting Sun Tzu.

'Right, right. You don't even know it's happened. You get taken over in a way that makes you think you chose it. That's the global conflict in which we're currently engaged ...'

The Chablis was finished.

'Shall I order another half?' Heller asked.

'Always were a man for doing things by halves,' Bill snidely reproached. 'Why so careful with the unvouchered funds? Somebody looking over your shoulder? They checking up on you, are they? That's how it starts. Checking your expenses with unusual rigour, that's when you know ... That's the sign they're thinking: this guy's no longer such a hotshot, when did he last come up with anything substantial? Let's take another good look at his track record, what's he done lately? Oh you'll see, you'll see. Little signs, little signs but they mean a lot. Hah-hah! Haaa!'

It was ridiculous to feel irritated by such gratuitous flea bites, but all the same Heller was thinking along the lines of bringing the dinner to as rapid a conclusion as possible; he had felt sorry for Bill, embarked upon his solitary gastronomic tour, and so had let himself be trapped into inviting him to dinner. A mistake. People like Bill were experts at making you feel sorry for them because they were down, and then kicking you from their prostrate position.

'I'm going to have to be back before ten-thirty,' Heller said. 'Couple of calls from Washington that I have to take.'

'Ah-huh! Ah-huh! Want to get rid of me, huh?' The kidding voice had a touch of freneticism in it now. 'Well ... that's OK. I been got rid of by better men than you, Gunga Din! Some of the Great Figures of Our Times have gotten rid of me, buster! Ha! Ha! See, once I made the mistake of saying things, certain things that are not said while the microphones are still live. That was my big blunder. Though they were things everybody knew were true. But not to be said, see, before a committee of senators, ye see. Those assholes have consciences too tender ... That's what it is. They want it done, but they don't want to know it's done, and I made the mistake of *not* lying to them. While the microphones were live. I'd had a little drink, ye see.'

'You had a pretty good run, Bill. You were almost seventy when you retired. Everybody knows what a very good job you did. And I include myself there. You taught me a great deal about this funny trade of ours. There's no question you were one of its greats. You were a star, Bill. A secret star, but a star.'

'Don't bullshit me, Heller. I was tossed on the junk heap. "You are required to vacate your office by five p.m.," was what the letter said. They said that to me! To ME! Who had ... who had ...

for fifty years . . . I did things those snot noses couldn't even have imagined.'

Looking at Bill now, Heller had to remind himself, yes, he really was one of the greats. He pulled off things that changed history. After the war, when there was a danger of Italy going Communist, and France too, Bill had agents in the Italian government, he had an Italian prime minister in his pocket . . . Bill believed in the anti-Communist cause with a passion. He *knew* about the Communists. He knew about Stalinism at a time when 'the piss-ant pinkos' were bending over backwards to blur the reality of what was going on behind the Iron Curtain, when they were all kowtowing to Castro and idolising 'Che' Guevara. Bill wasn't just interested in keeping Western Europe, he had aggressive ideas about 'rolling back the Iron Curtain' and bringing freedom to the Czechs and the Poles and Hungarians and Romanians and Bulgarians and Albanians and the people of the Baltic states, and in those days that was considered very dangerous jingoistic stuff. Bill was one of the people who wanted to deal with the Berlin blockade by sending in an armoured American division to ensure the trains got through. People said he went too far, that he was the sort who would land America in another war, with his crazy dangerous schemes. But it was recognised that his schemes were technically brilliant, that he was a kind of genius of the complex machination, that his elaborately devised masterplans structurally could not be faulted.

He was very thin and full of dynamism in those days, a man 'with a smell of burning rubber about him,' they said; imbued with fantastic energy.

In a mirrored pillar Heller could see into the narrow part of the restaurant, where there was a single line of tables parallel to the bar, by the stairs going down to the *vestiaire*. One of these tables was empty. He had noticed this before. It had been empty for some time: five minutes, ten . . . longer? That's what's wrong with this room, Heller considered. Outside, they had a sign saying the place was full, that there was a wait of an hour for a table, and here was an empty table.

Just then, two women in their mid-thirties came up from the cloakroom and sat down at this table. Simple explanation! They had made a long telephone call. They had powdered their noses. They had chatted about something private. Right, right. This was an example of the *psychose*. Quite innocuous things, like an empty table, took on an ominous meaning.

Bill appeared to have lost interest in the Third World War upon which the world was already unknowingly engaged, and his eye was wandering, balefully aglitter, to the mirror showing the two young women.

Why were they tense? They were not the most appealing examples of womanhood. Perhaps they were sexually frustrated. The blonde had the build of a bear, an irregular flush over neck and jowl, and her blonde hair was definitely out of a bottle. The other woman was small and thin and had brown hair and dark intelligent eyes. Both were badly dressed, the big one in a bulky open ski anorak, the other in a long, loose, man's jacket of the sort women were wearing now, and she wore a shirt and a tie. Heller speculated as to who they might be. A couple of secretaries from the provinces on a visit to Paris. From the northern provinces. They had the pallid dead skins of northerners, and a twitchy unease ... From somewhere close to the Belgian border, an industrial town where there was nothing going on. Did they come to Paris to get laid? Once or twice a year ... Well if they went to the Deux Magots they would get some offers. Bill seemed interested in them, Bill who had never been a 'player'. Perhaps that was something else he had taken up to fill his retirement years.

'One of them', he avowed, 'gave me the eye, God knows why she would, man of my age, but I promise you she did. The big one. The bear. Some of these young gals nowadays go for the older guys, don't they?'

'Want me to look them over for you?' Heller offered with a grin.

'Yes, you do that. I expect I have one or two rounds left in me yet,' Bill said none too surely. 'Ask 'em to join us for a drink.'

'Not sure they're exactly my type,' Heller said. 'And I've got that phone call to take.'

'I can take care of the two of 'em,' Bill boasted unconvincingly.

Heller got up to go to the men's room. He would have to pass the young women that Bill mysteriously fancied. Heller gave them a brief glance as he went down the stairs. Yes, he thought, they're looking for something . . . to shatter the dullness in their eyes, to set themselves aflame, yes, yes . . . How deeply unsmiling they are. And without grace.

He went down the stairs. A man was at the wall telephone alongside the cloakroom counter. He seemed to be listening and not saying anything. He was propped up against the wall in a sort of standing-up sprawl, his back to the stairs. The oddly silent call was still going on when Heller came out of the men's room. At any rate the man was still there, phone in hand, silently listening, or waiting.

Going up the stairs Heller became aware of an unnatural quietness, broken a moment later by an eruption of harsh and violent sounds, as if a group of clumsy furniture removers had set to work above his head. Shouts. Cries. Expostulations. Garbled utterances. It flashed through his mind that this outburst might have something to do with Bill. Maybe the old fool had made a clumsy pass at those two women and been insultingly rebuffed and it had led to a fracas. As he reached the top of the stairs, Heller saw that it was indeed to do with Bill, this thing that had happened, but the ferocity of it was out of all proportion to anything Bill could possibly have said or done.

One of the women, the big blonde, had got Bill's neck in a kind of garrotte-grip inside her elbow and was dragging him along. He was gagging and choking, his face a big red open wound. Nobody was going to his assistance. Heller started to push his way towards him. He saw people standing up, looking aghast, and then he discovered the reason why nobody was going to Bill's help. It was because the second of the two women, the twitchy brunette in the baggy man's jacket, with a tie, was holding a Czech 'Skorpion' submachine-gun in her left hand, swivelling around with it and menacing everybody in the restaurant. Heller calculated that he could take the brunette. The problem was the big blonde. She also had one of these Skorpions. She was holding it in one hand as she dragged Bill out. While Heller was dealing with the brunette the blonde would have a free field of fire. The two were covering each other. Bill was struggling against the garrotte elbow, a huge threshing machine of arms and knees, and the blonde bear used the stock of her Skorpion to smash Bill's face. The terrorists were shouting for people to stand back, shouting for them to lie flat. They were shouting that they were combatants in the struggle against the Fascist State. Their shouts went a couple of pitches higher and became screams, and then the voices went over the top, and he saw the open mouths of these women, their upper lips drawn back from their teeth, and there flashed through Heller's mind a piece of French folklore which says that a snake that rises up and shows its teeth is poisonous.

The craze for blood-letting was flowing down through their arms and hands, and then the Skorpions jerked about, and 'the Greek' was cleaved open at the chest and began to leak viscera all over the white tablecloth. His pretty companion had one side of her face shot away. The couple with the dog were thrown back against the wall of green palm trees and agaves, which began to sprout bits of their flesh. The mother of the homosexual, grandly gowned in Balenciaga, died where she sat, without budging, but the Skorpions passed over her son in their random sweep. They did not miss the American woman next to whom Heller had sat all evening.

The slaughter happened in seconds, and then the two women were dragging Bill by the throat and had dumped him like a garbage sack into a compartment of the revolving door and spun him out.

By the time Heller succeeded in getting to the door, Bill had been bundled into a Mercedes taxi that had drawn up outside. Heller caught a last glimpse of him tightly wedged in between the two furies.

TWO

Outside, sirens of varying rhythms and pitches filled the air. All along the boulevard St-Germain Heller could see the gyrating lights – blue, red, yellow, amber – of the emergency services. Soon after them came the TV live-broadcast vans: quickly they began unloading lights and cables and cameras. Electronic flashes lit up faces in shock.

The area in which the terrorist outrage had occurred was enclosed by metal crush barriers manned by police, and only those who had professional business there were allowed through.

The crowd grew all the time. People wanted to see the badly wounded being wrapped in gold foil thermal sheets, and the dead being put in plastic sacks. People were attracted by the calamity; they stood on lacquered rattan brasserie chairs to see better. And on table tops across the boulevard at the Café Flore. They stared out of apartments and hotel rooms. And all the time there was the mechanical wailing of two-tone air horns, a chorus crying woe.

Heller stood in the open, in the fresh light rain, taking deep breaths, dragging the air into the bottom of his lungs, and letting it out slowly, steadily. He had the collar of his raincoat turned up, kept his hands in his pockets.

In the crowd, a passageway had formed through which rolled a rough stone of a man, sweeping along with him four or five others – they stuck close to him and watched people's hands: eyes don't kill, hands do. Some of these men were dressed in the combat uniform of the special intervention force RAID, some were in plain clothes. While moving in his hurtling fashion, Commissaire Chaillet was looking around, taking everything in, talking into a walkie-talkie, asking questions, giving instructions. In front of Heller, he came to an abrupt stop, and his men piled up around him.

The Commissaire was short, but the force of the man made him seem bigger. He began, without any formalities, rapping out questions.

—*Qui êtes vous, monsieur? Votre nom, monsieur?*

—*Heller. Fred Heller.*

—*Vous étiez avec le monsieur qui a été pris? C'est un ami à vous?*

—*Oui. Un ancien collègue.*

The speed with which the Commissaire spat out questions in his strong Marseillais accent needed some getting used to.

Who was this former colleague? Bill Gibson. Profession? Retired. Formerly? Formerly with the CIA. Ah! Ah! And you, monsieur, you are? With the State Department. Ah yes, ah yes. Who were the people who did this?

—Two women.

—Describe them.

—Early thirties. One very large. A bear of a woman. Extremely strong. Fake blonde. The other thin and mousy and nervy.

—What sort of weapons?

—They were Czech Skorpions. VZ61s.

Chaillet slowed down like a car skidding to a halt, and then as if he had a bad taste in his mouth that he couldn't get rid of, asked:

—How do you know this?

—I've come across them before.

—What is it you do in the State Department, Monsieur Eller?

—I'm concerned with international security. I'm a special adviser to the Secretary of State on security questions.

—Ah! Ah! A "special", uh? Chaillet conferred with some of his men, who huddled around him. Then he said:

—You will come with us, Monsieur Eller. We shall need you.

15

You are not injured yourself? Good. I'm going to hand you over to Inspector Bosch here. He will look after you. If you need anything, ask him. Don't go away now. You have your passport with you?

—Yes.

—You give it to me, please.

Heller handed over his passport, and Chaillet glanced through it, turning the pages rapidly and scowling.

—You make a lot of trips, Monsieur Eller. To some very remote places . . . Not to say, exotic. No travelling for the present, Monsieur Eller. We're going to need you here. We keep this for now.`

He indicated the passport and handed it over to Inspector Bosch, who took it wordlessly and put it away in his pocket without looking at it. The inspector was a man in his early thirties with a habit of moving restlessly from one foot to the other as if walking on hot coals. He was prematurely grey of hair and face, and he had a mean, edgy look to him. To be handled with care, Heller noted to himself. The French police could play rough, very rough. The interview *musclé* was something of a French speciality.

Bosch sullenly explained that Heller would have to come back with them to the quai des Orfèvres, take a look at some photographs of women and make a statement. The photographs would not be up to *Playboy* standard, he apologised sarcastically. French women terrorists were not famous for the beauty of their centre-folds. He gave a low laugh of contempt. In a shoot-out, kill the she-swine first. That was his advice. The she-swine was the most dangerous of this particular species.

Bosch was a long sallow aggrieved-looking man, unshaven, with a winey acid breath.

—Do we have to stand here? Heller asked after five minutes had gone by.

—We'll have to wait until the Chief comes back. The Chief tells you what you can or can't do. That's how it works here in France. You see, we're in France here. Not in the United States of America. Understood?

This Bosch was a man of eclectic hang-ups and resentments, Heller noted.

The Chief, Chaillet, was going around asking questions, listening to accounts, picking out other witnesses who were to be taken back to the quai des Orfèvres.

It was another half an hour before he returned.

—Come, he said to Heller. You come with us.

Bosch drove the car, and Heller and Chaillet sat in the back.

A maniacal driver, this Bosch. Heller was accustomed to the craziness of French drivers, but Bosch, with *gyrophares* whirling and siren sounding, substantially surpassed his compatriots, while the unflinching Chaillet chain-smoked cigarettes, asked questions, and took cryptic calls on the radio-phone.

—Gibson is a close associate of yours?

—He was at one time . . .

—Does he still work for the CIA? Sometimes? Unofficially perhaps?

—He's retired.

—What was he doing in Paris?

—He was embarking on a gastronomic holiday, a tour of three-star restaurants.

—When was the rendezvous made for you to have dinner at Lipp?

—Sunday night.

—Where?

—La Coupole.

—Could you have been overheard, making this arrangement?

—It's possible.

—Did you tell anyone that you were meeting Gibson tonight at Lipp?

—No, I didn't.

—What was the purpose of this meeting?

—No purpose. For old time's sake.

—Old time's sake, uh? In the old times you have worked together, sometimes, you and Gibson?

—At times, yes.

17

—Were you on a mission together this time? A secret mission perhaps?

—No. Not this time. As I said, he's retired.

—What are you doing in Paris, Monsieur Eller?

—Giving seminars. On international terrorism.

—Seminars? *Ah bon!* On terrorism. So now you have some new material for these seminars.

—Yes.

Bosch was taking the narrow backstreets, and when he wanted to pass somebody, did not hesitate to go half on the pavement. He drove with a personal sense of hostility towards everyone else on the road, and finally pulled up with a squealing of brakes outside 36, Quai des Orfèvres.

They went in through the high gate, one side of which had been opened for them by the uniformed policemen on duty, and crossed a poorly lit courtyard, its cobblestones glistening with a gloomy wet light. In the central lobby there was a choice selection of Paris *truands* and *voyous*, some of them handcuffed. One was spitting blood into a big ashtray. Paper coffee cups and cigarette ends littered the floor.

Chaillet-the-stone continued to hurtle. Through the lobby. Up formerly grand stairs. Up into a luminous cloud of dust and cigarette smoke rising to the mezzanine. Creaking corridors. A Detectives' Hall noisy with the clatter of ancient manual type-writers as well as the fast high-pitched sounds of computer print-outs. An inspector of 'the Criminelle' fell in step with Chaillet and accompanied him up to his green-baize door, filling him in on 'developments' in coded *flics'* language.

Inside his office, Chaillet dropped down into a scuffed swivel chair on castors, and started rolling about on it here and there. He gave instructions for 'the calalogue' to be brought in. Ladies only. For the present. Phones rang, and Chaillet answered them as and when he felt like doing so. At times the telephone was placed on hold inside one or other of the Commissaire's armpits. The 'catalogue' started coming in: stacks of photographs in annotated folders, wheeled in on a trolley.

Chaillet and Bosch did the first sort-through, eliminating some of the folders and some of the individual photographs for unexplained reasons, while picking out others and placing them in a pile to one side. This second pile, when it had reached a certain height, was pushed across to Heller, who was asked to look and see if he recognised anyone. While Heller was studying the faces, Chaillet stood up, stretched himself, yawned noisily, and went across to the low window, through which he could only look out by stooping. The Left Bank was glitteringly illuminated, and tonight the light show was supplemented by the agitatedly spinning lights of emergency vehicles in permanent circulation.

When Heller had gone through the first pile of photographs without recognising anyone, a second pile was picked out for him and then a third, but he did not find anyone resembling the women who had abducted Bill.

—Bunch of unknowns, Chaillet said with disgust.

He rolled forward, placing himself intimately close to Heller, and gripping the wooden arms of Heller's chair, so as to lock the two of them into a tight little circle.

—Now let's see if I've got this straight. You arrive at Roissy-Charles de Gaulle Friday fourteenth November. Quite by accident you run into Gibson there. Then on Sunday, again by accident, you run into him at La Coupole and arrange to dine together at the Brasserie Lipp, 'for old time's sake'. Yes?

—Yes.

Chaillet rolled back behind his desk. Something had come up on his computer screen that he studied with a dark frown. He hit some keys and read off the unscrolling information. He shook his head, his lips tight and disapproving. Then he gripped his hands behind his head and put his feet up on the desk and sought to stretch himself out in a straight line.

—I have a message, he confided. From Claude Juvin. Of the DST? To the effect that he vouches for you. Frankly, Monsieur Eller, when Juvin vouches for someone it makes me suspicious . . . Now this type who was at the telephone. Making a phone call.

When you went down to piss. Describe him to me, Monsieur Eller.

—I didn't see his face.

—Colour of hair?

—Dark.

—Age?

—Hard to say. Not young. He'd lost some hair at the back. Quite a bit. Poor posture. Could be middle thirties to middle forties.

—Anything else you notice?

—Large feet. Shoes would be tens or elevens. Your size forty-five.

—You hear anything of what he said on the phone?

—He did not appear to be talking. As if he was waiting for something. Or someone.

—You say anything to him?

—No.

—No exchange whatsoever took place between you?

—None.

The Commissaire scratched his cheek stubble. By this time of night he normally needed to shave again to look presentable.

—They say that you are "a man of the shadows", Monsieur Eller. Like your friend Gibson. With such individuals you never know where you are, *especially* if Juvin vouches for them ... You may be an important man, Monsieur Eller. And I may be sticking my neck out. You see, I don't have a Arvard education. I'm not what you would call an intellectual. My education ... was the rue Budapest, and the Goutte d'Or. And before that, Marseille. The gangsters and *les putes*. That's where I learnt. I don't have any diplomas in the philosophy of crime. But I know about it. I know about it in my fingertips, Monsieur Eller. And there's something about this whole story, the way you tell it to me, the way it presents itself, even with Juvin vouching for you, that has a smell. There's something rotten here. As I say, maybe I'm sticking my neck out. I know that you people, you people of the shadows, you specials, you have certain arrangements, and maybe you have such

20

an arrangement with Juvin. I wouldn't know about that. I'm an ordinary policeman and I do my job, until somebody important enough tells me otherwise. You've understood?

—Yes.

—I have a hunch that the man you saw on the phone outside the men's room at Lipp was the chief of this terrorist group, and that he gave the signal for the action to commence. There was someone in the phone booth outside the brasserie. On the traffic island. Gave the signal to the Mercedes taxi to draw up. All carefully co-ordinated. And during this time what you were doing was having a quiet piss? Is that right?

—That is right, Commissaire.

Chaillet removed his legs from the desk and stood up, straightening out his shoulders and rotating his shoulder blades in a vain exercise designed to cast off the manifold tensions of the day. He handed Heller back his passport.

—Well, I expect things will become clearer, in due course. I let you get some sleep now. I imagine we are going to be talking together very soon. Myself, I've still got a long night's work ahead of me . . .

Heller walked back from the Quai des Orfèvres, and then along by the river, which in the reflected lights of monuments and street lamps looked pretty polluted tonight.

The streets were full of cops. He had never seen so many in Paris. They walked in twos and threes and fours, and in larger groups. The CRS all wore shiny action blousons, and over them, Velcro-fastened blue bullet-proof vests; they carried MAT49s and other types of submachine-guns.

The Palais de Justice was cordoned off – you had to pass through single-file passageways constructed out of crush barriers, controlled by gendarmes in combat green. You had the impression of being in a city under siege. A small number of terrorists had done this. Had brought the contamination into the city, and were spreading it, spreading the sickness . . .

He felt he was breathing it in.

He was trying to get to grips with the question: Why would they have taken an old lush like Bill, who's out of it all, rather than me?

THREE

IT SEEMED TO Heller that he had only just dropped off and was waking from a brief doze, but it was morning and outside it was grey.

The phone had woken him. The voice introduced itself as Gordon Welliver, from the American Embassy.

There was some formal enquiry as to Heller's state of health, and then Gordon, who sounded very young, said, 'I have some messages for you, sir.'

'Yes?'

'The French are calling a crisis council for this morning. That's their system, when they have a crisis . . .'

'Oh yes?'

'Charles Decourten. At the *Ministère*. In the rue de Varenne. Opposite Matignon. You know it, sir?'

'Yes, I know it, Gordon.'

'I believe you know the Minister, too, sir.'

'Yes, I do.'

'Well, they want you to liaise with him, sir. Washington. They want you to keep a watching brief on the Bill Gibson situation. And advise.'

'Where's this come from.'

'Comes from State. From the Under-secretary.'

'I'm supposed to advise him, concerning . . .?'

'I guess, what's to be done, sir.'

'Ah yes. Has Washington indicated any special concerns?'

'The telex is quite brief, sir. I expect they'll be in touch with you direct. The meeting's at eleven o'clock. It's all been cleared with the Quai d'Orsay. Your role. The advisory thing. I expect we'll be in touch again, sir. I've been sort of assigned to you. Help out in any way. Just give me a buzz should you need anything.'

'Be talking to you Gordon.'

From his hotel the Pont-Royal it was a few minutes walk down the bustling rue du Bac, with its *traiteurs* and its *pâtisseries* and its tucked away fruit and vegetable market, to the road-block on the corner. There the men in bullet-proof vests checked everyone wanting to turn into the rue de Varenne.

Heller observed that the *porte-cochère* of Matignon was open and that there was a continuous flow of vehicles in and out of the courtyard.

The Ministry of National Safety, across the road, was equally active, and Heller rode up to the Minister's office in a packed elevator that also carried Claude Juvin of the DST.

Juvin's smile of recognition on seeing Heller was somewhat remote, but that was the man's style. He was not renowned for his human warmth. A small, dapper man in a grey overcoat with a black velvet collar, carrying buckskin gloves, he did not look like a policeman. The other policemen in the elevator were much larger men and loomed over Claude Juvin. They did not, however, overshadow him. Though small, he was not easy to overshadow. Through a gap between all the bulky forms, he wagged his finger at Heller and murmured, 'Ah! Ah!' with a knowing glitter in his eyes. It was an old joke of Juvin's to greet acquaintances in this manner, an allusion to the fact that he was said to know everybody's unsavoury secrets.

'So you are going to help us out. *Mais c'est très gentil,*' Juvin remarked to Heller as both got out of the elevator. They were in the spacious gallery outside the Minister's office, beneath a golden ceiling depicting the marquise who had once owned this mansion 'offering herself to impossible desires'. There was a portrait of Talleyrand on one wall; rather a hero of Charles's, Heller recalled.

And there were plenty of Louis XIV *fauteuils*, though nobody sat in them. Everybody was facing the cream-and-gilt double doors, waiting for them to open. From behind acoustic screens came the restrained hums and screeches of communications machinery in full spate.

Juvin nodded distantly to colleagues from other branches of France's complexly interlinked police system: the Paris Préfet de police; the director of the national police; the director of the frontier police; the chief of the special intervention force of the gendarmerie; the head of the Président de la République's anti-terrorist strike force; the deputy head of the Renseignements généraux.

The double doors opened and the Minister's *chef de cabinet*, Le Quineau, a tall thin young man with steel-rimmed glasses tightly built into his face, came out to welcome the policemen and take them in.

As Heller entered Charles Decourten stood up and came round from behind his desk for a brief private word.

'Fred, it is good to see you are in one piece. What a horror! I went there last night, immediately I was informed. You had already left. Poor old Bill! Poor bastard! Thank God he has no close family. What an escape you have had! I am content that you will be helping us. It is your field and your advice will be valuable. For our part we shall co-operate fully. We must do everything we can for Bill. Everything we possibly can.'

Le Quineau asked them all to be seated on little gilt ballroom chairs that did not look sufficiently sturdy to bear such grim-faced, weighty men.

The office had an ornate ceiling and a lot of rouge marble. There were tapestries on the walls and full-length portraits of men who had previously exercised ministerial power in this room.

Behind Charles Decourten there was the battery of special telephones, the *réseau spécial* of the *interministériel*, linking certain high-ranking ministers with each other and with the main power and defence bases of the nation.

Charles's face was darkly handsome and stern.

Without any formalities, he called for up-to-the-minute reports from the men in a position to know what was happening throughout the land. First it was Chaillet who was put on the spot. He had nothing definite to report. It was too early, only a few hours since the *attentat*. The getaway car, the Mercedes taxi, had not so far been found. Nor had the weapons, the Skorpions. In accordance with usual practice, the sewers had been searched, and so had the obvious public places, but nothing had been found. He believed that the terrorists had not discarded their weapons. He believed they were keeping them, despite the risk this entailed of being caught in possession of weapons linking them with the murders. The death toll had gone up to eight. Several of the injured were in a serious condition. It was the most serious outrage since the explosion outside Tati in the rue de Rennes earlier in the year and the machine-gunning in the restaurant Goldenberg in the rue des Rosiers in 1982. At Goldenberg's the gunmen had swept the restaurant with gunfire, without taking aim and the target had clearly been the Jewish community. In so far as the Brasserie Lipp had a generic significance, it must stand for 'the political establishment'; it was widely known as a place formerly frequented by the Président de la République, and by other national and international political figures.

—Yes, they intend to strike at the heart of the State, the Minister said.

He questioned Chaillet about the search for the getaway car.

—As my colleagues here will bear out, a massive nationwide search has been instituted. I can assure Monsieur le ministre that none of us had much sleep last night.

—This is your famous *travail de fourmis*, the Minister remarked unimpressed. Let it not be too antlike, Commissaire.

Chaillet did not reply, but sat stony-faced, with all his rage in his seething ankles.

Charles Decourten turned to Juvin.

—Monsieur Juvin?

—The Department has nothing definite to impart for the moment, Monsieur le ministre.

That was all he said, and it was accepted. The DST did not share what it knew with a room full of fellow-policemen; it was not expected to. The DST from its inception had been a law unto itself, and it jealously guarded the privileges it had won. Among these was the right to safeguard its sources, to keep its information to itself, to refuse to answer the enquiries of other police departments, and when called upon to divulge what it knew, to do so only on the highest levels, privately, to the Président de la République, or to the Premier ministre, or to the Ministre de l'intérieur or the Ministre de la sûreté nationale. But most of the time the DST remained silent, answering not even to the highest in the land until it was ready to act.

Chaillet's disgust continued to show in his jerking ankle. The *police judiciaire* had to open all its files to the DST, if required so to do, while the DST's files were protected by *secret-défense* and didn't have to be opened to anyone. Certainly not to another section of the police. Nor was the DST under the direction of, or accountable to, a *juge d'instruction* as was the *police judiciaire*.

Juvin cleared his throat to no avail: as usual he sounded as if his words had been passed through a filter of dry desert sand, to purge them of unnecessary emotion.

—I ask myself: why was Gibson taken? A retired man. Old. Out of the picture now. Why him? Why not his companion, Monsieur Heller? A more obvious choice, since he is presently involved in combating terrorism. Was Bill Gibson a purely arbitrary choice? Would any American have sufficed for their purposes? The killings were random. Perhaps the kidnapping was too? This is what I ask myself.

—And what answer do you give yourself, Monsieur Juvin? the Minister wanted to know.

—It is not an answer based on any facts in my possession. It is based merely on my intuition.

—May we share your mere intuitions, Monsieur Juvin? Since that is why we are here.

—If you so wish. It is this. Bill Gibson is a man who has led so many secret lives, even he cannot remember what he did in all of them. But perhaps *somebody* remembers. These terrorists, from my experience, all possess elaborate grievances, they *cherish* the injustices to which they feel they, or others with whom they choose to identify, have been subjected.

—I tend to agree with that assessment of their psychology, Charles Decourten observed. But I am not sure how far it takes us ... Monsieur Miribel.

He turned to the head of the air and frontier police to provide the meeting with information of a more concrete nature, and Miribel proceeded to outline the special measures taken to prevent the terrorists getting away across the borders; all his forces were on high alert; an extra thousand men of the 11th Parachute Regiment and the 27th Alpine Regiment had been brought in to supplement the regular forces patrolling remote borders.

As he was speaking, Le Quineau came in and placed a buff folder before the Minister. It was opened and perused by the two men, with the *chef de cabinet* imparting information in the Minister's ear.

Charles Decourten raised his hand, stopping the director of the air and frontier police in mid-sentence.

—Messieurs. We have a *revendication*. I will ask Monsieur Le Quineau to read it out.

Le Quineau picked up the folder, and read expressionlessly:

—The strategic command of Attaque Contre l'Etat (ACE) announces the capture in the course of its armed revolutionary action of 18 November '86 against the centre imperialist Lipp, boulevard St-Germain, Paris sixième, of the American imperialist agent, CIA functionary and spymaster William Halliday Gibson. This action, executed by the *guérilla prolétarienne b2* of ACE, was in pursuit of our herewith declared policy of taking the armed struggle to the heart of the State. We declare that those who partake even tacitly, even by eating in its restaurants, in the conspiracy of the bourgeois State against the world proletariat, will be deemed guilty of participating *actively* in that conspiracy...

28

There was more in the same vein before the demands were reached.

The conditions which would have to be met before Gibson was released were:

1 The immediate release of the eleven individuals named on the attached list, presently serving prison sentences or under provisional detention for their part in the armed struggle against the oppressor State;
2 A contribution of $3,000,000 towards the Fund for the Revolutionary Struggle of the People;
3 The resignation of the Minister of National Safety Charles Decourten in 'recognition of his crimes'.

Failing a rapid response to these demands, Gibson would be executed, and further commando actions against the populace would ensue. Paris would be rendered totally uninhabitable.

Le Quineau finished reading and looked up, pressing the steel rims of his glasses more deeply into his eye sockets.

Charles Decourten had risen from behind his desk and was looking down into the courtyard where TV outside-broadcast vans were drawing up and discharging cameras and lights in preparation for the special interview with the Minister of National Safety to go out live during the one o'clock news.

Decourten addressed the policemen:

—The life of Paris must continue as normal, though with the maximum extra security in place. It is essential that we do not contribute to the *psychose* that these people seek to engender. I shall advise that all ministers keep to their announced public engagements. Your job, messieurs, is to quickly find the people who have perpetrated the Lipp horror and threaten further horrors, and bring the guilty to justice. No effort must be spared. I remind everyone here that no State functionary enjoys lifelong tenure of office. All positions are dependent on performance. As is a minister of the government. Indeed, the government itself . . . I mention this so that you do not lose sight of the extent to which all our futures are linked together. As to the question of how we should treat the kidnappers' demands, I will take observations.

He turned questioningly towards Chaillet, Juvin.

Chaillet said:

—We must try to make them get in touch. Every time they make contact it gives us a chance to intercept...

—Yes, yes ... Monsieur Juvin?

—I note they say they expect a response. Which suggests they don't expect *acceptance* of their demands. I agree with Commissaire Chaillet that we must make them come back to us, again and again. We must keep them on the hop.

—Fred? Any points?

—Only ... leave the door open a crack. It should be a big enough crack. Big enough to make them come back. And big enough for us to get Bill out through it, eventually.

—We are committed by national policy.

—I know. The formula I suggest you use is that in the interests of saving human life, you propose an intermediary. Propose me. I've done this sort of thing before.

Charles Decourten looked around at the others in the room, questioningly.

Chaillet said, holding himself firmly in rein:

—Personally, if you want my opinion, Monsieur le ministre, I'm opposed to letting things out of our own hands into the hands of ... *others*.

At which Juvin gently interposed:

—Of course, of course. But a representative of family interests is normal. One does not wish to stand in the way of natural sentiment.

—Gibson doesn't have any family, Chaillet grunted.

—Everybody has some family, Juvin said in a grandly vague manner. Aunts? Cousins? No?

—If we hand this over to the Americans...

Chaillet's voice was level but his ankle had gone into a little spasm of disgust.

—Not a question of 'handing over', Commissaire, the Minister said judiciously, but of permitting legitimate interests to find expression. I think Monsieur Heller is offering to act as intermediary in a purely unofficial capacity, subject to the normal controls one would expect to apply, and subject to French law, of course. I see some advantages in his offer. There are situations where an individual, acting alone, on behalf of family interests, has more room to manoeuvre. Therefore I have decided to accept Monsieur Heller's offer and would ask you, messieurs, to give him such assistance as you can.

The Minister stood up. The crisis council was at an end, and the police officers were filing out. Heller was leaving with them.

'Stay a moment, Fred,' Charles invited in a low voice. He waited until everyone else had left, and then said, 'This also came. A personal letter from Bill. I didn't want to read it out, you'll see why. In any case I thought you should have a look at it first.' He passed the letter across.

Heller read:

Dear Charles

I know you are going to find this hellish hard to accept, but there is no other way of getting out of this mess except by acceding to their demands. Bear in mind my age, my state of health (not good) and the fact that they have means at their disposal, including chemical means, that make it pretty silly for you to fool yourself with the notion that Bill's an old trouper, who'll hold out whatever they do to him. They are going to put me on trial, and at the end of the trial they are going to find me guilty (that's a foregone conclusion), and then they are going to execute me. Now you may be tempted to say, Poor ole Bill! and leave it there. But I don't think you should look at it that way, Charles. The way to look at it is that I may be the one they have got in their hands, with the threat hanging over him, but in every other way you are where I am. For I am standing in for you all. And a threat to me is equally a threat to you and others. Likewise, what's good for me, is good for you

31

all. What I'm saying to you, Charles, is don't think of this as being exclusively *my* problem. We're all in the same boat. If I go down, it's inevitable others will too. So try to work this out imaginatively. God be with you. And me!

Yours ever, Bill

Heller returned the letter slowly. 'That's Bill all right,' he said, 'don't need any handwriting experts. It's got his tricky ring to it.'

'What d'you interpret him as saying when he says, *you are where I am?*'

'I think he's saying, *get me out of this*. And he's trying to muster the best arguments he can find.'

'Is he threatening us? Old man, in poor health, can't hold out. Hold out concerning what?'

'I don't know. Bill's smart enough not to say. Let's *imagine* what we like. I guess he takes the view we will know what we don't want known. And that'll make us want to do something for him.'

'He's trying to blackmail us, then?'

'You could call it that. In other circumstances you might call it applying diplomatic pressure.'

Charles was looking at his watch.

'There is a crisis meeting at Matignon in five minutes' time, I have to give a report to the Premier ministre, and then I have the television interview to do. We are going to have to stand firm, you know. Whatever the consequences for Bill...'

'Or anyone else?'

'Or anyone else, yes. However, I am not closing any doors in advance. See what you can come up with, Fred. And I will consider it, if it's feasible.'

'Charles, I don't think we should write Bill off. I know him. And so do you. In my view I don't think he's going to let himself be written off.'

Charles Decourten said nothing. His face was solemn and statesmanlike.

FOUR

THE APPEARANCE OF Isabelle Decourten, daughter of the Minister of National Safety, on a public stage two nights after the horror at Lipp presented a major security problem, but the Minister had decided it was one that had to be confronted, to show that the country would not be intimidated by terrorists. If the first night were put off, or if his own attendance had been cancelled, then the signal would have been sent out that Paris was not a safe place. People would become fearful of going out – and if that happened, the life of Paris would be brought to a halt. Within a few months there had been the explosion in the Pub Renault on the Champs Elysées, the scare at the Eiffel Tower, the bomb in the metro, another at the Préfecture de police, and the slaughter outside the department store Tati. And now the Brasserie Lipp horror. The American tourists had stopped coming. It was necessary to send out a strong signal that Paris was safe, and what better way than by the Minister of National Safety attending his daughter's first night. The play was Sophocles's *Antigone*.

Arriving at the theatre ten minutes before curtain-up, Heller showed his special ticket to a member of the front-of-house staff at the bottom of the curving stairs and was referred to a bulky man in a bulging dark suit carrying a walkie-talkie. He examined Heller's special ticket, asked his name and checked it against a list; there was a brief exchange on the walkie-talkie and then Heller was told he could go up.

There were large men in dark suits on the onyx stairs to the mezzanine, and three more at the top, at the approach to corridor H. Outside *Loge* 1 there was Bosch, his breath smelling of wine; he gave Heller a surly salute.

Nobody was in the *loge*, and Heller went out again. He saw the ministerial party coming up the onyx stairs, a moving wedge contained within a phalanx of security men and preceded by Commissaire Chaillet, who was hurtling a little less rapidly than usual, out of regard for the occasion. Charles, when he reached the *loge*, welcomed Heller warmly, and introduced him to his wife Dorothy, his second wife, a good-looking American woman gingerly approaching fifty. She was wearing a long black gown designed to fall in sculptural folds. Tiny diamond pendants tumbled from her rather large earlobes, antique diamonds and sapphires sparkled discreetly on her hands. Nothing ostentatious. In jewellery, as in other matters, Charles was an admirer of lightness. Also in the Minister's party were a handsome young French couple, the Dubrelles, and a pretty woman in her early forties wearing a dress with a big taffeta bow in the middle. She was introduced by Dorothy as Edwige Maupeo d'Ableiges. She was related to the Guilhermys, Dorothy explained. There was also an elderly Englishman, Sir Anthony Braithwaite, wearing a wine-coloured *smoking*.

They were told by Chaillet that the Minister should not sit in the front row, and that no lights should be switched on inside the *loge* at any time. As the group went in Heller glimpsed through the open door of the adjacent *loge* two police marksmen with Cyclopean night-sight goggles strapped to their foreheads watching people take their seats. The atmosphere of expectancy appropriate to an important first night was mixed with a sense of apprehension.

As the curtain rose there was a burst of applause for the set by Chotard: the Palace at Thebes, a citadel beneath an overhang of sheer rock, an enclosed place of high walls and gates, a city under siege.

The first speech was Antigone's, and Isabelle Decourten spoke it in a fragile, exhausted voice: it concerned the deaths of her two brothers who had slain each other in battle, and the King's new edict prohibiting the burial of one brother, Polynices, who had attacked the State. He was to be left to the carrion, as an example to others.

The actress spoke her lines haltingly. She gave them a raw jagged edge. When she spoke of the King's order being directed against her, there was the sense of a mysterious resistance growing within her, of her dawning understanding that she must pit her frail self against King and State.

As the play progressed and Antigone found within herself the strength to oppose the edict of the State, even at the cost of her own life, Isabelle Decourten produced from within herself great outbursts of emotion, of anguish, hate, passion, determination. In her defiance of her uncle the King she was like a force of nature.

She spoke her line, 'I do not believe your edicts have the power to overrule the unalterable laws of God and Heaven', with the spiritual force of Joan of Arc vowing fidelity to her voices. The line that followed – 'Of course I know I shall have to die' – brought the audience back to a young girl who was vulnerable and afraid.

There was no interval. The play drove on relentlessly towards its terrible finale: Creon, unrelenting, embodying the absolute authority of State and ruler, imposing the terrible sentence. Antigone must be sealed up in her rock-vaulted tomb.

—*So to my grave.*

With this line she was overcome by uncertainty; the shining resolve was gone and suddenly she doubted herself. This was not Joan glorying in fulfilling the commands of her voices but a terrified girl being dragged off to a terrible death. Yet she must go through with it, she must ... She had buried her brother in opposition to the State decree and she could not back down.

Her physical state of terror as she was led away to her death was so real that there were those in the audience who experienced the bodily sensation of immurement; they felt there was not enough air in the theatre, that they could not breathe.

A minor commotion occurred as a woman in the auditorium, apparently feeling unwell, had to leave her seat and seek fresh air.

When the curtain came down the audience was at first uncertain in its response. The play had been performed, in particular by the actress playing Antigone, in a manner that was almost too realistic. Isabelle Decourten had drawn on something *in the air*, a certain mood of anxiety, and incorporated it in her characterisation of Antigone, and people had been made to feel very uneasy. They were not sure that they liked this. When the actors came on stage for the curtain call, the applause was respectful but not fervent. Then Bernard Lapallière, who had played Creon and directed the production, appeared, and the applause built up. He was an actor greatly admired.

There was still no sign of Antigone. Was she not going to appear? People in the audience looked at each other questioningly. Finally Isabelle Decourten did come on. She shuffled on to the stage looking fragile and exhausted. She did not bow and she did not look around the audience as the other actors had done, but remained quite still, staring straight ahead and breathing hard. A single cry of *Bravo!* came from one part of the audience, and was taken up in other parts. They were sporadic, isolated shouts at first. But as Isabelle Decourten remained expressionless, the shouts of *Bravo! Bravo!* started coming from all sides, as if the audience was determined by its enthusiasm to kindle some emotional response in the actress. At last, she inclined her head forward in modest, tired acknowledgment of the applause.

Then the curtain came down, and when it rose again for – the appaluse had continued – she was no longer there, and although Lapallière and other members of the cast kept gesturing to the wings inviting her to reappear, she did not come on stage again.

Before the final curtain call, the Minister's party was ushered out of the *loge* and, once more encapsulated in the protection unit, moved rapidly down the onyx stairs, which had been kept clear for their descent, and then through a door marked *Privé* and out of the ambience of red carpets into the bare corridors leading to the dressing-rooms.

Because it was considered inadvisable for the Minister to hang around, the usual custom of waiting a short while before going backstage, so as to give the actors time to recover and change out of their costumes, had been dispensed with on this occasion and the Minister's group was taken straight to Isabelle's dressing-room.

Inspector Bosch was outside the door, and the smell of wine on his breath had increased.

Isabelle was still in costume and make-up. Her eyes were framed by thick black lines which joined other lines coming from her eyebrows. Though it was only minutes since she had seemed so emotionally drained, she had now undergone some quick inner readjustment and was revived and in lively spirits. She appeared to have the capacity of some actors to come rapidly down to earth after a harrowing, emotionally consuming performance.

Heller offered his warm praise.

'Oh really? Really?' she said as if she could not believe such compliments, and added: 'I'm so glad you came, Fred. So glad.'

'You have become a wonderful actress.'

'Thank you. Thank you. You are sweet. You are all very sweet and adorable. Thank you all so much.'

Dorothy approached to introduce the Dubrelles, and Edwige in the taffeta bow, and Sir Anthony. The praise flowed richly, and Isabelle submitted herself to it with an air of resignation and humility.

Dorothy was a backstage gusher. 'I really don't know where you get it from, honey. That POWER. WHAM! you just hit us with it in the solar plexus. It's scary. When they take you off to the cave, I can tell you, it gave *me* claustrophobia. Where'd you get that from?'

'Oh you know Dorothy, you draw on things,' Isabelle said vaguely.

'How d'you make it so real?'

Isabelle was smiling evasively, wanting to change the subject. She looked towards Heller. It was not really possible to talk. She was being polite to Dorothy, but Heller could see that it was an effort for her. She had, he recalled, a reputation for being determinedly private, hated to be photographed, or for people to pry into her personal life – or to ask her about her acting. A lot of good actors were like that, did not like to explain how they had done a particular performance, perhaps not even to themselves. They tended to be fearful that such explanations dry up the magic, interfere with those subconscious processes by means of which the actor is able to project himself into somebody else's skin. There were things they did not want to render conscious, for fear that the clear light of day would sap the essentially dark and mysterious gift of impersonation that had been granted to them.

Dorothy was continuing to insist in her kiddingly pushy American way that Isabelle give them the 'low-down'.

'You've heard the story about Laurence Olivier and the Method actor?' Isabelle asked.

'I don't think so.'

'Well ... the Method actor, who shall be nameless, says to Olivier, "Now the way I approach it, Larry, is this way. First what I do is, I first of all consider the motivational ..."' Though she had said that the actor would be nameless she had a talent for impersonations, and her listeners had no trouble identifying the American actor as Dustin Hoffman. Catching his voice brilliantly, she expained how he looks into the character's relations with his mother, and so on. That was how he prepared for his part. 'Olivier listens politely,' she continued the story, 'and then *he* says ...' And now she assumed Olivier's grandly resonant tone, '... he says, "Well, that's absolutely fascinating, Dustin, but wouldn't it be a great deal simpler to just do it?"'

Dorothy laughed. 'Oh you're a cagey one. You don't like to give away your secrets. That's mean.'

'If you really want to know I will tell you how I approach this part.'

'Sure we want to know.'

Everyone was waiting expectantly for the revelation.

Isabelle began: 'My lovely old acting coach in New York, he taught me always to start with the sensation ... the concrete.

And so I remember something. A certain sensation ...'

'Yes, dear?' Dorothy asked. It did not seem to be the eye-opener that she was expecting.

'You see, actors are like that, Dorothy. They use anything that works. Their worst fears. A mother on her deathbed. Anything. Nothing is too private or too shameful.'

Charles had been listening. He smiled. 'Isabelle won't tell anyone her secrets. Not even me. She believes in being a mystery. *C'est vrai?*'

—*C'est vrai, Papa.*

She appeared to have thrown off the last vestige of her tragic stage role. She drank a little champagne and seemed in good form. It was difficult to relate this poised and beautiful actress to the tomboyish bold and awkward teenager Heller used to encounter all those years ago – the devilish pool player! – at Charles's house in Washington. Ah! the sneaky way time passed, changing everything.

People were beginning to leave.

'Oh Fred,' Isabelle said, seeing that he also was about to go, 'we haven't had a chance to talk at all. I'm really happy to see you, Fred. And to see that you're all right. I was so worried when I heard that you were at the Brasserie Lipp, when it happened.' She gave him a hug. 'It's been such a long time. Perhaps ... I know you must have a lot of pressures right now, with this awful thing ... and poor old Bill! God! *J'en ai eu des cauchemars.* If you have any time at all ...'

'Soon as things let up a bit. I'll come and see you. I want to see you in the play again. It's a marvellous performance you give. And I want to see *you*. Have a chance to talk. So much has happened.'

'Promise?'

'If I possibly can.'

'The way the things turn out. It is the way you expect it and yet not the way you expect it,' she reflected with an air of sadness.

'What sort of things are you thinking of?'

'Oh life. Not now, this isn't the moment ... but one day,

Fred, if you have the time, we'll have a long talk? Like we used to? Yes?'

Her eyes clouded over, and he thought: yes, she used to be very moody as a young girl, bursting with exuberant energy and joyousness one moment and down the next, with tears quickly following: he thought of something that had been written about her – an actress who even in the full glare of the limelight retains a quality of being 'in hiding'.

The Minister's party was leaving. The visit to the theatre had brought out the press and the television and radio news programmes, and there was a storm of camera flashes as the party, still ensconced in high security, made its way to the waiting cars. The Minister spoke briefly into the microphones being held up all around him, putting across his message that the normal life of Paris must go on.

Heller did not leave with the ministerial party but stayed outside the theatre watching the crowd slowly disperse as the television lights went off and the media people left. Around the stage-door entrance, a handful of fans remained waiting for the actors to come out.

Heller went back into the theatre, across the now deserted lobby. He tried the doors to the auditorium and found one that was open and went in. The theatre was empty. With the departure of the Minister and his party, all security measures had been abandoned. He peered around. In a stalls *loge*, *bombé*-fronted and decorated with gilt garlands, a shadow stirred. Heller froze, a prickly sense of unease along his spine. Heller's unease was a sensitive instrument of measurement that he had learned to heed. He had felt uneasy at Lipp before the horror happened.

A figure emerged out of the dark interior. It was Juvin, wagging his finger: 'Ah! Ah!' What the knowing gesture was supposed to be reproaching him for, on this occasion, was not clear to Heller. The joke was now so firmly established it had become a little ritual with him.

'What brings you here, Claude?'

'To observe, Fred, to observe ...' he declared enigmatically.

'And *Antigone* is such a very profound play. So meaningful for today's audience. A story of terrorism against the State, and the State having to defend itself, even at the cost of an innocent – but wilful, stubborn – young girl's life. Much as I admire Antigone, of course, I have sympathy also with Creon. He is required to safeguard the security of the State in the face of attack by insurrectionists and terrorists. The edict of the council is that the murderous opponents of the State shall not be given the burial that is the right of honest citizens, and Antigone ignores the edict, buries her dead brother. What is Creon to do? If he concedes, he loses authority, loses face ... *Raisons d'état* compel him to impose the terrible sentence and send Antigone to her death.'

'Always knew you had no feelings, Claude,' Heller said lightly, avoiding being drawn into a discussion.

He looked around the empty dark theatre, his eyes tracing the rows of *loges* on different levels: intimate boxes for two, royal boxes that could hold up to twelve. Some of these boxes were situated far back from the proscenium, high up, with poor sightlines, while others virtually overhung the stage. From any of them, though, a terrorist would be able to choose his moment to strike. And someone on stage would afford a very conspicuous target.

'I notice there's no security any more, now that the Minister has left,' Heller said.

'Well, the police can't protect everybody,' Juvin said. 'The Minister is the one who has been threatened ...'

'You don't think there's any danger of them striking at him through his daughter?'

'There is no way of knowing what those sorts of people will do, but it is not possible to cater for every possible contingency.'

Heller nodded, and remained silent.

'Any developments, Claude?'

Juvin said blandly, 'One must not cast one's line precipitately or one may catch a minnow and lose the big fish.'

The man's evasiveness could be maddening. 'Come on, Claude. Goddammit, I didn't fob you off in the case of Legrand. I gave you the goods on him.'

'So you did, so you did! And we are profoundly in your debt for that. Profoundly ... If I were in a position to ...'

'And that wasn't the first time and I don't expect it'll be the last ...' He put a very slight question mark on the 'expect'. 'Claude, I have a report to make. At present I don't have very much to put in it that they can't read in the press. You could tell me what's going on ...'

Juvin considered the request, and painful though it was to him to give anything away, he had to acknowledge that Heller had a point.

'We have made a certain small progress,' he conceded. He paused for a long moment, and Heller had to prompt him.

'Yes? Tell me about this small progress.'

'We found an apartment in the dix-huitième. Empty, but containing some interesting literature and equipment.'

'What sort of equipment?'

'A range of alarm clocks.'

'Yes?'

'And batteries ... mercury elements, metal springs, threaded caps ... We are testing for fingerprints. The place has an air of having been evacuated in great haste.'

'And the literature?'

'Newsletters, private circulation newsletters.'

'Point to anything?'

'Here is a sample.'

He took out of his pocket a single sheet of paper, unfolded it and handed it to Heller, who read it slowly, translating sentence by sentence:

Hunger and fear are the great catalysts that change society. Since in contemporary France we cannot engender hunger on a sufficient scale to move the masses to action, we have to seek to create fear. Fear is a cost-effective weapon. In the safest countries, the sense of security can be undermined by actions which impress upon the populace that they are not safe anywhere. Not safe in their own homes, or the trains that take them to work, or the cinemas or theatres to which they go for relaxation. These must all be our targets, and we must select targets with maximum publicity value so that our message will be most widely disseminated. Since we have not the means for conducting a blitzkrieg, we must use psychology to play on people's inner fears and create a climate of terror. Our purpose is that people shall not feel safe inside their own skins. Only from profound discontent with one's lot does there arise the unstoppable momentum towards fundamental change. A fearful person is a discontented person . . .

Heller looked up; he had reached the end of the page.

'The rest is much in the same vein,' Juvin said. 'An inclination to repeat themselves is characteristic of these fiery minds . . . What do you make of it?'

'Quite well expressed. Educated. Could be a schoolteacher?'

'Could be, yes.'

'Does it fit?'

'Possibly. The fingerprints will confirm. They can't have obliterated every last one.'

'When will you know?'

'The labs are going to work all night. By tomorrow we may have some idea. If you like, I will send my car for you in the morning. We can have a look round. I will tell you where we have got so far.'

When Juvin had left, Heller again made his way backstage, going the way he had come with Charles and his party, and then along the corridor which widened out to serve as a repository for stage scenery and props. A medieval throne in need of re-upholstering. Free-standing Grecian pillars. Painted backdrops of pastoral scenes. *Commedia dell'arte* masks hanging from overhead lines. Nobody was stopping him, and Heller was becoming increasingly concerned about the lack of security. The stage-door keeper was at the artists' entrance, but anybody could come in from the theatre itself, through the door marked *Privé*, which was not locked.

He rapped perfunctorily on the door of Isabelle's dressing-room and without waiting to be asked to come in, turned the knob and entered. He wanted to see how easy it was. It was very easy. He did not like this at all.

Her dressing-room was empty of visitors and she was sitting facing the mirror in the act of removing her make-up. She seemed to be just staring at herself in the glass and for some moments was not aware that he had come in.

He said, 'Sorry to barge in like this. I thought Charles might be here still.'

'No, he left a while ago.' Her voice was flat, dull. It was not just her voice, her whole appearance had become curiously flattened out. Apparently the allure that she could summon up for an occasion she could also quickly discard when the occasion was over. Devoid of make-up her face seemed featureless, like un-worked clay. She appeared to be in a kind of mild trance. He wondered if she might have taken something, a tranquillizer of some sort. She was definitely not in her outgoing, scintillating mood now. In the harsh light of the naked electric light bulb dangling over the dressing-table mirror, she looked small and fragile and, he thought, frightened.

'You're not supposed to see me like this,' she reproached, 'when I haven't got my face on.'

'Sorry about that,' he said.

He slipped out, feeling that he had seen a ghost.

FIVE

WHILE ISABELLE DECOURTEN was giving her shattering
performance as Antigone, in Washington, where it was six
hours earlier, Arthur Simpson, Vice-president of the United
States, was back from lunch and seated behind a desk in his staff
offices in the Executive Office Building. Later in the day he was
going to be standing beside the President, in the rose garden,
fielding questions from the handful of privileged journalists
invited to these off-the-record chats. The understanding was that
the President would be described as 'a high-placed source in the
White House'. It was a rule of these get-togethers that the press
would show restraint in its pursuit of delicate issues, and that for
his part 'the high-placed source', and anyone who accompanied
him, would not tell outright lies. If lies were told and the press
found out, it deemed itself free to pursue any leads it had previously obtained under the seal of confidence, wherever they led.

The Vice-president was a veteran of the political scene and
familiar with the Jekyll and Hyde nature of the press; one moment
they were your friends, the next they were out for your blood. He
was aware, too, that while he already had an office in the White
House, across the corridor from the President's, crossing that
narrow divide and getting to sit in the office on the other side was
a major journey, fraught with possible mishaps. The President,
though old, was in sturdy good health, and unlikely to die in
office or to be shaken out as Nixon had been. So the Vice-

president's sole chance of getting to sit in the office across the corridor was going to be by convincing the electorate to vote for him in sufficient numbers in 1988, and to that end it was important that nothing happened to rock the boat between now and then.

He turned away from his contemplation of the desirable residence across the way to remark mildly to his friend General Riflin, 'Bill's been writing a darn lot of letters. Writing to everyone. Written to the DCI, the DDO, the President. Hell, he's written to the Pope ... '

'To you too, Arthur?' General Riflin asked.

General Riflin and the Vice-president were old friends and colleagues from way back, from CIA days, when Riflin had been Director and Arthur Simpson had served under him as Deputy Director in charge of covert operations. General Riflin, the older man by some fifteen years, had considered his young deputy to be promising material, had thought he might rise to succeed him as Director of the whole outfit some day, but had not really pictured him as President of the United States. Chance and an image of cleanness had got Simpson selected as the present President's running mate for his second term, and now the general poor quality of potential candidates had suddenly opened up the prospect that, simply on the basis of being there, and being known to the public, he might get the nomination, and from there go on to win in 1988.

'Bill knows a lot of people from the old days,' the Vice-president said. 'I expect he's written to all of them, given the situation he's in. Can't blame him exactly. It's the cry of a man *in extremis*.'

'Has he written to you, Arthur?' General Riflin repeated his question.

'Yes.'

The Vice-president hesitated, puckering his lips and shaking his head up and down in a way that his media advisers had warned him not to, because it suggested indecisiveness. If he wanted to be elected in '88 he had to project an image of knowing his own mind and not wavering. Rather than waver, do a U-turn. U-turns if quickly executed were hardly noticed, whereas wavering was highly visible. He had tried out different stances and postures and expressions on a sample audience, whose reactions had been analysed by market researchers with fancy new monitoring equipment capable of recording subliminal responses, and these potential voters had definitely given the raspberry to his little peevish *moue* of complaint with the puckered lips. Real men not only didn't eat quiche, they didn't pout peevishly, his media experts had told him. But in the privacy of his office he couldn't help puckering his lips. Nobody was watching now, except old trusty Ed, who had served under five presidents and was planning to serve under a sixth before finally retiring. General Riflin had a vested interest in Arthur Simpson's election. Arthur had promised him State if he got in, and that was, thought Riflin, a fitting climax to a life of service to the nation.

'We've got to put an end to all this damned letter-writing of Bill's. There's no knowing who he might write to next, and what he might not say.'

'What d'you have in mind, Arthur? How do we stop him writing these letters?'

'Get him out.'

Riflin shook his head solemnly. They had been through all the options in the case of William Buckley and had found no way of bargaining for his life with the Presidency committed to a stance of 'No negotiations, no ransom.' The stuff coming out about the Iran initiative had already shaken the administration's credibility and where all the fall-out was going to settle, finally, was still an unknown factor. Some of it was bound to settle on the Vice-president. Riflin hoped to limit the damage and get it well over with before '88. To risk another initiative that might break during the run-up to the primaries would be courting disaster. If the Vice-president could distance himself from the Iran play, he might be able to ride out that particular storm by '88. But Bill Gibson was a whole new can of worms; opening it was not the way to keep the Vice-presidential image shiny clean in accordance with what the market researchers were saying the electorate wanted.

The electorate might not know this itself, but motivational research showed that whatever they might declare their preference to be in opinion polls – and Arthur Simpson for the present didn't figure very highly in those – what they wanted deep down in their hearts was 'Gary Cooper'. That was the image-makers' conclusion and that was the image they told Simpson to aim for: a decent man, strong, resolute, contained, of unquestionable integrity, morality and honour: 'Gary Cooper'. If 'Ronald Reagan' worked there was no reason why 'Gary Cooper' shouldn't. The thing to remember, the experts had told him, was that 'Coop' never draws first.

The Vice-president clenched and unclenched his hands nervously, another mannerism of which he was required to rid himself, and asked, 'Ed, how much real damage d'you suppose Bill could do, if he started spilling beans in earnest?'

Riflin pondered the question. 'Bill's big action phase was in the forties, fifties and maybe a part of the sixties, and much of that now is ancient history. A lot of those actions have matured or come to nothing. But there is some long-term stuff he had going in Eastern Europe. Some of that still hasn't surfaced. I don't know if it ever will. Yes, there could be damage there . . . I wouldn't know how bad. Then there's the level of image.'

'I'm not talking only of damage on an operational level, Ed,' the Vice-president said, showing some irritability (another trait to be suppressed) at Riflin's failure to comprehend the real issues.

'Well,' Riflin said with a chuckle, 'he certainly knows where a lot of the bodies are buried, and I guess if he starts telling tales out of school there will be some red faces around town.'

'I don't appreciate the lightness with which you take this, Ed. Maybe you consider the post of Secretary of State a light matter. The office of Secretary of State has a great deal to do with imagery, projecting the right image of the United States, and anyone who doesn't understand that is not motivationally qualified for the post.'

'I am very aware, Mr Vice-president, of the power of imagery and of its importance.'

The secret of Riflin's survival throughout five presidencies, of accommodating himself to the differing styles, priorities, policies and ambitions of those five very different men, was quite simply that he had no opinions of his own and was a natural mimic who could without difficulty identify with whoever was his current master. He now identified himself totally with the aims and objectives of the man he was determined would be his 'sixth president', and he therefore understood at once that their problem was one of 'imagery'. Arthur Simpson had got to be made to look presidential.

'You know as well as I do, Ed, that once the press see a loose thread they can't resist pulling. They'll pull everything undone, everything we've been building up.'

'Are you concerned about some particular loose thread?' Riflin asked, focusing on the political problem.

'I can think of some. Expect you can too.'

'Anything Bill says under those sorts of circumstances can be very plausibly denied ... '

'Provided the press don't get it into their heads to follow up the clues.'

'What you have in mind we do?'

The Vice-president folded his arms and pondered. 'Fred Heller?' he asked. 'What d'you think of him?'

'A good man.'

'Reliable?'

'A reliable man, yes.'

'And he knows Bill. Bill was by way of being his mentor. Gives him a good personal motive to get Bill out ... '

'I suppose so ... '

'Well, look, Ed. Supposing Heller got it in his head to act on his own initiative ... to save his old friend and mentor. Affected by the spectacle of what he witnessed at Lipp, he takes it upon himself to ignore strict orders and pursue his own line. He raises the money, he ... Could that be done?'

'I think that could be done, the money could be raised. But they are asking for a lot more than money.'

'Well, that's where the bargaining comes in. I should think one or two of the people on their list who haven't yet been formally indicted could be released, the judge might find nonsuit ... '

'And the resignation of Charles Decourten?'

'That'll be the tough one. But he might be prevailed upon, in the interests of France and the United States ... '

'You want Fred Heller to handle it?'

'I think he should be encouraged to do whatever has to be done. Naturally, he has got to do this on his own. You think he can ... handle it?'

'If anyone can ... '

'He's completely sound?'

'One of the best.'

'Blind spots?'

Riflin thought about this.

'Every man has his blind spots,' he acknowledged. 'What Heller's are I wouldn't care to say.' He thought back. 'He has been known to lose his head over a woman in his time, go off the rails a bit. Yes. Women. Women are his "blind spot", if he could be said to have one at all.'

'Well, that sounds like a pretty human weakness, if it is a weakness,' the Vice-president said, relieved that nothing worse than this was known about Fred Heller. 'In fact,' he added 'it's a "weakness" – impetuosity – that would fit the profile of a man who disobeys orders in order to save a friend, wouldn't it?'

'I think you've got something there, Mr President,' Riflin acknowledged, making a sly old fox's slip of the tongue.

SIX

WHEN JUVIN SAID morning, he meant morning. He was reputed to get to his office at six; his car was outside Heller's hotel at 7:15. There wasn't time for coffee.

'We will have one somewhere on our way,' he said vaguely, a man indifferent to the rituals of meals; he waved to his chauffeur to drive off. 'They have held Bill in that apartment in the dix-huitième. It is confirmed; some of the fingerprints we found are his.'

Heller was silent. 'You got there just too late, huh?'

'We are not the US Cavalry, Fred.'

Juvin wasn't volunteering more than this. Heller prompted him:

'Find any other prints?'

'One that is of interest. We believe it is of the man you saw at Lipp, making the phone call. His name is Gavaudan. We think that he is the author of the pamphlet I have shown you, who signs himself "Marduk".'

'Marduk?'

'That is the pseudo he uses. You remember your mythology, Fred? Marduk was an early Babylonian god, who went around "arrayed in terror". He fought his great battle against Tiamat, the sea, a female god, and a representative of the feminine principle – chaos, blind nature. Marduk was the organiser, the maker of order out of chaos. He slew Tiamat, "splitting her skull open and cutting the arteries of her blood" and in her corpse conceived "works of art".'

'Sounds like our man's style. What d'you know about Gavaudan?'

'He was a teacher of history in a small school in Nevers. Where he lived from the age of seven till he went into the clandestinity. Up till then – nothing to attract attention: married, with two children. Then, in January 1977, he has packed up bags, left his wife, his children, disappeared. Has changed his life and become somebody who lives as a vagabond. Lived here, in this area.'

The car was going along the boulevard Magenta. Beyond the Gare du Nord the streets were teeming. In the boulevard Barbès Juvin's driver took a right turn to enter the Goutte d'Or, an area resembling an Arab souk.

'This is where they have held Bill,' Juvin said, pointing to a building ahead on the right. 'We can go up to have a look. But you will not see much. Our technicians went over it thoroughly.'

If Juvin said thoroughly that meant thoroughly. It was in one of the better buildings, quite reasonably maintained, with high, shuttered windows giving on to shallow wrought-iron window-boxes. There was a double wooden entrance door framed in ornamental *fin-de-siècle* plasterwork.

'I'd like to see it,' Heller said.

Sun Tzu said that if you knew his psychology you had the man, and Heller's system was to put himself in the other guy's shoes, to try to think the way he thought, understand his viewpoint and his feelings, get into his milieu ... into his skin. If you could succeed in doing that, then a point sometimes occurred when the character 'came alive' and you knew what he would do next.

Juvin's driver dropped them at the café-tabac on the corner, and they walked three doors along and went in by operating the door code.

There was a DST man inside by the row of wooden letter-boxes. They walked up four flights of stone stairs to the apartment that took up the whole of the top floor. It was opened from inside by another DST man.

They looked around, and Heller saw that the DST had stripped the place bare. Chalk markings indicated where things had been. A light grey chemical powder lay over shelves and ledges and door knobs and window frames and light switches.

Searching for the shadows that people leave of themselves, Heller could find no trace of the turbulent characters who had lived here with their hostage. The DST had been thorough.

It was an apartment of three rooms, kitchen and bathroom. The oven looked unused ... they must have lived a lot on cold cuts and take-aways, and out of cans.

'How long were they here?' Heller asked. 'Do you know?'

'They were here eight months. And before that they lived in another smaller apartment, just two streets away. They probably moved here because they required bigger accommodation to carry through their plan.'

'How did you find this place?'

'In their hurry to leave, they left a bath tap running. The bath has overrun and the water went through the floor and people below, since they couldn't get any answer, called the *pompiers*. The *pompiers* broke in and when they'd turned off the taps they noticed the alarm clocks etcetera, and they found the literature ... and called us.'

Heller opened the door of a built-in clothes cupboard. It was empty. There were chalk-circled dark-coloured stains on the wooden floorboards.

'This where they kept him, this where they kept Bill? In this closet?'

'Yes. The stains are blood. The blood type matches Bill's. He must have been still bleeding when they got him up here.'

'How did they rent this place?' Heller asked.

'Perfectly legally, giving bank references, a deposit against breakages, proof of income, and the rest.'

'The person who rented it has to be traceable.'

'Yes, we have traced her. But it does not help very much. You know the system they operate, the system of the pyramid?'

Juvin remained quite still, explaining, while Heller walked

about looking at everything, running his hands along walls, opening doors and drawers, sniffing around. Putting himself in this environment.

'At the top of the pyramid,' Juvin was saying, 'is the command structure, a handful of people, and at each level there are just one or two people who communicate with the level above and the one below. At the bottom, at the base, are the foot soldiers, arranged in separate cells, none of more than five people. The people of one cell are not known to those of another cell. The people at the bottom do not know who the ones are at the top, and vice versa. If the pyramid is penetrated from outside the most that can be given away is one compartment. The compartment of the person who has rented this apartment is certainly a compartment of the foot soldiers, and perhaps she is not even one of those, perhaps she is only a camp follower.'

'Who is she?'

'*Une petite bourgeoise*. One of these mixed-up young women with woolly ideas about making a better world. In love with the idea of revolution. Not someone you would think of as a terrorist. She has slept with somebody in the pyramid, and has run errands for them. She found this apartment and rented it in her name. She passed money for them through her bank account with the BNP. That sort of thing. We do not touch her, we watch her to see what she will do ...'

Heller went to the window and looked out. He thought about Nevers, in the cold damp centre of France. A place steeped in provincial inaction and darkness. Nothing going on. A dead place. Occasionally a fair would have visited the town, and Gavaudan the schoolteacher, the teacher of history to bored and inattentive little boys and girls, would have visited the shooting alleys and punctured some caricature faces with the pellets of an air gun, turning the target papers to pulp, obliterating eyes and noses and mouths in his secret ambitions and rages.

Down below, in the side street, there was a small Arab greengrocer and general store, with vegetables and spices ranged outside in crates. He could smell the North African spices in the apartment. Next to the greengrocer, there was a Tunisian place selling take-aways, *beignets* of every sort, round bread loaves stuffed with meat balls and chopped salad; plates of what looked like red beans . . .

There were some dingy bars in the street. A seedy hotel. A shop selling long colourful North African robes – from the iron stays of the awning hung rugs and other textiles. A shopkeeper in a fez lurked amid his bales of cloth and his baskets of beads and his skeins of gold and scarlet thread. Further down the narrow street there were abandoned buildings that had been taken over as squats.

An African in a burnous came out of the store that sold robes and rugs and for a moment his eyes went to the fourth floor window where Heller was standing looking down. The carpet-seller in the fez emerged from his shop, and there was an exchange between the two: it seemed that the black man was asking a question, and the man in the fez also for a moment glanced up to the fourth floor. Then he bent close to the black man and whispered something to him, and the black man's ivory necklaces and bangles clicked like castanets as he listened, while his body was in sinuous motion.

'What else did you find here, Claude, apart from the bomb-making equipment and the pamphlets?'

'Books. Manuals for the revolutionist. And other texts.'

Heller thought: I know Nevers. It's a town where the fountain in the main square switches off at nine p.m. Nothing doing after that. A place in which to dream of bombs and revolution and sudden death.

'What other books?'

'What you would expect. The usual library: *What We Can Learn from the Tupamaros* . . . *Small-Scale Warfare Instructor* . . . *The Urban Guerrilla* . . . *Armed Rebellion* . . . *The Coup d'Etat* . . . *Modern Explosives Technology* . . . the standards . . . and oh yes, yes . . . *Moby Dick.*'

'*Moby Dick?*'

'With certain passages heavily underlined. Relating to Captain Ahab . . . Gavaudan – we conclude it was he – had copied in the

55

margin a quotation from Melville, to the effect that it would not detract from the character of Ahab if either by birth or other circumstances he has a certain half-wilful overruling morbidness at the bottom of his nature, for – and this sentence was underlined three times – all men tragically great were made so by a certain morbidness.'

'Yes,' Heller mused, 'I begin to see him, don't you, Claude? Our man Gavaudan. He's emerging.'

He watched the black man in the burnous shimmy down the street, ivories going click-click like balls on a pool table.

Aspects of Gavaudan's history started coming to light in the course of the next few days, and Juvin, as he had promised, kept Heller in the picture. (Not fully, of course: that would have been contrary to Juvin's principles and character, which required him always to hold back more than he imparted, but he gave Heller the basic storyline of the terrorist's life, as it was becoming revealed.)

The beginnings were in 1977, with Gavaudan leaving his wife and family and coming to Paris to adopt the life of a drifter in the squats of the dix-huitième arrondissement. The area was a multi-racial melting-pot that attracted every sort of marginal: hippies and druggies and drop-outs. And cranks. And bearded ecologists, and environmentalists, and young girls of good families seeking new sex thrills in the workers' communes where they, as well as money and goods, were supposed to be shared equally. Maybe Gavaudan was attracted by the communal sex, the girls worship-ping at the dirty feet of the Trotskyists and the Maoists and the worker revolutionists . . .

This was the time when Action directe was being born, in a volatile coming together of various strands of the far-Left move-ments. There was one section led by Jean-Marc Rouillan that had its origins in GARI (Groupe d'action révolutionnaire inter-national), born out of the Spanish anarchist movement and the anti-Franco struggle. Another section, led by Régis Schleicher, traced its origins back to the abortive 1968 students' uprising in France. There was a group that called itself NAPAP (Noyau armé pour l'autonomie populaire). There was cross-fertilisation with adherents of CCC (Cellules communistes combattantes) from Belgium, the Red Brigades of Italy, and the Fraction armée rouge of West Germany.

Prior to 1979 most of the actions undertaken by these diverse groups in their various ad hoc combinations were against mainly symbolic targets. Gavaudan must have seen in the temperaments of the anarchistic types with whom he was thrown in contact a reflection of himself. Their ideas corresponded with his own: they had in common, hatred of the Americans, the bourgeoisie establishment, the Zionists, the gigantic multinational corporations, and the CIA with its fingers in every pie.

The earliest strikes were against Interpol; l'Office national de l'immigration; le ministère du Travail; the right-wing weekly, *Minute*; Dassault; Elf Aquitaine; the Agence spatiale européenne.

The movement beginning to unite under the banner Action directe was not categorised as an illegal organisation. Juvin's people were keeping watch, but not able to act effectively, since what was in the course of forming was still in an embryonic state and it was not yet clear who were the people who constituted serious threats to the State.

Juvin had considered it best to let the movement develop into a single organism rather than try to stamp out all the disparate elements which were in the course of uniting. He considered the best plan was not to drive the movement underground too soon.

When Gavaudan visited comrades in jail, he was, in common with dozens of other visitors, fingerprinted (without his knowledge), and his prints were filed away in the DST's great computerised archive. The files gave no indication of Gavaudan's direct personal involvement in the earliest terrorist outrages; there was nothing to connect him with the murder of the two policemen in the avenue Trudaine on 31 May 1983. Nor was he thought to have been involved in the nine attacks with explosives that occurred during 1984 against a variety of targets, or in the murder in January 1985 of General Audran, the man at the Ministry of Defence responsible for the sales of arms abroad, or in the attempt on the life of the controlleur-général des Armées on 26 June of that year. But, during this time, Juvin believed he must have become involved in the political struggle going on within the movement. This was increasingly taking the form of a conflict between what were known as 'les mous' and 'les durs', the softs and the hards. The hards in 1985 had gone international, allying themselves with the Fraction armée rouge, the name under which the group formerly known as the Baader-Meinhof gang now operated in Germany. This 'internationalist' group was behind the murder of Audran in France and the slaying of Ernst Zimmerman in Munich.

Juvin told Heller:

'We lose sight of Gavaudan at this point. He is not seen with any of the leaders. He seems to have disappeared. His limited file peters out. At the time, it was thought that he had broken with the terrorist movements. But it is clear now that that was the wrong reading of his 'disappearence'; he was not breaking with them – he was setting up his own group of ultra-hards.'

Further details turned up by Juvin's men had some bearing on this turning point in Gavaudan's life, when he chose between the softs and the hards, and came to the decision that he was to be harder than the hardest.

Yes ... people suddenly 'crystallised'. 'Murbak' arrayed in terror. Nakedly seen in the mirror. A perfect fit. The lost twin. The anarcho-terrorist Priapus refusing to be quelled. A new identity baptised in semen. *This is who I am. Yes. Yes.*

Juvin's people had got hold of Gavaudan's wife in Nevers, and she provided them with photographs of him dating from 1977 when he left her.

He had a rather weak face then, prior to the decisive moment of self-revelation. During the period when he was a husband and father and schoolteacher, leading a provincial family life, the photographs showed a clean-shaven face, unfocused eyes with a certain slyness in them. And then, in the very last snapshot, taken some days before his unheralded departure, he was beginning to grow a beard, a red beard on his weak jaw line and receding chin, a beard that fringed his face with a tenuous fire, and the eyes had a new focus, a focus of contempt.

His wife said that he had always entertained extreme ideas, but had never shown any signs of taking actions. He had railed constantly against the Americans and the CIA and the multi-nationals and the Zionists. Between them they were the cause of much of the evil in the world. He held the conviction, his wife said, that Hitler was the manipulated puppet of American capital-ism, which needed a world war to get back on its feet after the Depression years. The war was to be the engine of business expansion. It was good business for America, according to Gavaudan, the history teacher.

It seemed from what his wife said that the Americans had been a lifelong obsession of his, the bogymen of his private world, behind all sorts of questionable and devious events.

Heller's instructions had been to keep a watching brief, to liaise, to advise the French, to be available for consultation. And to devise a plan to get Bill out. General Riflin told him that it had been decided at the 'highest level' that he was the best man to find the solution. The play was with him. This was a mission that needed his special skills. 'My view's always been to leave the details to the man on the spot,' Riflin claimed untruthfully.

'What are my guidelines? Are you saying to me I'm to ignore stated policy . . . ?'

To which Riflin had replied, 'Fred, you're not going to get me to hold your hand on this. The ball's with you and you've got to run with it.'

SEVEN

'THEY IGNORED THE no entry sign and came along here into the rue Mabillon,' Juvin said, steering Heller through the backstreets behind the boulevard St-Germain. 'We know that now . . . and one or two other things.'

'Glad we know something, Claude.'

'Ah yes. The invisibility of the obvious! Hmm?'

On their right was the arcaded Marché St-Germain, with stalls selling fruit and vegetables, fish, cheeses, meat. The market had formerly extended the entire length of the rue Clement, but a large part of it had fallen into disuse and become wasteland, with only the graffiti-covered arches remaining. This eyesore had been turned into a temporary action playground by the ville de Paris.

There were now a number of police cars in the rue Clement, their roof lights whirling and flashing. Uniformed police guarded the way into the desolate open space.

Juvin led Heller across the litter-strewn ground, stepping around puddles of stagnant water, avoiding oil patches, motor-cycle parts barnacled in rust, broken bottles, items of clothing in an advanced stage of decomposition. Those arches that remained standing were buttressed by steel girders and the entire area had been fenced off from the street to hide it as much as possible from passers-by.

The Mercedes taxi was behind one of the blocked up arches, where it could not be seen from the street. A filthy plastic car hood, patterned in pigeon droppings, lay near by on the ground.

The Mercedes was being gone over by half a dozen forensic scientists, while policemen went through the playground, examining fencing and gates, outhouse buildings, the littered ground. Chaillet was squatting, studying tyre marks, touching them lightly with his fingertips.

'This was where they switched vehicles,' Juvin said.

With the tip of his shoe he shifted a mass of sodden newspaper from his path and looked down the steps by the side of a squat shed-like structure made of breeze-blocks and cement.

'Down-and-outs sleep here. Some of our new *misérables*. The playground is closed and locked up during the night-time. But they have ways to get in. A policeman found one sleeping inside the Mercedes this morning. He had been 'dossing' in the *luxe* for the past few nights.'

The down-and-out was in the centre of a group of plainclothes men from Chaillet's anti-terrorist squad; they were walking him around in an endeavour to sober him up. He was quite young, dressed in what had once been a decent blue suit, a once-white shirt, a striped tie, and a ragged overcoat. Coffee was being poured down his throat, but he had difficulty remembering what had happened last night, let alone four nights ago. The attempt to sober him up had evidently been going on some while.

'Earlier he talked about a van,' Juvin said. 'But whether he was talking of that night or some other night is not clear. Very little sense of time. One day is much the same as another to them, I expect, in their circumstances. Not an unintelligent type. Fell through the gaps in the system.'

Heller accompanied Juvin to the Mercedes. Using paintbrushes, the forensic scientists were dusting the inside of the vehicle for fingerprints. The upholstery and floor were being gone over with a small vacuum appliance. Samples of hair and fluff were extracted from the waste bag and anything of potential interest picked out with surgeon's tweezers and put in plastic containers.

The down-and-out had been made to empty out his pockets

and the contents were arrayed on a plastic sheet spread over the bonnet of the Mercedes. Empty wine bottles. A roll of toilet paper. Bits of mouldering bread. String. A coverless porno mag. A Bic ballpoint pen. Matches. A collection of cigarette butts, with a few smokes left in them.

Among these cigarette ends Heller spotted one which had been rolled by hand and had a home-made funnel mouthpiece.

He was reaching out to examine the butt when Chaillet came up and stopped him, saying not to touch anything. He stared at Juvin. The warning was meant for him as well. Chaillet was a man of territory, and this was clearly his.

—I expect, said Heller, you'll have that analysed.

—I'm sure we will, Chaillet said. I'm sure we will. But I can tell you now what it is. They like a little smoke. And some of the harder stuff too. According to what I hear.

'No more we can do here,' Juvin said. 'This sort of thing is Chaillet's field. I propose we go for lunch. Something I want you to see.'

Heller accepted, surprised at the proposition. Juvin was not a man for lunches, normally.

The cable-car surged up through the lattice-work iron structure and Heller saw the patterned ground opening across the Seine to the fountains of the Trocadero and the white concave of the 1930s Palais de Chaillot. An imposing view that illustrated the French love of symmetry, of balance and counter-balance: the design of the Trocadero's geometrically laid-out gardens was continued across the river in the Champ-de-Mars, completing with schematic *élan* the pattern begun on the other bank. This form of French logic extended right up to the Ecole Militaire.

They went up through the intricate airiness of the Eiffel Tower, resting so lightly on its four feet that the pressure per square inch exerted on the ground was said to be no greater than that of a man seated on a chair. Through clinging steel mesh and the *belle époque* iron arch, up to the second floor, where the broadly based structure narrowed to a high perch. From there the tower tapered abruptly to the communications platform at the summit.

The restaurant was very full, very smart: tones of grey and black, halogen lamps, black china, black-stemmed tulip glasses. Grey napkins matched the grey mist through which Paris appeared matchlessly blurred. The view was something even on a day when you couldn't see anything much.

An expensive restaurant. Heller wondered whether the DST picked up these sorts of bills or did Juvin pay them out of his own pocket. He was a wealthy man. It was said that he did his job out of a sense of public duty, believing that the defence of the Republic against internal or external threat was a task for lofty, disinterested minds far above the common struggle for position and wealth. A mind such as his.

They examined the menu.

Duck terrine with pistachio. Braised bass with vin jaune. Ginger-scented sweetbreads. Bresse squab.

'Are you an amateur of oysters, Fred?' Juvin inquired solicitously. 'I am going to have some myself. They are light.'

Lightness, when it came to eating, was the overriding consideration, as far as Juvin was concerned.

'Oysters for me, too,' Heller said, opting for lightness.

With the oysters, Juvin ordered a Puligny-montrachet '82. A light wine. A wine of finesse.

From within this glass cube poised high above Paris, they could see laid out, as in an old map, the serpent's crawl of the Seine, the Bois de Boulogne compressed into a vertical layer of green, and beyond that, the new skyscrapers of La Défense.

'By most artistic standards, quite hideous really, this tower of Monsieur Eiffel's,' Juvin remarked. 'Yet it has a beauty all its own. Don't you think? Perhaps the beauty of what it stands for. I know I have become exceedingly fond of this pile of old iron. It has come to stand for France, and the French tradition, and when you look down and see spread out, below you, this amazing city, with its two-thousand-year history of literature and art and the struggle for human equality and freedom, I do feel a sense of . . . personal duty: to stop these maniacs who want to smash what others have created.'

'"Marduk" wants to create new works of art in the corpse of the old ...'

'We must stop him, mustn't we?'

'We're agreed there, Claude.'

Heller wondered whether the lunch on the second floor of the Eiffel Tower was solely to impress upon him the glories of France and of its capital, or was there also a more practical purpose to this somewhat unusual choice of restaurant? Juvin had a certain eighteenth-century aspect to him, a fondness for form and cere-mony, and was not to be hurried in coming to the point; Heller raised no professional issues during the second course.

'Claude, it was a good lunch, thank you,' Heller said when coffee was brought. 'But you never eat lunch just for the sake of lunch. And why here?'

'On the night of November 11 Bill dined here. He ate the ginger-scented sweetbreads, drank a bottle of St. Emilion, Grand Cru. Took a Hine with his coffee ... He was alone.'

'I'm impressed, Claude. The details that your flies on the wall put together!'

'No, no, we were not here. This is something we have only just discovered ... I am reconstructing. From the bill and other sources.'

'Ok, you've got me in suspense, Claude. What happened? He orders a second cognac and falls flat on his face?'

'Not exactly.' Juvin had received his bill, and was paying with cash. 'Let's go, Fred.'

He led Heller out towards the elevator, the special elevator rising from the south *pilier* and serving only this restaurant. With a slight gesture towards it, he explained:

'The night of November 11, that is a week before Lipp, there was an elevator failure. Everybody up here was trapped for two hours. Well, most of the diners did not suffer too greatly. The management offered them liqueurs, petits fours. Most people were calmed down. But not Bill. Bill was not willing to sit and wait until the elevator was repaired. He became quite agitated . . . '

The elevator had arrived, its doors opened, but Juvin took Heller's arm and steered him away, took him to the fence of steel mesh to look down vertically into the viscera of the tower through which the massive counterweights were rising as the passenger lift descended.

They could see within the intricate system of rivetted angle-irons that made up the tower's innards, the spiral of narrow stairs rising up to the top.

Juvin pointed to the stairs.

'Bill decided to walk down the stairs, since the elevator wasn't working. These very narrow stairs that wind down, as you see, in a precipitous fashion inside the skeleton of the tower. Only the stairs were blocked off: locked iron grilles denied access to them. A security measure apparently. Bill was furious, demanded that the grilles be opened, to allow him to leave. He suffered from asthma, he said; he could not remain in a confined locked-in space without air . . . Bill can be very insistent, as you know. At any rate he did by these and other threats induce them to get hold of keys and open the grilles. And he went like the devil himself was after him, clattering helter-skelter down those hundreds of stairs, this big man, who had had a fair amount to drink. A miracle he did not fall down the stairs and break his neck. But he was determined to get out. Why so impatient to leave? Instead of accepting the management's offer of liqueurs on the house. Why?'

For a moment or so there was a silence as both men looked out through the latticework of iron into the slanting grey rain. Below, Paris was an underwater city, an aqueous blur of buildings running into each other.

Juvin took Heller by the arm and directed his attention to the big red pulley wheels above them, thick oiled cables drawing up the lift, lowering the counterweights. Above the pulley wheels there was a small service platform reached by an iron ladder.

'The problem with the elevator mechanism was traced, eventually, to the pulley wheels. A blockage. And from that it was not long before they found ... the bomb in the elevator shaft. Fortunately not a very sophisticated bomb, a primitive detonation device that the experts were able to dismantle. Since there was no injury to anyone, the episode was kept quiet, the newspapers carried a story of an elevator breakdown, but that was all. For us it was a sign of what we had to contend with, but the investigations did not lead anywhere. We had no solid indication about who was behind the attempt. That is ... until this morning, when I learn that Bill was dining here that night, and that he ran out when the elevator mechanism failed.'

Heller was staring down into the interior of the tower, picturing Bill clattering down the stairs. Bill must have become aware of the planned *attentat*. He was not one to run needlessly.

Making connections is what this trade is all about, Bill used to teach. Seeing the precursors. Following the thread. Because every event has an aetiology.

'He may have seen something,' Heller said, 'put two and two together, realised they were out to get him. It is too steep a coincidence that there should have been this attempt on November the eleventh, while Bill is dining here, and then a week later when Bill is dining at Lipp there's the second *attentat*. Both places were on his itinerary and the Crillon made the reservations.'

'We are looking into who at the Crillon had access to Bill's itinerary.'

Heller nodded. 'So they were after Bill. He wasn't chosen randomly, simply because he was an American with some past CIA connections. He was picked because he was William Halliday Gibson. They were determined to get *him*.'

'Yes, that is what it does very much look like, Fred. It adds an extra dimension, doesn't it?'

Yes it does, Heller thought. It certainly does. It adds the dimension that for Gavaudan Bill is ... the white whale.

—What does the lab say? Heller asked Chaillet when he finally succeeded in getting the Commissaire on the line in the late afternoon.

—What I have thought. The lab report says the active ingredient is tetrahydrocannabinol. THC. Cannabis. High-grade shit is their smoke. They smoke Sensimilla. They spoil themselves. The grains of white powder we got off the upholstery were cocaine.

Heller took the metro. The No. 4 line (Porte de Clignancourt–Porte d'Orléans) was known as one of the main drug-dealing circuits in Paris. Street dealers operated on the platforms and in the corridors, on the escalators, in the toilets. They also operated in bars and cafés at selected spots around certain stations of the No. 4 line.

He got off at Barbès Rochechouart and walked through the packed streets.

The far-Left 'hards' would readily resort to bank hold-ups (dubbed 'proletarian reappropriation'), but regarded drug dealing as 'dirty', participating in the capitalist system. Their relationship to drugs was strictly as consumers.

Heller pictured Gavaudan and his small band of followers 'living in the populace like fish in water', in accordance with the revolutionary teaching of Mao: going to the corner café for cigarettes, to the poky little supermarkets for their provisions, frequenting the neighbourhood brasseries, finding their pleasures and amusements in this environment. They would have sought to 'disappear' while 'Marduk' dreamed his violent dream of the new order, of social justice arising out of the dead body of the old. Heller saw a man with a permanent grudge. There were rages that fitted neatly into any delusional system. As he went around in these streets, an alien spirit among aliens, he would have taken a harsh and bitter pride in his outsiderism, in not belonging anywhere, or to anyone, in being part of this tide of drifting washed-up humanity. And he would have found in clandestinity his natural habitat.

This would be where they shopped for their drugs, right here, on street corners, in bars and cafés, in the doorways of derelict buildings.

Some way into the dim interior of one of these disintegrating piles, a dark face glimmered momentarily in the light of a match, and Heller saw the litter of syringes on the ground. He took a couple of steps into the dimness, smelling the decay coming out of the walls. He murmured into the dark:

—Sensimilla? You have Sensimilla?

—What you looking for, mister? You looking for something special?

—Yes, something special.

The man came forward into the light. He had the red-rimmed eyes, the bombed-out face and the sickly skin of someone hooked on his own dope, and the dirty little bags he fished out of his pocket to dangle with obscene provocation in front of Heller did not inspire confidence.

Heller said, Maybe another time. He walked on.

Rubbish bins overflowed in the narrow streets between squats where ground and first floor windows were all bricked up with breeze-blocks. In the boulevard de la Chapelle the metro trains rumbled overhead, and a heavily concentrated smell of offal rose from butchers' slabs.

In the dim backstreets *maghrébin* men were huddled around upended cardboard boxes marked out with squares; money was placed in these squares, dice rolled, cash changed hands. Heller noted which men had the fattest money rolls in their hip pockets and the fastest rotating eyes as they placed their bets, the ones who met his eye as he looked around searchingly and were ready to detach themselves from the game at a moment's notice.

He was identifying them one by one, on street corners, in bars, in parked cars, in entrances. He saw the deals being done, a quick turning of backs, and a huddled conference, faces to wall. A transaction followed: a package for a roll of bills. A familiar ritual of urban life anywhere.

Once or twice he came close to some of these men, murmured, Sensi? and watched for a reaction. They always said Yes, but it depended how they said it, with what degree of conviction. He hadn't got a really convincing Yes so far.

He went into a brasserie with a curved wooden bar; mirror

68

mosaics were coming away from the walls, but there was a spanking new Wurlitzer Lasergraph belting out American rock with accompanying visuals. People stood at the counter, where drinks were cheaper.

Heller took a table in the corner, with a view of the door. A *maghrébin* boy with dark and daring eyes and long eyelashes came to take his order. Heller ordered a glass of red wine, and when the boy came back with the drink, asked him if he'd seen Click-Click.

—Click-Click?

—The black man. The black man with all the ivories.

—I don't know who you mean, monsieur.

—You know who I mean. What's your name?

—Achmed.

—I was told to come here, Achmed. I was told he comes in here.

He slipped a 100 F. note across the table to the boy, in payment for the drink, and told him to keep the change.

After ten minutes a black man came in and exchanged some whispered words with Achmed. Achmed looked towards Heller and his long eyelashes fluttered, his eyes flashed.

The black man went to one of the pin tables and began to play the game of Royal Flush. He played excitedly, talking to himself, urging himself to win. He was in spangled jeans, leather jacket, and spangled boots, but he didn't have any ivory bangles or necklaces and he didn't go click-click as he moved. He moved soundlessly.

Finishing his game of Royal Flush he ambled by Heller and in passing informed him:

—I must go to make pee-pee.

—Is that a fact? said Heller.

He followed the black man down the stairs to the toilets, stood at the next bowl to him.

—You are looking for something? the black man asked.

—Sensimilla, Heller said.

—Sure, sure, the black man said. He held up the fingers of his left hand. *Cinq cents balles.*

69

—OK, Heller said.

The black man put out his hand.

Heller held back.

—Let me see.

—I give it to you. What do you want?

The fingers twitched impatiently, aggressively. Heller took out a 500 F. note. He held it loosely without letting go of it, and the black man fished up from his groin a little packet of something that looked like blue tea. At the same time he grabbed the 500 F. note from Heller's fingers and pocketed it.

He was turning and going up the stairs as Heller opened the packet and smelled it.

He came after the black man and took hold of his arm.

—This isn't Sensimilla. This is ordinary shit.

—You're in France, the black man said. This isn't the USA, friend. This is what you get for your money in France, understand?

—You said it was Sensi.

—This is French Sensi, OK? the dealer said.

—No, not OK. I don't want this. Give me the money back.

The black man said he didn't give refunds. A knife had appeared in his hands, its blade catching the light.

—OK, listen. Tell me where I can get the real stuff. Tell me where I can get Sensi and you can keep the five hundred francs. Tell me and you get another five hundred.

The black man folded his knife away and walked slowly up the stairs.

At the top he said, smiling contemptuously:

—I don't know where you can get this Sensi, I never even heard of this shit.

The phone was ringing as he got to his room.

Heller said, '*Oui?*' and there was a silence which lasted for several seconds.

Then a girl spoke. She spoke in French, in a flat, low voice:

70

—I have something for you.

—Who are you?

—It does not matter.

—What have you got for me?

—You must meet me in five minutes at L'Escurial.

—How do I find you?

—Just tell the waiter who you are and that you are expecting someone.

She had hung up before he could say anything else.

Well, blind dates were an aspect of the business he was in. He slipped the Browning automatic in his jacket pocket and took the elevator down. The Escurial was on the corner of the rue du Bac and the boulevard St-Germain, and from the Pont-Royal it didn't take more than a couple of minutes to get there.

Heller went in slowly, noting carefully where the exits were; he twice changed his mind about where he was going to sit, finally selecting a seat between rubber plants, with his back to a wall covered in a blue cloth material. The whole café was in tones of blue: walls, carpets, chairs, banquettes.

He ordered a coffee and told the waiter that his name was Heller, that he was expecting somebody, a girl, and to direct her to his table. The café wasn't very full and Heller systematically examined every face.

Presently the waiter returned with the coffee and set it down, slipping the machine check under the saucer. Then he felt inside his pocket and handed Heller an envelope, saying he had been told to give it to him. Who by? Heller demanded, looking around. But the waiter couldn't see her any more. She must have left, he said. What did she look like? Heller asked. He was told: about thirty, brown hair, medium height, wearing a raincoat. A very nervous young lady. Heller sipped his coffee and regarded the blank self-seal envelope carefully, on both sides, before opening it.

The letter inside was written on graph-lined paper torn from a *brouillon* exercise book. There was a date but no address. The letter was from Bill and the handwriting was shaky, very shaky. Bill's hand hadn't been too steady at the best of times.

71

Heller read:

Dear Fred

They are allowing me to write this – it's my idea to establish an alternative circuit, a hot-line between you and me. Because my experience is you can't trust the French! They are a whole tricky bunch.

Fred, my time is running out. They are going to execute me in seven days' time, if they don't have a satisfactory response before then.

Ever since I was taken there has been a deathly silence from all my so-called friends and former colleagues. Those fuck-faces in Washington, they have done nothing, and the French the same. None of the people I've gotten in touch with, people I know well, people in positions of power, who owe me, for whom I have done things in my time, has made one move, sent out one signal to get me out of this. The bastards are going to write me off. Well, I tell you this, I'm not ready to be written-off so easy. I'M NOT GOING TO GO QUIETLY. I know that if you're in my position you are supposed to take the rap without complaint. You're supposed to do that. You're supposed to accept that they put the bullet through the back of your head, you're supposed to be dignified when they bundle you up in the trash can like so much refuse and blow your brains into the left-overs of their breakfast. The French did a deal over Peyroles. They let Abou Daoud go when they had him in their hands. They set him free in return for an understanding to keep France out of the firing line. So don't tell me that they don't do deals ... If there is going to be an A-list and a B-list when it comes to whose life is considered worth saving, I don't intend, after my record of service, to be B-listed.

Now the way to see my situation is this way. Morally you are – and they are, our lords and masters in Washington and our friends and allies in Paris – where I am. Exactly where I am. Because I am being condemned for what I have done as *their* representative, for carrying out their orders and if I go down, others will go down with me. Arthur Simpson can say goodbye to his presidential ambitions, and Charles to whatever are his. I AM GOING TO ROCK THE BOAT, YOU BET I AM! I am going to rock the boat so fucking hard it'll make Watergate and Irangate look like storms in a teacup. Skeletons are going to come tumbling out of cupboards, Fred. The world's going to find out about some people's pasts. It's going to find out the truth! The world's going to find out what went on in France during the war. And after. This is going to be a psychodrama about the old times. And will it make waves! The French don't like to face up to the truth of what happened during the war, they keep the Gestapo files tied up with string, buried in deep cellars, unopened. The occupation was a time of shame and they don't want to open pandora's box, but I'm not so lily-livered, with seven days left to go. Make that clear to them, Fred. Make it real clear. I AM AT DEATH'S DOOR AND I AM NOT GOING TO BE A GOOD SPORT ABOUT IT, FRED!! I'm not going to go not saying anything. Yes, I'm bitter. I'm bitter as hell. They abandoned me, threw me on the JUNK HEAP after I gave them FORTY YEARS OF SERVICE, after I served them well, as well as I know how, and if I say so myself after having done some services for my country that will get a line or two in history. After all that they kicked me out with nothing. Just kicked me out. They showed me no generosity and I owe them no loyalty. The loyalty I owe is to my country, not to individuals who are serving their own personal interests.

Everybody seems to be united in wanting my death – the people who hold me here, and the rest of you out there; you all think it's going to solve something if I die, my captors will have made their point, that they mean business, and the French and American governments will be seen to have stood firm, and all will be forgotten by the time of the presidentials in '88.

I want to disabuse everybody of that cosy scenario, Fred. That may be the way it's written, but it's not the way I'm going to play it, and I remind you I AM THE STAR PLAYER! If I go, I will not do so absolving others with my death, I will not

73

discharge them of their guilt by dying for them. No. If I have to go down it will create a WHIRLPOOL and others (SOME IN VERY HIGH PLACES!!!) will go down with me. There are things I will talk about before I go. The people concerned know what those things are. I will talk to the cameras and I will tell everything. And however much Reagan says it's not good ole Bill talking, it's some brainwashed and programmed zombie who's not to be believed, I will give chapter and verse which the media can pursue and check and they will want to pursue and check this stuff, I promise you. Oh yes!

Fred, I am not getting at you in any of this. Your hands are clean and I regard you as a friend, a trusted friend. Perhaps my only friend now. And as an honourable and able representative of the interests of the United States, which both you and I have always served and continue to serve, as God is my witness.

See what you can do for me, Fred.

Now to some practicalities. Keep this letter to yourself, it's personal to you. Act on it but don't show it.

A signal must come from the French government. Indicating that they are willing to meet the terms.

To get in touch ring the telephone number below and leave a message for 'Elvire' and you will be rung back. You have to phone before 13:00 and then allow at least two hours for the phone call to be returned. Don't try to find 'Elvire'. She is a circuit-breaker and can't lead anywhere, except to my death. If you make any moves to find her it will be taken by my captors as a sign of bad faith and they will implement the sentence immediately instead of waiting seven days.

That is all for the present, old friend.

As ever, Bill

Heller thought of Bill in his heyday, so confident and arrogant in his manipulation of others, so certain of his cause. And now here he was reduced to this pathetic plight. Did he really mind so much about dying? Or was it being on the B-list that irked him most? The worst thing for him would be the humiliation, the helpless-

74

ness. Being dependent on them for the alcohol he couldn't do without. Finding his craving reducing him to a state that he would despise in himself.

Heller looked at his watch. Seven days to go.

He paid for his coffee and went to the Embassy and put through a call to Washington on a secure line. He was calling a special number at the White House, and when he got through he asked for General Riflin. Riflin was the troubleshooter, he was the man to talk to about something like this. He was the one who would entertain 'unorthodox' solutions.

Riflin listened to Heller's account of what was happening, and said he would take some soundings and ring back. He told Heller to stay by the phone.

Two hours later he rang back.

'The monetary aspect is running positive,' he said. 'Has got to be worked out. May take a while. See if you can hold things whilst that's happening. See if you can get our friends in France to meet some of those other conditions.'

'I'm thinking of one condition that I cannot see our friends meeting.'

'Lay it on strong, Fred. Appeal to his patriotism. Indicate to him that Franco-American relations are at stake. He has got to be made to face what the consequences could be of this thing. We've got "Irangate" on our hands, we don't want "Parisgate" as well. Pull out all the stops.'

As soon as he had put down the phone to Washington, Heller called Charles Decourten's private number.

The person who answered said that Monsieur Decourten was unable to come to the telephone. He was occupied. Could he be given a message?

—Tell him it's Fred Heller, that I have to see him urgently. This evening.

—I doubt if that will be possible, Monsieur Heller. Monsieur Decourten has guests.

—Please give him the message. I'll hold on.

Heller waited holding the phone. He could hear the discreet

75

low buzz in the background. Charles had always given good parties. In his Washington days he was considered a bit of a celebrity snob. And a lightweight. Not one to rise to great heights. Perhaps not ambitious enough, though Heller had known that wasn't true. Charles had made his way. From being a dashing young *chargé de missions* for de Gaulle, after the war, to his present key ministerial position. He had benefited from what de Gaulle called 'the element of genius that is chance': in his confrontation of the terrorist menace he had placed himself in the forefront of the public consciousness.

The man on the phone said:

—Monsieur Decourten has asked me to tell you that he is very occupied this evening. However, if it is a matter that absolutely cannot wait until the morning, he will try to find a few minutes this evening to see you, Monsieur Heller. If you will come here . . .

—I'll be right over, Heller said.

EIGHT

CHARLES DECOURTEN'S PRIVATE apartment was in the rue de Lille, behind the quai Voltaire, in a *quartier* where there were still a number of *hôtels particuliers* that had belonged to the likes of the Rochechouarts and the Montesquieus and the Bourbon Condés.

There were crush barriers both sides of No. twenty-nine. Heavy security. Heller had to show his passport and he saw the police check his name on a list.

The building that Charles lived in was one of the smaller eighteenth-century mansions in this street. It had been converted into spacious apartments, each one with its own entrance from the courtyard. Heller took in the graceful façade, the intricate iron-work of balconies, the rich corbelling, the perfectly proportioned high windows. Superb! Oh Charles knew how to live! Always had done. He had flair and he had style ... and this was the grand style.

Inside, there was the cluttered and somewhat faded and even slightly shabby pomp of a princely line. The sort of place you could imagine having been in the family for centuries. Nothing suggestive of the *nouveau riche* for Charles. There was heavy old damask wallpaper coming away from the walls in places. Some sun-bleaching, and penetration by rainwater. No need to repair and re-polish everything as if you were an interior decorator. There were a lot of bronzes, a wing-footed Hermes on a plinth, a

Venus in a pillared niche, smaller figures of horses, huntsmen, athletes. The bust of a Roman general looked down from a high corbel. Satyrs and nymphs displayed on glass shelves in recesses. Surfaces were crowded with chinaware and small busts and carved ivory figurines. Bronze encrusted furniture, tortoiseshell inlaid with brass, brass inlaid with tortoiseshell. A little palazzo.

The place was large enough not to seem full, even though it must have held more than forty people. A formal party. Men in dark suits, many in dinner suits, a few in dress shirts with winged collars. The dominant note in the case of the women was elegance and restraint.

Heller spotted Charles in a group that included his American wife Dorothy, who wore her jewels without any inhibitions tonight. Among these people the flaunting of wealth was hardly a problem. These people were old money and old power. The French political and financial ruling class.

Seeing Heller, Charles frowned very slightly and indicated that he would be with him in a moment, and when able to do so without undue abruptness, extricated himself from his guests and came to the door.

'Well, Fred. What was it could not wait until tomorrow? As you can see . . . '

'Let's talk somewhere more private.'

'I will be with you shortly, Fred. I must have a word with Le Quineau first. Ah, Annette, chérie . . . ' A tall woman, all in black, with a choker pearl necklace forming a clasp around her swan-like neck, had approached. 'You have met Annette? Annette du Breuil-Hélion de La Quéronnière. Fred Heller of the State Department.'

The woman with the very long name was in her sixties, with finely engraved lines in her white features, which contrasted strikingly with her black hair.

'You have seen the television, monsieur?' Annette du Breuil-Hélion de La Quéronnière enquired conversationally of Heller. This could refer only to Charles's recent appearance on *L'Heure de vérité*.

78

'Yes, I have.'

'What was your opinion?'

'I thought Charles came out of it pretty well.'

'And what was your opinion of that man from *Le Monde*? Beaucousin. He has some grievance against Charles, do you think?'

'He was trying to rattle Charles. But that's normal enough. Makes good TV. Any case, Charles wasn't being rattled.'

It *had* been good TV, the moment when Beaucousin, with his provocative, knowing air, said:

—You have to admit, Monsieur Decourten, that in France we are none too keen to get to the bottom of things. We keep our skeletons locked in the cupboard, wouldn't you say?

—These skeletons you refer to, Monsieur Beaucousin. Perhaps more correctly described as phantoms? Of the journalist's sometimes overheated imagination.

Though Charles had neatly turned the question, a feeling had been left that this man Beaucousin knew things that he wasn't revealing. Annette of the very long name had evidently been angered by the journalist's insinuations.

'You know Charles well?' she asked Heller.

'Yuh, we've known each other a long time, nearly twenty years, it must be.'

'I have known him for . . . forty years.'

'That *is* a long time. You must know Charles better than he knows himself.'

'He is very popular with the French people. Public opinion is very much behind him. In what he seeks to do to fight terrorism. They see that he is a pragmatist, not an *idéologue*. They trust him, because they see he is a man who believes in what works, and not in arid doctrinaire notions. You know that he is talked about as a possible future *premier ministre*?'

'I've heard that said.'

'It is not just talk.'

Charles had returned. He asked Annette to excuse them and led Heller through rooms that displayed a taste for the over-elaborate

Napoleon III style, with the pom-poms and the tassles and the heavy braiding and the sinuous curves. A slow progress, with Charles stopping to flatter, to charm, to make witty remarks. Heller saw Isabelle arrive. She was having her coat taken and being offered a glass of champagne by a waiter. She must have come directly from the theatre and was looking tired, but as she entered the party ambience she threw off the tiredness, put on allure. Someone who could rise to occasions, summon up beauty by an exercise of will. With her was Jean-Pierre Duru, the young actor who played Antigone's fiancé, Haemon. He was dressed with rather aggressive informality in a buckskin blouson and Kenzo jeans. The blonde girl who played Ismene, Antigone's sister, followed them in, and with the arrival of these actors the mood of the party turned decidedly more boisterous. Jean-Pierre's jeans had developed tears just below the buttocks, to which Isabelle was laughingly drawing attention. Becoming aware that Heller was observing her, she wriggled her eyebrows Groucho Marx fashion. Heller thought: one minute she's this unquiet spirit, the next she's a clown. A roller-coaster temperament.

He approached her. She seemed glad to see him, had not expected him to be there.

He said that he had some matters to discuss with her father, but would come and look for her when he was through.

'Promise,' she urged. A shadow passed over her, wiping away the summoned-up high. 'You won't disappear?'

'I won't disappear.'

Jean-Pierre had come to her side, and she was clowning again. '*Mon fiancé!*' she declared with a send-up flourish of the hand. 'I'm his luckless love. We are married in death. And it is no Fun, believe me. But *he*' – another Groucho wriggle of the eyebrows – 'is fun. Glug-glug-glug! Aren't you, Jean-Pierre?'

Jean-Pierre parted his luscious lips and showed perfect white teeth in obedient demonstration of how much fun he was.

Others crowded around, and Heller extricated himself to rejoin Charles, who had finally succeeded in making himself available. They went into the study. Charles seated himself to the side of his desk and indicated an adjacent chair for Heller.

'Well. What is it has happened?' he demanded, dropping the charm.

'Charles, I have received information – don't ask me the source but it's reliable – that they're going to execute Bill in seven days' time, unless their demands are met. Bill is in a pretty embittered state, ready to make some last confessions that will rock boats. We're talking about stuff that will have international repercussions. Affect the American government. Affect the French government. Affect individuals ... Something is liable to blow up that'll be more serious than the Iran initiative.'

'You have been talking to Riflin.'

'Among others.'

'Fred, certain people have a tendency to scream before they are hit. Riflin is one.'

'He says we don't want to wait till the shit hits the fan. Thinks something has got to be done now.'

'What, for instance?'

'I'll lay it out for you. In order of rising unpalatability.'

'Very well, Fred.'

'One. Prevail on the Président de la République to send out certain signals. A reference to his willingness to help resolve the hostage crisis by the exercise of the Presidential pardon. Tell him that we are not asking for a commitment, only for a signal, a tactical move. He's a tactician of genius, he'll understand. But it has to be done fast. They have to see it as a response to their demands.'

Charles had picked up one of the porcelain cranes from his clear desk, a desk that bore only objets d'art and a large number of photographs in filigree silver stands. If Charles worked at home, there was no indication of it; he must have kept his papers locked up in drawers. The antique silver pen and ink stand, with its finely curved penholders and intricately carved inkwell lids, didn't look as if it had been in use for the last couple of hundred years.

Charles gestured elegantly. 'That could only be a stopgap. Between an illusion and the fact there is a huge distance. The

President could not pardon certain individuals specifically to free Bill, while leaving the French hostages in Lebanon to their fate. Their incarceration has gone on much longer than Bill's and naturally weighs more heavily on French consciousness.'

'It's to buy time. Enable us to implement other steps.'

'Which are?'

'There looks like being a possibility of some sort of monetary package.'

'I would not wish to have anything to do with such a "package".'

'There would be no need. You've asked me to be the intermediary. I'll take care of it, Charles.'

'What other steps?' Charles asked, his brusqueness increasing.

'If one of their people could be released. If the *juge d'instruction* found *non-lieu*. I'm not talking about leaders . . . but somebody on the fringes. As a gesture. A tactical gesture.'

'The *juge d'instruction* is independent in France. We have no control over his decisions.'

'That's a problem that could be left to Juvin to handle, provided he didn't encounter any ministerial opposition . . .'

'If these are supposed to be the more palatable solutions, what is the *less* palatable?'

'That certain rumours appear in the press. In the *Canard*, say. To the effect that you are contemplating resigning from the government. For personal reasons. That'd give Attaque the impression they're winning, that they can get everything they want if they hold out long enough. It buys us time. Whatever the final package is, I need more than seven days to put it together.'

Charles Decourten's head was nodding sagely while he turned the exquisite crane over in his hands, fondly examining the reign marks in Chinese calligraphy on the base.

'Superb, isn't it? Ming – sixteenth century,' he intimated in a delicate undertone. He returned the crane to its place on the desk. 'Am I actually expected to resign, at some stage, to fit into your "package", Fred? Or are we simply talking of a rumour that will turn out false?' he enquired in the same delicate undertone, with a dismissive little pass of the hand.

'Would depend on how things develop. If I can win some other points and trade them off . . . '

Charles's fine hands lay interwoven upon his lap. His attitude was statesmanlike. He pondered for a while, nodding, regarding his fingers carefully. The timbre of his voice did not change.

'It looks to me as though some people in Washington are suffering from very early pre-election jitters. Arthur Simpson is not even a front-runner at the moment. The panic is uncalled for, and premature.'

Heller said, 'Two years before a presidential election may be premature in France, it ain't in the United States.'

Charles stood up and began to pace slowly, deliberating, the elegant frown tightly compressing his brow. Heller thought: yes, he has increased in stature, there is hardly any vestige of the lightweight left now. If great events produced great men, Charles may at last have found the events he needed. This was the stern and yet compassionate expression that looked so good on TV. The image he had left of himself in *L'Heure de verité* was of a dynamic man, poised for action, but calm and serious and reflective. Not one to overreact. Not one to be panicked. At the end of the programme the viewers had been strongly in his favour. Seventy per cent of the 500 polled saw him as a future premier ministre, 85 per cent approved of his handling of the terrorist threat. In the atmosphere of intangible menace which the terrorist outrages of recent months had engendered in France, Charles Decourten was someone who reassured people. He had the gift of calming. Even in the face of Beaucousin's allusions to cover-ups and matters never gotten to the bottom of in France, Charles had scored, making a point of placing the national interest before the press's hunger for sensation.

'The *Le Monde* man, Beaucousin,' Heller said, 'gave the impression he knew more than he was saying.'

'It is that sort of journalist's technique to give such an impression.'

'Will you think about it?' Heller began, but Charles stopped him. He had the TV look now: all directness and strength and unflinching resolve. His hands became fists.

'Fred, these terrorists of Attaque have an especially ferocious – obsessive – hatred of everything American. The Americans are their bugbear. And because I have shown my "pro-Americanism", am married to an American woman, and have shown a determination, which perhaps goes further than that of some of my predecessors, to destroy them, they are bent upon removing me from the scene, be it by obtaining my resignation ... or my death. The idea that one might accede to such people in order to buy off their menaces ...' His hands flew up vigorously, showing the contempt he felt for any such tactic. 'It's out of the question. Riflin – and the Vice-president – must be made to understand that making concessions to these sorts of people, in order to save the life of one man, and possible embarrassment to some others, places in peril the lives of hundreds. They have tried to blow up the Eiffel Tower. Remind them in Washington of the numbers of American tourists, men, women and children, who would have lost their lives, or been appallingly maimed, had that succeeded. The bomb in the elevator shaft was primitive but had it gone off I am told the tower would have broken off like a beanstalk, it would have been carnage ... The political ambitions of individuals cannot count when weighed against these sorts of risks ...' He paused momentarily in his powerful rhetoric, and Heller quickly cut in.

'Charles, you agreed I should be the intermediary. I think I have a way in to them now, it's tricky, very tricky, but I can see a glimmer of a chance ... Only ... I can't go to them empty-handed. I have to bring them something. You have got to give me *something* to hold out to them, for me to be able to get my foot in the door.'

Charles Decourten considered this, his head nodding. 'What I will do', he said, 'is I will go to see the Président de la République and I will say to him that the government is working on a plan to resolve the hostage crisis. I will say that some public reference from him to the presidential prerogative would be helpful ... he will understand, he will not wish to be left out of any possible solution ... Now I must get back to my guests. Why don't you stay a while, Fred? Have something to eat. A glass of wine.'

The sound level in the next room had noticeably increased.

'I expect more of Isabelle's actor friends have arrived,' Charles said with a smile. 'Unwinding, I think it is called. There will be some pretty girls. The party risks to become quite lively in due course ... once the gerontocrats have departed.'

'Thanks, Charles. But I should be going. This is a good time to find people at their desks in Washington.'

'Well ... if you change your mind, you are most welcome to stay.'

'Another time, Charles.'

Left alone in the study, Heller thought: all the same, a glass of wine would not go amiss, it has been one hell of a day. There were days when nothing happened, when it was all waiting in the dark, and days when it was one thing after the other.

His eye was drawn by the photographs on Charles's desk. They constituted a sort of pictorial chronicle of Charles Decourten's rise in the world. Some of the earliest showed a very youthful-looking Charles with General de Gaulle. Then gradually, very gradually, he was seen to grow older, invariably in the company of the great: Kennedy, Nixon, Kissinger, Gromyko, Mao Tse-tung, Chou En-lai, Pompidou ... Giscard d'Estaing. Mitterrand. There were also some very early photographs of Charles in the Resistance. One in particular caught Heller's attention. It showed two men with pistols and Sten guns, wearing Resistance berets and arm-bands. In this photo Charles couldn't have been more than twenty-two. He was looking with hero-worship at the other person in the picture, who bore a striking family resemblance to him.

'It is Charles with Henri,' a woman's voice explained.

The speaker was the woman with the long aristocratic-sounding name and the white face and the black hair.

'His brother Henri?'

Heller picked up the silver stand and looked at the photograph more closely.

'I've heard Charles speak of him.'

Henri had the appearance of someone brimming over with self-confidence and daring. Striking eyes. A compelling personality. Sure of his destiny. Next to him Charles looked unformed.

'What happened to Henri?' Heller asked Anette du Breuil-Hélion de La Quéronnière.

'He died. During the war. Was murdered by the Germans. It was a great tragedy. He had tremendous . . . charisma. The power to lead and make others follow. If he had lived, he would have been a major figure in France's history.'

'Really?'

'What I find so interesting about history, Monsieur Heller, is what it tells you about the future.'

'And what is that, madame?'

'Oh that there is an unseen thread of continuity linking the past and the future. You must know the Russian saying that the man who waits long enough by the river bank will see the body of his enemy floating by.'

'Depends how good a connection your man has with the KGB, I would say.'

'You must have a look at the Fragonards, Monsieur Heller,' Annette du Breuil advised, 'if you have not seen them. They are charming.'

Heller went into the salon and took a glass of wine from one of the tables on which the buffet supper was laid out. He held up the glass to the light. The wine had a pretty colour, and when he sipped it, presented a firm fleshy taste to the palate. A Burgundy of a good year, maybe a Nuits-St-Georges. He drank one glass rather faster than such a good wine should have been drunk and poured himself another to make up for this lapse. He felt the wine entering nicely into his bloodstream, softening hard edges with its rich dark spice. He was tired, pretty damned tired, he realised, and it went deeper than this one day of confused developments. He was getting tired of his strange secret stardom in the grey area

86

where things had to be done that could not be seen to be done. There were some days ... oh there were some days when he would have gladly quit. The job wasn't even well paid, and there lay the whole problem. He couldn't quit. Didn't have the money to quit.

A girl with chopped off hair, an adherent of the androgynous look, bright as metallic paint, came up to him and asked if he knew where the 'dirty pictures' were. He took this to be a reference to the Fragonards. He said he did not know but offered to join her in the quest. Her name was Flo, and she was an American actress working in Paris. She signalled to Jean-Pierre Duru, indicating Heller. '*He* knows where they are.' Perhaps this falsehood was to lure the actor with the luscious lips, who seemed much in demand.

Actors were not the only ones who needed to unwind. Heller followed them through sumptuous rooms of kingwood and tulipwood and Carrara marble. The Fragonards were found in a bedroom. Stolen kisses. A basket overturned in the course of some suggested activity in the background. A dreaming nymph on a bed, legs widespread, approached by an angel with a flaming torch – *Putting the Flame to the Powder*, the picture was called. Charming, charming. Flo was disappointed, though. Not what people cracked them up to be, she said.

He caught sight of Isabelle in a group of older men; they were the sort of men who ran Dassault, and Elf Aquitaine, and Paribas, and the Banque de France, and France itself probably, but maybe were not the most amusing company. She appeared tense and nervous and bored and was glancing around. Seeing Heller, she used this as an excuse to remove herself from the unamusing company.

'You were going to leave, without even talking to me,' she said accusingly.

'No, I wasn't going to do that. Definitely not. I was looking for you. Are you all right?'

Her eyes were going around the room in a restive way. She was very pale and swaying slightly and for a moment he had thought that she was going to faint. The high spirits seemed to be all used up.

'What was it you had to talk about, with Papa?'

'I liaise with Charles concerning Bill Gibson.'

'Has there been a development?'

'Nothing solid.'

'You know they have given me a bodyguard. Because of the threat to my father. Did you know?'

'Yes, I had heard that. It's a good idea. Who've they given you?'

'It's an Inspector Bosch. He's the principal one, there are others.'

'Bosch. They've given you Bosch, have they?'

'You know him?'

'I've run into him,' Heller said unenthusiastically.

'You don't like him?'

'Maybe I do him an injustice.'

'He has his good points.'

'Will you tell me what they are.'

'He is very devoted to me. Very protective.'

'That so?'

'He has told me I mustn't go out with men until he has checked on them. Cleared them. It's like having a Victorian father. He thinks I could put myself in danger.'

'Do you?'

'I give him the slip,' she said mischievously.

'That would seem to defeat the object.'

'Fred?' She was swaying again.

'Yes?'

'Would you see me home, Fred? I'm not feeling well.'

NINE

Outside, on the stairs, they found Bosch disconsolately lurking.

Isabelle said she was going home now, and told him the way she would take. Bosch seemed resentful.

—He's going with you? he demanded, jerking his head at Heller.

—Yes, Isabelle said.

Bosch told her not to go taking any funny routes, or he'd lose her again. He couldn't be responsible if she did things that were not correct. A sullen glance towards Heller indicated exactly what he considered 'not correct'.

Isabelle did nothing 'funny', driving back the short distance to her apartment in the rue Monsieur le Prince without taking any unusual ways, and she made sure the whole time that Bosch was close behind her.

Outside her apartment she waited in the car, doors locked, engine running, until Bosch came up. Only then did she open the doors and get out. She handed her car keys to the bodyguard.

Heller took her to the *porte-cochère*.

—Is he going up with you? Bosch demanded.

—Yes. Monsieur Heller is going to have a drink with me, Bosch.

—It's late, madame. It's after midnight. I think Monsieur Heller should be going back to his hotel, madame.

—He's having a drink with me first, she insisted.

Bosch scowled. He said nothing.

—What are your plans for the morning, madame?

—I don't know yet.

She was tapping out the entry code on the panel beside the entrance: 809GD. There was a click and the heavy door opened to pressure.

—Madame, Bosch insisted. You must let me know in good time what your plans are. I need to know, madame. I can't do my job, if you don't tell me. I can't protect you, madame, if you don't co-operate.

—I will tell you when I know, Bosch.

They went in through the unlit courtyard. There was a pollarded chestnut tree in the centre with a circular iron bench seat around it. The building was eighteenth-century, somewhat run down, stucco crumbling away, but with a lot of charm. There was no elevator and the stairs were black until Isabelle had found the timed light switch and pressed it in.

'It's a very fast switch,' she said. 'You have to run up the stairs...'

He made her walk at a normal speed and noted that the light went out before they got to the third floor. Someone could have been lying in wait for her there, in the dark of the landing: Bosch hadn't gone ahead to check the inside of the building. Relying on the entry code to keep out intruders. Not very secure, that. Of course, full-scale round-the-clock protection would have required a team of twelve men. They probably considered she didn't need anything like that. They wouldn't have the resources to provide protection on this scale for every member of a minister's family.

'Anyway, he parks the car for you,' Heller observed. 'Means you don't have to walk back in the dark. That's useful.'

'Yes,' she agreed.

Her apartment consisted of one spacious studio room, with windows two storeys high. The ceiling had been removed, so that the room extended upwards to the rafters. It had been an artist's studio once. It had an iron spiral staircase that went up to a gallery,

90

where there was a futon covered with Kelim rugs and cushions. Privacy was afforded by a pair of Chinese screens. In the main room the kitchen units were concealed under a zinc-top bistro bar, cupboards were built in.

The windows worried Heller. Until the ancient wooden-slatted venetian blinds had been wound down, a slow business, it was possible to see into the apartment from the other side of the courtyard.

'Who lives across from you?' he asked.

'It's an apartment that's rented out to visitors.'

'At the moment?'

'It's empty at the moment, I don't think anybody lives there. Do you want cognac? Or – Calvados?'

'Calvados, please.'

He looked around as she went behind the bar to fix the drinks. Books were overflowing the bookshelves and were piled up haphazardly on the floor. She seemed to read several books at the same time, judging by the number lying around open, or with markers inside them. There were boxes and bundles and items of clothing scattered about ... Coloured stickers on the wall to remind her of things she had to do. You could see that it was not a very tidy life that she led, a life of sudden impulses.

She brought him the Calvados and then went to the venetian blinds and looked out at an angle into the rue Monsieur le Prince.

'No sign of Bosch,' she observed. She was tense.

'I expect he's there somewhere. How you feeling now?'

'Feeling?'

'You weren't feeling too well, before,' he reminded her.

'I think he's getting his revenge on me, Bosch. Because I let you come up with me.'

'What?'

'He's like that. Any man comes near me, he's furious.'

'You should ask to have him replaced. He sounds crazy.'

'He's very jealous.'

'Jealous? How can he be jealous? What sort of relationship does he think he has with you that he can be jealous?'

'I don't know. But people get things in their heads when they're around you all the time. When they have to know intimate things about you.'

'Yes?'

'Anyone shows any interest in me, that's suspicious to him. I can see he's very suspicious of you.'

She went to her telephone answering machine and pressed the playback key.

The voice of her father:

—Mon amour . . .

He'd hardly had a chance to talk to her all evening. He thought she looked tired and tense. He asked her to phone him when she got home, no matter how late. He sounded concerned.

Next message: a young man's voice . . .

'*Salut, Isa! Tu étais ravissante ce soir . . .*'

She grinned at Heller and did a piece of dumb show, tightening her long sweater-robe about the hips and performing a male wriggle; Heller gathered it was the luscious-lipped young actor with the torn Kenzo jeans who was being maligned.

After the caller's first few words, once she had identified who it was, she did not listen to the whole message but wound further back, as if searching for a particular call. Finally she reached a silence on the tape and listened intently.

'Somebody calls me and doesn't say anything.'

'There are people who feel uncomfortable talking into a machine.'

'I can tell that sort,' she said, turning to face him. 'But this is different. Has a different feeling. These silent calls . . . there's a sort of tenseness about the silence that I can feel. It's someone . . . I'm sure it's always the same person. I think it's a woman. I don't know how I know this, but I do. She's ringing up to see if I'm in. She's checking up on my movements.'

'Could be a fan of yours', Heller said, 'who just wants to hear your voice . . .'

'When I pick up the phone she hangs up immediately. But when it's the answering machine she listens right to the end. It is somebody who want to do me harm. I know that.'

On the dusty blinds, with the backdrop of the dark courtyard visible through the open slats, he saw a vision of the furious women, these furies with their bared gums and their bodies racked by the spasms of the Skorpions: women in the throes of painful orgasm, you might have thought, from the way they shook, from their contorted faces. These murderous women had sunk below the level of his conscious mind, and were no longer entirely real to him, had already become partly myth.

Isabelle was staring at the same spot, as if she could see them too.

'I think they're following me.'

'Who?'

'Those women . . .'

'Why would they follow you?'

'I don't know. It's not just recently, I've felt it before. Before what happened at Lipp. Sometimes I . . . get the feeling when I'm in the street or in some public place that there are people I don't know who know me, and that they know things about me that I don't know, and that they're watching me.'

'Well, you're an actress. You have a public. Of course there are people who know you that you don't know . . .'

'It doesn't have that feeling. I can't explain it. Oh I have got to put those things out of my mind,' she said determinedly, 'otherwise I can't live.' She lit a cigarette, made an effort to shift moods. 'What's been happening to you . . . all these years? The way I remember you, you used to be . . . spikier. Very go-getting. Oh you were such a smarty-pants. Knew all the answers. Look-out-I'm-on-my-way-and-here-I-come . . .' He made an apologetic gesture. 'What was I like? I expect you don't even remember.'

'Oh I remember. You were very young . . . but I remember thinking there was something very special about you. That you would succeed in whatever you did. I wasn't wrong.'

'Remember the night I took all my clothes off and was jumping about outside in the rain . . . during the thunder storm . . . when there were all those people in the house . . . you remember that?'

'Yes.'

He remembered a close southern night of rumbling incipient storms and heavy heat. In the billiards room there was a wooden ceiling fan moving the cigar smoke around, stirring it into the warm dense air. The storm wouldn't come. It was building up and building up. Then it finally burst and a gentle torrent fell. And suddenly, outside the French windows, there was this watersprite, a glistening naked form, all bony knees and shoulders, turning cartwheels on the sodden lawn. A schoolgirl breaking bounds in a show of irrepressible high spirits.

'I made you hypnotise me,' she reminded him.

He remembered that too. The game with a sense of danger to it. Look at the spot on the ceiling! Don't blink! Works by tiring the optic nerve. Mustn't blink. Keep staring. Your eyelids begin to feel very heavy, very heavy ... Amazingly, it had worked. He had never hypnotised anyone before, but her eyes were glazed over, her body slumped in the chair, and when he snapped his fingers in front of her eyes she was completely out, ready to do his bidding. He'd made her prick her finger with a needle and she hadn't felt a thing, and after that her eyes had flipped over into her skull, the pupils virtually vanishing, and she was in a deep trance. And when he tried to, he couldn't bring her out of it. She wasn't waking up when he commanded her to wake up. A dangerous game to play with an overexcited young adolescent girl on the brink of womanhood.

'You thought I was going to die, didn't you? When you couldn't bring me back?'

'You scared the hell out of everyone for about five minutes.'

She laughed guiltily. 'I will tell you a secret.' She started upon a gaspy giggle, quickly suppressed it, and the 15-year-old peeked out ...

'You didn't,' she gasped, 'you didn't hypnotise me, I was acting it. I had to act *comme une folle*, when I stuck the needle in my finger, because it hurt. I was acting that I didn't feel anything. And then I pretended I was in a deep trance and couldn't come out of it.'

94

'Sly thing to do. Very sly. Scaring everyone. Why? Why'd you do that?'

'Oh I expect what I was doing was having a little flirt with you. Funny way of doing it, I know. *Mais les jeunes filles de quinze ans!* Peculiar little beasties at that age. You didn't know I used to have a crush on you?'

'Really?'

'You never got the letter I wrote you?'

'No.'

'Anyway, you didn't reply.'

He remembered the letter she had written him, in green ink, in a wild, schoolgirl's handwriting, and left in his car. He had ignored it. He'd decided that was the best thing, pretend he hadn't received it. She was fifteen! And she wasn't any Lolita. She was an ordinary teenage girl and Charles's daughter.

'You didn't see anything peculiar about me, the way I acted around you? Or were you so used to young girls falling in love with you that you didn't even notice?'

Bill was there that night, at Charles's house, Heller recalled. Bill was often there. Yes: Bill was there when the storm burst and the lightning squiggled across the sky. Could be that he had first got to know Charles through Bill . . .

She went to look out of the window again. She seemed very keyed-up.

'He's not there. I think Bosch has gone to a bar to get drunk. To spite me. Because I . . . asked you to come up with me. He doesn't approve of that. He says he can't protect me if I deliberately put myself in danger.'

'Is it putting yourself in danger asking me in for a drink?'

'He would think so. People used to say things about you . . .'

'What?'

'That you were not to be trusted where women are concerned.'

'Is any man? And, well, that was a long time ago. Anyway, people exaggerate.'

'Do they?'

She looked at him very directly. She had an actress's gift for making somebody else feel what she was feeling, and she was conveying to him very clearly with her bold look that she was reaching out towards him, and it made him remember a time in his life when love with someone new could be an instant physical thing, a matter of strong young bodies homing in on each other. She was making him feel in the league of the young again.

'What?' he asked.

Her nervousness seemed to have increased. Her eyes were wide the way a woman's eyes are wide when she is afraid, or aroused. She was white and tense and trembling. He touched her cheek, smiling. It was meant to be comforting, because she really did look in need of comforting. She kept still, looking up at him with solemn fearful eyes as he kissed her lightly on the mouth, it was supposed to be a friendly reassuring sort of kiss that said, you're a lovely girl, relax, it's not so grave. Only she wasn't ready to be reassured in this friendly light way, and her mouth clung to his, her eyes intense. It got out of hand. And he wasn't able to keep it light any more. She seemed to get paler, and both of them were rapidly becoming very breathless. Then they were on the spiral stairs and getting to the top was not easy in their breathless state, with her pulling her dress up as she went. By the time they were at the top it seemed as if they had both run for miles, and then there was the guilty joy like a dark secret between them, and at the height of it she was saying, '*Fais-moi mourir,*' over and over, and other such things, and he thought: yes, there are women who want to die of love. Though she clung to him and seemed transported and spoke passionate words designed to inflame, he had a peculiar sense of her being absent, up on a stage, while he was down in the audience. Afterwards, when the craziness was over, she told him, quietly, that she believed she loved him, and demanded if he loved her, to which he replied kiddingly that he would have to think about that.

Yes, he was going to have to think about it. He wasn't sure what he was getting himself into. He was a man of settled ways. His equilibrium had been hard-won over the years, and he wasn't sure he wanted to expose himself to something that might get out of control, on her side or his. She was evidently someone of very intense feeling. Someone who wanted to die of love. Heller didn't know if he wanted anything like that, that sort of upheaval.

'For you it was not the same,' she accused softly. 'For you it was just a little Paris one-night adventure, with a wild crazy French girl who has thrown herself at you?'

'Was kind of spur of the moment,' he said trying to be light about it, and yet not too light. 'Let me get used to it. The *coup de foudre* takes longer at my age.'

TEN

NEXT MORNING SHE woke up late and slowly. As if coming out of a coma. In a deep fog she felt around for cigarettes, lit one and dragged in smoke. Her head was shaking.

'Coffee?' he asked.

'Strong and black.'

'Sugar?'

'Yes. Lots of sugar.'

He brought her the coffee and she drank it silently, uncommunicative in word or looks.

She seemed to be under a shadow, and after a while he asked her if she was all right.

'I . . . take long to surface in the morning.'

'OK, OK. Only I'm going to leave pretty soon.'

'That's all right, go whenever you like.'

There was a flatness about her now that dismayed him.

'How about some breakfast?' he asked.

'I have got nothing here.'

'What do you do?'

'I go down the road. To a café.'

'Shall we do that?'

Some activity seemed called for; it might arouse her from the stupor. He didn't want to leave her like this.

She dressed quickly, pulling on jeans and a shirt and a leather flying jacket. She didn't bother about make-up, ran her hands through her hair, that was all.

'You'll have to put up with me without a face,' she said.

They walked up the rue Monsieur le Prince towards the place Edmond Rostand. There was a brasserie looking on to the Luxembourg gardens that she liked.

Several times, as they walked, she looked around.

'I can't see Bosch.'

'Maybe they've put on somebody else this morning, someone you don't know. They probably watch over you from a distance. Since you don't like them breathing down your neck.'

She didn't seem very reassured. And there was no increase in her communicativeness.

In the café he saw her eyes go searchingly around the old cinema posters and linger on the image of Arletty, in *Le Jour se lève*, the classic shot of her sitting on the bed, putting on stockings.

Isabelle was becoming restive.

'Let's go,' she said, before finishing her croissant. She started for the exit while he was still waiting for his change to be brought.

In the street the fine rain and the cold air seemed more agreeable to her than the atmosphere in the café.

'It was close in there,' she said distantly, from behind the edges of the eclipse that now hid her.

'Yes, a bit.'

They crossed the *place* and went into the Luxembourg gardens and strolled. Vaporous spray encapsulated evergreen shrubs. They took a long straight path under the plane trees.

'What is it this morning?' he asked her.

'*Rien!*'

For the moment, the princess was inside her castle, portcullis lowered against all intruders.

The gardens were very misty and she kept looking around all the time.

'What are you afraid of, Isabelle?'

'Earlier, when we were going to the café, I had the feeling of being watched.'

'Probably Bosch's people.'

'No. It did not feel as though it's them. I get this feeling . . .'

'Yes? This feeling?'

She didn't answer; they walked on in silence for a while, and then she said:

'I had a bad dream last night. I think that is what has upset me.'

'Want to tell me about it? Would that help?'

She continued to walk, staring straight ahead into the misty distance.

'I have had this dream before. Begins in slightly different forms. But it always ends the same way. I'm in a fine apartment, filled with beautiful objects, works of art, magnificent furniture inlaid with ivory and mother-of-pearl. Everybody is beautifully dressed. There is wonderful wine and food. Everything is beautiful. But all the time I am in this beautiful apartment I know, though for long periods I forget this and then the reminder comes as a terrible shock, that in the attic there is a mouldering body under a pile of old clothes – they are my mother's clothes – and I know that one day this body will be found, and we will be accused, and our beautiful life will end.'

He said with a smile: 'Ah yes! The skeleton in the attic. All the best families have one.'

She gave a little uneasy laugh and took a deep breath, determined to shake off the bad dreams.

'You live alone, Fred?'

'Yes.'

'No girl in your life?'

'My marriage broke up. Since then I've lived alone, though at times I have overnight guests to stay. There have been women who've stayed a while . . .'

'What you call a while?'

He was defensive. 'It's not a big apartment, and I'm often not there. I tend to live everywhere except at home. The work takes me off a lot . . .'

'And when you go, they move out, these women who have stayed a while?'

'I'm never sure when I'm going to be back.'

'I suppose they must mind that. And you? Do you mind to live like that?'

'I guess it must appeal to something in my character, keeping moving. Or I wouldn't do it. I could have a desk job in Washington and live a more regular sort of life. Sometimes I think about giving up the work altogether. But I'm pretty good at it, and I don't know what else I'd do. I'm too old now to start on anything new, and it seems early to retire, and there's the problem of money ... That *is* a real problem, because I have got used to living a certain way now, drawing on funds that are provided for you, when you're on a job, and I'm not too good at changing my old habits.'

She said, 'I can see your life's all set. You wouldn't want anything to change. Fred, we don't need to see each other any more. You don't want to get involved with someone like me.'

'What d'you mean?'

'I'm ...' She didn't finish saying what she was.

'What?' he prompted her.

'I ... I think is best you forget about me.'

'You're not so easy to forget.'

'Last night you were pretty cool about what happened.'

'If that's your idea of cool ...'

'I mean afterwards. You wanted time to think. Wasn't that what you said?'

He gave a defensive laugh. 'Thinking doesn't hurt. If we'd both thought a little more, my ex-wife and I, before ...'

'It was no good, your marriage?'

'It was good for a time.'

'What went wrong?'

'There were things I hadn't seen.'

'Such as?'

'She wanted to be free. To be free the way she thought men were free. To have affairs *and* a marriage.'

'You were having affairs?'

'Not at the time.'

'But she was?'

101

'She was.'

'And that was something you couldn't put up with, even though you loved her?'

He laughed. 'That's right. I couldn't. The fact is, I finally hit somebody. One of her lovers. He . . . he was at my house, and he was flirting with her, sort of in a kidding way, when he knew that I knew and that everybody else knew, and then he spilled some wine over me. That was sort of kidding, too. It was my wine, my house, my wife. And so . . . I sort of hit him. Kiddingly, you see, but hard. Cracked his jaw. It was a pretty weak jaw to start with . . . Trouble was, he as an assistant secretary of state, and it got around that I was someone who sometimes "loses his head" when it comes to women. That's how I got the reputation that I was a violent type and all.'

'Is it true? Do you lose your head over women?'

'Yes, sometimes.' He smiled. 'I think I could be in danger of that with you.'

'Why you say in danger?'

He held back, not sure how honest he wanted to be about this. Then he said, 'Oh, because I'm almost fifty, and like someone once said, past fifty everything's a bonus. That you're not entitled to. So . . . something like this is either very light or very important, and I don't know about that. I don't know. I can't quite make you out. That was some pretty strong stuff you said last night . . . I mean on the physical plane and the, uh, sentimental? But now, I don't know. You keep changing.'

'It's true I . . . I feel everything very strongly at the moment, and then afterwards it changes for me.'

'What has changed for you since last night?'

'It was you who said you wanted to think about it.'

'I thought about it.'

'And what have you decided?'

He hesitated, advising himself not to go too far out. Last night she must have looked at him through the eyes of a young girl in the grip of her first big crush, seen him as he was eighteen years ago, when he was on his way, thrusting out, one of the best in his field. OK, so last night she hadn't noticed the wear-and-tear that had occurred since then, in body and mind. But eventually she would. Perhaps she had done so already, and realised her mistake. Last night had been a little piece of the past brought back, something that derived its peculiar potency from the length of time it had lain buried. Last night was a flashback, a piece of cinema.

He said, 'Yes, I've thought about it. And . . . I know I want this thing with us to go on. I think I probably want it to go on more than I dare admit to myself, if you want to know the truth.'

'Then we just have to see what happens,' she said.

Gordon Welliver, the individual at the Embassy assigned to Heller, turned out to be a tentative young man with a tendency to phrase even declarative statements as if they had a question mark after them, including the seemingly straightforward assertion:

'I'm Gordon Welliver, sir?'

'Are you now, Gordon.'

'Yes, sir?'

Gordon must have been recently appointed to whatever was his position, because he did not look more than twenty (though he must have been at least thirty); it was the unmarked-by-life downy smooth face, with a tendency to chubbiness, that gave him the air of a young seminarian. He was wearing a suit of plain light-grey virgin wool that blended perfectly with his virginal blandness, a plain grey knitted tie, white button-down shirt. His large black-frame spectacles gave him an earnest Harvard Business School look. Probably had taken some postgraduate course in insurrectionism and counter-insurrectionism.

'Sir, I've been assigned to you?' he announced with his usual upturn at the end of the phrase and the eager air of an aspiring slave. Heller wondered if Gordon was, with a question mark, gay.

He gave Gordon various things to do that were not too demanding: files to find, information to access, phone numbers to obtain.

While awaiting fresh developments, Heller studied the latest news of the Iran initiative. Poindexter had resigned, criminal charges hanging over him. Ollie North was suspended from his functions. A special committee of inquiry was in the course of being set up under Senator Tower. In Nicaragua Gene Hasenfus, caught delivering arms to the Contras, had been given thirty years. Latest opinion polls showed that in the month of Irangate Reagan's popularity had slumped from 66 per cent to 43 per cent. Not a good month for another American to get himself kidnapped.

The question that kept hammering in Heller's head was: why did they take Bill and not me? What makes him the white whale? This was a mystery in which the clues were locked up inside people's heads.

What made him think there was a connection between whatever haunted Isabelle Decourten and the terrorists holding Bill Gibson?

What?

A hunch. A feeling he had that she knew something, without knowing that she knew. That her *angoisse* had a secret history.

She was an intuitive actress, not the kind who works out her characters by analysis and reasoning. Antigone was a character she claimed not to understand. She said she did not *know* why Antigone went to her death. She did not understand her wilfulness, or what the meaning was to her of burying her dead brother, and why she should do this in defiance of the State edict, thereby incurring her terrible death-sentence, the living death of immurement in the cave. And yet, though she did not know with her reason why Antigone did these things, could not explain it, she did know on another level, knew enough to 'become' Antigone on the stage, to make her 'live'. She had found this Antigone within herself, and acted her with such conviction that the audience saw and understood why Antigone did what she did, even if the actress claimed not to. So – an intuitive actress, Heller argued, and like all outstandingly talented artists she had ways of knowing unfathomable things, of making mysterious cross-connections.

On this tenuous basis, Heller, who also could make mysterious cross-connections at times, when his form was good, concluded that Isabelle's intuitions – apprehensions – had to be heeded. If she had the capacity to draw a stage character solely by these means, might she not be able in the same way to draw herself, to see her fate, from her unconscious knowledge of herself? She would 'know' what seeds had been planted in her and what fruit they must one day bear.

Heller asked Gordon to find the address of the 'contact' phone number in Bill's letter. It turned out to be a bar in Les Halles called Le Forum.

Bill had warned not to try and find the messenger. Had said she was a circuit-breaker. Still, Heller had nothing much else to go on, for the present. So he phoned the bar and left a message for 'Elvire' to telephone him back – urgently.

She phoned back within two hours as Bill had said she would. She had a flat voice. It was like talking into an answering machine. He told her that he was interested in their offer concerning the Oldsmobile. Provided a price could be agreed that was *feasible*. He was making arrangements for a transfer of funds. Might take longer than the time they'd stipulated in their announcement. But she must know what banks were like. He wanted assurances that the Oldsmobile would not be disposed of while he was making the arrangements. Because he was really very interested. Of course, as part of the deal to be worked out he'd have to test drive it, or else be given other proof of its soundness. Had she got all that? She said, Yes.

—We'll need to keep in close touch if this is going to work out. How can I get you again?

—Leave a message.

—The same number?

—Yes.

—I may know more by tomorrow. If I leave a message at that number, you'll ring me back? Within the hour?

—Allow two hours for me ring back.

The smartening-up that had occurred almost everywhere in the vicinity of redeveloped Les Halles, with its vast new below-grounds shopping arcades, and its gardens and carousels on top, had not impinged upon Le Forum, which remained, in its narrow little street, defiantly shabby. It was a long narrow place, with a new copper bar, the one concession to modernisation, running the full length of it. The barmen served with an air of urgency. The customers drank urgently. Even apart from the fact that it had no outlook and that there was nowhere really to sit down (just two or three very small hemmed-in tables), this was not a place for a leisurely drink. It was too crowded. There was too much coming and going, with some pressing to get in and others to get out through the same narrow space. A continuous squeeze of bodies. Whatever the appeal of this little bar, it could not have been its ambience. It must clearly be famous for something else, judging by the people eager to get into it.

Heller, arriving at 12.45, made a quick tour of the place, upstairs and downstairs (downstairs there were toilets and telephones), looking at faces. Most of the customers were men, and of the two women one was a blonde who looked like a model from a 'Life Show', and the other was a bag-lady the worse for drink. Neither looked like being Elvire. He noted where the bar telephone was by the big old-fashioned chromework cash register, and left.

He might have two hours to wait, if the system worked. If it didn't he would have hung around for nothing. He began to while away the time, without ever taking his eyes off the entrance to Le Forum for more than a few seconds.

Opposite, there was a dim little shop selling men's shirts, ties and underwear. At 1.45 Heller went in and embarked upon the difficult business of selecting a shirt and a tie to go with it. He stood in the light of the window to assess how well the colours matched.

At 2.10 he saw a young woman in a brown raincoat, collar

buttoned tight across her throat, go into Le Forum. She had mousy hair and tired, bruised-looking eyes. He made her out at the bar, near the telephone, waiting to get one of the barmen's attention. She lit a cigarette and smiled briefly whenever a busy barman whirled past her banging down drinks. Finally she caught an eye, was served and, in response to another brief smile, given a chit of paper with her messages. Looked like her.

Heller left the shirt shop hurriedly, without buying a shirt or a tie. He stepped out into the narrow street. Elvire had paid up and left the bar. At a distance of ten metres he followed her to the boulevard de Sébastopol. There she stopped at the first decent brasserie and sat down at a table looking out on the street. Heller stood at the bar, behind her and a little to the side. She ordered a drink and immediately, chit in hand, went down the stairs to make her phone call.

After a couple of minutes, she returned and sat down again at her table. She looked at her watch and asked the waiter for a menu. The message she would have been given at the Pont-Royal was that Monsieur Heller had been delayed.

She gave her order to the waiter and he returned with a carafe of white wine and a *croque-monsieur*. She ate disinterestedly, mechanically. To Heller she looked like any number of single girls that you saw eating alone in Paris cafés and brasseries, depressed girls with an air of being at the end of a love affair, wallowing in inner emptiness. He reminded himself that this Elvire, however low down in the pyramid, was a terrorist, and that the two women who had sat across from him at Lipp hadn't looked like Gorgons with snake hair, had looked pretty ordinary, at first – schoolteachers from Lille, he had supposed, on a monthly outing to Paris.

She was given to starts, Elvire. A sideways jerk of the head. Or a complete turnabout. Heller had to turn round fast himself to avoid being spotted. As she twisted in her seat, he saw her hand go inside her big floppy leather shoulder bag, and he supposed she would have a gun in there. Perhaps one of the evil little Skorpion submachine-guns that this lot seemed to go in for. He remembered Bosch's advice to kill the she-pig first, the female of the species being the most dangerous, according to him.

You would not have thought so, looking at this one. She looked nervy and 'fragile', and unfocused. Confused. The sombre dullness of her eyes suggested to him somebody who has sat too long in dark cinemas watching mesmeric-bright images on a large screen, whose eyes have not yet readjusted to normal light, to the human scale, to real life. Very concentrated on her inner script. Very jumpy at the same time.

She came back into reality, looking, hungering, fearful. The slightly protrusive eyes and the bulge of the neck indicated a metabolism veering between the overactive and the underactive.

At 3.30 she went down the steps to the phone again, and returned soon afterwards looking disgusted. She paid her bill and left.

Heller followed her at a distance. One minute she was wandering slowly, looking in shop windows, and the next she was hurrying. She seemed undecided about where she was going. She went from one phone to another. Once or twice he was able to watch her making calls. They were not long. And they seemed to give her little satisfaction. Her face remained blankly unanimated. She was walking along the rue de Rivoli in the direction of the Marais, again looking in shop windows, sometimes abruptly looking around, almost as if sensing that somebody was following her. He did not believe she had seen him. But suddenly she made a dash across the road at a pedestrian crossing where the light had gone red against her and the traffic had got off like from a starter's gun. He followed, dodging between vehicles, and saw her go down the stairs of the Hôtel de Ville metro. He had no metro ticket and was obliged to buy one, and by the time he was through the turnstyle there was no sign of her, either on the platform for direction Pont de Neuilly or on the other for Château de Vincennes. At this time of day trains came every minute.

In case she had used the metro as a diversion tactic, he went up again to street level and looked around outside the Hôtel de Ville.

But there was no sign of her.

When he got back to his hotel, he phoned Le Forum and left another message for Elvire, saying he had been unexpectedly called out of town but that everything was on course. And he'd be in touch soon to finalise the deal.

ELEVEN

MONTPARNASSE WAS VERY lively, racy: 'fun' in the new mode-word appropriated by the French for their own special use. They mingled in the crowds around the oyster bars, the cafés and restaurants with famous names. La Coupole was a steamy bath of celebrity, and there was the usual panic at the various points of entry to the vast restaurant area, with people just arrived unable to get a table and being cursorily informed that there was an hour's wait. Heller wondered how Isabelle would react to that, since she didn't like to wait for anything. But it turned out she didn't have to: being a well-known actress counted for something, and they were quickly seated. Heller had a vision of Bill Gibson rising up from his corner banquette, a saturnine presence with his glimmering and gloomy redness, his high blood pressure, his contemptuousness. This was where I ran into Bill the third time, Heller reminded himself, where we made the arrangement to dine at Lipp. Fateful encounter. And now Bill is in the bad shit. At the mercy of this man Gavaudan, terrorist and teacher of history. Organiser of the furies. Heller was beginning to perceive the man's distinctive silhouette. Someone living on his stored-up grievances. A man for whom the world had become such a bad place that no act was too terrible to put right the wrong. How low would he not be prepared to sink to remedy the baseness of the world? To make a new world in the corpse of the old.

While Heller's thoughts had taken this grim turn, Isabelle seemed to be in a sunny phase. She ordered *saumon fumé artisanal* with *blinis à la crème*, and suggested to him that the Pouilly Fumé was quite OK.

She was taking pleasure in being with him, in being seated at a prominent table where she could be seen, and having people turn and stare politely, smilingly; no sign now of the 'Greta Garbo complex' she was supposed to have, of her hatred of being recognised and photographed.

'Lucky I was with you,' he said, 'or I'd have had to wait for an hour.'

'It has some uses being known,' she conceded. 'Gets you tables in restaurants. Mind you, it's only because I was in that film, that's how they know me.'

'What film was that?'

'A *policier* called *Image dans le miroir*.'

'Oh yes, four or five years ago? I saw it. You play identical twins, one of whom is a murderess, and the audience doesn't know in some of the scenes which one is which. You make them think it's one, and it's the other ... And then it's not. A lot of twists, I remember.'

'It was very successful.'

'It was a good part for you. You played it very well. The change of character from one to the other was brilliant.'

By the time they were having their second bottle of the Pouilly Fumé, Banquo's ghost had quit his corner seat and somehow that made things easier for Heller, he was feeling more relaxed and talking of his work, the theory, the practice.

'At the beginning you're making your reputation and you want successes. There's the element of high adventure, the Great Game. All of that. See, you're playing for high stakes. You can change the world, you can write history. I learned the trade from Bill Gibson, and there's undoubtedly a swashbuckling element in his methodology. At least that's the way you do it when you're young. That was the faith we lived by, and as a young man I was a believer ...'

'No longer?'

'Oh, up to a point. But not up to the same point as at the beginning. Let's say ... I can still see the Bill Gibson argument. His argument was there has to be a class of individual, apart from the rest, with more ... balls, and more dedication, that would be in the business of rectifying history's mistakes. Wow! That was a wild idea, and at the time I was very taken with it.'

'I hear disillusionment?'

'No, no ... not exactly. Experience. Experience of how things go wrong. Because when you get into it, you see that nothing is ever for sure, and the human factor being what it is, nothing quite comes out as in the scenarios you have so meticulously constructed. A lot of those "surgical actions", you end up removing the wrong kidney. And the operation, even if successful, always has side-effects that you haven't anticipated. Therefore "rectifying history" is not so straightforward. Look ...' He leaned towards her. He was saying things he had not said to anyone as openly before. 'I've seen what happens to people. I saw what happened to Bill. Bill used to be one of the greats of this profession. But finally he got lost out there. What happens is people can't live with the ambiguities, balls they started rolling come full circle. It's a phenomenon for which we have a name. It's called Blowback. When something you set up, "comes to life" so well you believe it and are taken in. Finally, you lose the thread. Forget the premise. And then when you're all washed up, can't stand the inner dizziness the way you could in the beginning, that's when they dump you, as they dumped Bill. It's a thankless business. Now that Bill's life is on the line, they won't lift a finger to save him. Sorry. This is a lot of shop talk, I got carried away. This probably doesn't interest you at all ...'

'I'm interested. I'm interested in what affects you, Fred.'

Heller looked at her. She was a lovely girl, a truly lovely girl. And she loved him, she said. That was what she had said. Though the morning after hadn't been so great. All right, even supposing this love of hers was mixed up with her feelings of long ago, the volatile immature feelings of an adolescent girl, so what? Were people's love feelings ever straightforward, ever entirely one-to-one? There were always the ghosts of others standing behind. Sometimes this was in your favour, sometimes it wasn't. You had to take the advantages that came your way, as you had to take the blows.

He was getting in deeper with Isabelle. He wasn't managing to keep it light. He knew his own pattern, and he realised that he was liable to lose his head.

Heller shifted in his chair, turning to see, as a matter of inbred routine, where the exits were. In doing so, he crossed sightlines with another man who seemed to be doing the same thing, while he stood chatting to two young women lunching together. The curse of Heller's work was that you could never exactly switch off. You had to be alert to dangers the whole time. No, he decided, this guy with the two women was just looking around to see who was there, to see if there was anyone better to talk to.

'Shall we go?' Heller asked, feeling despite his explanation to himself a vague ruffling of his early warning system. You had to live with the false alarms if you wanted to receive the real ones in time. As he got up, he made an automatic mental note of the guy talking to the two girls: his own age, grey hair, medium build, 140lbs, dark eyes, blue blazer with navy buttons, grey pants, small feet, wearing moccasins with tassles.

This noting was done in a small corner of Heller's mind, the larger part of it dwelt on the notion he had been entertaining throughout lunch of taking Isabelle back to his room at the hotel. Why the prospect of this change of lieu for their love-making should carry so strong an erotic charge, he did not know. Perhaps because it changed the scenario in his head, turned the continuation of an affair into a fresh and exciting after-lunch adventure. It restarted the action at the beginning, contrived to bring back the exquisite shock of the new. The idea of this had given him a delicious buzz that he was nursing along nicely, only a minute portion of his mind concerned with fire exits.

'Come back to my hotel,' he said, as if she were someone he hardly knew and was boldly propositioning for the first time. The real first time it had come from her. Now he was making the move and that gave it a whole new feeling. She seemed to understand the script and to be willing to play the part.

Waiting for a taxi he felt the terrible sweetness of this affair, even with all the tensions and background dangers; they contributed to the adrenaline flow, heightened the charge.

A taxi came and they got into it. Going through the rain-spattered streets, Heller, sitting circumspectly apart from her, uttered various warnings to himself that he had no intention of heeding: it's going out of control, you're completely in the grip of this thing now and truly hooked. If you had to slip off the hook, you couldn't to save your life. This is the formula for a fall. This is the total abandonment of all the rules about keeping the upper hand in relationships and not becoming fixated.

The ruminations were brought to a halt by their arrival at the Pont-Royal and the mania taking over. They weren't saying a word to each other, eyes not even meeting. The guilty pair. He marvelled at her complete collusion with him in this erotic plot, her genius in understanding without direction how the scene had to be played. What an actress!

When he opened the door to his room, she understood that there was nothing to be said, that the strengh of the scene lay in there being no talk. They had just met, had felt some overwhelming physical attraction for each other, and she had agreed to return to his hotel room with him. That was the story in his mind and hers, and it was having a powerful effect on him.

The skirt that she wore was too tight to pull up easily, but there was a line of buttons down the back.

She said, 'You know what this sort of skirt is called? Men-are-always-in-a-hurry. That's what the buttons are for.'

Once undone, one side of the back of the skirt lifted aside neatly like a tent flap. There was no question of getting even as far as the bed. That wasn't in the script. In the erotic script in his mind she had to stand. And she had understood that. Christ! he might be fifty years old but he was an old hound of hell let loose, and she understood perfectly, had a special aptitude for love-making, a natural French lack of puritanism about bodily things, and went along boldly with the passion that gripped him.

The frenzy over, they had finally taken to the bed to rest and she let him fall into a mind-blown sleep for several minutes. When he woke up she said in his ear:

'You make me happy.'

'I do? It was not too violent, it didn't go too far? I was sort of afraid you might...'

'No, with some dishes a coarse wine goes better,' she said.

'Oh and you are some dishes!' he told her.

While he was with her she never answered the phone. She would switch on the answering machine and later decide which callers to ring back. Several of the social calls were from Annette du Breuil and Isabelle said she'd like him to get to know Annette. '*Elle est chouette*. She's really very nice, *je l'aime beaucoup*. She's probably my oldest and closest friend. I've told her all about you.'

'All?' he queried.

'I'm very open with her, she knows everything about me – oh I've known her since I was a small child. She is practically family.'

'I thought she *was* family. Your father introduced her to me as his relation.'

'Oh well she may distantly be related, somewhere along the line, very distantly. You can have no idea how beautiful she used to be. Ten, fifteen years ago she was a real beauty, and when she was young she was a true knock-out.'

'I can well believe that. She's still a handsome woman.'

'And she was amazing during the war. So courageous! You are always amazed when you find that someone you know very closely could have done these courageous things. Once she was arrested by the Gestapo, they tortured her in ghastly ways, holding her head under water, things like that. Subjected her to dreadful humiliations ... But she didn't break. She is very strong. I'd really like you to know her. We should take her out to lunch.'

'Sure. Whenever you like,' he offered.

For the lunch with Annette du Breuil, Heller chose La Biblio-
thèque, a small distinguished restaurant in the government
district, where the tables were sufficiently far apart to permit
private conversation.

Heller and Isabelle arrived early and were installed in an alcove.
Annette du Breuil-Hélion de La Quéronnière made her appearance a few minutes later, and it was a striking appearance with her
blazing anthracite black hair and her face the white of washstand
marble. She wore black too, to emphasize her dramatic colouring
even more: a long black tailored coat-jacket that moulded her
long slender figure, and underneath, a knitted jersey dress with
high collar and a pearl choker around her swanlike neck.

She apologised for being late and as Heller held her hand in his
said with a warm and personal smile how happy she was to meet
him again.

The menus were brought promptly, and Heller suggested:

'If you like your oysters simmered with seaweed ...'.

'Ah but how else? Oh I am game to try,' said Annette of the
very long name.

Isabelle more conservatively ordered a *bouillon* to start and
Heller *escargots*.

While he was mulling over the choice of wine, Annette du
Breuil said she permitted herself to tell him that he must be good
for Isabelle, not for a long time had Isabelle seemed in such good
form and so happy.

'I better make her happy,' Heller said, taking Isabelle's hand,
'because I've fallen in love with her, you see.'

'Oh I do see.'

The conversation quickly and easily slipped into concerning
itself with Isabelle's personal life.

'Annette is the one person I can go to and tell anything to and
not feel *judged*. She is such a wise and tolerant person ... Papa I
adore, of course, but he is not someone you can talk to easily. He

116

is too formidable, too judging. And he hasn't the time . . .'

The conversation proceeded in this personal way, and Heller had a happy feeling that it was not only with Isabelle that he was having this love affair but also with France and French life, and French food, and French *mœurs*, and French history. His affair with Isabelle seemed to give him admittance to a new life. The wine he had extravagantly chosen (being extravagant with State Department funds) seemed to him to have a savour of almonds and black truffles, a noble French wine. The love affair with all things French was proceeding apace. The fricandeau of turbot and veal that he had ordered was delicious. Into the second bottle of Gevrey Chambertin a most noble French haziness was clouding his senses.

'I have heard some things about you, too, Annette,' Heller said. 'Things you did in the war. That you were tortured by the Gestapo.'

'Unfortunately that was quite a commonplace event.'

'Isabelle says you held out in a very remarkable way.'

'It was my love for Henri Decourten enabled me to hold out. I could not let him down. He was an inspiring man. There are such individuals, who inspire an almost mystical devotion in others. Obviously de Gaulle was one. Henri was of the same mould.'

'Yet someone betrayed him. Was it discovered who?'

'Oh yes. It was quickly learned. It was that sordid man Mont-carbier, the owner of the bar. In collusion with the barber Godin, a miserable wretch! A straightforward crime for money. For the money that the Germans paid to informers.'

'How did it happen?'

'There was a meeting. Of the leaders . . . the leaders of the two main Resistance groups in the area, to discuss the merging of forces. It was in the barber's shop, this meeting. One has always to choose places where a group of men could sit together without drawing attention. The barber Godin was considered a trustworthy man, one of us. Nobody believed that he would sell us out for money. When we arrive . . .'

'You were with them on the day it happened?'

'Yes. I was in the first car with Henri . . .

She stopped to take a sip of wine for her throat which had gone dry with emotion.

'You truly wish to hear what happened? It is not a story for the lunch table.'

'I would like to know. If it doesn't upset you too much telling it.'

She seemed to be steeling herself, drank more wine for her throat.

'These things are still painful, more so than I realised. . . . You cannot know what it means, Fred. Cannot know what it is to be an occupied nation. America has never been in that position, has never had such a trial of its nationhood. It is a prescription for the worst excesses of the human being. Both for the noble and the ignoble . . . I relive it now and all the hurt and the suffering is still there, yes after forty years . . . so if you do not mind? One day I will tell you the story, if still you are interested in it, but not now, please.'

'It does interest me . . . it's sort of part of Isabelle's inheritance, isn't it?'

'Yes. Part of all our inheritance. But please, let us now be a bit more gay, please. I do not want our lunch, and meeting you Fred, meeting you properly, which I have so much looked forward to, and enjoyed, finally, to be marked by this one note.'

That night Heller was in the audience seeing Isabelle as Antigone for the third time, and half an hour into the play he saw that something was wrong. She was having trouble with her breathing, and in getting her lines out. Was she sick? She was trying to deal with her malaise, whatever it was, by merging her own difficulties with Antigone's anguish. A white follow-light held tightly on her wherever she turned. There was no escaping it, it pursued her like some terrible manifestation of the furies. He saw that Isabelle's mouth had filled with saliva, making her cough and choke. Some of the audience turned away with distaste at seeing such clinical acting, such an unnecessarily realistic depiction of a woman gripped by the fear of death, spittle running down her chin, making awful whooping sounds as she gasped for air. Not everybody cared for such strong acting; they considered it inappropriate in the case of a classical play whose speeches were often 'sung' by the traditional French actor. The bodily nature of this performance, the way the actress seemed on the verge of vomiting her insides out, was rather overdoing it, some in the audience considered. The awkward breaks in her speech disrupted the poetic flow of words, gave them a hard jaggedness. Antigone was being played as a hysterical young girl struggling not so much against the autocracy of the State as against her own internal tormentors. But nearly everyone felt profoundly moved by Antigone's eventual recovery of her calm, and her dedication to her cause. The quiet dignified rendering of 'So to my grave,' was heart-rending.

Heller rushed backstage immediately the curtain came down. She was shaking and he poured her a large vodka.

'Did they see? she asked, and he said, No, it had all, somehow, fitted in with the character of Antigone and her plight.

At this she gave a sly smile, as if she had cunningly arranged the whole attack to aid her performance.

'Was I good, Fred? Was I good tonight?'

'You were superb.'

'In the end I overcame it.'

'What was it that happened to you?'

'*Le trac*. It was stage fright.'

'But you're a very experienced actress. Novices get stage fright, but not an experienced actress like you.'

'Lots of actors get it, Olivier used to get it.'

'What produced it tonight?'

'I don't know. It sometimes happens simply because you think it is going to happen. It can be self-fulfilling like that.'

'There has to be some reason behind it.'

'It has to do with being on-stage, exposed to all those eyes. Everybody seeing you.'

'That's what happens every night.'

'Sometimes I feel trapped on the stage. It's claustrophobia.'

She was still distressed, and he tried to comfort her. 'You overcame it. And gave a brilliant performance.'

She let out a hollow knowing little laugh. 'This is what Jouvet meant when he said that the actor turns hysterical symptoms into performance. The panic method of acting!'

TWELVE

HELLER WAS BACK in the shirt shop when Elvire arrived at Le Forum for her messages. This time he bought a tie, an expensive silk tie, with diagonal azure stripes on a dark red background. But he was undecided about the shirt, he said. Could not make up his mind. The way things were developing, he thought he had better give himself the cover of an eccentric, so he could return to the shirt shop, again and again.

—*Concernant la chemise, je vais reflechir encore . . .*

Elvire remained in Le Forum longer than yesterday, a good ten minutes, and for some of that time she was not at the bar. Afraid she might have slipped out by some exit other than the one he had been watching, Heller risked going into the bar to check. After a couple of minutes he saw her come up the stairs from the *sous-sol*, where the toilets and telephones were. He turned away and in the press of people she brushed by him. He hung back, and observed which direction she took when she got outside. As he waited, he glimpsed coming up from below a tall black man in a burnous, ivory necklaces and bangles clicking. One of Click-Click's places! It figured. It figured, too, that Elvire had been down below, to see the dealer. And it figured that this bar was so busy and that the customers didn't stay long. Heller would dearly have liked to try Click-Click on the subject of Sensimilla, but he couldn't do that now. He had to keep after Elvire.

He followed her as he had done before. She seemed still in a daze, to the point of being disorientated at times. It suggested that her depressed and anxious state yesterday had not been a passing thing. Her 'retreat from reality' could be due to drugs. Or to psychological factors. Or to a combination of both.

Once more there was the ritual of telephone calls, made from three or four different phones along the way. Adrift though she might be, she was at least nominally keeping in touch with base. He would have liked to have been able to trace the numbers she called, but her conversations were all brief and the telephones she used were not the same as those she had used last time.

Today she wasn't looking around, her daze appeared to have deepened, and he felt in little danger of being spotted. She wasn't seeing people straight in front of her, let alone behind her. When she crossed roads she didn't see the traffic coming and once or twice narrowly escaped being hit.

Even so, she took elementary evasive tactics when she went into the metro, getting in one train, emerging two stations later, as the doors were closing, and then jumping on a train going in the opposite direction, and doing it after the sound signal had gone to warn of the doors closing. Obviously such practices were in-grained now.

Heller found it easy enough to follow her.

She left the metro at Ségur and walked along the avenue de Suffren. Here she did turn her head to see if she was being followed, but it was a cursory look. She left the avenue and made her way through streets of fine *belle-époque* apartment buildings to the rue César Franck, where she stopped outside No. thirteen. She tapped out a code by the door, and went inside. Heller had positioned himself no more than a couple of metres behind her at this point and was able to catch the heavy iron and glass door before it had swung completely shut. He prevented the lock from engaging by quickly inserting metro tickets in the catch, and waited, back turned, until she had taken the elevator up. Then he followed her into the small mirrored entrance hall and peered through the ornamental ironwork of the elevator shaft to see on which floor the elevator stopped. The fourth.

He took the elevator up. There were two apartments on this floor; the name plate outside the one on the left said, Paul Utudjian; the other, France Thurillet.

He took the elevator down again, walked rapidly to the nearest phone kiosk and called Gordon Welliver; he told him to get on to his contact 'in the Renseignements généraux for a couple of quick identity checks. A Paul Utudjian and a France Thurillet. Nothing in depth, for the moment. Speed was of the essence. He would phone back in half an hour.

Heller returned to the rue César Franck and watched the fourth floor of No. thirteen until half an hour had gone by, and then he returned to the phone box and called the Embassy again.

Gordon had got some information. Utudjian was a retired Turkish businessman, born 1903, unmarried. France Thurillet was a widow, aged sixty-two, with one daughter, Marie-Ann, born 1957. The widow had a *maison secondaire*, an apartment in Cannes, where she lived during the winter months. She was 'without profession', i.e. lived on private means. She was registered as being liable for French 'wealth tax', which meant she was worth in excess of 4,000,000 F. She owned an Audi 90. Gordon furnished phone numbers for both Utudjian and Thurillet. Heller said good, and to conduct a check on the daughter of France Thurillet.

'See what you can get on Marie-Ann. I want it today, Gordon. Latest by this evening.'

When Heller phoned him back a couple of hours later, Gordon sounded pleased as hell with himself. He had found out some things. Marie-Ann's address was 17 bis, rue Gros-Caillou in the septième. She had a small private income, derived from a trust fund set up for her by her late father, a manufacturer of bottle tops for Vichy water.

A 1984 *blanc* supplied by the Renseignements généraux stated that she had visited in jail one Henri-Georges Olanier, then being held in connection with the placing of an explosive device outside the offices of El Al. The device had been discovered and dismantled by Israeli security men before it went off.

'OK. OK.'

The *blanc* stated that Marie-Ann Thurillet had attended rallies organised by SOS-Racisme, had done voluntary work for Amnesty International, and for Greenpeace, and was known to associate with men active in Combattants pour une nouvelle société.

She had worked from time to time in temporary clerical and secretarial jobs, the *blanc* stated. One job was with a Yugoslav travel agency, another with the personal announcements columns of *Le Nouvel Observateur*, another with a visiting Italian theatre company. She had also been working in the office of the Crillon Hotel, as a replacement for staff who were absent.

'Now we're getting someplace,' Heller told Gordon, and instructed: 'I'm going to need a car. Have it laid on for tonight, will you?'

He was outside 13, rue César Franck that evening, in the small Fiat that Gordon Welliver had obtained for his use, and when Marie-Ann Thurillet, or Elvire, left in her battered old blue 2 CV, he followed.

He noted that she had got herself dressed up a bit; she had put on make-up and her hair was freshly done. Instead of the brown raincoat, she wore quite a smart black overcoat, and since it was open as she came out of the door he saw that she had on a black sheath dress with a hemline that was well above the knee. She wore crocodile-style leather shoes. Looked like she was going on a date.

Heller followed her to Montparnasse, where she left her car badly parked in a side street, half on the kerb. He parked his car equally badly, close by, half on a pedestrian crossing, and followed her on foot. She walked hurriedly. He was sure now that she had a date. She looked neither to left nor right. A lady with a purpose. A minute later it became clear where she was going, and it wasn't to meet anyone. She was going to the cinema, and it seemed she was going alone.

The film was a reissue. *La guerre est fini*. A film by Alain

Resnais about an ageing Spanish revolutionary, played by Yves Montand.

Heller followed her inside. Maybe the film was a blind, maybe she was meeting someone in the darkness of the auditorium. He sat down in a row behind her, slightly to her right, and watched her closely. She was completely involved in the story. Mesmerised. Her seat was at the end of a row, with nobody in the place next to hers. Nobody spoke to her.

At the end of the film, as the audience was leaving, a man did start to talk to her. He was well dressed, in his late fifties, with white hair. He started talking about Resnais's other films. A film buff, evidently. He talked of *Hiroshima mon amour*, of *L'Année dernière à Marienbad*, and the more recent *Mélo*. It was conversation with an underlying purpose. It appeared that the film buff was trying to pick her up. The pieces of his conversation that Heller overheard ruled out the possibility that this was some kind of a drop, nobody except a comic impersonator could have contrived such a brilliant imitation of an intellectual *dragueur*.

Marie-Ann was unresponsive. She was focused on her inner plot. The outside world hardly made any impression on her. Undaunted, he continued to expatiate, with elaborate gesticulations, while she with a faintly derisive expression walked away. She was walking back to where she had left her car. The film buff, impervious to the fact that she was taking no notice of him, walked alongside her, and went on talking.

Heller, following, catching the occasional word, noted that the tone of the seductive chat had coarsened. Now it was no longer about *Hiroshima mon amour* and other masterpieces of French cinema, but concerned the sheer poetry of the pornographic imagination, and the erotic quality of wetness that was shared by milk, tears, saliva, urine, semen, and female come. A sex buff as well as a film buff.

Marie-Ann was back at her badly parked car and about to get into it, still not having said a word to the man. He proposed something to her, with a sort of philosophical half shrug and a spreading of the hands. For the first time she looked at him, as if she hadn't really noticed him before or heard what he was saying. Her expression was one of contempt. The white-haired man was however undeterred; he moved his arms a lot, in lofty, elegant, explanatory gestures, smiling, philosophising, expounding. He seemed to make no impression on her contempt, but he had the sort of eye that could see she was lost, and so he started to half lead, half playfully drag her towards a taxi he had signalled with his clicking fingers, and she went along with him, as if she had decided that what happened to her was of little importance. Within moments the taxi was in the thick of the slow traffic of the boulevard.

Heller followed in the Fiat.

Ten minutes later the taxi stopped outside a fine apartment building in the seizième, overlooking the Seine, and Heller saw the white-haired man get out with Marie-Ann. He was still gesticulating, still philosophising and expounding.

Heller waited in the Fiat. It was close to midnight.

At 01.17 he saw Marie-Ann come out. She was dishevelled, and not only her clothing and hair, her whole being. There was blood on her, she had no overcoat, her dress was torn in places and stained, and she was staggering and gasping and having to hang on to railings and lamp-posts to stop herself from falling.

The long quiet residential street was empty.

Heller approached her, took her arm and held her up. Gently he helped her to his car.

—Who are you? she asked as she got in.

—Someone who can help you, he said.

She slept deeply for nine hours, sleeping off her drugs. When she emerged there was the incipient panic.

It was either daze or panic and she preferred the daze; she was searching the apartment for the *hasch* that she had hidden somewhere. When she couldn't find it she became furious. (While she had been in her coma-like sleep, Heller had taken the precaution of removing all the drugs that he could find.)

126

Gradually, with coffee and food, she was becoming more focused:

—I know who you are, she said. You are the American. The one I talked to on the phone. What are you doing here? How did you get ...

She looked around as if only just taking in where she was: the flowery patterns of curtains and sofa covers, the magenta fitted carpets, the Chinese rugs, the Louis XV-style furniture. The Art Deco ceiling lamp in the form of a suspended flower bowl. The reproduction painting of Tahitian native girls. Her mother's apartment. The rue César Franck.

—You remember anything of what happened to you last night?

Things were filtering through and she turned her head away from his intrusive gaze. He forced her to face him.

—Listen to me, Marie-Ann. You need help. You need medical help. You need psychiatric help. You need legal help. And before all that, you need my help just to stay alive.

—Your help? she said without any expression.

—That's right. I can help you. If you help me.

She shook her head in rebuttal of what he was saying, and started violently to sweep cushions from sofas, to bundle up rugs, to sweep delicate china figurines from mantelpieces and other tops, looking for her fix.

—You won't find any, he told her. I got rid of it all.

—Bastard! Bastard!

—I need your full attention, he said. So no drugs. No alcohol. Listen. If I wash my hands of you, you're a dead duck. What chance d'you think you've got? You know what's been happening to you. How long d'you think you can last out? Between the drugs and the perverts. Next time you'll find somebody who'll finish you off while he's about it. Why d'you think you go in for things like that? The demeanment. The other stuff. Why d'you think? I'll tell you why. Because when you were working at the Crillon, in the office, you supplied your friends with Bill Gibson's restaurant reservations, and so you hold yourself responsible for

127

what happened at the Brasserie Lipp. Right? In part, you are responsible. In part.

—What's that supposed to mean?

—Listen to me, Marie-Ann. This is the way I see it. You got sucked into this thing. You were on the fringes. At the bottom of the pyramid. How you got into it doesn't matter now ... some misguided ideas. A love affair. A man in a maroon polo says to you don't you want to create a better society. If so, first step is sleep with me. Right? And then you get into it. It gets to be an *amour fou*, and OK, you believe him when he says everything's the fault of the American imperialists, and you want to do something, you want to do something to fight for the underprivileged of this world ... I know the story, Marie-Ann. You're not the first one who has got led into something like this. And before you know it, you're running errands for them, picking up suitcases, lodging comrades, passing their remittances from abroad through your bank account, rendering them other little services of one type or another. Like passing them lists of visiting Americans. With their itineraries. That's how it happens, and then one day you wake up and read eight people have been shot dead at the Brasserie Lipp ... If the French police get you, you are going to do ten, fifteen years ... On the other hand, if you co-operate with me, I can promise you your case will be treated leniently. You'll get ... two, three years' suspended sentence. Something like that. You can make a new start. Your life's not over.

—What d'you expect me to do?

—Help me get Bill Gibson free.

She laughed at him.

—They would kill me.

—You'll be protected. I can arrange that.

—They'll kill you too.

—I can look after myself. We'll put you in a safe house. Nobody'll know where. You make your phone calls. You relay our proposals, and their answers. As you have been doing. Only we'll be monitoring every stage.

—And then?

—You leave the rest to ... others, those qualified to deal with this sort of thing.

—You mean I give them away. I betray them. Give evidence in court.

—That would be part of the deal, yes. If you want a reduced sentence.

—I can't do that. I can't give away my friends.

—They're murderers. They killed innocent people, who were simply sitting in a restaurant eating. They're torturing a sick old man to make him say the things they want him to say. These are your friends?

—I can't, she said flatly.

He nodded impassively, and said:

—OK. OK. But you have got to realise that if we don't work something out, I have to hand you over. Without any conditions. That's your choice and you'll have to make it.

—If you hand me over, they call off the negotiation. They execute Gibson straight away. And release the tapes of his trial.

—That's right, everybody loses. I say we have to think about it. Calmly. But we haven't got long.

She was between impossible choices, did not know which way to turn. She was also all alone, had at least partly abandoned a world that had turned poisonous for her. Now she had no place to go, but could not bring herself to take the inevitable step forward to free herself. Could not. She must have been in this state of deep isolation ever since Lipp, fearful of all normal human contacts, and therefore prey to men like the film buff.

Dazed, she switched on the TV and sank into the sofa. She did not want to have to think. She wanted to escape. Escape from the inescapable things that confronted her. She was a channel-hopper, frequently switching channels with the remote control, and hardly noticing the change of programme, watching everything with the same fixed stare, as if it was all one and the same story to her.

—What did they mean to you? he asked her at one point.

—They were my 'family'. I belonged to them.

—Yes, I see that. And now?

—I don't know.

—You're a big TV watcher, aren't you?

—Yes, it distracts me. And it passes the time.

There was a video-recorder on the shelf below the TV set, and several shelves of video-tapes, tightly arranged like rows of books, with the recorded programmes marked on the spines. He glanced along the rows. *Shogun*. A Maigret series. Variety. French soaps, American soaps. Crime. Ballet. Concerts. – Old movies. American movies, French movies.

The titles of the programmes were all precisely inscribed on the spines, with cast details and dates of production. Must be the mother's work. He did not see Marie-Ann being so meticulous.

He noticed a blank spine. Why had the mother not noted the contents of this box, as in the case of the others? Was this a blank tape? He took down the box and extracted the cassette. Nothing written on the label.

Marie-Ann seated on the floor close to the TV wore her mesmerised look.

He inserted the tape in the video-player, rewound, and then shifted to play.

Numbers unspooled across the top of the screen, and Heller saw a figure not entirely in focus stepping out of a car. The angle of the shot was awkward, and the face was not visible. The camera rolled on nothing in particular, people in a street, then swung and caught another glimpse of the original man, an equally poor shot. Other cloudy shots followed. The camera followed individuals doing nothing more special than going into buildings or coming out of them, stepping in and out of cars. Some were filmed entirely from behind. Nothing was seen of them except their receding backs as they went along a street. The American Embassy in the place de la Concorde: people going in and out. The Hotel Crillon. The doorman opening car doors, a man stepping out, entering the hotel. It was Bill Gibson, twitchy with impatience. A bulky overcoated figure. The camera caught him in the rue de Varenne, outside the Ministry of National Safety. Then at the foot of the

Eiffel Tower, about to take the elevator up to the second-floor restaurant.

Marie-Ann had come out of her trance. She realised what she was watching now.

'This is evidence,' Heller said. 'Ties you in with the Lipp *attentat*. It's enough to get you fifteen years.'

Still she hardly reacted, remained locked inside her deep daze. Nothing made any difference to her in the state she was in.

On the TV screen he saw Isabelle's dim, wavering face. She was emerging from the artists' entrance at the theatre. She was walking towards her car. She was getting into it. She was going towards a metro station. She was in the rue Monsieur le Prince, outside her apartment. She was in the Jardin Luxembourg, walking under the plane trees. The camera followed her. She was seen from a distance, in the same unvarying follow-shots and panning shots, as she wandered about immersed in her thoughts, oblivious of the unknown filmer.

Marie-Ann sat up. Her head trembled. The glimmering of some reaction was forming on her face.

Heller turned on her.

—You filmed Isabelle Decourten for them. The way you filmed Bill Gibson, and the others. The potential victims. You followed them around with the camera, to find out where and when they were most accessible, most vulnerable. Why her? Why Isabelle Decourten? What was the point of that? She is not a political figure. She's not one of their targets. What is their interest in her?

She seemed to have come out of her daze with the mention of Isabelle, her eyes had begun to focus and lose their dullness, and he saw the beginnings of consternation. So she was capable of that.

She said:

—They wanted to strike at her, because of her father. If necessary, they were going to kill her.

THIRTEEN

Juvin had the fast flicker of the eye, which was as far as he ever went towards betraying excitement. Heller concluded that there had been developments, important developments they must be, considering how rarely Juvin's eye flickered, how firm and fixed it normally was in its unwavering world-wide view. It was astonishing to Heller how this man had banished the carnal passions in himself, was content with a cactus-like existence. At times it gave rise to an unearthly flowering: a flickering of the eye when something was brewing. To Heller, Juvin sometimes seemed like a person from another planet, all cerebrum, and with a whole different immune system from the rest of humanity. Inconceivable that Claude Juvin could suffer the pangs of love – inconceivable that he could love anything, other than his collection of glass. There was a story told about him that Heller remembered now: the world's most powerful leaders are meeting and get to boasting about their trusty subordinates. 'I have a man,' says the Soviet leader, 'who, if I told him to, would sit on a spike of ice until it melts.' To which the French leader replies, 'I too have such a man, his name is Juvin, he would sit on the spike of ice just as long as your man, only in Juvin's case it wouldn't melt.'

Juvin and Heller were standing together outside the Brasserie Lipp. Juvin had suggested they meet here. The place was all fixed up and business was better than ever, tables even harder to get. Everybody wanted to eat at the scene of the horror.

'We won't go in, I try to avoid lunch if I possibly can. Otherwise one is always eating,' Juvin said. 'I can vouch for the fact that it is all back to normal inside. The blood has been cleaned off the banquettes, the mirrors have been replaced and the *prunes de Souillac* are in their jars of *eau-de-vie*, and all is again for the best in the best of all possible brasseries. The *choucroute* is as good and plentiful as ever, I am told. You know in France nothing is allowed to interfere with lunch.'

Juvin looked up and down the thronged boulevard, surveying the tumultuous flow of Paris in its relentless seeking after pleasure.

'Do you know any other city', he asked Heller, 'that makes such an art of pleasure, and so much fuss about it?' He nodded his head thoughtfully. 'I suppose it must offend the puritan spirit of the revolution, so much eating, so much conspicuous consumption. The consumer society in all its moribund glory. The over-bountiful breast, detested for its sheer endless flowing abundance, while the rest, the poor little orphans of the world, must starve ... Ah yes, it is very unjust. They have a point, of course.'

'Of course.'

'Know his psychology and you have the man, hmm? Isn't that what you always say? Well, we're beginning to know these people a little, our murderers of the over-bountiful breast. Aren't we? Our history teacher Gavaudan, who wants to teach us all a lesson. A very bloody lesson. He's a psychopathic idealist. Wants to reorder the world for its own good, no matter the cost. Those are the most dangerous, the ones who know they are in the right. They can justify anything. In a despotism, violence is a legitimate defence. And since even his own will of yesterday becomes a kind of despotism today, you can see how violently he is able to live, and justify himself according to his point of view.'

When Juvin had something to reveal, he did it in his own good time, with fitting introductory remarks. No use pressing him, he would go at his own sedate, correct pace, in the spirit of the heart surgeon who has an intricate action to perform in thirty seconds and knows that he can do it provided he doesn't hurry. That was

Juvin's attitude. When crucial things had to be done, the proper amount of time had to be taken.

He paused and turned towards Heller, and something resembling an emotion showed in his face. It needed deciphering. Heller deciphered annoyance.

'I am disappointed, Fred, that you decide to pursue your own paths without having the courtesy to inform me. Since I have been so meticulous in keeping you in the picture.'

'What are you talking about, Claude?'

'I am talking about Marie-Ann Thurillet.'

'So you are on to her too.'

'We have known about her before you, Fred. And we have certain advantages over you. We are able to listen-in to her telephone conversations. Some of them, at least. So we know what has been going on.'

'Then you know about their plans to kidnap Isabelle Decourten?'

'Those plans were superseded. They chose Bill Gibson instead. Now they have their hands full with him and won't be contemplating other action. They don't have the resources. They are short of funds, very short. That is why they are amenable to your approach. An approach that we find most disquieting, I have to tell you. The prospect that they have such funds at their disposal, to finance their murderous activities, is not one I can view with equanimity.'

'Every move entails certain risks. The plan is to hand over the money. Not that they should keep it.'

'A plan that often backfires on the planner, Fred.'

'Life's a risky business, you die of it sooner or later ... So what've you done with Marie-Ann? She doesn't phone back any more. Doesn't pick up her messages.'

'You scared her, Fred. She has run.'

'Where?'

'Her mother has other apartments. She has taken refuge in one of them.'

'How do you interpret that?'

134

'I interpret that you convinced her with your argument, and she is making the break. That is why she does not pick up the messages, and does not make the phone calls to base. She is going to break away. But her way, not yours.' There was again the rather faster flicker of the eye, the dry restrained touch of excitement. 'This is where I think we may have an opportunity. She is their banker. A substantial remittance from Libya has just been paid into her account, by way of the Credit Suisse, Geneva. Marie-Ann's friends, even if ready to let *her* go, will not let her go with their money.'

'What's your plan, Claude?'

'They will look for her. And in due course ... will find her. If need be, we will arrange that. And when this happens ... ' – he shrugged – 'we will be there.'

What Juvin said about the risk to Isabelle being small, made sense. Even so, Heller was worried. What made sense was not always what occurred.

In her mysterious intuitive ways Isabelle had perceived that she was in danger, had correctly understood that the silences on the telephone answering machine were those of somebody intending her harm; and she *had* been followed by the furies, they had filmed her with their video-camera, as they had filmed Bill Gibson and others on their list.

That night he asked her if she was still getting the nightmare of the body in the attic. She said, yes.

'As bad?'

'It has become worse.'

'In what way?'

'I know whose body it is.'

'Whose?'

'Mine. Or rather ... '

'Tell me.'

'It's like when I get the stage fright. A feeling of being trapped. Inside this person, this dead person.'

'You should have woke me.'

'I did.'

'So you did?'

'Yes.'

'And that . . . chased away the bad dream?'

'Yes.'

'What you say is . . . make me die.'

'I know.'

He had observed that there was a high-strung sexual quality to her anxiety; it was when she gave out the most alluring signals of her desire, was most expressive of her need of love, hungered for mind-blowing sensations. It was when she was most beautiful. And it was when she was in a state of *angoisse* that she spoke in intense crude language of the extremes of physical love, at the same time saying that she loved him, that he was the great, great love of her life.

Since 'losing' Marie-Ann Thurillet, he had left messages every day at the Forum bar in Les Halles for Elvire to call him, but there had been no response from the terrorists. They were not picking up their messages.

The deadline for Bill's execution passed and Heller did not know if Bill was still alive or not.

In a television interview Mitterrand had said, speaking generally, that if he could save the lives of hostages by pardoning 'one of the imprisoned', if he could be of any use in this respect, he was willing to consider such a step. Heller hoped this might have helped gain a reprieve for Bill. If they were being logical, the terrorists ought to take the view that since the breakdown in negotiations was due to the defection of their messenger, the deadline had to be extended. That was if they were being logical. All he could do now was wait for the next move.

The heading across four columns, towards the bottom of *Le*

Monde's typographically sedate front page, conveyed the whiff of sensation.

AMERICAN HOSTAGE'S REVELATIONS
Threat to Vice-president Simpson's presidential hopes

Heller's eye went quickly down the report by Jean-Luc Beaucousin, skimming it for new elements.

Police investigators had made no solid progress in discovering where the former CIA man William Gibson was being held by the terrorists who kidnapped him on 18 November in the *attentat* at the Brasserie Lipp ... He was facing trial before a People's Court ... According to information reaching *Le Monde* he had been speaking freely before the video cameras recording his trial, and was spilling beans that would prove of serious embarrassment to the American government and in particular to Vice-president Simpson, who had served as Deputy Director CIA, in charge of covert operations, at the time Gibson was most active.

Gibson had been talking about past CIA operations, revealing the full extent of American interference in the internal affairs of its close allies. He was said to have talked in detail about how in the immediate post-war period he and James Angleton fixed the Italian elections to ensure that the people the US wanted in, got in, and that the Communists were kept out. Similar actions on the territory of other friendly powers had been revealed.

Gibson had been one of the men most prominently involved in using the services of Nazi war criminals in operations against the Soviet Union.

While it was widely known that such things had happened after the war, Gibson's confessions for the first time gave full details, naming those presently in high office who had been involved. Some of the most unsavoury CIA operations were mounted under the authority of its then Director of covert operations, Arthur Simpson.

Heller decided that he'd have to see this Jean-Luc Beaucousin of *Le Monde*.

★

The journalist was about forty; he wore a striped shirt with fashionably narrow collar, meagre tie knot. He had a shock of carelessly curled black hair, styled to give the uncombed look. The image was of sexual dash and intellectual seriousness, or perhaps sexual seriousness and intellectual dash. He wore expensive blue suede shoes. The smell of cigarettes persisted around him. And so did the faint sneer. It was built into his persona. A man who finds the world absurd.

'Tea, Monsieur Beaucousin?' Heller asked. They had sat down in the inner lobby of the Pont-Royal, which was usually empty at this time of day.

'I prefer a whisky.'

'Sure.'

'You want to know where I get my story from? Let me save you the question. The police have already asked, and I've told them I can't reveal my sources. Obviously I'm not going to tell you. I will tell you this, though. It's solid. My information is solid. Now let me ask you something. How much ransom you are ready to pay for Bill Gibson? How much the old bastard is considered to be worth?'

'American policy, as you know, is not to pay ransoms.'

'Like Irangate proved. Well, sometimes the left hand does things that the right hand doesn't need to know about, isn't that so?' He lowered his voice and said a little gloatingly, 'It's what the left hand does that I'm interested in.'

'You don't want to have the responsibility for a man's death on your head, do you, Monsieur Beaucousin? I certainly don't. So I wouldn't want to say anything to you that might result in that.'

'But you want *me* to tell *you*,' Beaucousin said with his faint sneer.

Heller allowed himself be drawn out a little. Let the reporter think he was getting things out of him. They talked about Bill Gibson's supposed 'damage value' and about 'public benefactors' in the US who were sometimes willing to subscribe ransom money for hostages, which the government could not be seen to provide. About Mafia connections in high places.

'You and I know this happens,' Beaucousin asserted, and Heller allowed himself to be manoeuvred into admitting it tacitly. The rule was if you had to make a discreditable admission, admit something already known. He said on no account to quote him by name, demanded assurances of this, as if he had recognised having made a slip and was trying to redress it. At the same time gave the impression that further slips might be in prospect. Then he switched over.

'These people – Attaque; what's the aim of killing innocent people in a restaurant? What do they hope to achieve by that? And now these alleged confessions of Bill's. What do they want ultimately?'

'This type ... we are talking about. This type of activist. Terrorist. Whatever you like to call him. He sees the domination of ordinary people by great inhuman corporate interests. Preeminently American interests. Yes, yes? America "sewed-up" the post-war world for its own benefit, and hangs onto that benefit on the basis of the rationalisation that what is good for General Motors is good for the world. Yes? All right, he – our hypothetical terrorist of the left – he sees American actions in El Salvador. In Guatemala. In Nicaragua, in Cuba. He sees ... knows how the Americans subverted the crucial 1948 elections in Italy. He knows how they put the Shah in power. How America infiltrated the French trade unions after the war. Bought union leaders. He sees how everything is subordinated to the interests of American business. He sees the United States administering a pedagogy of terror through its agents and client states. These are the triggers.'

Heller nodded. He had heard not just reporting but the hard ring of ideas formed long ago.

'That's the way you see it too, isn't it? So where do you part company with them? If you do.'

'I part company with them on many things but above all their methods.'

'At one time you also believed in violence.'

'That was May '68. A lot of us who subsequently amended our

139

views believed then that a better, juster society could not be achieved without blood. Don't forget we are the *héritiers* of 1789. We are the product of revolution, so for us the *idea* of violence has legitimacy. Remember what Lenin said? "Violence is the midwife of history."'

'And Brecht said, "With whom will the just not sit down to remove injustice?" You subscribe to that?'

'Up to a point.'

'What point?'

'Violence is justified in combatting a tyranny. We live under a democratic system that is unjust and defective, but it is not tyranny. Hence violence is not justified. But almost everything short of it is.'

'I think I've got the picture.' Heller paused. 'You seem to know these terrorists of Attaque pretty well. If you are in touch with them directly and not telling the police, you're running a risk, not only vis-à-vis them but also with the law. I don't need to tell you that.'

Beaucousin delicately felt the length of his thin fingers and then lightly clenched and unclenched his hands.

'I am not in touch with them,' he said categorically. 'I don't know where they have got Bill Gibson. I don't know where their hideout is. What I do know, in part, is what Gibson has been talking to them about.'

'How?'

He hesitated a moment, and then said: 'I have seen a video-tape. Of his "trial".'

'Yes ... The videotape has become a favourite weapon of terrorists the world over. It's the Kalashnikov – and the Sony! I expect you know about how such tapes can be ... uh "edited" ... played around with to make them tell the story that *somebody* wishes to have told.'

'I'm satisfied this tape has not been faked.'

'How'd you get hold of it?'

'I am not in a position to reveal that.'

'I see. Well ... ' Heller stood up. 'We've had an interesting conversation, Monsieur Beaucousin. Thank you for coming.' He was starting to turn away. 'Of course you're quite sure that the person on the tape is Bill Gibson. You've met him recently?'

'No, I have not met him. Ever. But I do know what he looks like.'

'From photographs? Most of those photographs are ten or more years old. He's older . . . he's got fat. Used to be a lean man. But drinking the way he does. Puts weight on you, alters your appearance. And he's been sick. A person's appearance changes . . . Those old photographs of Bill . . . he's never been a photogenic subject. Doesn't reveal himself to the camera. I'd advise you to be very careful you're not being set up, Monsieur Beaucousin. That has happened to you, hasn't it? You wouldn't want to place yourself in that position *again*. Whoever it was gave you this stuff has an angle. There are no Deep Throats without angles. I seem to recall that last time, too, certain faked material was planted on you. I'd be damn careful, if I were you, before rushing into print with any more of this sort of stuff.'

Beaucousin said tiredly: 'You know, Mr Heller, in France we are not too good at getting to the bottom of things. There are many matters that are never cleared up. Remain forever un-fathomable . . . This suits a lot of people. But I do not intend for the Bill Gibson "affair" to be one of these cases . . . Of course I will be "damn careful", as you advise. Goodbye, Mr Heller.'

He was tired-out and he and Isabelle slept chastely in each other's arms, and then in the morning he was sufficiently restored to respond again to her closeness.

He had a feeling he was going to lose her and this aroused a wildness in him. They were all over the place. Afterwards, she went to the high windows and pulled the cords of the venetian blinds, changing the slat positions to admit the maximum amount of dusty cold northern light. She peered out between the slats at the windows opposite and the rooftops of the other buildings forming a square around the courtyard.

Her face darkened and he saw a shiver pass through her, starting at the neck. Though she was naked it was not a shiver of cold: it was very warm in the room, she always kept the central heating thermostat on high. In a moment her mood had changed, her sunny world had clouded over. She reached for a towel and wrapped it around herself.

'There are men on the roof opposite,' she said. 'You think they were watching us?'

'There are enough shows in Paris, I don't think they need climb on roofs . . . '

'I hate to be spied on.'

He saw the shadow then, very clearly, a sudden eclipse that hid her from him.

'Any case, I don't think they can see through venetian blinds.'

'There is nothing over the top of the windows. From the roof, from that angle, they could see in. I'm sure they were watching us,' she said.

He went to the window himself now, but not too quickly, in order not to alarm her by showing undue concern – she was so quick to sense other people's states of mind and to be influenced by them – and put his arms around her, in a comforting way, and only then did he casually glance up to the roof opposite. There was no one. Grey slates covered with hoar frost.

He looked at her and shrugged.

'Nobody there now.'

'They were there a minute ago,' she said, eyes burning, 'I saw them. I didn't imagine it. I am not a paranoiac.'

In the evening he telephoned her just before she would be leaving for the theatre. He got the answering machine. He frowned, a vague worry beginning to form. The curse of his profession was that you were obliged to entertain the most outlandish possibilities. No, he told himself: she has just left for the theatre a little earlier than usual, perhaps had some things to do on the way. None the less he did phone the theatre at just after eight to ask if the curtain had gone up, and was told it had. To make quite sure all was well he asked who was playing Antigone. They said, Isabelle Decourten. So all was fine.

He poured himself a scotch from the mini-bar and lay on the bed and closed his eyes. When he woke up it was after eleven. He was refreshed and hungry. He reached for the phone and dialled Isabelle's number.

Again he got the answering machine, and this time he left no message, realising that he was thus adding to the 'silent calls' that so perturbed her. He rang once again five minutes later and it was still the damn machine. He let fifteen minutes go by before calling once more. Isabelle's recorded voice answered. He telephoned the stage door of the theatre and was told Isabelle Decourten had left an hour ago. That was worrying. It didn't take an hour to get from the theatre to her apartment. It didn't take half an hour. It didn't take fifteen minutes, normally.

Of course there were all sorts of possible explanations to account for her not being home yet. She might be having a drink with someone. Her car might have had a breakdown ...

The thing to do, he decided, was to go round to her apartment. When he reached the rue Monsieur le Prince he saw the unmarked police car, a white Peugeot 205, its motor off, Bosch at the wheel, outside her door.

—*Elle est revenue*?' he asked Bosch.

She was back, yes, Bosch said surlily.

Her phone doesn't answer, Heller said. Was something wrong with the phone? *Une panne?* He pressed the bell of the entryphone and waited for her voice and the click of the *porte-cochère* opening. But there was no voice and no click.

He turned to Bosch in the car, puzzled.

—She's not answering.

Bosch had a hard little acid-etched smile on his lower lip, which was turned downward.

—She isn't seeing anybody, he said.

—Including me?

—Including you, Eller. That's how it is.

—Come on. This is ridiculous. There's some mistake. You saying she doesn't *want* to see me?

—Well, you know how changeable women can be, Bosch said smirking. The bastard was really enjoying this.

Heller went to the gate and tapped out the code of the security lock.

Bosch called from the car:

—Wouldn't advise you to go up unannounced. She's got company.

Heller heard the click of the lock opening, but did not go in. Slowly he turned round.

—Who's up there?

—It's that young guy. The actor, you know the one. He's the new love in her life. The one with the gorgeous ass.

FOURTEEN

S INCE HE HAD not succeeded in establishing contact with Isabelle by telephone, Heller decided to go round to the theatre and see her after the play.

To avoid having to pass the stage-door keeper, who would have checked with Isabelle before admitting him, Heller went through the auditorium and the door marked *Privé*, which as usual was unlocked, and made his way along the dim passageway lined with the scenery of old productions. At the door of Isabelle's dressing room he saw Bosch, drowsy from wine, heavy eyelids closing and being forced open in a vain struggle against falling asleep on the job; the sight of Heller woke him up. Animosity flared in his red eyes.

—You can't go in, he said, savouring his guardianship of the door. No visitors.

—I'm not a visitor, Heller said. She doesn't tell you everything, Bosch.

Bosch was lounging against the wall as Heller knocked on the dressing-room door and called through, announcing himself. Without waiting for an answer he opened the door with his other hand and was inside before Bosch was firmly balanced on his two feet. Not the most brilliant of bodyguards. To make up for it, he came after Heller, with gun drawn.

'Explain to this asshole that you were expecting me,' Heller told Isabelle.

—*Ça va, Bosch. Ça va.*

Bosch did not take this well. He complained bitterly about the way she changed her mind all the time. How could she expect the police to protect her, if one minute she said a certain person was not to be allowed in and the next she was letting him in. Bosch slammed the door.

Isabelle said, 'Pour me a vodka, will you, Fred? I have the feeling I will need it.'

He poured it for her without saying anything, while she continued to remove her make-up. He thought, she fits Jouvet's description of the actor: 'an empty vessel waiting to be filled'. He set down her vodka amid the clutter of brushes, creams, pan sticks, eyeliners. Her wig of long black tresses was up on a block, her costume on a tailor's dummy. When the last of the stage make-up had been removed, she was once more 'herself', whoever that was. He didn't know, and perhaps she didn't either.

'How was it tonight?' he asked neutrally, with determined calm.

'Terrible,' she said. 'I was terrible.'

'Why so terrible?'

'It was flat. No terror.'

'You can't win, can you? It's either too much or too little.'

'That's right. There is no straight road. You have always to steer. Tonight she did not go to her death. She only went off-stage ... Flat. I am a very bad actress tonight.'

He let a silence ensue, during which she was slowly starting to put herself together again after the emptying out on the stage. She drew hard on the cigarette and blew out smoke into the light from the electric light bulb dangling down over the mirror. Her eyes closed momentarily.

'What's going on?' he asked. 'Why can't I get you on the phone? Why don't you answer the door to me? What's happened?'

'What are you setting me up for?' she threw back, staring at him in the mirror with bitter eyes.

'Setting you up for?'

'Those people spying on me with their telescope zoom lenses...'

'What? What people are you talking about?'

She said angrily: 'Those people on the roof. Who were photographing us together.'

'Photographing through venetian blinds – this is crazy! Why would I have people photographing us make love? In any case, there was nobody there...'

'There were people there. I was not the only one who saw them.'

'Who else saw them?'

'Bosch.'

'And he said that it was my doing? He's mad. You know he hates me, he hates me because I'm American and because he has got a thing about you.'

'To you everybody else is mad. You probably think I am mad, too. That I have a persecution mania. Is that what you think? Because I see people on the roof who are not there? Well, they were there, there is proof...'

'What proof?'

'The apartment opposite, those two men who rent it are Americans. They are CIA,' she said with grim satisfaction.

'Where d'you get that they're CIA?'

'Bosch.'

'It all comes down to Bosch.'

'No. I asked my father. He made enquiries. He confirmed that both men work for you, for the American government. For a foreign aid agency. They use those jobs as a cover, Bosch says.'

'That's what Bosch says, huh? Look: whoever they are and whatever they were doing on the roof, they are nothing to do with me.'

'That is what you say.'

'You don't trust me? How is it that suddenly you don't trust me? Twenty-four hours ago you said I was the love of your life, remember? Does nothing you say mean anything?'

She blew out a sigh of anger. 'We hardly know each other,

Fred. I . . . I don't know you. I don't know who you really are, what you do. You aren't the person I got it in my head you were . . . all those years ago. You are someone else entirely. I have no idea what you are doing here. With me. With my father.'

'Look, it's straightforward . . .'

'It's not straightforward at all. At all.' She became heated. Anger flared through her. 'You're plotting against my father. I know that now. You've been using me to . . . to get things against him. Because the CIA want to destroy him. I've heard of that happening. When somebody doesn't suit American policy, he's got rid of. That's what you're here for. That's your mission. And I fell for it. I was your means of insinuating yourself into our family circle.'

'You're forgetting who made the first move. Anyway, why's the United States supposed to want to get rid of Charles?'

She said nothing, was in eclipse with no light reaching her. He let the silence go on, and when he could not stand it any more, he said:

'What's all this saying, Isabelle?'

'I . . . thought I loved you, Fred.' Her voice was implacable. He saw she had become a wall against which he would beat his head to no avail. She had undergone some sudden change of heart, and was telling him that this was how it was, nothing to be done, no use arguing.

'You *thought* you loved me. A few days ago you were pretty sure.'

'I made a mistake, Fred. I admit the first move was mine, I admit that. I was in a very strange state that night, after the party. I was terribly anxious. Panic-stricken, really. About those terrorist women, I suppose. And there *was* a very strong chemistry that I felt with you, a very physical thing, which is something that happens to me when I'm afraid . . . And you were there, Fred.'

'And now the zest has gone out of it suddenly? Like your performance tonight. No terror equals no juice. Everything is a performance for you. And when it's over it sure is over. Curtain

148

down, off with the make-up.' She did not say anything. 'So now it's luscious lips?'

'Now it's Jean-Pierre.'

He felt the air reduce in his lungs, the arteries to his heart narrow dangerously.

'*Salope!* What a little whore you are! The day before yesterday there was all that stuff – that I was the great love of your life.'

'That was the day before yesterday.'

'And tomorrow?'

'I don't know. Tomorrow I may be dead.'

'But tonight Jean-Pierre is going back with you?'

'Yes.'

'Does he make you go out of your mind?'

'Yes.'

'You say those words to him?'

'Yes.'

He pushed his hand roughly between her legs and felt her grow moist and was exultant. 'Do it with me,' he said in a low harsh whisper. 'If you want to be a whore, be a whore with me. A last time. Then you can go to Jean-Pierre with your guilty secret. I want to hear you say those words again.'

'No, Fred,' she said, matter-of-factly disengaging his hand as if her bodily response was of no significance: freeing herself from him. She had some of her father's gift for lightness, at times. She could make light of some pretty heavy stuff when it suited her.

So it was over between them, all in a moment, like a sudden death, and he felt a vast emptiness, a raging ache at this loss, which seemed so arbitrary, so meaningless, so wanton and cruel.

He poured himself a hefty vodka. Then he spoke in a calmer voice, the voice of the calm solver of puzzles.

'How can you go from one extreme to another so fast?'

She gave the question her serious consideration, and then she offered her considered answer: 'I think I must have difficulties when somebody wants me too much. It gives me claustrophobia. I feel I am trapped and then I have to escape.'

He got up to go. He knew from her tenseness that it wasn't over

149

yet between them. When it was he would know. But it wasn't yet. She was too tense for it to be over. There was too much electricity still. It wasn't the end. It was a piece of the zigzag in her mind. So he told himself.

FIFTEEN

AFTER LEAVING THE bank with the 50,000 F. that she had withdrawn, Marie-Ann Thurillet went straight back to the empty apartment in which she had been living and no more was seen of her for the rest of the day. She did not emerge again until the early evening. She was wearing her brown raincoat with the collar buttoned up around her neck. Hard, cold, slanting rain was coming down. It carried a foretaste of ice and snow. She went to where the 2 CV was parked: it spluttered and wheezed a long time before starting.

She jolted and rattled through the streets of the quinzième, vaguely heading in the direction of Montparnasse, but not following the most direct route, and indeed changing direction several times, as if going somewhere else. It seemed to be a pretty haphazard route she was taking, and finally she reversed dangerously around a corner for no other reason, it seemed, than because she had spotted a parking space. There was a bar-tabac on the corner, and she went inside and ordered a glass of white wine at the counter. After she'd drunk a few sips she asked where the phone was. They showed her and she went to use it; a few minutes later she returned.

She kept trying the phone every five or ten minutes, without success. She had drunk a number of glasses of wine by now and decided she had better eat something: she ordered a mushroom omelette. When she had finished it, she went once again to phone, and this time got through. It was nearly eleven by then, and the telephone line of the bar Jean Bart was now connected with a room reserved for the use of the DST at 51, boulevard Latour-Maubourg. The police officer to whom the Jean Bart had been assigned, seeing the small red bulb light up on his console, proceeded to note down the conversation on a pad before him, while at the same time it was recorded on one of a bank of permanently turning tape-recorders in the adjoining room.

The conversation was quite brief and the familiar 'tu' was used:

—You know who this is?

—Yes.

—Tell him I want to see him. Tell him I have something to give him

—Yes.

The other voice was also a woman's: brittle and with a quality of tense nerviness. She sounded in a hurry to leave and spoke fast.

—It's what you're waiting for. You understand? I want to give it to him.

—Where?

—In the usual place. Tomorrow at eleven. In the morning. Eleven in the morning.

—In the usual place, all right.

—I just want to give it to him, and then I want to be able to go. You understand? I don't want to talk. When I see him, I'll just leave it and go, I don't want to have any more to do with ... I've been sick ...

The other voice cut in: tense, hurried.

—Understood. I confirm: tomorrow at eleven in the usual place. You'll leave it there. Where? How?

—It will be in an airline bag. A blue and white plastic airline bag. An Air France bag.

—Understood.

Within less than three minutes twelve unmarked police cars were at the Gare du Nord. Armed plainclothes men rushed through the station towards the public telephones. When they arrived at the one to which the call had been traced, the booth was empty.

Saturday morning Marie-Ann Thurillet left the apartment before nine. It was raining out of a sombre grey sky. The rain had a wintry edge to it and there was some fog and a gusty wind. She did not take the 2 CV. She followed the streets running parallel with the avenue de Suffren, as far as place Henri Queville. There she walked beneath the grey cast-iron and stone viaduct carrying the metro rail-line across this part of the city. She went as far as the rue Lecourbe and into the Café du Nord, where she drank a coffee, standing up at the bar, and ate a hard-boiled egg from the rack.

Leaving ten minutes later, she looked around, searching both sides of the street, scrutinising passing faces. She waited until all the loiterers in the vicinity, all the people looking in shop windows, all those seated in stationary vehicles, had moved off, but she could not look inside the backs of closed vans without windows.

Going on her way, she continued to exercise a high degree of caution, first starting out in one direction, then abruptly turning about and going the other way and looking to see if anyone else had made a similar about-turn. She noticed nothing to disturb her.

She was not concerned about the black girl with dreadlocks, a Walkman clamped to her head, who went into the metro Sèvres Lecourbe. For a while the two girls walked alongside each other in the same direction, the black girl moving rhythmically to her music. They parted ways when Marie-Ann took the direction Etoille, and the black girl, Nation. Marie-Ann saw her on the opposite platform. She seemed to be murmuring to herself the words of the song she was listening to.

Marie-Ann, after changing trains twice, got off at Barbès Rochechouart. Leaving the station, she lost herself in the back and forth flow of the boulevard Barbès. She was swept along by the crowd and arrived at the department store Tati with its many entrances and exits. She went in through one door and moments later exited through another. Even so, she was still being followed as she left. Now it seemed she was finally going to her rendezvous.

Chaillet had been brought into the operation. Chaillet's division within the brigade criminelle was the most trained for actions involving dangerous criminals. Chaillet's men were expert marksmen, and of a high level of physical fitness. They had undergone intensive training for actions against terrorists and hijackers and insurrectionists. They were part of the *police judiciaire*, and were responsible to a *juge d'instruction*, whereas the DST, protected by the law of *secret-défense*, was responsible to the Minister of National Safety, the Minister of the Interior, to the government, to the Président de la République, but not to any little judge. There was a lot that the DST could do without asking anybody's permission, but when it came to arrests involving the possibility of gunplay, the French system called for the presence of a police force that was accountable to the high law officers of the land. It was therefore considered correct to alert Chaillet's forces, and to bring them in as 'reserves', though no showdown was envisaged at this point.

Juvin's plan was to let Marie-Ann Thurillet hand over the money, and then for his men to follow the recipient back to the terrorists' hideout. It was meant to be a high-grade surveillance operation, nothing else. At a later stage the question of a raid might arise, and Chaillet's men would then be expected to carry it out, since that was what they were trained for. For the present Chaillet's men were to be there solely as observers, and as reserves in case something went wrong. Their instructions were to lie low and not to intervene unless called upon to do so by Juvin. It was his operation.

Once she felt confident that nobody was following her, Marie-Ann took a metro train in the direction of République, and Juvin, receiving the report of this, concluded that she was going to Père Lachaise.

The sky was black and it was beginning to rain again as Marie-Ann walked slowly along the avenue Principale with the pillared family tombs on each side. The rain did not seem to bother her and she had not thought to open her umbrella as she walked with the blue and white Air France bag dangling from her left shoulder, the collar of her raincoat buttoned up to her chin, hands deep in pockets. She was going towards the Monument aux Morts, with its grief-stricken figures hiding their eyes before the black doors of death.

She turned briefly off the main avenue in order to see Colette's grave on the corner, and then she went on again. She stopped at Rossini's tomb to peer through the rusting iron grillwork, in which a fresh carnation wrapped in cellophane had recently been inserted. She was trying to make out the inscription on the faded tombstone inside. The next grave she stopped at was Alfred de Musset's.

Once or twice she looked at her watch and then glanced around to see if anybody was coming. She saw no one.

She walked on, slowly, dragging her feet through the fall of yellow leaves that made a straggling trail along the sides of the main avenue. She was still early for her appointment. It was only five to eleven.

The DST observers in the Citroën hearse held her in the sights of their special binoculars, while the vehicle proceeded, at a suitably funereal pace, in the direction of the Chapelle. They alerted their colleagues, placed at the exits of the cemetery, and at key points in the streets all around, when two young women in jeans and anoraks, with ski hoods over their heads to protect them against the light rain, approached Marie-Ann Thurillet and spoke to her for perhaps two minutes. Nothing, however, was handed over to them, and the encounter ended with Marie-Ann pointing somewhere to her right and the two girls going off in that direction. They were kept under observation until it had been established that they had found the grave of Jim Morrison and placed on it a white rose and a picture postcard with a message of love.

After talking with the Jim Morrison fans, Marie-Ann began to hurry along the avenue Principale. As she passed the Monument aux Morts, mourners started coming out of the Chapelle, above her. There was a large Citroën hearse waiting at the bottom of the steps, densely hung about with funeral wreaths, and cars parked all along the avenue de la Chapelle as far as the carrefour du Grand-Rond. And now the mourners on foot were crowding the avenue, following the cortège, which had begun to move off.

Marie-Ann appeared not to know what to do; she was searching the faces of people in the funeral crowd, and then pushing in among them, but did not find the person she was looking for. She decided, after glancing at her watch one more, to stand by the tomb of Géricault, alongside the statue of the lounging artist grasping palette and brush. Anybody looking for her would be bound to see her there.

She moved the strap of the airline bag on her shoulder to a more comfortable position. She examined the dates on Géricault's headstone, calculating the length of his life. She looked left and right and all around.

A second hearse was stopping at the bottom of the Chapelle steps, and she presumed it was waiting for another coffin to be brought out.

There was no sign for the moment of the person for whom she was waiting. The sky was getting blacker the whole time, and as the rain began to fall more heavily, she opened her umbrella.

Feeling suddenly too conspicuous where she was, now that the bulk of the funeral procession had passed her, she went off the main avenue and into the leaf-cluttered paths alongside it. In this part of the cemetery the graves were in a state of disorder. Moss-speckled headstones tilted weirdly, tombs had sunk, paths petered out. She was more concealed here, and the men in the observation vehicle kept losing her. They picked her up again as she stopped at the simple column designating the spot where Kreutzer was buried – born 1766, she read. Died Geneva 1831.

Calculating the length of his life, she saw below her a group of bulky men in overcoats and hats standing in a kidney-shaped segment where music-lovers were often searching for the grave of Chopin. These bulky men were getting wet, they were not moving, and they did not look like music-lovers to her.

Then she saw wild-haired Marco coming towards her along the avenue de la Chapelle, and she closed her umbrella twice to warn him, but he seemed not to understand and carried straight on towards her, walking fast. When he was a few steps away from her, she slipped the airline bag from her shoulder and placed it on Kreutzer's column. She started down the rough stone steps between tilting headstones towards Chopin's grave. The flowers on it were fresh and abundant, yellow, white and gold irises, mauve chrysanthemums, yellow roses, a wild orchid. Before she could get close enough to see the faces of the men standing there, Marco had caught up with her and grabbed her arm and was dragging her towards the broadly curving avenue Casimir Perier. The men around Chopin's grave did nothing, treating the fracas as a private matter in which they did not wish to become involved.

The rain was getting heavier. A red loamy haze rose from a recently dug grave. Across the burial ground, to the right, she saw a long line of open black umbrellas moving in a solid phalanx, returning from an interment to rejoin the avenue Casimir Perier.

With an abrupt violent wrench she succeeded in breaking free of Marco and started to run towards the umbrellas. It must have seemed to her that she could find safety among these mourners, that she could not be snatched out of their midst: it looked as if it was the funeral of someone important, the press were there, and television cameras, and the Minister of Culture, and two gendarmes of the *garde portière*.

To the sound of the rain was added the hard patter and rattle of hail. The hailstones were large and soon some umbrellas were in tatters, fluttering uselessly about metal ribs, and mourners were being struck stinging blows to the head and face. To protect themselves people were taking off their coats and draping them over their heads.

The observers in the surveillance van in the lay-by on the other side of the avenue du Puits had lost Marie-Ann as she entered among the mourners caught in the hailstorm; the light-enhancing telescope isolated and refined one or two faces in the grainy mass, but Marie-Ann couldn't be found. The surveillance telescope swivelled, searching in the blur. People were making tents of their coats and faces vanished from sight.

Under a tent of metal-studded black leather, the surveillance telescope picked out a big woman's heavy, large-boned features, lips rising high above the gums and pulling back. The teeth became prominent; and then the whole face seemed to be convulsed with the force of some action, the nature of which remained unknown until the telescope, tilting jerkily down, brought into vision the image of a pistol with a long silencer. The trailing smoke made a dark little squiggle in the frosty air. People were running. There were frantic, confused movements. Then, through a blurred undergrowth of rushing feet, the telescope found a woman lying in a heap of yellow leaves in the muddy path with a rushing stream of rainwater lapping against her body.

SIXTEEN

HELLER LEARNED OF what had happened very soon afterwards; radio had the bare bones of the story – a shooting at Père Lachaise, a young woman killed – within half an hour of the event. And when he was able to get through to Juvin, about an hour later, he was told the rest.

A very bad outcome, said Juvin. In the thick rain, which was throwing up a mist pall, the terrorists had vanished amid the tombstones. They were accustomed to meeting at the cemetery and knew its topography, whereas the police did not.

A man fitting Marco Vougny's description had been seen coming over the wall and dropping down to the boulevard de Ménilmontant. Gisèle Chenu, who had fired the shots, was thought to have disappeared into the Jewish section of the cemetery and to have proceeded along the periphery, past the tomb of Rachel, past Rothschild, and then up by way of Héloïse et Abélard, along rising ground to Modigliani, then past Edith Piaf to the Mur des Fédérés. Witnesses had seen a woman of her large build, in a black leather jacket, at points along this route.

The whole thing was a fiasco, disastrous for the police's image, Juvin said. But he was as always philosophical: they had lost Marie-Ann Thurillet but not the war. The number of every banknote drawn by Marie-Ann was known, and as these banknotes were used, they would begin to turn up in banks, and then ... Juvin could always look on the positive side.

Heller was listening to the latest about the murder at Père Lachaise on the car radio as he drove out to Villacoublay military airport. He had received a message, via Gordon Welliver, to be there at 15.00. He would know whom he was meeting when he saw him. He was to go to the airport with a hire car. A comfortable car was specified.

Heller had a pretty good idea whom he was meeting. The cult of anonymity was Ed Riflin's style. And at 15.00, there was Ed, waddling across the tarmac from the Mystère 20, carrying a metal valise and a smaller attaché case. Seemed like a lot of luggage for one of Ed's famed flying visits.

The military jet was Ed Riflin's preferred mode of transportation – he didn't care for the publicity that flying by scheduled airlines entailed. For a man in his position, with his delicate missions, publicity was anathema. The people to whom he brought messages often were none too keen to be seen to receive them, and so presidential and prime ministerial jets were placed at his disposal.

Ed wasn't saying much as he got into the Mercedes and Heller did not ask him anything.

When the Mercedes was out past the military turnpikes, Heller did however ask what direction he was supposed to take.

'Head south. We're going to the Morvan,' Ed said.

'To see Decourten. OK. That figures. Got a message for him, Ed?'

Ed didn't answer. If Ed didn't want to answer, he didn't. No avoiding the question, just didn't speak. Blunt in silence as well as speech.

He was staring into the monotonously unfurling grey distance, not looking at Heller; then slightly adjusting rimless half-lenses and addressing the damp landscape passing by them, he said:

'Got a message for you, too, Fred. I have to tell you there's a feeling in certain quarters that your performance in this instance hasn't been up to it: you've allowed private matters to get in the way, and that's something none of us is entitled to do, OK?

Anyone may fuck-up once in a while. Everybody's human, and the flesh is weak, OK. Allowances are made. But the operative word is once in a while. Recall a couple of previous occasions when similar things happened. One was a regrettable instance of personal loss of control – another time ... Look, Fred: the word is that you may have run out of motivation. Or, even worse, gotten in a state where your motivations are confused. That you've lost track ... of the primary purpose. That happens and you're all washed up.'

'Ready for the junk-heap, huh? Like Bill was.'

'That's what some are saying. I'm just delivering the message ...'

'Well thanks. Thanks for giving me the message, Ed.'

'My personal advice to you, Fred, is forget about the delectable Isabelle. It doesn't help any that she's Decourten's daughter. The view is taken that you may have a conflict of interests, and that we may be getting second best from you.' Ed paused a moment, thoughtfully. 'Fred, I'm no puritan,' he avowed, 'but when it comes to a choice between a distinguished career in public service such as you have had and a ... roll in the hay, however exhilarating the latter may be, I can tell you what takes priority in my book.'

'Ed, you never gave a damn about women, you'd rather have a good dinner, you used to say.'

'And you always were liable to lose your head over them, I recall. Get off the hook, Fred. This gal is going to destroy you.'

'I expect you wouldn't believe me if I told you I can't, I can't get off the hook. All right?'

'So be it! As long as you realise what you're letting yourself in for.'

'I realise.'

While holding onto his calm, Heller had now the prickly feeling along his skull which told him they were getting ready to dump him. If things went wrong, badly wrong, he had the perfect profile to take the rap ... A man who lost his head over women.

Ed was giving his poisoned, godfatherly advice. 'All right. Leave the girl out of it. Your affair. But what you've got to do, Fred, you see, is prove all these people wrong, take charge of your career structure, show you can deliver.'

'Deliver what, Ed?'

'Well, Bill for one.'

'Don't have a lot of time there,' Heller said. 'They're going to execute Bill tomorrow at noon. That's the new deadline we've been given.'

'And what are the French doing about it?' Ed asked derisively. 'Their Minister of National Safety goes fishing!'

'Yes, that's playing it very cool,' Heller said.

'Too damned cool.'

'Nowadays, thanks to the marvels of electronic technology, you go fishing and stay in touch, even on the river bank. My assessment is that ...'

'Speaking of staying in touch,' Ed interrupted, 'you been reading *Le Monde*?' He had a copy of the newspaper on his lap, the crucial – dangerous – passages marked up with yellow high-lighter. Ed tapped the paper. 'How does *Le Monde* know what Bill's been saying to these terrorists?'

'Seems Beaucousin has seen a videotape.'

'He must be in league with 'em, how else would he have seen the video? He's serving their cause. What are the police doing about it? What's the government doing? What are *we* doing?'

'Ed, it isn't *our* country. We're not free agents. Every move, I have to persuade somebody else to make it.'

Ed tapped the metal case between his feet.

'In case you think my pyjamas are in there, they aren't ... nor yet my toothbrush. What's in there, Fred, is a million bucks in used French franc bills. OK? Near enough six million. OK? Contributed by a public-spirited individual with Bill's interests at heart.'

'Not solely Bill's,' Heller couldn't resist saying, mildly, in accordance with his policy of mildness, and added: 'A million may not be enough. They're demanding three, as you know.'

'Can you bargain them down?'

'I'm trying, I'm trying. But there isn't a lot of room to manoeuvre, and they want the other things: the release of their people in jail. I don't know how I'm going to get that. The resignation of Charles Decourten. If we don't deliver on those two demands, and I don't see how we can, then we may have to step up the money.'

'We're going to have to persuade the French government to be more helpful. That's what I propose to discuss with Charles.'

'Not a lot of time left to persuade him.'

'Let's not get ourselves into a mode of negative thinking,' Ed said, closing his eyes. He announced: 'I'm going to have a catnap. We have a fair way to go still, haven't we? Wake me up when we get there.'

Heller drove chauffer-style at a steady 110 kph and let Ed Riflin sleep. Let sleeping dogs lie. He was a dog, Ed. A mongrel. He had known Ed a long time, had known him when he was a skinny, gaunt-faced, ambitious military attaché in Vienna. Had known him as one of Allen Dulles's men in the early CIA. The time of Bill's glory. Ed had never been an original like Bill. When Ed became, for a while, a caretaker Director of CIA, it wasn't because he was brilliant, or insightful, it was because he could run things and take orders. He wasn't difficult to control from above, the way some others were. He was a dog who barked exactly how and when his master told him to. That quality had equipped him to be a presidential envoy/messenger entrusted with delicate missions. Now he was in line for another career leap: to be another kind of dog, a Secretary of State dog, if Vice-president Simpson became President in '88. The secret of Ed Riflin's success was that he executed the wishes of his current master without interposing the impediment of his own thought processes.

In the thick rain forms appeared indistinct. Heller had a sense of the car's wheels not being in contact with anything solid. He was going through screens ... endless screens of rain.

He had a feeling of dizziness, of driving in a dream ... the dream in which he was driving along a wide highway that without warning became a precipitous ledge with no room to turn around . . .

The hypnotism of the *autoroute* was getting to him inside the cocoon of this luxurious car, with its excellent power-steering and its super-soft suspension, its highly effective sound insulation; hardly anything was reaching him from the outside, and for a moment he must have dropped off.

He jerked back to full alertness, and pinched his cheeks to snap out of the state of mind-drift he was in.

At Avallon he exited from the *autoroute*, and soon the rich Burgundian lands with their great estates had been left behind and they were in the harsh and rocky Morvan region. The countryside here, with its granite rock formations protruding through skimpy coverings of poor soil, had no notable vineyards, and not much agriculture of importance. Heller saw cows, a few sheep grazing in muddy fields, the constant movement of water in streams and ditches and along lanes and paths.

Nimbostratus rain-cloud laid a low turbulent lid over the landscape, ending only at the horizon, where the rainfall could be seen as black smudges spreading down from the cloud mass into the narrow rim of light over the earth's curvature.

Frequent and heavy inundations were the condition of life in these parts with, in the highest places, rain or snow 180 days out of the year, and Heller could see the inhospitable climate and the ungenerous earth reflected in the faces of the people who lived here. People made sturdy by the harshness of their lives.

Passing through a succession of tiny stark stone hamlets, he began to appreciate this land, which was so unpampering, so meagre in what it offered its inhabitants; they must have learned over the generations to make a living on the basis of minimal resources. This was where Charles came from: one would never have thought it, seeing the polish and opulence of the man now.

The name Decourten, Heller recalled, was a derivative of de Courtenay and hence of the Pierre de Courtenay who, back in the thirteenth century, had built a feudal château at Nevers, on the site of which (of the original castle nothing now remained) there

164

stood the Palais ducal that dominated the town today. Heller remembered stories of ancestors: one had been the king's master of the waters and forests in the seventeenth or eighteenth century. Despite the impressiveness of the lineage, Heller had had the impression that there wasn't much money around when Charles was young, just the dilapidated old castle that had been in the family for centuries.

Ed Riflin slept fitfully, emitting powerful snores like someone noisily breathing his last, the triple chins giving jellyish quivers as his chest heaved. Sometimes he actually seemed to stop breathing altogether, and then he woke himself up with a start, took a breath, and dropped off again.

They were going along straight narrow roads that cut through muddy meadows and rough grassland and woods, with some very poor hamlets strung out between. Streams and ponds and water-falls and marshes linked everything up with a watery thread. The cultivated fields were overhung by brownish-red rain-mist.

The dense forests of this region had afforded good hideouts for the Resistance during World War II. It was an area that had seen a good deal of action. Sabotage by the Maquis, barbaric reprisals by the Germans.

Higher up in the hills, Heller saw, the rain was falling as intermittent snow, and the stark lines of bare-branched trees were impressed on a pallid sky. He could feel the cold thickening whenever he opened a window to get his bearings.

After Onlay, he began to look out for the war memorial by the side of the road, immediately past which he would have to make a sharp right-hand turn. Those were the directions that he had been given for getting to 'the rock', which was how the locals referred to the château on the hill, above the village of Courteny.

Some minutes later he spotted the Resistance memorial, a monolithic mass by the side of the road, topped by the cross of Lorraine Free French symbol.

He pulled up and Ed jerked awake, focusing slowly. To get his bearings and see better where the road turned right and rose towards 'the rock', Heller got out of the car. He swung in a half arc and saw the road he would have to take. A *table d'orientation* gave the principal landmarks.

The memorial was dedicated to those who had fallen in the ambush of the *trois chemins*, 18 May 1944. This must have been the ambush in which Charles's older brother had died. Going round to the side of the monument, Heller saw a bas-relief representation of an octopus in the form of a swastika spread out over a map of France. A muscular male figure with an axe was depicted hacking at the portion of tentacle which enclosed the region around Courteny. Below were inscribed the words of 'General Amourot' (Henri Decourten 1916–1944):

Rise people of France against the Oppressor. A life given in the cause of Liberty is not a life lost but a life gained. Rise to destroy the occupier of our homeland. Death to the invader! Death to every invader in every time! Count not the cost, for it is the price of Liberty.

The rain had eased up a little and Heller could better see the rising road he had to take. He followed the long loop with his eyes and made out, on a rocky promontory above the village, the château of Courteny starkly outlined. It had the rather grim look of a feudal fortress, with ramparts and crenellations and circular towers.

Heller got back into the car and pointed the place out to Ed Riflin.

'That's it.'

'OK, let's go fishing,' Ed said.

The château was seen intermittently from the rising road, an isolated mass on a plateau, approachable only from one side. On reaching the plateau, Heller drove across an open expanse of ground to the massive iron gates where two gendarmes with submachine-guns stood guard. They looked at the visitors' identification and then spoke over their walkie-talkies. There was a couple of minutes' wait and then the gates opened electronically from inside. They closed again as soon as the Mercedes was through. A narrow, modern asphalt road led up to a second entrance, an archway of vermiculated stonework, with a gate of wrought iron rising to a gilded crest of crossed swords beneath a crown. Video cameras attached to the archway surveyed the approaches to this gate. It, too, was opened by remote control, the gates beginning to swing apart as the car came within five metres.

Heller drove past a shuttered gatehouse and across a cobbled forecourt ringed by cone-shaped shrubs.

As they approached the main entrance, Le Quineau emerged from inside to welcome them and take them up to the first floor.

They were kept waiting a few minutes and then led into a spacious room, its walls lined with finely bound volumes, where Charles Decourten was seated behind his battery of telephones. He was dressed for the country: green Barbour waxed jacket, cavalry twill breeches, black leather riding-boots.

He apologised for keeping them waiting, and welcomed Ed Riflin with a sturdy handshake .

'*Mon général*. A good flight?'

'Yes, thank you, Charles. Thanks for laying it on. It's a nice plane, that. The Mystère. Any news?'

Charles's face took on its stoniest aspect. 'There has been a further phone call from Attaque. To confirm that the execution was taking place – they used the gerundive – tomorrow at noon, and only what they call a definitive response could now arrest this process. They made reference to a train moving towards its pre-determined destination. Only acceptance of their demands could stop the train.'

Heller asked: 'What answer were they given?'

'They were told to phone at 19.00 for our reply.' He looked at his watch. 'I wanted to talk to Ed first.'

'That was thoughtful of you, Charles.'

On one of the phones a light winked silently; Charles picked up the receiver. He made a few cryptic utterances and listened, his head just barely nodding. At times his eyes closed and he massaged his eyelids.

167

'Hmmm ... hmmm ... hmmm. *Oui.*' He replaced the phone somewhat wearily, but quickly recovered.

'Martini, Ed? The way you like it, very dry?'

'If you're having one.'

'I will have one to keep you company, Ed. And you, Fred?'

'Yes, I'll have one.'

Charles busied himself at the marble console where the drinks were, pouring and mixing and stirring with his light touch.

'What are you going to tell them, when they call at seven?' Ed asked. 'What's your final offer?'

'I thought I would pass them on to Fred. Or you, Ed. You make the final offer. Bill is your ...' He spread out his hands, leaving blank what Bill Gibson was to the messenger from the White House. He handed Ed the dry Martini. Ed took a sip and approved.

'Perfect! You could always make a great dry Martini, Charles.'

'You are a great flatterer, Ed.'

'The thing is, on the Bill situation: there are elements of that not within our control, which is why the offer has got to come from you, Charles. Nobody else can deliver on what they're demanding.'

'Deliver?' He gave Heller his dry Martini and took his own with him to the vacant high-backed chair opposite them. He sipped his drink questioningly, a very long sip. 'In what respect? The policy of both our nations ... is not to negotiate with terrorists, not to submit to their demands.'

'Yes, that's our policy,' Ed agreed. 'But we're not talking about policy, we're talking about practicality. In a war the policy is to win, but practicality may involve strategic withdrawal to a more defensible position.'

Charles laughed. 'Your military metaphors are ... a little inappropriate at times, Ed.'

'Monsieur *ministre*,' Ed said, becoming ominously formal, and slapping down his copy of *Le Monde* with the highlighted passages. 'This guy, this Beaucousin, last year brought down one of your senior ministers. There was a lot of fall-out as I recall, a lot of dirt spilled before the gentleman in question, who by then had got himself completely tied in knots, finally decided to quit. It would have been less damaging all round, and more dignified for him, had he resigned sooner. Now I don't know what Beaucousin has got hold of exactly this time, and how much there is to it, but I do know that once the press get hold of a thread, they pull. That's the nature of the beast. And this Beaucousin seems to have got hold of a thread and is pulling. These sort, they pull and they pull. Until something is pulled undone. Maybe not what they were pulling at in the first place, maybe something else, but somethin' ...'

Ed Riflin had a mimic's aptitude for speaking with the voice and the words of his master. Heller could hear the Vice-president's characteristic inflections in what Ed was saying. 'They start looking into areas of coincidence, areas of financement, private life. Nothing is sacred when they smell a big story. Mr Minister, I know that in France you are accustomed to stories blowing over, to the use of certain governmental prerogatives, but it'd be a mistake to rely on this one blowing over. As you correctly point out, Bill is ours, and therefore of interest to our media, and they're not in the habit of letting things blow over. No sir.'

Charles got up from his chair and thoughtfully began to pace before the life-size portraits of the Decourten line. Darkly dressed men of the Morvan, the product of dark skies and infertile lands, and rain. Lots of rain. Dourly provincial, stubborn men, un-budgeable men.

'*Mon général*,' Charles responded, finishing the rest of his dry Martini in a single hasty, though elegant, sip, 'whatever Bill may have said – may say before they execute him – can have little credibility, even for the American press. Which so prides itself on getting to the bottom of things. But in so doing often gets it all wrong. It is obvious that Bill is a man destroyed, an old drunk, brainwashed, fighting desperately for his life, ready to say any-thing for a whisky.'

'The press will follow up what he says,' Ed said.

'Yes, yes. Perhaps. But all they will find will be the fabrications of am embittered old man who has forgotten his own lies! People like Bill finally become occupational *mythomanes*. They believe the tortuous scenarios they have themselves devised, even when nobody else believes them.'

'You are remarkably sanguine, Charles. You always were. I am not so sanguine ...'

'You never were.'

'Even if things don't turn out as bad as the worst projections, it's necessary to have some fallback position, in case,' Ed said.

'What do you have in mind?'

'First let's try to get Bill out. Whatever it takes to do that. Official, unofficial. Seems to me that a gesture could be made by the French government. One of the Attaque people held in jail, say this Thérèse woman, whatever her name is, who lodged them, at times, ran errands ... Another Marie-Ann Thurillet type ... The *juge d'instruction* could find *non-lieu*.'

'I have already thoroughly discussed with Fred the obstacles standing in the way of such initiatives ...'

'Obstacles can be overcome, given the will ...'

'And on the question of my resignation, which they also demand: how is that obstacle to be overcome?'

'We may be able to get them to drop that demand, if we give them the other things. However, if we can't ...' He paused, his teeth clicked; no matter how unpalatable the message, Ed Riflin delivered it. He wasn't a man to shirk what his role demanded of him. 'Alternatively, Charles, you might consider giving them what they ask. A resignation as a humanitarian gesture, to save a man's life, would be a praiseworthy step, one that I should think would be recognised by everyone as altruistic and disinterested. At the same time Franco-American interests would be served, and I think those interests would be only too eager to have a man of such evident moral stature at the head of one of the great international corporations that depend for their success on Franco–American understanding.'

This sort of thing happened. The United States sometimes applied pressure for a stumbling-block in the way of better understanding between itself and another nation to be removed.

Evidently Charles was now perceived in Washington as being such a stumbling-block.

He was livid as he walked across to the window and looked out into a valley hung with straggling mist patches. He turned around:

'Inform Washington, Ed, that I am not contemplating resignation. As far as Bill's fate is concerned, when the call comes through at seven, I will let you speak to them. See what you are able to achieve. Now you will excuse me. One of the workmen on the estate has died. He will be buried in the cemetery here. I must pay my respects to the family.'

At the door, he had another thought. 'Stay for dinner if you wish. It will be *en famille* – just Dorothy and myself and my daughter, Isabelle, who is coming down from Paris. I take it you will be remaining at least until seven, for the phone call?'

When Charles had gone out of the room, Ed Riflin remained staring at the long rows of leather-bound volumes on the library shelves, shaking his head.

'Hubris,' he said as if the books had given him this insight. 'Hubris. Charles has the foolishness of great arrogance. Thinks nothing can touch him. That he can charm and wriggle his way out of everything.' He was silent for a while; he rubbed his brow. 'When the call comes through at seven, Fred, you better take it. This is your ball and you got to run with it.'

SEVENTEEN

THE CALL CAME through first to Paris, and from there was
re-routed by way of the *interministériel* connecting the château
with the Minister's secure internal line. It was exactly seven. Le
Quineau answered and said: '*Je vous passe Monsieur Heller.*'

Taking the phone, Heller said:

—*Oui. C'est Fred Heller à l'appareil. J'écoute. Allez-y! Allez-y!
Qui êtes vous, monsieur?*

The person at the other end replied in English:

'I am the one that you must speak with, if you are interested to
save you friend.'

'All right. I'm listening.'

'I give you a warning, I say this to you in English, so there will
be nothing misunderstood. Do not make any mistakes.'

'Uh-huh.'

'The sentence is being carried out at noon tomorrow unless our
demands have been fully met.'

'Let us talk about this,' Heller said. 'Let us talk about ways and
means. Do you understand? First, before anything else, we require
proof of life. This is essential.'

At the other end, outrage, suppressed, but perceptible from the
man's breathing.

'So, so – now we get more of your American dirty tricks.'

'No, no tricks. It's self-evident that we require this proof
before . . .'

'Do not make the mistake to think I do not know of your "techniques". I have studied them. I know them. Your "tradecraft". I know them of a long time ago. So! Go on, go on. Before . . .?'

'. . . before going to the next stage.'

'Which is?'

'You have to understand. There are things I can do and things I can't do. It is only worth continuing to talk if you accept the reality of that.'

There was a silence at the other end, a long silence. Heller looked towards Charles listening in to the conversation on an extension handset, seated with his light and charming frown beneath the mediocre portraits of his mediocre ancestors, these men and women of the *petite noblesse*, these provincial nobles, with their pretensions written on their faces, in their pompous cravats, in their over-adorned women, possessions among other flaunted possessions.

'You wish to break off? Then you are sentencing your friend to have his brain blown out. Tomorrow at noon he will be a bloody mess on the dung-heap. Our people must be released and we must receive the money for our fund and . . .'

Heller cut in. 'I'm not breaking off. But regarding the release of people in prison, you must appreciate that this is outside my control. In any case you must know that the release of prisoners is a complex process and can't be achieved between now and noon tomorrow.'

A contained explosion. 'Then put on the Minister. It is not outside *his* control. Why does he pass me off to you, if you cannot do *anything*?'

The sense of outrage. He was making no more than a just demand. And he was being tricked. Subjected to the American dirty tricks. This was a man who knew he was in the right. Offences had been done to him, he had been patient. Had been patient all his life. Waiting to change the world. And he had now got to the limits of his patience. No more concessions. No more offers of life to these American tricksters.

173

Heller thought: yes, it's him. Must be. I can hear his morbid joy in the quest for the white whale. It's the sound of Marduk who is going to remake the world in spilt blood. This is Gavaudan. Something has been festering in him from birth – the Ahab morbidity. He has a mad part with its own delusional logic that you cannot address . . . but another part is sane.

'You must see the technical problems,' Heller said. 'There are problems of time, of procedure. Of contact. Of implementation.'

The rule was wrap it up in technicalities.

'You have been talking only of what you cannot do, and what I must do. This does not move us forward. Our demands must be fully met or there is no solution . . . except the dung-heap.'

It would not be a dignified execution for Bill. He would have to be demeaned, the American devil would have to crawl in the dirt to satisfy this reformer of the world. *To what baseness will I not sink to cure the world of baseness?*

Heller deliberately kept silent; he let the silence grow. The voice in the microphone inserted in his left ear was telling him to delay, to spin out the conversation. Ed Riflin, also hooked into the telephone line, was impassive, mouth down, thumbs down.

The voice on the phone mocked: 'You can make spin out this call as much as you like you won't succeed to trace it.' At this moment Le Quineau, who had been on another phone, placed a scribbled note before Heller, which confirmed what the man presumed to be Gavaudan was saying: that the call was untraceable. Probably, said the note, they had hooked themselves up to an overhead telephone line.

Heller broke his silence. He said:

'I'll come to the part of your demands that can be met and can be met in the short term, given the fulfilment of certain basic technical conditions.'

'Tell me of the demands that can be met,' the voice on the telephone taunted.

'People, private individuals – family and friends – who wish to do something for Bill Gibson have succeeded in raising a certain sum of money. Let me say straight away, it is not the sum you ask for, it is not nearly that amount, but it is a substantial sum and it is the best we can do, given the fact that Bill Gibson is not a rich man and that no other funds are available.'

'How much is it?'

'I had made available to me half a million – dollars, that is to say. Amounts to three million francs, after expenses.'

'This is not enough. This is very far from enough ... It is no good to make these contemptible offers.'

'That is what I have. I have it here, now. That's what you can have immediately. If you want me to go back for more, try other sources, all right, but that is going to take more time.'

'Then your friend is going to die tomorrow, and the media will receive his detailed confession.'

'Since we are short of time, let me stop you there,' Heller interrupted him. 'I ask you to reflect. I have made you a certain offer, which is a private offer, got up by Bill's friends. I'm acting purely as a private individual in making you this offer. As Bill's friend. Bill's retired, the government's not interested in him. If you don't take our offer you're back with officialdom, and official policy is that the national interest comes above the private, and you know what that means in this case. Cancel tomorrow's execution and we can talk, and maybe start to get somewhere. Carry it out and you've got nothing, nothing to bargain with.'

'You are a very tricky man, Mr Heller.'

'No, this is straightforward, and it's the only way that's open.'

'You will hear from us should we decide to continue.'

'Has the sentence of tomorrow been lifted?'

There was a silence of several seconds, and then the phone was put down.

Ed Riflin said he was not able to stay for dinner. He had urgent matters to take care of in Paris.

'Supposing they don't accept half a mil, Ed? All right, I go up to a million. And then? If that's still not enough, given that their other conditions are not being met? What's our next move then?'

'Let's see what happens.'

'Where do I find you, Ed?'

'I'll be in touch.'

'I may need to get you in a hurry. We may need to finalise our offer before noon.'

'That's as maybe. Let's not anticipate what can't be anticipated.'

'What's your final word on it? Can I upgrade the offer, if I need to? Beyond the million mark?'

'Fred, you've got to decide how you play it.'

Heller thought: they're distancing themselves from me, in case I fuck up and have to be dumped. I'm working solo, without a net. Without back-up. Because they've little faith that it'll come out right. They're readying their worst-case script.

Dinner in the vast dining-hall was not gay. Isabelle had arrived, accompanied by Annette du Breuil, and Heller was painfully conscious the whole time of his sense of loss. It was a hurt to which there was no end in sight.

Isabelle was not making any effort, *en famille*, to raise the mood of the evening. She gave off no spark of her famous electricity. To the remarks that Heller addressed to her, she offered minimal answers.

'I am sorry it has not worked out with you and Isabelle,' Annette du Breuil said to him confidentially at one point.

'You know about that?'

'Yes. Isabelle told me.'

'She sure changes her mind,' Heller said.

'That is because she does not know who she is,' Annette said. 'Therefore how can she know whom she loves?'

'That's tough,' Heller said, 'on those who love her.'

'Yes, yes it is. But that is how she is. She can't change.'

'What d'you mean by that?'

'It's her inheritance, she is a child of the war.'

Charles was in and out all during the meal. He ate little. There were a lot of phone calls. But no developments. None that he

176

would talk about, anyway.

'You'll stay here to see what happens tomorrow?' he asked Heller at the end of the meal.

'Yes, I think I'd better. In case ... well ... I'd better stay until noon at least.'

'Yes, that might be advisable.' He pondered grimly, and then demanded with suppressed anger. 'Why have they sent Ed? Why do I represent a threat to them? They want me out of the way, don't they?'

'I don't know, Charles. I expect it's like you said before. Very early pre-election jitters ...'

EIGHTEEN

Heller was awake long before daylight. A slow feeble light glowed inside a mist bowl and the countryside gradually emerged. He dressed thinking about the sort of preparations Bill would be making. Six a.m. Six hours to go. Six hours to noon. How did you go into the long night? Drunk probably, in Bill's case. Maybe he'd made a deal with them – his final tricky deal: a last-minute, soul-cleansing, dirt-spilling confession in return for a bottle of Scotch.

Charles was up as early as Heller, wearing the Barbour waterproof, and Wellingtons. Having a hearty breakfast. Ready to go fishing. The insupportable lightness of the man!

'I see no point waiting around here,' he said. 'There's a CFTR Fly-Away in the Range Rover, which gives us full communications, should there be developments during the morning ... Why don't you come? It is not useful to anyone that you sit here biting your fingernails.'

'All the same, I think I'll stay here. Fishing's not my thing.'

Once the fishing party had driven off into the mist bowl, the château was quiet. Nobody else up this early on a Sunday. Heller walked in the grounds, in the unearthly silence, amid the shaped hedges and trees, restless. Periodically he came inside and buzzed Le Quineau on the internal phone, to ask if there had been any calls over the special lines, and each time was told no, nothing. He looked in the breakfast-room. Nobody.

It was ten by the time Dorothy and Annette du Breuil were down. Then Isabelle arrived, as distant as ever. Two hours to go and no acceptance call. If they had decided to accept the postponement, they wouldn't say so in advance. They had nothing to lose keeping you wound up tight, not knowing. They'd let you go through noon thinking the worst, and deliver the reprieve afterwards. Or the body. Whichever it was. That was the way they operated. He thought: I should have gone fishing.

Heller found Isabelle on the vast terrace which dominated the valley. In the hills there were new pine forests, rising in neat serried lines to the summit. The old forests were not so neat. They formed impenetrable areas of dense vegetation that could be traversed only by following the laid-out paths or by hacking one's way through jungle.

'Is it going to be a permanent vendetta between us?'

'I don't know what you mean.'

'You know what I mean. This coldness.'

He saw Dorothy approaching, threatening to make early morning conversation. 'Tell Dorothy you're going to show me the château,' he said urgently.

'Fred has not seen the château,' Isabelle explained to Dorothy, leading him out of reach of the threatened conversation.

'I would like to see it,' Heller said. 'Will you show me round?'

'Yes . . . all right.'

She showed him, first, the fourteenth-century five-storey tower with its brown tile roof and its archers' loopholes and its casemates and narrow winding stairs within thick walls. He thought of her going up the spiral stairs in her apartment, that very first time, and the memory was strong and painful.

He told her: 'Look, I've now got reason to think you may have been right that somebody was spying on us, taking pictures. Only it had nothing to do with me. The truth is it was probably me they were spying on. Trying to get something on me.'

'Why would your own people spy on you?'

'Oh you'd be surprised.' He gave a sour laugh. 'Anyway, they're not exactly "my" people. The State Department doesn't control the CIA. The Agency has its own prerogatives, special unto itself. Why on me? Because – I don't know – they may need a fall-guy. If this whole thing with Bill goes wrong. The name of the game is saving the Chief. And the fact that I am in over my head with "a beautiful French actress", that's good casting for them and maybe fits their lousy script. That's all I can imagine. There could be an even more tortuous reason that I haven't thought of.'

She said, 'Do you want to see the rest of château or not?'

'Yes, I do.'

They continued the tour. The atmosphere between them remained cold and tense.

'Did you live here as a child?'

'No, I never have lived in this part. This part was all in ruins then.'

'Show me where you lived.'

'It is not interesting.'

'I'd be interested to see it.'

She shook her head. For some reason she did not wish to show him the part of the house that would hold personal memories for her.

'It has been closed down,' she explained, like a tour guide. 'It is no longer in use. You see, it is not *bien exposé*. North-east. It will be cold and damp. And it is locked. I don't have the key.'

'Could you find the key?'

'Why d'you want to see where I have lived?' Her suspicion was acute. At least this was contact.

' . . . I want to know about you.'

'For what reason?'

'You know for what reason.'

They went down the tower stairs, and he said he did not want to see the cellar dating from the thirteenth century with its broken-barrel vaulting. And he did not want to see the *arretoirs*.

'I want to see the place you grew up. I don't mind how cold or damp it is, or how *mal exposé*.'

At the bottom of the tower, she led him along the main façade to the east wing, and then round the back to an extension that had been made to the château in the nineteenth century. She went into a dim closet with many old rusty keys hanging from numbered hooks and she selected those she needed, after consulting a hand-written chart. The first of these was for a heavy old iron door that unlocked with difficulty. It was rusted into its frame. Heller put his shoulder to it, and it came open with a resounding clatter that echoed through the whole north-east wing. There was a dark corridor beyond, its ceiling running with condensation. Exposed water pipes and ancient electric wiring ran overhead, carrying the damp in droplets. They went into the kitchen where there was a system of bells on coiled springs for summoning the servants to the main part of the château. One bell was marked *Salle de Bains, Madame la Marquise*. That made Isabelle laugh.

'There were no servants when I lived here,' she said.

'Who was Madame la Marquise de Courteny?'

'I don't know.'

'You're not interested in your ancestors?'

'No.'

She took him up stairs smelling of mildew, to the first floor, the main living area of the extension.

'This was where we lived,' she said, her eyes beginning to come alive with a rush of memories. 'Before the other part was restored. You see, it's not at all special. Rather ugly, in fact.' But she had a smile of recollection on her face.

The rooms they went through were mostly bare, with furniture piled one piece on top of another.

'I remember I used to like this table,' she said, running her fingers through thick dust. 'And this cupboard. Look—someone put a padlock on it! Can you imagine that! On a lovely old oak cupboard! I kept my dolls in it.'

She forced open a stuck window and leaned out and smelled the air. The grounds here had been left wild and overgrown. The gardeners who so meticulously maintained the geometrically laid-out gardens on the southern and western sides of the château did not occupy themselves with the area behind the north-east extension. This part, here, was the Morvan of old, a mixture of marshland and granite sand: spongy soil engorged with water. The ground was a stirring compost heap of fallen leaves and fungi and rotting dead wood, cemented together with coagulations of spiders' eggs. Tree trunks were covered with barnacle-like outgrowths of fungi. From the dead bracken and tangled briars there rose a fetid smell.

'Oh I remember this smell,' she said, excitedly, breathing in the taint in the air. 'I remember this so well.'

The smell was the sweet and pungent smell of dense vegetation not much exposed to sunshine and not freshened by winds, because of the high walls.

Her mood had changed. There was still a tension in her, but her eyes had brightened in response to these potent stirred-up memories. Impulsively she went from room to room, eager to discover other traces of the past, touching, smelling, looking.

'This was their bedroom. The bathroom was next to it. And my bedroom was the other side ... this was it here.'

Her face went bright, and she laughed happily. He smiled, glad to see her like this again.

'Oh I have such a clear clear picture suddenly,' she said excitedly. 'It's July or August. Everything still and quiet. We are all in the garden drinking *citron pressé* and tea and eating almond cake and orange cake. I think it may have been my birthday. Yes ... there was chocolate cake as well ... There was Mama and Papa and Annette ... I remember the stillness. Nothing moving. Not even birds. The high grass didn't stir – not a puff of wind. The branches and leaves not budging, the clouds fixed like in a painting. Total stillness. It was perfect peace. I wanted it to go on for ever, I wanted for nothing ever to change ... '

'What changed?'

She did not answer for several moments. 'My mother died,' she said at last.

'How did she die?'

She was darkly suspicious of him again, and he could hear the persecuted sound in her voice when she spoke. 'Why are you people probing into my life? You shouldn't snoop around in other people's lives. People who do that discover things they would rather not know.' Her voice had a lecturing tone, the voice of a schoolteacher laying down moral guidelines.

He watched the flickering of her mood, going from dark to bright and back. You never knew what role she was presently playing.

She said in a rush of excitement: 'I want to go up to the attic. Come on, come on . . .' Now she was like a schoolgirl proposing a dare.

They went up narrow, steep wooden stairs where they had to bend their heads because of the lowness of the ceiling.

In the attic there were two big brass-bound cabin trunks with metal reinforcements at the corners, covered with the labels of ocean liners, some good leather suitcases, hat boxes, metal boxes, wooden crates, the cardboard packing cases of furniture removal companies. The small windows were a mesh of spider webs on glass that was opaque with grime. She pushed open one of these little windows to let air into the musty space.

The window gave an outlook beyond the enclosing high wall to a patch of ground behind the north-east extension, as far as the small private cemetery on the other side.

'I hate to think of her being in the cold earth. She was so warm, so full of life. Wanted only to be loved.'

A funeral was taking place, must have been of the estate workman who had died: the cortège was making its way along the avenue of bare-branched plane trees beyond the wall, led by a portly old priest swinging a smoking censer from side to side. The coffin was carried by six pallbearers from the village, ruddy-complexioned men in dark suits, with black armbands and fresh soup-bowl haircuts. The workman was going to be buried amid the impressive tombs of the sires of Courteny.

'Sometimes I used to watch funerals from up here,' she said, 'and I used to tell to myself: *voilà!* that's what it all comes down to in the end, *that!* You are put into the cold earth. Ugggghhh! I'd deliberately scare myself, thinking about how it "felt" being dead

'... Oh children can have very morbid minds ...'

In search of more cheerful memories, she opened trunks and suitcases and looked inside them, rummaging under layers of clothes, finding school exercise books, letters, diaries, address books, scrapbooks, photographs, and other mementoes. He watched her face in swift succession light up and fall with the strong play of memories and emotions.

'What happened to your mother?'

'A car accident. She drove into a tree. She was very unhappy, poor thing. She drank a lot, and she took pills. It was because of Papa, because of all his women.'

'Did that threaten the marriage? Was he going to leave her?'

Isabelle said nothing, she seemed unwilling for these matters to be discussed.

'There were crises ... I don't want to talk about it. I find it very upsetting to talk about.'

'You don't want to see what's under the piles of old clothes,' Heller told her. 'In case it's the skeleton in the dream, which is going to destroy your beautiful life.'

She flared up at him. 'There are some things that are private, that I don't tell to anyone. I'm not a tell-tale.'

She had undergone a change of role again; now it was the priggish little girl, giving herself airs.

'I can just see you,' he said.

'What can you see?' she asked, annoyed. 'Oh you don't know me at all. At all.'

'I had the impression I knew you quite well, in one respect at any rate.'

'If you think *that's* knowing somebody ...'

'What is it then?'

'Fucking,' she said. 'Which is nothing to do with knowing.'

'Call it carnal knowledge.'

'Yes, you have that knowledge of me,' she said with a coarse little giggle.

'And would hope that knowledge is not finished,' he ventured, coming up to her close. 'Is it still working with the actor?'

184

'Fantastic.'

'I wish I hadn't asked. Like you say, ask questions, you get answers you don't want to hear. It's going well, is it? Damn him!' She made no reply. 'You say those things to him? You ask him to make you die? Do you? And the other stuff? Do you say all that to him too?'

'Please don't probe into my private life.'

'Right. I'd forgotten how much you cherish your privacy. But I'm not the press, you know, and just a few days ago I was part of your "private life", and I thought a pretty important part, from what you said . . . I miss you, Isabelle. I miss you like hell. Even not knowing where I am with you is better than knowing it's nowhere at all.'

'I think the tour of the castle is over, don't you?'

He wasn't ready to go yet. There was too much unfinished business left in this attic. He felt it in the musty air. He looked around.

'This is the setting of your nightmare. Your mother's old clothes. The rest of it. The morbid games. Imagining what it felt like to be dead. Etcetera.'

Suddenly the priggish little girl was replaced by the wicked child. She shot him a glance of confession.

'I used to come up here when I wanted to be private. I always had very intense *phantasmes*. Sometimes they seemed more real than my real life.'

She remembered something and got on her hands and knees and listened with her ear to the floorboards. 'Their bedroom was just below here and if I lifted up one of the floorboards I heard everything.'

'What a bad child you were.'

'Oh I was, I was.'

She regarded him with overbright eyes, a long intense look in which he could perceive the actor's movement, the change of skin. She wasn't breaking the look, and he felt the roller-coaster ride start all over again. He reached for her hand and she didn't pull away. She said, 'I think I do love you, Fred. I think I do.' But immediately added: 'Oh this is impossible, this can't be. This can't be. This is mad.'

'Make it be,' he pleaded. He kissed her and touched her, but though she let herself be touched as he wished to touch her she remained unresponsive, in a kind of trance of disengagement, and he could not reach her.

He let go of her; she moved away deeply preoccupied and stood above her parents' bedroom listening intently, as if she could listen to the past.

'"*Fais-moi mourir!*" she used to cry out, and other things too.'

'That's where you learnt that stuff.'

'She was a passionate woman . . . He did make her die. He made her drive into a tree. "*Assassin! Assassin!*"'

This last was not said in the voice in which Isabelle had begged him to make her die of joy, there was no enticement in it, no loveplay, no rapturous invitation: it was not her voice, it was the mother's voice, and it was a shrill hoarse cry of accusation. Isabelle was shocked, he saw, by the way the words had spilled out of her, drawing on things in herself that she had not known she knew.

'She called him a murderer? You heard that?'

Isabelle was silent, back in her own skin, solemn with recollection. Her eyes moved searchingly around the attic. She gave a strained little laugh and said sheepishly:

'I . . . I expect I made it up. Children are like that. Aren't they? They have morbid imaginations. They invent all sorts of things about their parents. They hear these strange cries at night that they don't understand and they think somebody's being murdered. The things that were going on in my head! I'm sure I . . . I made it up, Fred.'

'OK.'

'We should get back. People will wonder where we have got to.'

There was the distance again, the full distance.

'All right.'

Nothing remained of the previous mood of enticement in

186

which she had thought, briefly, that she loved him after all. That moment was already past. She was beyond his grasp; as soon as he tried to hold her she slipped through his fingers, became somebody else.

NINETEEN

THE FIRST THING Heller did when he got back to the main part of the château was to check with Le Quineau if there had been any phone calls from Attaque. There hadn't been. Their technique was to keep everyone in the dark. The unknown was a potent weapon, and they knew how to use it. To go fishing was probably the best way of dealing with this pressure by silence.

Annette du Breuil was leaving for the village to buy bread. He offered to accompany her. It was a way of avoiding the silence.

'What was it you meant yesterday, about Isabelle's "inheritance"? That she's a "child of the war"? You never told me what happened here during the war, the story of the betrayal and the ambush. You found it too painful for lunch.'

'Yes, yes.'

'Are you going to tell me? You said one day when ...'

'I will take you to our little museum in the village. It is all told there. You will see.'

The museum was in the principal street which ran from one end of the village to the other in a straight line. It was in a handsome private house of the 1920s, set back behind iron gates, with a small front area consisting of flower-beds and a small patch of lawn, in the centre of which there was a bronze statue of 'General Amourot'.

The museum appeared to be closed. They had to ring the bell several times before the doors were opened. The woman seemed surprised to see them. There were not many visitors at this time of year. Today they were the only ones. The exhibition rooms were dark. She sold them two admission tickets, and went around switching on lights. They cast a yellow glare on institutional scruffiness: parquet flooring marked with cigarette burns and a pattern of high-heeled shoes, walls flaking, cracked window-panes framed in crumbling putty, dust, museum dust.

They went into the first of the exhibition rooms and peered at a dimly illuminated letter, under glass, from General de Gaulle, regretting that official engagements prevented him from attending a memorial ceremony in honour of 'General Amourot' – M. Henri Decourten – but saying that his heart and thoughts were with the villagers of Courteny on this day of solemn commemoration.

Blobs of electric light bounced off the dusty glass of framed photographs and the glass tops of display counters containing documents. There were photographs of Resistance fighters, men and girls, but mostly men, wearing armbands, rifles slung over shoulder, munition belts around the middle, around the neck.

Displayed under glass, inside the counter tops, were maps, charts, operational logs, a tattered manual of guerrilla warfare, issued by the local branch of the FIP (Francs-Tireurs et Partisans). There were last letters of men about to be executed:

—My dearest Mama, embrace my brothers for me, hold them tight, old Jacque and Jean-Paul, and Grosjean. If they send you my things, there will be some tobacco for them. In times of crisis it is good to laugh a little/My dearest little wife, I say goodbye to you. There is only a short time left now, but I wanted to say to you, whom I have loved so much, that should you find a companion worthy of you, don't hesitate, my darling one, to remake your life with him. You are still young, and what we have had together must not be the whole of your dear life. Don't worry about me. I have a little knot in my stomach now but am not afraid. I think I will manage to die with courage, and please pardon me the little miseries that I have inflicted on you . . .

There were other moving last letters of this sort. Some of those

189

about to die were youths in their late teens or early twenties. One lamented that he was going to die without ever having known love with a woman. He was philosophical about it, surprisingly so: he had had a great deal in his nineteen years for which to be thankful, you could not expect to have everything in life.

There was a photograph of members of the Milice executing a young boy of the Resistance. Other photos of Miliciens in their turn being executed by the Resistance. A time without pity unfolded in the form of photographs and journal entries and last letters and town hall documents and eye-witness accounts and extracts from trial testimony.

Annette du Breuil had been forged in the fire of this time and she seemed proud of having come through.

'*This* is our inheritance,' she said, a sweep of the hand encompassing the exhibits. 'All of this which has happened. Even those who were not born then have been marked by it. France has not faced up to it, and perhaps will never be able to.'

Heller nodded. Juvin had once told him the story of how, after the war, the heads of French intelligence, confronted with ten tons of secret German papers relating to events of the occupation, had made the decision not to open the mouldering bundles. A preliminary sampling had revealed that men who were currently prominent in government and business and other spheres of public life had been collaborators, had been involved in fraudulent land appropriations, had profited in illicit ways from the occupation, had been guilty of acts of betrayal and vengeance and murder. Juvin had been in agreement with the decision not to open the German papers. Let them remain sealed and buried. Let them gather dust. In a hundred years' time, they could be opened. But not before. To open them earlier would inflict terrible injury to the French nation. It would be an act of self-mutilation. Juvin still believed that the decision taken after the war was correct. Better injustice than disorder! What happened during the occupation could not be judged on the basis of normal moral standards. France had been in a state of civil war. It was a time of hot blood and vengeance. Politically what was at stake was France's survival as a free nation, and many things had been done which in more normal times would be judged unspeakable. No one who had not lived through those times could judge them. In some areas, the local Resistance had the intention of declaring independent republics when the Germans were driven out. Communists, taking their orders from Moscow, were behind these movements. There was a big danger that when the German occupation crumbled, a general take-over by the Communists would follow. Terrible choices had to be made, and terrible acts were perpetrated: by the Germans, by the Gaullists, by the Giraudists, by the Communists, by the Milice. And by the Allies.

'Few,' said Annette du Brueil, 'came out of this time with clean hands.'

She and Heller had come to a sepia group photograph, somewhat over-exposed, not very sharply focused, showing about twenty people, in two rows, wearing berets with badges, FTP armbands, carrying guns, breech-lock rifles, pistols, in some cases Stens. The man in plain centre wore bandoliers across his chest. He looked every inch the bold bandit chief, with his dashing smile, and his air of being in charge.

'That's Amourot.'

'Yes.'

'You couldn't mistake him. I mean about the charisma ... It's apparent even in a photo.'

'Yes.'

'Who made him a general?'

'He made himself a general.'

'Is that you in the front row, the lovely dark-haired girl?'

'Yes, that is me.'

'And the other girl, in the back row, next to Charles ...?'

'It is Sybille. Isabelle's mother.'

'She and Charles were already together, then?'

'It began then.'

'She was pretty, but you were the beauty, Annette.'

'You think so?'

'Oh I do, I do think so ... So naturally you ... you went to the

Chief. That's how it goes, huh?'

'I loved him.'

'Because he was the Chief.'

'I don't know. I was twenty years old.'

'What did he have? What was his charisma?'

'He could make people do what he wanted, love him, follow him. Die for him. Accept his ideas. Obey him. That's what leadership is, isn't it? He was a swine.'

'And you loved him?'

'Yes.'

'In what respect was he a swine?'

'He wanted everything. All the women, all the power, all the glory . . .'

'Sounds familiar. Anything you *liked* about him?'

'But I liked that he was as he was, this great hunger of his for everything. And his ruthlessness. It was very thrilling. As well, he could be very tender, very loving, if he wished. And he had great courage.'

'Give me an example of his ruthlessness that you admired.'

'One day . . . he declared himself commander-in-chief of the area and issued a general order of mobilisation, demanding that the populace join him, bringing their own supplies, arranging transport, lorries, vehicles, fuel. People must uproot themselves, burn their crops so that the Germans would not have bread, and come into the forest. Those who did not respond to his order were considered to be traitors. Their fields were burned, their homes dynamited, or they might receive a visit from the death squads who rode around in doorless Citroëns . . .'

'Charles supported that?'

'Charles loved his brother and followed him as we all did, but Charles, when he thought for himself, was more . . . roundabout. He was not so inclined to go head-on at things. He believed more in waiting, and seizing a chance when it presented itself. When the moment was ripe and we had some kind of temporary superiority of numbers or position.'

'Were they in conflict sometimes?'

'No. Never. Charles avoided confrontation. His character was to go round. To wait. Not to have showdowns ...'

'Yes, that's Charles ... You must have heard him quote that Russian proverb. About he who waits long enough on the river bank seeing the body of his enemy float by.'

'Yes, I have heard him say that.'

The second room of the little museum was larger than the first and contained, in addition to photographs and letters, an ancient 1910 Maxim machine-gun on a two-wheel cart mounting that had been obtained by General Amourot and used in a pitched battle between his forces and the Germans. There was an Underwood typewriter on which General Amourot's orders were typed. One of these proclaimed the creation of a free republic of the Nièvre under his presidency. It had never been signed, because of his death in the ambush of the *trois chemins* on 18 May 1944.

The exhibits in this second room included equipment from VENGEANCE's arsenal. A British-made suitcase transceiver with headphones, a Wel Rod silent pistol, an Indian wrist dagger, various kinds of disguised igniters and detonators, a hand-pump Phillips torch, Sten-guns, rifles, some of them of the straight-pull bolt action type, dating from the time of the Austro-Hungarian Empire, false identity cards. The weaponry conjured up pictures of the kinds of actions that VENGEANCE must have undertaken, led by the bold and charismatic General Amourot.

There was also on display a German belt-fed light machine-gun, mounted on a bipod, an M34, of the type used in the ambush of the *trois chemins*.

The centrepiece of the room consisted of a display of two cars. The first was a black 1936 Renault of angular outline, with back-slanting radiator grille, side-opening bonnet. It was a big car, a five-seater, with a running-board on which the spare wheel was mounted. The second car was smaller, a blue Peugeot of around 1938. These were the cars which had been transporting members of the VENGEANCE group when they were caught in the ambush of the *trois chemins*. The first of the cars was badly shot up: its chassis had been riddled with scores of bullet holes; the windscreen and side windows were shattered; the upholstery was scorched and holed by maching-gun fire, and in places darkly stained by blood. The front part of the car had partially telescoped in on itself from an impact that it had received.

The commemorative plaque said that in this vehicle on 18 May 1944 the heroic Resistance fighters listed below had died in the ambush of the *trois chemins*. The list was headed by the name of General Amourot, and after him came four other Resistance names (with their real names in brackets): 'Lafite', 'Bertrand', 'Lapin', 'Brochette'.

The second car, the Peugeot, was not in such a bad condition. Its windscreen and side windows, though hit by bullets, had held together in loose webs of fractured glass. There were clusters of bullet holes high up in the front and rear doors. But it wasn't a wreck as the first car was. The plaque said that in this car four other members of the group had escaped from the ambush, through their great daring and courage. Heller read the Resistance names.

'Who was "Antigone"?'

'I was Antigone.'

'You were in the ambush?'

'Yes.'

They walked around the two vehicles, and Heller gave a low whistle.

'You were lucky to have been in this one, instead of the first.'

'Yes, I was. In the first car nobody survived.'

Maps, diagrams, scale models and personal accounts told the story in detail. How the VENGEANCE group had arrived in Courteny in two cars, the Renault and the Peugeot; how Amourot and two others had gone into Godin's barber shop for the meeting with the Communists; how the meeting had turned acrimonious and broken up. There were descriptions of the ambush on the road out of Courteny, where the German lorries and staff cars were waiting beyond a bend. There were accounts of the executions of Godin and Montcarbier, the German informer. Godin was dragged out of the barber shop the same day, stood up against his own wall and summarily executed. The barkeeper was executed some days later in a small hotel in Autun, where he had gone to hide.

'How is it you were there that day?' Heller asked Annette.

'I ... went everywhere with Henri. He liked to have me at his side.'

'Not always, presumably. Since you say he was such a womaniser.'

'No, not always. But a lot of the time I was with him. And that day I was.'

'But not in the car with him. Not in the Renault. You were in the second car, in the Peugeot with Charles.'

'I came in the first car with Henri. But then, at the barber, they thought I might draw attention, a girl sitting in a men's barber.'

'Yes, you were someone who would draw attention.'

'Henri sent me out to change places with "Lapin", who had come in the second car.'

'As a result of which you were saved, and "Lapin" died.'

'Yes. That was the destiny.'

Heller looking at his watch saw that it was five to twelve. He went to the entrance of the museum and asked the woman if he could use the phone. Le Quineau, when Heller got through to him, said there had been no word of any sort. The Minister was interpreting this as a reprieve, a further postponement of the execution. Because if they intended to go through with it at noon, they would surely have tried at least one more phone call to put on pressure for an improved offer. Heller wished he could be as certain of this interpretation as Charles seemed to be. He thought: it's going to be noon, and we won't know, we won't know if Bill's dead or alive.

Annette du Breuil and Heller left the museum and went out into the main street of Courteny.

While Annette went to the *boulangerie* to buy bread, Heller looked around. The village did not seem to have undergone great change in the past forty-two years. The barber's was now a *salon de coiffure* for both sexes, with tessellated floor, plastic-helmeted hair-driers and a range of beauty products in glass cabinets. The display photographs showed the latest hairstyles, including the currently fashionable boyish haircut for women. The name on the sign was Ponsard. The shop would have been sold after the execution of Godin. In a small village the family of an executed traitor would not have been able to continue a business.

The bar across the road from the barber's also still existed.

The lookouts would have been posted at vantage points on both sides of the main street on 18 May 1944. They would have been watching the one road along which any vehicles entering the village would have had to come. Someone posted outside Montcarbier's bar could have kept the other lookouts in view, and if they had signalled the approach of a German patrol, the men in the barber's could have been quickly alerted.

Several of the village shops were now closing for the lunch period. Shutters were being put up, iron bars slid into slots under end panels.

There would have been a lot of shuttered windows in 1944, with fear abroad and vengeance and reprisals creating an endless spiral. People would have kept to themselves, and been suspicious of others. They would have hurriedly gone indoors after their essential shopping. Mostly women and old men in a place like this. The able-bodied young were either in the forest with the Resistance or had been transported to Germany for forced labour.

Annette du Breuil came out with the bread and she and Heller walked towards the river and the railway tracks. The line here had long ago been closed down and the carriages in the station brightly painted and turned into stalls selling local craftware and pottery. In spring 1944, with an Allied invasion of France expected any day, the railway line joining the important centres of Nevers and Autun would have been of vital importance to the Germans and hence a primary target for the Resistance.

Once the Allied landings had taken place, a major Resistance in this region would have drastically affected the Germans' ability to bring supplies up to their fronts in the north and impeded the evacuation of their troops from the battle zones. The village of

Courteny straddled the German supply route and their line of retreat. So the removal of an effective and popular Resistance leader like General Amourot was of great importance, and the Germans would have put a high price on his head to tempt someone like Montcarbier to betray him.

Heller said: 'This barber, Godin. He must have been trusted if such an important meeting was held in his store.'

'Yes. We were very dependent on the villagers,' Annette said. 'We could not live entirely in the forest. It was not a hermetically sealed and separate existence that we had. There was contact all the time between us and the villagers. The populace supported us and supplied us, otherwise we could not have held out. There was always a risk of betrayal. It was a risk we took. Godin was one of those who was trusted, and that was why his place was chosen. But there is always the chance that a person will be corrupted by a large sum of money.'

'How did you find out who the informers were?'

'During the course of the meeting between Henri and the Communists, Godin left to go across the road to Montcarbier's bar to buy cigarettes. I was standing outside, that was where I had been posted as a lookout. I saw him go in, I saw him talking secretively to Montcarbier, and then Montcarbier disappearing inside his quarters at the back of the bar to make the phone call betraying us to the Germans.'

'Did he confess, did Montcarbier confess?'

'He closed his bar and went into hiding. That was enough confession. We traced him to Autun. He was executed in his hotel room by one of our units. They gave him the miniature coffin and he knew he had been condemned, and then they shot him. It was quick. It had to be.'

They had reached the war memorial at the entrance to the village, the point at which the road split into three, one going up to the château on the rock, the other going right towards Château-Chinon, left to Moulins-Engilbert. It was the left turning that Amourot and the others had taken on 18 May.

Heller and Annette du Breuil started to walk along it.

'It happened along here?'

'Yes, a few hundred metres beyond the village.'

They walked in that direction. Beyond the village, the road was bordered on both sides by open ground, agricultural land on the left, rising ground on the right, open for about fifty metres and then becoming forest.

The road began to curve almost at once. There was a sharp S-bend. Just beyond this bend the German troops were lying in wait: an open truck on one side of the road, then three staff cars in the middle, and a second open truck on the other side. These vehicles had all their doors open and were arranged in zigzag formation. By the side of the road, at the bottom of the slope, there was a deep drainage ditch and here Germans with MP43s, capable of single shot or automatic fire, lay hidden. This much Heller had gathered in the museum, from the scale models and the diagrams and the eye-witness accounts.

As the Peugeot she was in entered the bend, Annette said she glimpsed a flash of glistening waterproof capes, camouflage green and brown, coming from the ditch. The Peugeot was going at about sixty or seventy kilometres per hour. Amourot was sixty metres ahead in the Renault, probably doing eighty or ninety by then. Rounding the bend they saw the German trucks, a massive blockade, a formidable army presence on this quiet country road. They were a Waffen-SS unit. It was too late for Henri to stop and reverse out of the trap, Annette said, and characteristically he did not even slow down. Instead, as he saw the trucks loom up ahead out of the grey wet morning, he put his foot down on the accelerator, taking the car past 100 kilometres per hour.

'How's it you all escaped in the second car?' Heller asked.

'We had more time. And also with Henri keeping straight on, the Germans had to cope with that. We got down low ...'

'Who was driving?'

'Charles. We were saved because of Charles's presence of mind.'

'What did he do?'

'He has gone into reverse and backed the car around the bend ... once we have turned the bend we were out of their fireline ...

it was only twenty, thirty metres . . . which was a very long way, I can tell you, that day.'

'How's it he didn't get hit, Charles?'

'He was down on the floor. Like all of us. He steered the car from the floor, by the overhead telegraph wires, which he could see through the window.'

'Like you say, great presence of mind.'

Heller let Annette return to the château alone. He said he would walk back. It was after midday now and it was obvious there was not going to be any phone call. They were going to play the game of maintaining uncertitude.

He went back to the museum; the woman was locking the doors. He said he had lost something, something of value, and he must look and see if he had lost it there. He would only be a minute, he said. He gave her 50 F. and she let him go back in. He went straight to the first room and made his way to the sepia photographs of the VENGEANCE group. The photographer had focused on the most important figure in the centre of the first row, General Amourot, and not paid much attention to figures in the second row, especially those at the ends. Some of these were blurred. Others had been caught with eyes closed, or turning away.

Annette du Breuil was very clear: she was in the front row, squatting so as not to conceal the person standing behind her. She was holding an automatic pistol in one hand, raising it smilingly, almost coquettishly, to the camera. Her sidelong glance was on Amourot, and it was a glance that showed her passion. Squatting next to her, his arm in comradely fashion around her shoulders, was a boyish Charles, maybe twenty, maybe twenty-two, very handsome, and he also was looking towards the group's centre, older brother Henri, the Chief, pistols stuck flamboyantly in his trouser top, trousers tucked into fine leather riding-boots that must have been appropriated from the body of a German officer.

Though looking towards his brother, Charles's eyes were concealed, and Heller thought: his Resistance name was 'Fabius', a name well chosen in the light of Charles's subsequent career, for

Fabius, the Roman general, was a man of clever stratagems. He had harried Hannibal's armies, avoiding direct confrontations that he could not win, attacking only when the moment was opportune, when the numbers were in his favour, the terrain of his own choosing: smart guy Fabius!

'Fabius' in the photo had a comradely arm around the beautiful Annette's shoulder, while Sybille, his wife-to-be, glowered in the second row.

Heller was looking carefully along the second row. The photographer had not taken trouble with Sybille. Heller examined her face keenly. It showed signs of an untranquil nature. She did not look happy. She did not have the radiance of Annette du Breuil.

Right at the end of the row was the face that had brought Heller back to the museum.

Poor though the photograph was, there was no doubt now in his mind that this bare-headed, clean-shaven individual, partially concealed behind somebody else, was the young Bill Gibson. His posture, his whole attitude, conveyed the feeling of someone who has discovered his vocation, who knows what his life is going to be about. This was a Bill who was young and slim and bright, and had discovered his love of the labyrinth, his ability to tolerate situations of complex ambiguity; who knew he could withstand 'inner dizziness'. No advance sign in this photo of the heavy-drinker's terracotta complexion, of the puffy jowls and the bloated ungainly body. This was Bill in the making, Bill in the pink, with the fresh eager face of an ardent young priest secure in his faith.

The thing Heller wanted to know was what Bill Gibson was doing in occupied France, in the Morvan, in May 1944, out of uniform, and therefore liable to be shot as a spy, if caught by the Germans.

After leaving the museum Heller went out of the village the way he had come with Annette du Breuil. Annette du Breuil de la Question Mark Question Mark! He came to the entrance of the village, and past the war memorial turned left along the road that Amourot and the others had taken forty-two years ago.

There was a ragged edge to the cloud that extended across the sky. Wispy black threads of rain or snow spilled into the bright band above the horizon. Snow had been predicted. And it was certainly cold enough. Heller felt the wind curl around him as he walked along the drainage ditch towards the S-bend. He walked right through the bend and saw the road become a long straight undulating line, a white slash through dense forest. Hills like whales' backs submerging in a spreading white spume. Nothing moved along the road down which the German trucks had come on 18 May 1944. Heller thought about shadows in wrong places – the de Chirico effect. A car came from behind, very fast. Thchchioumpptchchioumpp! He felt the backwash of its air displacement roll over him. The whale-hills were diving into the white.

Heller jumped over the drainage ditch and began to climb to the forest edge, looking around him, reconstructing the past. He climbed rapidly, determinedly, feeling his breath deepen and the chill of the air in his lungs and heart. His heart had an uncomfortable beat. Those wrong shadows, not matching with the position of the sun. Sleet fell, liquifying on contact with his face. The wind was getting stronger. He thought about five men struggling to reach the protective shelter of the woods above them. Only fifty metres. But fifty metres was too far on 18 May 1944.

He was seeing the ambush in his mind. It was his methodology to visualise, and to put himself in other people's places ... Mist. Rising from the river and straggling across the road in patches. The Germans had belt-fed machine-guns on both the open trucks, MG34s that fired 850 rounds a minute. He'd seen the machine-gun in the museum. Accounts spoke of Amourot swerving wildly, making the machine-gun units swivel frantically to keep the Renault in their sights. They were firing off short bursts, and there was also the rifle fire from the ditch.

The testimony of those in the second car described Lapin and Brochette hanging out of the rear of the Renault, firing back with Stens, and Lafite, sitting next to Amourot in the front, firing his pistol.

The Germans in the staff cars were firing through the open doors at the wildly veering mud-caked black car hurtling towards them.

Motor screaming.

The road has been laid with tyre-piercing treads and to the high scream of the engine is added the sound of tyres bursting as they go over spikes.

Heller saw it all play before his eyes like film in a cutting-room. Frame by frame.

The Germans realise the Renault is not stopping. It's coming at them like some lethal projectile. They start scrambling out of their vehicles, panicking, throwing themselves clear.

They're thinking: these bastards have pulled the pins of their hand grenades, they're going to blow us all up.

Are doing a kamikaze act.

Amourot steering straight into one of the Vs of the zigzag. Where the rear ends of two staff cars are in soft contact. Sound of tearing metal.

Open doors ripped off.

He crashes through the soft V point. Is through to the other side, the Renault riding on its wheel-rims in a mess of shredded, smoking rubber. It keeps on another twenty or thirty metres. An out-of-control metal-tearing slither. Arrives with its front end in the drainage ditch.

Despite the salvos fired off at them, and the wounds that some of them have sustained, all five of those in the Renault are still alive at this stage and able to scramble out.

They crawl from the ditch and, encrusted in mud, start the desperate climb over rough rising ground towards the forest. The fire power of the zigzag is pointed the other way, and this gives Amourot and his people a faint hope that they have a chance of reaching the forest.

They spread out and keep low and work their lungs to bursting-point, climbing, staggering, stopping to let off bursts from Stens and automatic rifles.

They are only a few metres from the shelter of the trees by the time the Germans have regrouped on the other side of the zigzag and swung the machine-guns around.

There is a one-minute burst of concentrated non-stop fire and at the end of it all five Resistance men lie dead on the rising ground at the fringe of the forest, their bodies ripped apart by saturation machine-gun fire.

Heller was trying to find an entry point at the forest edge. There were no paths. Densely interlaced and plaited thongs of rampant vegetation created impasses. Thorn bushes reached higher than a man's height, and you could wade up to the waist in stinging-nettles. If Amourot and his men had got this far, they would have been able to disappear, knowing the forest as they did.

Heller continued along the perimeter of the forest until he found the vestige of a path. Stooping under matted sinews of creepers, he found a way in. The gorged ground was soggy with rain-rotted material.

This was their terrain, this was where they had led their hard forest existence, the Maquisards, where Amourot had known the exaltation of command, and Charles had learned about waiting, about avoiding head-on confrontations until you possessed superior strength. And Bill had learned his vocation.

Somewhere in there was the ruin of the Maquis encampment – it could be found quite easily provided you began at the correct starting-point and followed the marked trail. On the road he had seen signposts for the start of the trail. He didn't suppose many people took it these days. It was three kilometres over rough ground and there couldn't be that much to see. A few fallen down walls, a roofless hut, primitive defensive ditches and outposts.

But Heller wanted to see it. Following the laid-out trail, it took him a little more than half an hour to get to the camp … it was close, very close to the village. And Godin the barber would certainly have known that, if he was someone they trusted sufficiently to hold their all-important meeting in his place. In his presence. They would have been discussing the details of the merger in front of him while he cut their hair. He was bound to have known how near the camp was. And knowing that, would have known how quickly vengeance would be visited upon the traitors.

Annette had said he was executed the same day, after being dragged out of his shop. He had made no attempt to hide, to save himself, to claim the blood-money. How could he have felt so sure he was safe? He must have seen Montcarbier quickly close his bar and leave, even before the sound of shooting was heard. And when the whole village learned of what had happened, Godin must have seen that Montcarbier was suspected of being the informer. And if Godin was in with Montcarbier, would he not have panicked seeing Montcarbier run? Was it possible that Godin would have remained oblivious to the danger to himself? And yet, according to Annette, he had carried on cutting hair until the moment they came for him with the miniature coffin.

Annette was accompanying Heller to his car. They looked up at the blackening sky; snow clouds were lengthening across the landscape.

'All right, you showed me the museum, Annette. You told me the story. Now tell me what haunts Isabelle.'

'What haunts all of us. The past.'

'What in particular of the past?'

'Do you know how many books and articles have been written about the ambush of the *trois chemins*? So many "solutions"! You can imagine that some of them are very disturbing to read, if you are the daughter of someone who was involved. Even if the "solutions" are absurd, they can put into your mind doubts, shadows about the people you love. You know what a tangram is?'

'A Chinese puzzle.'

'A puzzle that can be put together in several different ways.'

'Some people think Godin and Montcarbier weren't the informers?'

'Well, if you are going to write a book about it, you have to say something different. Something sufficiently startling, or else there

204

is no book to write. You must say that innocent people were executed. Or who would want to read it?'

'What do they think, the ones who think Montcarbier and Godin were innocent? What are the other "solutions" on offer?'

The beautiful face of Annette du Breuil sometimes seemed curiously without age, as if preserved by some catastrophic event that had fixed her permanently in a moment of time, not allowing her to develop beyond it. Heller supposed she must have had a face-lift, perhaps several. That would account for the uncanny feeling she gave of being out of this time.

'Oh there are almost as many different "solutions" as for the Kennedy assassination,' she said, avoiding a direct answer.

'Tell me some of them.'

Her eyes in the marmoreal whiteness of her face glowed with the pride of one who had experienced great and terrible events. She seemed peculiarly excited. Wispy filaments of blood stirred here and there in the deep pallor.

'In one version, it has been suggested that I was the informer. I have betrayed Henri because he has betrayed me with another woman. That was one of the theories put about.' She laughed derisively. 'You see how absurd.'

'And the others?'

'That it was a husband Henri cuckolded. In another, that it was a farmer whose crops had been burned ... That Henri was a homosexual, that he had a lover who ... I have forgot. All very crazy. In one "solution" it is implied that it was Charles.'

'Why Charles? Henri was the older brother he looked up to and loved.'

'Yes, it is difficult to see why. But it is no more absurd than some of the other "solutions". If I remember rightly the case rested on there being always an element of envy and hatred in hero-worship.'

'This is what Isabelle grew up with, these village tales. That's what you're saying?'

'She is an actress. An artist who lives by her imagination.'

'Do you have a favourite among all these theories, Annette?'

'There is one that it was you the Americans. That the OSS were behind it. As it was thought they were behind the assassination of Admiral Darlan in Algiers. Henri was a danger. He was playing into the hands of the Communists. And so had to be removed . . . Which of the "solutions" you prefer, Fred?'

'I don't know, Annette. I don't know yet,' Heller said. 'I think . . . I have a preference for the one in which it's you.'

'Why?'

'I suppose because that would make it a very dark love story. Whereas the last "solution" takes it into the category of a political thriller. Depends which genre you prefer.'

TWENTY

Heller was coming into the Pont-Royal, crossing the lobby towards the elevator.

'Monsieur *H*eller!' The name was pronounced with an ironic inflection on the H, as if being called Heller with an H was a matter for satiric comment.

'Yes?' He did not slow his step until he was at the elevator.

'Could we have a word together, Monsieur *H*eller?'

Heller stopped, back to the elevator doors.

'What d'you have in mind, Monsieur Beaucousin?'

'Is it absolutely necessary to stand before the elevator?' Beaucousin asked. 'Or is it feasible to sit down?'

Heller nodded to Beaucousin silently and led him to the innermost of the Pont-Royal's lounges, the one that was nearly always empty.

'A Scotch, huh?'

'Yes, a Scotch.'

The journalist did not look in too good shape: he had a forty-eight-hour's beard, his eyes were red-rimmed, and his hound's tooth cashmere jacket was very crumpled. Looked as if he had slept in it the last couple of nights. His mauve-striped shirt with the fashionably narrow collar opening and the fashionably narrow tie-knot were not fresh, and his expensive blue suede shoes were dusted with cigarette ash. The smell of cigarettes persisted around him. Jean-Luc Beaucousin appeared to be suffering from a long-standing hangover. This hangover could have been going on for days. He squeezed his forehead, massaged the scalp a little. A rough weekend, evidently. Whether in the pursuit of work or pleasure was a matter for conjecture.

'I have a proposition,' he said. 'Here is what I propose. I expect you like to get a look at the Gibson tape, for your own interest.'

'Could be of interest,' Heller conceded.

'Here is my proposition. I let you see parts of the tape, and you verify that the person is Bill Gibson. That it is not an imposter.' He laughed at such a notion, with an air of humouring so melodramatic a possibility for the sake of his cynical proposition. 'Seeing the tape in advance – mind you, only parts – gives you the time to cook up your repudiations. OK?'

'So you have some doubt that it is Bill Gibson.'

'*I* have no doubt. But . . . *Le Monde* is a newspaper that checks its facts. And double-checks . . . '

'Well I'd very much hope so.'

Heller thought: OK, Beaucousin is in a hurry, and for 'an American spokesman' to comment on any part of the videotape would authenticate it. Beaucousin had been the victim of a disinformation ploy before. He was playing it safe.

Heller said: 'I'll have a look at it for you, all right.'

They found a taxi outside the hotel.

Beaucousin lived in Montparnasse, behind the station, in a pre-World War I apartment building. There was a glass-panelled entrance door. He tapped out the code and a faint click announced that the lock had disengaged. They went in. A dark hall, dark stairs. A timed light switch. A narrow elevator.

Beaucousin was on the top floor. Two rooms, small kitchen, toilet and shower. The accommodation had a defiantly Bohemian sort of shabbiness. There were a couple of big lumpy sofas, a round pedestal table that served partly as a desk, partly for eating on. Piles of stuff everywhere: books, files, newspapers, reports, journals and magazines, government bulletins, telexes, faxes . . . The bedroom, seen through the open door connecting the two rooms, was in a similar state of chaotic overflow, with the unmade bed functioning as a repository for still more clutter.

Beaucousin cleared a sofa in a flurry of dust and crumbs, offered Heller a seat, himself a whisky. He drank the whisky neat, in a determined gulp, and extended the bottle to Heller, who accepted for the form of it. Drinkers distrusted people who didn't drink, so Heller drank, at the same time noting the names of some of the authors on Beaucousin's shelves and floor: Marcuse, Reich, Marx, Heidegger, Sartre, Camus, Chomsky, Lacan, Gramsci, Brecht, Proudhon, Stirner, Debré . . .

'Who does Riflin work for?'

'Far as I know, he works for the President. Of the United States. Check out with your reliable sources?'

'This President of the United States or the next?'

'This one, and he hopes the next. He thinks ahead, Riflin. At least as far as the next elections.'

'If Simpson is the next President.'

'That would help, yes. Simpson and he are close.'

'What does he think he is going to get? If Simpson is the next President?'

'I do believe he has his heart set on the State Department.'

'Secretary of State? Riflin? That's what he is playing for?'

'I don't think he's playing. Riflin doesn't play. Even when he's playing he doesn't play . . . Are we going to see this video-tape then?'

Beaucousin tilted back his chair, head turning, looking over the many piles of his unorthodox filing system, trying to think where he had put the tape. There appeared to be some order within the chaos that was known to him alone. He looked under books, ashtrays, cups and saucers. He looked under the table, where there were fruit boxes used as 'in' and 'out' trays. He looked under his chair. He was blowing out and rolling his lips. A faint ray of recollection penetrated the cloud banks in his brain, and he said with clicking fingers, '*Mais oui!*' and went off into the bedroom, and Heller saw him on his hands and knees, excavating. Finally he found the tape. It was in a blue and red Sony box.

He returned with it and squatting a little unsteadily before the

TV-video unit, began to fiddle with the controls. He inserted the cassette, and switched the TV set to the video mode. As the tape was fast-rewinding, he said:

'Did you know that Bill Gibson and Charles Decourten knew each other forty-two years ago? That Gibson was in occupied France, in the Morvan, in the same group as Decourten? Did you know that?'

'Matter of fact, I did.'

'Do you know what he was doing there, in the Morvan, in the group VENGEANCE?'

'I would guess he was their "Jedburgh." Gibson was in OSS, and we had Allied military advisers, training officers, with a lot of the Resistance outfits.'

'He was not in uniform. Consequently could have been shot as a spy.'

'Bill was never very meticulous about the correct forms of dress. And I don't think Hitler was either. People he felt like shooting he shot. In or out of uniform.'

Beaucousin had got to the beginning of the tape. He pressed the 'play' button.

Jagged horizontal lines rolled down the screen, becoming coloured, and a moment later a face formed out. The shot was shaky. There was a lot of hand wobble. And a strong microphone hum on the soundtrack. The camera was being moved jerkily, amateurishly. Then the fuzzy face became clearer. Heller frowned. It was Bill and he was not in good shape. His face was puffy, his breathing laboured, and there was an accumulation of water in the pouches under his eyes; his lips looked blue.

He was seated behind a table that blocked off the corner of a room, forming a sort of dock; behind him was bare white wall. The table was a metal camping table. There was a glass of colourless liquid next to him.

No way of telling if it was day or night. The lighting on Bill was crudely direct. He was in an overcoat, an ill-fitting overcoat, and had a scarf around his throat. He seemed to be hunched up shivering and sweating. He kept his hands in the overcoat pockets much of the time. When he reached out for the glass, his hand shook violently. The fingertips, Heller noted, looked white, bloodless. Sometimes the picture went out of focus. But the camera remained relentlessly on Bill: his questioners and judges were never seen.

From off-screen a harsh woman's voice ordered the accused to stand up, reminding him that he was before a People's Tribunal.

Bill gave a bloodless smile with his blue lips and did not budge or say a word. He gestured with one feeble mocking hand towards the voice, as if excusing himself for not rising in the presence of a lady: alas! his hand indicated, he was no longer capable of such feats of gallantry. He drank from the glass before him while a murmur of low voices sounded on the tape, and then he gestured pointedly towards the empty glass.

There the shot froze, though the voices continued, and one, a man's, emerged as predominant. This seemed to be the prosecutor. The proceedings were in English: under the stress of circumstances, Bill's French must have gone completely. He would have managed not to understand the questions, thus forcing them to speak a language that was not their own. Obviously Bill had not lost his appetite for small advantages.

There was a preamble in voice-over. Heller was pretty sure it was Gavaudan's voice, accusing, self-righteous, filled with unshakable conviction. He was rolling off the crimes with which Bill was charged: the usual catalogue ... the crimes of American imperialism.

During the reading of the charges, Bill's features remained frozen, and then the features unfroze and the 'trial' got under way. Heller noted that during the freeze Bill's glass had been moved, it was now in a different position on the table, closer to him, and when he spoke his voice was slurred and he rambled and had to be repeatedly brought back to the subject. Clearly he had done some kind of deal with them; they were providing him with alcohol, vodka or gin, judging from the colourless liquid in the glass, and he was 'confessing' in return. He's singing and they're pouring, and when they stop pouring he stops singing. Hence the peremptory gesture: refill my glass! Hence the frozen shot, while Bill imbibed.

Beaucousin stopped the tape with the pause button. 'It is Bill Gibson you have to agree ... '

'I haven't heard him speak yet. And the lighting's pretty strange ... I can't say yet.'

Beaucousin gave a cynical smile and wound fast-forward.

'You are going to get your money's worth, yes? I warn you, I will not show you the whole tape. I shall not fall for that. I am prepared to show you some extracts, a sample ... That will have to be enough.'

Beaucousin was stopping and starting the tape, looking for a particular section. He recognised the lead-in that he wanted and pressed 'pause'.

'I show you the part where he talks about May 1944. You will see that is not a very nice story. With not very nice sub-plots. And you won't be able to say you don't recognise him, because you will see that it is him. The old devil himself, without any question or doubt ... '

He released 'pause', and on the screen Bill began to fidget in his chair, move his hands around. The glass on the table was empty. He was mumbling a lot, running his words together. At times he was incomprehensible. But having got his fix, he was now singing to order.

'Now see Communists trying create momentum of uprisings and vengeance, vensheance ... brought on retaliashon, and that more vengeance see, see, this was'n their'nterest, this was the scenario see for taking over France ... This General Amourot – a madman, megalomaniac. But th'young fellows he'd got round him, they thought he was God. All under his spell. When he ordered burning farmers' fields, they burned the damned fields. See he was loved and he was hated see. And was'dissaster. Dissaster! What-a-d'ssaster! He w's goin't'be used by the Communists and then took over, and way I saw't *my* task was t'remove him 'fore that happened.'

212

The prosecutor's voice demanded: 'How you did set about "removing" him?'

'Did what had to be done,' Bill said in reply. Behind the glassy eyes, his brain was in an advanced state of dissolution, in alcohol. But his words had become clearer.

'What was it you had to do?' the disembodied prosecutor insisted in voice-over, and in the absence of any image other than Bill's dissolving face, it might have been his own voice hammering at him inside his head.

'This was war. There were overriding factors. There were long-term considerations, the geo-politics of the whole thing ... '

'The details,' the relentless voice of the unseen prosecutor demanded.

'Well, if you want to know,' Bill said, 'I thought about killing him myself. But he was well loved by his men, he'd his body-guards round him the whole time. And would've been counter-productive, an American killing a French Resistance leader, wouldn't have achieved our aims. So I'd to find'nother way solve th'problem.'

'What was this other way?'

A look came over Bill's face that Heller recognised: it was the look of one who has learned the rules of the labyrinth, knows his way around in it, and has come to have a perverse sort of love for its dead ends, its false exits, its tortuous paths.

His voice was a lot clearer now.

'First rule of clandestine action is moving hand that writes mustn't ever be seen. Don't want ter spoil the Punch'n Judy show, do ye? Gott'be spontaneous.'

Beaucousin had pressed the 'stop' button.

'This is enough for you to see,' he said. 'You can certainly identify him from what you've seen so far.'

On the frozen screen the colours were all out of true, giving Bill a very gaudy aspect, a scarlet complexion, purple lips. He really did look like an old devil. His contempt shone nakedly in his eyes. Everything showed.

Heller said, 'The physical being is Bill, yes. But how much is that really saying? Considering the state of that physical being. You saw what was happening. You saw the image freeze, and then he came back and was "co-operating", with his voice getting slurred and the glass on the table emptying. This is a man who has been taken over. He's been given a script and he's saying it in return for his fix. Whether the things he's saying have any credibility or are just total fabrications, calculated disinformation they've put in his mouth, or whether it's something Bill is making up – could even be a code – I can't say, because I've only seen these snatches out of context, nothing substantial enough for me to arrive at a reasoned judgment . . . If you want me to comment . . . '

'You are raising the price,' Beaucousin said.

'You have to show me enough to enable me to form a judgment.'

'I will show you one more piece,' Beaucousin said.

He started winding the tape back and forth to arrive at the section that he was willing for Heller to see. Because of Bill's tendency to ramble, Beaucousin could not quickly find the part he wanted, and there was a lot of winding fast-forward and then back, and what Heller saw was a rush of hectic grimaces.

Old devil though he undoubtedly was, you couldn't help feel pretty sorry for him now, in his awful plight. He was a man who had had no ordinary love in his life. Had a wife one time. Strange wisp of a woman, faded as a dried flower, who used to go around tilting like a sinking ship, until she sank one day, without trace, leaving him a widower. Heller had never imagined that there was anything like love between them, not in the usual sense of the word. At any rate, not on Bill's side. She was more like a spinster aunt looking after a troublesome, demanding boy. Cooking him those awful meals, one or two of which Heller had been obliged to sample. Over-boiled cabbage predominated in Heller's memory, followed closely by over-roasted lamb, and tinned peas swimming in their juice. Heller remembered the house. In Philadelphia, on snobby Chestnut Hill. Rather run-down and in one of the frowzier streets. Strange-looking. With gargoyles and curlicues. American rococo. Full of cats who roamed the four floors at will.

Bowls of cat food standing around everywhere. The father had died and Bill had inherited the family residence. The mother was alive and inhabited one of the upper floors, a presence as dim and fleeting as a ghost. The Gibsons' fortunes appeared to have been in decline for a couple of generations. Bill had gone to the university in Philadelphia, instead of to Princeton or Yale. Money must also have been the reason why the Gibsons stayed in the declining city as the municipal rot spread and the old families who owned the city moved out to the Main Line suburbs. In his youth Bill would have heard Roosevelt called 'a traitor to his class' at the Penn Athletic Club, and Truman referred to as 'that little haberdasher', and he would have picked up a bit of 'gentlemanly' anti-Semitism, and some thinly veiled contempt for Negroes. Perhaps Ethel, the wife who faded without ever having bloomed, had loved him, otherwise why put up with such a difficult prickly man? But he hadn't loved her. Of that Heller was sure. Because Bill wasn't able to love human beings, that was obvious to most people who knew him. His mouth had difficulty forming words of respect, approval, tenderness. Instead there was contempt.

All he could love, and he loved that quite shamelessly, was his country. That was his one true love. That was what brought tears to his eyes, and gave him a feeling in his heart, his country the USA. To a lesser degree, he felt that way also about France and the other 'bastions of European civilisation'. He did whatever he did because he believed that he was helping to save Europe from the yoke of Stalinism, and of course he knew better than most, and earlier, all about that. He was amazed and appalled by the whole 'piss-ant pinko establishment' that refused to heed the truth of what he knew. Springing from this central love of his life was a related love for those who worked with him for the same end, as long as they didn't let him down, didn't betray him. Bill felt strongly about agents he sent into the field and exposed to dangers, and would feel a personal – a paternalistic – sense of responsibility towards such men, and do everything he could for them if they got in trouble. A good man lost was a heartfelt blow, and in such a situation he could show emotion, weep openly. But not otherwise.

Beaucousin had found the section he was looking for, and the narrative picked up once more. Bill was mumbling a good deal in this part. It seemed to be a continuation, after some gaps, of what he had been relating about his mission in France in 1944.

He was telling how he had exerted influence in order that an important meeting between the Communists and Amourot and his people should take place in Courteny. The barber shop was proposed as the meeting-place. The barber Godin was a trusted man. It was safe to meet in his place. The Montcarbier bar was across the street. Perfect for Bill's plan. It was the place to post one of the lookouts. The principle was to spread the lookouts around, so as to cover all approaches and have men in reserve at concealed vantage points, in case there was trouble.

Bill didn't really look too stricken now, he loved the laying of plots, the secrecy, the stratagems for getting all the pieces in place. He explained, almost boastfully now, that he had known from the start that the only way of removing Amourot was to get one of his own people, somebody close to him, to do it. There were different possibilities. Amourot was a womanizer and had taken the women of some of those in the group – so there was that angle. And there were women he had loved and then abandoned. So there was that, too. Jealousy, human emotion, Bill always worked on the human element, twisting it to suit his purposes.

Amourot had burned farmers' fields, so that the Germans would be deprived of bread, and some of those farmers were ruined. They had sons, and some of these sons were with Amourot in the forest. He had ordered the killings of German officers and officials, and whenever that happened the Germans took hostages and executed them, and there were in the forest with Amourot fathers who had seen their sons executed, sons who had lost a father or mother or sister in this way. All potential material for Bill to work on.

'Like I say, he was a man who was loved and hated. Even by the same person.'

Bill was staring into the camera, dead eyed, his face a mask of disgust. Heller could see the decision, the moment of strange joy in the downfall of another.

'During my working life,' Bill was saying, counting off on his fingers, 'I owned a cardinal in the Vatican, a Greek communist guerrilla leader, a king or two, a hell of a lot of Labour leaders in different parts of the world, Latin American dictators, Italian cabinet ministers ... and a man who was the right hand of de Gaulle. Yeah, yeah ... '

Beaucousin stopped the tape, and stared at Heller.

'You have heard enough? Too much, perhaps? In any case, that is as much as I'm ready to let you see at this stage. I'm ready to let you see more once you've kept to your side of the bargain.'

Heller stood up slowly, head nodding. He paused and stroked his face tiredly. 'I could comment on this or that aspect, but no point: my overriding impression is that this is an elaborate manipulation. You know the old rule. It's not the information itself that defines its credibility so much as who supplied it, and why. *And why*! I'd want to know who has provided you with this material to be able to arrive at a view of what the sting is. What I'm sure of is that if you print any of this you are lending yourself to a classic disinformation exercise.'

'What Gibson says will be checked.'

'You have a lot of checking to do, Monsieur Beaucousin. I'll leave you to it.'

Heller had stood up and was leaving.

'Some of it I have already had corroborated,' Beaucousin said.

'Some of it? What?'

'I don't think I want to go into that now.'

Heller stepped gingerly between piles of the journalist's papers, books, junk. He was almost at the door when Beaucousin called out, 'Wait!'

Heller saw that the rain and sleet had turned to snow, and that it was coming down in a murky dense fall in which car headlamps were diffused.

'Yes?' he said.

'Stay, have another drink,' Beaucousin said. He was refilling his own glass. Heller could see why Beaucousin had a permanent hangover. Why was he drinking this hard? Beaucousin was not as cool and casual as he was affecting to be with his informal dress and his uncombed look and his unstructured lifestyle. He was under a lot of stress, dragging on his cigarette with nervous intensity. Beaucousin was fearful about something. And it occurred to Heller that the journalist had not got him here only for the reasons he'd said, but rather because he was a man in the dark, not sure what he was getting himself into. The guy was seeking help.

'The reason you got me here,' Heller said, 'is because you've realised there's something fishy about this videotape. You know where you got it, I don't. Also you've played it right the way through, so you have a better idea of how it's been tampered with.'

'What do you know about the dollar devaluation in 1971?' Beaucousin threw at Heller.

'Not much,' said Heller. 'I remember its happening. But I didn't have enough dollars for it to make much difference to me. What do you know about it?'

'It made a difference for some,' Beaucousin said. 'Knowing the exact amount, the exact date. For the Banque de France. The Banque de France received its information from Pompidou, from the President in person. He received it from Marenche, then the head of foreign intelligence. As a consequence the Banque de France made a killing, enough to pay for the entire foreign intelligence budget for several years. This is according to Marenche himself.'

'I guess insider dealing when it's in the national interest is considered legitimate.'

'Some others, beside the Banque de France, have benefited from the foreknowledge.'

Heller nodded, returned to the middle of the room, sat down on the lumpy sofa again.

'What did you want to ask me?'

'Who would know of something like that? Impending

218

economic changes such as a devaluation? America coming off the gold standard? Who would know it for sure? Sure enough for the President of France? For the Banque de France? And some others?'

'I don't know who.'

'Somebody French foreign intelligence could get to.'

'I don't know.'

'Might Bill Gibson have known?'

'I can't see why Nixon would have taken Bill into his confidence about his economic strategies.'

'How about Arthur Simpson?'

'Your guess is as good as mine.'

A nervous tic developed in Beaucousin's unshaven chin. The man was really tensed-up to a high degree under the layer of cool. The cool was a fake.

Heller was once more about to leave; Beaucousin urged him back to the sofa, at the same time insistently refilling his glass.

'I've talked to them,' he said.

'You've talked to who?'

'*Them!*'

'How'd that happen?'

'Telephone call.'

'To what purpose?'

'They wanted me to print something.'

'Ah! And?'

'I refuse. I say I was not there to print what they want me to print.'

'And what did they say?'

'They say I am in the pay of the capitalist press, which I suppose, speaking literally, is true.'

'They issue threats?'

'Yes. That comes natural to them.'

'You tell the police about this phone call?'

'No.'

'I think you should. To protect yourself.'

'The uncanny thing about this telephone call,' Beaucousin said, 'is I knew his voice.'

'We are talking about Gavaudan?'

'He didn't say who he was, but seems to me it must have been him.'

'You knew his voice?'

'Yes, from a long time ago. A voice can leave a kind of recording in your brain, and when you hear it again ... '

'From how long ago?'

'From eighteen years ago.'

'Sixty-eight – the student uprising.'

'Yes.'

His chin was twitching and he was looking at his watch again. He seemed to be divided in his mind between keeping some appointment and a need to talk.

'He was someone I saw once or twice in our group. We were twenty years old, sitting around planning the Revolution. He looked ... quite small. No beard then. But red hair, yes ... I remember the red hair and the fiery temperament. I remember he used to say very pretentious things. He said once that he considered Antigone his mythic fiancée from far in the past. Whatever that was supposed to mean. He talked about the Eiffel Tower and wanting to blow it up. Creative destruction, he called it. He thought it would be an important symbolic act to blow it up. I remember he talked about "the need of the first death", after which one is across the threshold and can go on to however many deaths are required.'

'And how many is that?' Heller asked.

'I don't know,' Beaucousin said, a blood-surge bringing a coating of sweat to his face.

He's afraid, Heller thought. The guy's afraid of something.

'What was your overall impression of him?'

'Of a man who was not just talking. As the rest of us were. A man who was prepared to go through with it.'

Heller went to the door. This time he was determined to leave. There were things to be done.

'I would inform the police about the phone call,' he said. 'Maybe you should have some protection.'

TWENTY-ONE

IT HAD TURNED very cold in Paris. The ground had kept its hard surface of overnight frost, and in the Champs-Elysées the wind had a straight run from the place de la Concorde all the way to the Etoile and could get up speed. It must have been minus eight by the oval lawn in the allée Marcel Proust, allowing for the wind-chill factor. Heller estimated this on the basis of his sorely whipped ears.

General Ed Riflin jun. was wearing a long army-style blue overcoat, the high collar buttoned up under his considerable jowls, a Persian lamb fur hat suitable for Moscow, fur-lined boots and heavy gloves, and so was not bothered having meetings on park benches on a cold day such as this. But Heller had not come so well prepared. He had on only a raincoat, was gloveless, hatless. He proposed breakfast at the Crillon, a stone's throw away.

Riflin didn't like the idea of that. 'It's not secure,' he said.

'Get the Embassy to give us a room to talk in,' Heller suggested as another alternative, but this didn't suit Ed either.

'Don't see the necessity of bringing the Embassy into this,' he said. He paused. 'What's your problem? Feeling cold or something? Let's not waste time. Now since *they* haven't got in touch with us, we don't even know what the state of play is, whether Bill is still alive. We're in the dark. Is there a way for us to get in touch with them direct? Without going through the French. I'd sooner leave the French out of this, they're tricky sons of bitches, the French. Byzantine in their ways ... '

'I leave messages at a contact number that I have. I have to wait for them to respond.'

Ed Riflin shook his head sombrely somewhere within the flurry of light snow that the wind was blowing up around their faces. Heller stamped his feet. He filled Riflin in about the meeting with Beaucousin and the salient features of the Bill Gibson tape. He mentioned Beaucousin's interest in the dollar devaluation of 1971 and in who might have known about that in advance. 'This Beaucousin,' Heller said, 'won't be fobbed off.'

'Yes, yes. A real hungry sewer rat,' Ed Riflin said.

'I think I have bought us a little time,' Heller said, 'by putting it in Beaucousin's head that he is being set up. It's happened to him before, and so he's wary. He has a fair amount of checking to do before he goes to press with what he's got. But finally he'll get it all checked out.'

'How long do we have?'

'Hard to know ... '

'Tell me about this Beaucousin.'

'One time Marxist. In his student days. Top of his profession. Cynical. Clever, but ... careless. Not much money. Likes the whisky – a little too much. About forty. Smokes a lot. Screws around a fair bit, I would guess. Gives an impression of cool but I'd say is under a lot of stress. From what I don't know exactly, though I have one or two notions. My impression is of someone who, under the cool, is running scared.'

'OK, OK,' Ed mused. 'I've got the picture.' He was silent, contemplative for a minute or more while the snowflakes began to build up on Heller's head and shoulders. 'The reason he's under this pressure is that he's in the rat race and has got to keep running. Right? Journalists at the top lead very hectic stressful lives. Have got to top themselves all the time. Secretly they have the desire to get out. Now suppose you went to Beaucousin and said to him, instead of chasing your tail trying to prove this cockamamie story of yours, that nobody'll believe, here's another idea. Drop the story and write it instead as a work of the imagination. Make it fiction, and we'll arrange the sale of rights. Tell him we'll get him a good price. Guaranteed advance of say . . . half a million.'

'Francs or dollars?'

'Dollars. We're not going to be cheap about this. It's for world rights. An outright sale. No author's royalties. We own the material . . . I'd say that was a pretty good offer. Enables the rat to come out of the sewer.'

By now Heller was very cold, and something was sticking in his throat, and there was a bad taste in his mouth that he would dearly have liked to be able to spit out, except you couldn't spit out General Ed Riflin jun., he had a way of sticking in your throat. Till he choked you.

Heller remembered when Ed Riflin had been a scrawny army captain in Intelligence, ready to do anybody's dirty work for them if it enabled him to move up the ladder. And he had moved up, moved up to general without ever having set foot on a field of battle or learned to fire a pistol. Won all his battles by means of licking asses and stabbing backs.

'Anyway,' Ed blithely allowed through the thickening snow-fall, 'this is only an idea of mine. In any case we first have got to get Bill out. While they've got him, no matter what we do to stop the outlet, we still got the *source* of the leak to contend with, and you know how water finds its own level. It's a real pity you let this thing slip through your fingers when you had them. You had them on the phone. You should have clinched it there and then. I'm sorry to say it but you really fucked up there, Fred. You should have offered them more, you should have offered them a million instead of futzing around *bargaining*.'

The shiny metal suitcase was between his feet. He had lugged it all the way here. The case that did not contain his pyjamas or toothbrush.

'Pick it up when you leave here,' Ed told him. 'You know what's in there. If it's not enough, tell 'em you can get more, tell 'em it's a first payment, but they've got to give us solid watertight guarantees. And see if you can't get Beaucousin to agree to our publishing offer. I'll come up with the advance. Henceforth he can be a gentleman author instead of a sewer rat.'

'And if he doesn't want to be a gentleman author?'

'Then we'll have to think again,' Ed said.

Heller's breath balloons were expanding in the sub-zero temperature in proportion to the rising anger he was trying to hold down. The cold was heading. He could feel the 'inner dizziness' that was said to beset people in his profession when they could no longer keep all the ambiguous elements of the job juggled in the air.

'Ed,' he said. 'Give me a good reason why Arthur Simpson has got to be the next President of the United States, and why you have got to be Secretary of State. Give me the reason.'

'We think we can serve our country – now if you don't think you can, and some people have already drawn that conclusion from your recent performance, you maybe should think about taking early retirement and devote yourself to messing about with boats.'

Heller could see his breath clouds envelop him, and it was a moment like the one when he punched that assistant secretary of state on his receding jaw. He drew his breath deep into his lungs, and let it out slowly, slowly, very controlled. It steadied him seeing his breath reduce from a puffy envelope to a smooth jet. Control. He spoke in a measured tone.

'When I decide to quit, Ed, I will let the Department know. Meanwhile I will try to do what I consider to be my job, which includes getting Bill out, if I can, and includes protecting the interests of the United States, but does not include saving Arthur Simpson's ass, or yours, Ed.' He gave a frozen lopsided grin. 'I don't know about you, but I'm getting out of the cold.' He picked up the metal valise. 'I've been told that if you've once got close to real power, mere sex pales by comparison. Well, Ed, you may just have to settle for the paler vice. For once in your life.'

Heller went straight back to the Pont-Royal. He didn't put the valise in the hotel's safe. In a situation like this it was best for no formal record to exist.

He telephoned Le Forum and left a message for Elvire to phone him back. They might be picking up Elvire's messages again in the hope of unblocking the bargaining process.

Then he opened the money case. The money was in used 500 F. notes. Non-consecutive numbers. Notes in bundles of twenty. Should be six hundred bundles. He didn't count them but made a rough check. The amount seemed to be correct and he spun the combination number lock, put the case in the closet, locked it and pocketed the key.

The sky was darkening as he took a taxi to Beaucousin's apartment in Montparnasse. Feathery snowflakes were floating down and the roads were becoming slippery. He saw a few skids on the way, and some stalled cars; others with bumpers entangled. The weather was definitely worsening.

Beaucousin was not in. There was no reply when Heller rang the bell. Arriving without an appointment was a long shot.

He could see that there was a light left on in Beaucousin's apartment and it occurred to him that Beaucousin might not bother to respond to the entryphone, if he was not expecting anyone. Worth a quick check. Heller tapped out the entry code – G449J – and went up in the elevator to the top floor. He rang the bell of Beaucousin's door. No answer. He rapped on the door with his knuckles. No answer. He listened with his ear to the door for voices. It was silent in the apartment.

He took the elevator down.

There was a busy brasserie across the road, from which Heller could keep a watch on the entrance of Beaucousin's building. Sooner or later he would be back.

Heller ordered a coffee and settled down near the window, behind a copy of *Le Figaro*.

At 17.20 he saw Beaucousin pull up in his racing green Alfasud and get out carrying a Vuitton bag elegantly suspended from his shoulder. He went hurriedly into the building. You would have thought that he had an appointment and was late for it.

225

Heller paid for his coffee. He left a modest tip, crossed the road and arrived at the door of the apartment building just as the elevator with Beaucousin in it was going up. Rather than wait to have Beaucousin open the door for him, Heller tapped out the entry code; he felt his way towards the elevator, pressed the button, and kept his finger on it. He remained in the dark, waiting for the elevator to come down. He was not going to bother to search around for the time-switch.

When he got to the top floor, he saw that the door of Beaucousin's apartment was ajar, the key still in the lock. He could see the Vuitton bag thrown down on the floor, just inside, and could hear Beaucousin moving about and talking angrily to himself. He sounded outraged about something.

Heller rang the bell and heard Beaucousin call out, *Putain de . . .* The curse was cut off by an explosion.

It was the old solid oak entrance door that saved Heller from the blast, the flying glass and debris. He had spun round, covering his face and head with his arms. In doing this he had a sloweddown glimpse of a mass of fragmented glass billowing towards him, saw chairs, tables, lamps, books, files, opened-out newspapers and journals flying through the air and pile up at the far end of the room, like unwanted objects tossed on to a rubbish dump. Beaucousin was deep inside this dump, his head at an unnatural angle to his torso, face and hair turned albino-white as a shower of powdery plaster and masonry dust fell on him out of the torn-open ceiling. Heller could see that Beaucousin was not moving. His eyes, though open, had a fixed opaque look to them.

Heller examined the dim room through 180 degrees; he stirred the rubble cautiously with the toecap of his shoe, and a little way into the apartment recovered a three-pronged antenna. Further on he found pieces of a metal spring. Pressure bomb. Put under a sawn floorboard. Step on it and you pressed down the metal prongs of the detonator, compressing a spring. That released the striker against a percussion cap. Required around twenty pounds of pressure. Stepping on it was more than enough.

He had the impression that Beaucousin had stirred, but there was so much masonry dust in the air and the little remaining daylight was so reduced in a sky heavy with snowcloud, he could not be sure if what he thought he had seen was the movement of somebody still alive or just the body's subsidence in the debris.

He moved forward gingerly, putting one foot before the other with the absolute minimum of weight on the first foot, transferring his full weight to it only when he felt that the floor beneath was solid. He had taken two steps towards Beaucousin in this way when his descending foot evoked a cat whine. He froze, keeping his forward foot light, all his weight on the other. In the cold apartment sweat prickled his face and scalp. He felt around for somewhere to put down his foot. Wherever he put any weight there came the animal howl of loose floorboards. In the fast fading light, his vision flickered like a compass needle. Nothing was solid, nothing was focused. Perhaps the whole fucking apartment was booby-trapped. There were those who liked to make really sure. With the sweat running into his eyes he could hardly see a thing. Crouching down within the tight circle that was supporting his weight, steadying himself with one hand, he felt around with the other hand. Gradually, very gradually, he increased the weight on the forward foot, searching for a section of floorboard that did not creak on contact. He edged forward, edged forward . . . inches at a time. In this way he gradually got close enough to be able to touch the unstirring form in the rubble, to feel around for an arm, to find a wrist, to search for a pulse. He tried one grip on the limp wrist and then another and another: no pulse, no pulse. Shit! Shit! There was no responsive movement to the contact. One of Beaucousin's hands was clutching a cigarette lighter. Heller extricated it from the tight fist. He struck the lighter, raising the light to the encrusted white face. No movement. Oh shit!

He raised the cigarette lighter in a semi-circle, increased the flame to maximum. Some of the dust had settled, the air was less dense now, more permeable to sight. There was a clearly defined area within which the explosion had had its worst effect. Beyond this area debris was loosely strewn about but damage was superficial. He could see scattered files and folders and the weird

227

concertinas formed by computer print-outs.

Somewhere in all this mess there was a little red and blue Sony box containing a cassette that Heller would have dearly liked to have in his possession.

He began to feel around, with the lighter raised. He could hear shouts from the stairs below, anxious voices, cries, hoarse hard-edged demands. He knew he did not have long. Calculating on normal fearfulnes at the scene of an explosion, people would probably keep their distance for a while. But soon they would start coming up ... They would have called the police and the SAMU emergency service by now. So there was little time.

The bedroom. That was where the tape had been, before. In one of the piles on the floor, left of the bed. If there was any order in chaos ...

To get to the bedroom meant crossing the living-room with the creaking floorboards. He moved cautiously on hands and knees, feeling ahead of him. Feeling the carpet. His fingers touched loose strands of carpeting, he felt further and found a ragged edge that lifted up when he tugged. A rectangular flap was coming away. He directed the lighter's illumination downward, and his fingers feeling carefully under the flap touched fresh sawdust. He found the line where the floorboard had been recently sawn through and traced out the loose rectangle. It sunk a little, and pressing on it very very lightly he felt more give there, nothing holding it – except three metal prongs. Three metal prongs that would retract with 20 lbs of pressure and force down a spring ... The second bomb. There won't be three, he decided. He entrusted himself to the logic of the economy of means, and giving the wobbly rectangle of floorboard a wide berth, walked lightly but quickly to the bedroom and opened the door.

The bedroom door had been closed, yet the bedroom was almost in as bad a state as the living-room, with all the various piles toppled over and everything scattered around.

Heller cautiously investigated the mess. There was no debris. No ceiling plaster, no broken glass, no splintered wood. Just overturned chairs and chests. The contents of drawers. Bedding torn from the bed lay all over the floor, the mattress was upended. This was mess made by human hands. He made a further search for the Sony box. But after a few moments he saw there was no point continuing. It was clear someone had got there first. He could hear the different sirens of the emergency services swelling up and converging as he retraced his steps across the living-room floor.

He went out of the flat. There were people on the half landing below, faces upturned, peering anxiously up the stairwell, talking in high nervous tones. It was dark on the top landing and they could not have seen more than a vague form. They called out, asking what had happened. Monsieur Beaucousin? Monsieur Beaucousin? Jean-Luc? Is it you? When they received no answer, they demanded who was there. What was he doing?

Heller had his finger on the elevator button. Excruciatingly slowly, cumbersomely, the elevator rose within its narrow shaft: thick oily black cables moving, the rattle and clank of machinery, counterweight sinking.

One or two people were beginning to come hesitantly up the stairs, calling out, asking what had happened. A plump woman in a bathrobe, her hair turbanned with white towelling, hands outstretched, was looking for the light switch.

The elevator arrived. Heller got into it quickly, pulled the accordion door shut, pressed the button for the ground floor and turned his back as the elevator started to descend. Out of the corner of his eye he glimpsed people peering through the leafy ironwork of the elevator cage. He kept his face averted and didn't answer the shouted questions.

Heller reached the ground floor. It was dark and he did not put on any lights.

Swiftly he crossed the narrow hall.

As he slipped out of the entrance of the apartment building the first of the SAMU ambulances arrived and white-coated paramedics jumped out. Then the police cars came.

Snow was falling with exquisite slowness out of the freezing air, big dry adhesive flakes that attached themselves firmly to everything they touched, staying firm on the ground, on roofs and cornices and string-courses and on window-boxes and flower-pots. A sedate white innocence was beginning to cover Paris.

At the first public phone box Heller telephoned the Embassy and asked for Gordon Welliver.

'Gordon,' he said, 'find out something for me. Find out where General Riflin is staying in Paris. Get me a phone number where I can reach him.'

After a minute Gordon Welliver returned to the phone.

'General Riflin is not in Paris,' he told Heller.

'When did he leave?'

'I'm told he hasn't been in Paris recently. You must have been given some wrong info about that, sir. I'm told you can reach him in his office at the White House. I expect you have that number, sir.'

TWENTY-TWO

THE PHONE WAS ringing as Heller came into his room at the Pont-Royal.

He thought: this will be it! Things come together. And then the waiting ends. The voice was immediately recognisable: the argumentative tone, the certain knowledge of being in the right. The sufferer from injustice.

'You have left a message for Elvire to call you,' he complained, 'and then you are not in.'

'Something came up,' Heller said. He added, 'I'm glad you've called.'

'You are ready to meet our terms?'

'I take it, then, that the Oldsmobile is still for sale, and in working order?'

'At the present moment.'

'Well. I'll need proof of that.'

'You going try the dirty tricks again?'

'No dirty tricks. No dirty tricks, either side.'

'Everything must be done very quick. You have the money? How much?'

'Six million. That's the best I can do.'

There was a silence at the other end, which Heller interpreted as a good sign.

'You have to follow the instructions, in all respect.'

It was messy, with large areas of uncertainty. But there was no foolproof way of retrieving a hostage. The rule was: live with the uncertainty. Cross each separate bridge as you come to it.

'How d'you want to do this?'

'You follow the instructions.'

'What sort of instructions?'

'You will see.'

They wanted him to accept whatever they were going to tell him to do. It was risky, very risky. They could end up having two American hostages instead of one; two lives to bargain with. But he couldn't see any other way. He could say, No, this isn't prudent, this is taking unwarranted risks with a second person's life, mine. But where would that get him? Back to square one, as far as Bill was concerned. Moreover, he had got the message from Ed Riflin that if he couldn't deliver on Bill, he, Heller, was for the junk heap.

Heller said: 'I will follow instructions to do with mechanics. Time and place, that sort of thing. But I'm not going to walk into a trap. If it looks like that, I'll back out and it's all off.'

'And to remember that you try any of your tricks, your friend find his brains in the trash can, understood?'

'What d'you want me to do?'

'Go down to the lobby, to the desk. Now. Straight away. Make no phone calls. They will give you an envelope, with instructions. You must follow them in totality. Any divergences and we will know this immediately. To remember: somebody watch you the whole time and any funny business, it's the end for your friend. We don't allow you to benefit of the doubt. If you make us nervous, it will be bad for your friend. You must keep to the timetables. Otherwise it will make us nervous . . . '

'I'll try not to make you nervous, Gavaudan.'

'What makes you think I am Gavaudan?'

'I recognise the voice. See, I have a theory which says no man can conceal himself.'

'We have not time to discuss your theories, Heller. Each stage will be timed. Go down now to the lobby. And remember you are being timed.'

The phone was put down.

Heller started to move fast. He unlocked the clothes closet and took out the money case. He set the combination number lock to 984, and then spun the numbers. They would have to break open the case and that would give him extra seconds. He opened his black Gladstone, prised up the lid of the false bottom and took out the two guns: the 9mm Browning automatic and the Smith & Wesson 357 magnum. He took extra ammunition clips for the automatic and a box of cartridges for the revolver. One had to be in a position to conclude the negotiation by other means.

He put the guns in his raincoat pockets, picked up the case and went down in the elevator.

There were times when events converged in an irresistible way and you were carried along by the force of circumstances ... useless to argue with circumstances.

At the desk he asked if there were any messages for him, and while the clerk was looking to see, Heller glanced around the lobby trying to pick out the person or persons who might be there to watch him. Men with cameras, with *Herald Tribunes*, with open street plans of Paris. A middle-aged couple, waiting to ask something at the desk. A small dapper man in a navy blazer, turning to and fro on his heels like a weathercock. A slightly built *Maghrébin* in a Prince of Wales check sports jacket. A brunette window-shopping for jewellery at the glass display cases, and casually looking around from time to time.

Maybe nobody was watching him, but he couldn't be sure of that. He had to proceed on the basis that he was being watched and that any departure from the instructions he was given would result in the consequences of which they warned. They had shown that their threats had to be believed. He couldn't count on them behaving rationally ... he was at the mercy of their obsessions, their aberrations, their paranoia. Whereas he being rational would have to behave as such, which meant predictably. A definite disadvantage.

He was handed an envelope on which his name had been written in capital letters with a biro. Inside there was a single

233

sheet of cross-lined paper torn from a school exercise book.

His instructions were contained in two hand-printed lines, and Heller assumed they would have been dictated to whoever was the messenger in the lobby.

GO TO PHONE BOX OPPOSITE L'ESCURIAL.
THIS MUST TAKE YOU NO MORE THAN 58 SECONDS.

Heller hurried. It was best to be seen (if he *was* seen) hurrying, so as not to make them nervous. Since they were making a point of the fifty-eight seconds. They had to be made to feel they were winning. They had to be made to feel confident, unthreatened.

He hurried, lugging the valise stuffed with six million francs. Six million francs was no small weight to lug around.

The phone was ringing as he got to it. He unhooked it, looking at his watch: sixty-eight seconds!

'You are late,' the complaining voice said.

'Allow for warm-up time,' Heller said. 'And for the fact that I'm not as young as I was.'

'You must go to the Elf garage in the avenue de Suffren. A car is there for you. You must rent it at your own expense. You have fifteen minutes. When you receive your key, open the glove compartment. Inside you find further instructions.'

They were turning this into a sort of insane treasure-hunt, with clues and directions at each successive step of the way.

Heller started looking around for a taxi; a woman was getting out of one at l'Escurial and he succeeded in grabbing it before anyone else. That put him a few minutes ahead. Except that if he was being watched, his watchers would report at what time he had got the taxi, and taking too long to get to the avenue de Suffren would be considered suspicious. Would feed their paranoia.

At the Elf garage the woman in the office said that his car was ready. It was a little red Renault 5. She gave him the papers to sign, and he paid with a Visa card.

The car was waiting for him in the display court. In the glove compartment he found another envelope containing another sheet of paper. A sheet of plain white A4 on which his instructions had been typed on an old typewriter with a used-up ribbon.

GO TO PERIPHERIQUE FOR NORTH. EXIT PORTE DE LA CHAPELLE
SIGNPOSTS TO LILLE AND A1 AUTOROUTE.
TAKE AUTOROUTE DU NORD DIRECTION LILLE.
BEFORE COMPIEGNE, STOP AT LAYBY AIRE DE ROBERVAL–EST. GO TO
WOMEN'S TOILET. ENVELOPE WITH FURTHER INSTRUCTIONS
BEHIND WATER CISTERN.
DO NOT STOP FOR ANY REASON.
DO NOT SPEAK TO ANYONE.
IS ESSENTIAL TO HURRY.

He considered leaving some sort of message with the woman in the Elf office but it was risky. He could not know what arrangement they had come to with her. Even if she had no direct involvement with them, she might have been induced by one means or another to report back to them. Or they might have some plant in the place. The guy washing the cars. Too risky to try anything.

He followed his instructions. He drove along the *quais*, past the Eiffel Tower, and then across the bridge to the place de la Concorde. He was going to drive right by the American Embassy, but there was no way of stopping, no way of leaving a message. Too risky. He might have a tail on him. Then again he might not. But he couldn't chance it.

Going around the *place* the small car was buffeted by the rush of wind coming out of the funnel of the rue Royale. Presently he was passing through the working-class districts of north Paris: streets named in honour of Moscow and Stalingrad; flea-markets, launderettes, poky little supermarkets; American-style fast-food places; beer barrels being rolled down ramps; twitching net curtains ...

The Périphérique was clogged with heavy traffic: great monsters of the road, their engines panting and throbbing and spewing out lead and carbon monoxide. The big vehicles lurched dangerously in and out of their lanes, going too fast for their size and the prevailing road conditions and the visibility, air-brakes hissing, massive road wheels churning up slush. Heller was receiving a lot of it on his windscreen. For seconds at a time he was driving blind. Going into the unknown. Which sometimes had to be gone into, like it or not. When you had no other choice.

Heller drove opportunistically, bettering his position whenever he could, going through any gaps that offered themselves, gaining a little distance here, some more there, until the overhead signs warned of the Porte de la Chapelle coming up. This was where he had to exit.

In a short while he was driving through the grey-white outskirts where the Paris overflow became a continuous clutter of transport firms, railroad goods yards, industrial zones, construction sites, factory chimneys, underpasses, overpasses. Ramps. Road bridges. High-rise tenements − stark concrete eruptions ringing the outskirts, topped by huge advertising signs: TOSHIBA, VOLVO, TECHNICS, SAAB, PUMA. Cranes slashed the sky.

Presently there were wide meadows, and snow-dusted bushes, trees edged with white, and steel towers with their skeins of frost-coated high wires passing over cornfields.

The dull gleam of water in fields. Here and there the road surface showed black skid marks, the deposits of locked brakes. The past left its mark, crude or brutal or hidden. The past was a Chinese puzzle.

Heller owed it to Bill Gibson, his one-time mentor, to try and buy back whatever portion of his lousy life he might still have remaining to him. Owed it to him because they were in the same difficult dubious business. And because it was a matter of professional pride for Heller − and of survival! That too. Bill's survival seemed to have become tied up with his own.

Passing Le Bourget. A big Airbus hung heavy in the sky, static with weight before rising.

Heller was all the time looking in his rear-view mirrors for the cars that might be tailing him. He was supposed to stop only where they said. They had picked the car that he drove – not very fast or powerful, incapable of throwing off a Lancia HPE like the one that had been sticking close behind him the past five minutes, making no move to overtake.

An overhead electronic message board gave the temperature as −9, and warned of fog. Freezing fog.

He could feel the wind battering the little car, making it shake and wobble and move in abrupt sideward shifts.

Senlis coming up.

The *autoroute* had been swept and salted, but there were spots where the salting had been ineffective, and blowing light snow gathered up from trees and hedges whirlpooled out across the road, concealing patches of black ice.

He pushed the Renault up to 120 kilometres per hour to see what the Lancia HPE would do, and it increased speed as well, to keep the distance between them the same; 120 wasn't any problem for the Lancia. Heller took the Renault past 130, at which point its road-holding was far from firm.

He felt the loss of grip between tyre and ground, the beginning of the sinister slide, and then he was in a high speed side-spin, careering towards the centre verge. He tusselled with the steering-wheel, driving into the skid, working the brake on-off, on-off, on-off, while the little car slid about, spinning out of control, on a collision course with the oncoming traffic the other side. Would the barrier hold, or at the speed he was doing would the Renault go summersaulting to the other side? A concerted outburst of hooting klaxons. He struggled with the car.

The light progressive braking was working. And then he had control once more, the wheels steered ...

In his driving mirror he saw the Lancia HPE was still on his tail, but had dropped back a bit, for safety's sake. He must have made them nervous: taking unwarranted risks with their million bucks.

The fact that the Lancia had hung back while he was fighting the skid was proof enough for Heller that it was *them*. If it had been anyone else they would have given the skidder a wide berth, passed him comfortably and left him far behind. But this Lancia was sticking close.

Past Senlis.

Compiègne coming up.

High winds of twenty or thirty knots were scattering fine grey powdery snow across the World War I battlefields. He thought of trenches and thick mud and young men dying.

The landscape had become a grainy war newsreel of a time when the world was not in colour. It was a blanched place. Woods, hedges, farmhouses, trees, sky, ground, streams. A matt uniformity. You could not see where the sky ended and the ground began.

He saw the P 1,000m sign for Aire de Roberval-Est and began to pull in and slow down. He stayed in the exit lane and took the gently curving slip-road into the lay-by and picnic site. There were a couple of trucks drawn up alongside each other on the crescent, in front of the frost-topped picnic tables – a Daf with its cargo covered in flapping yellow tarpaulin, and a Scania. Their drivers were biting on long *baguettes* of ham and cheese, which they washed down with coffee from thermoses.

Heller parked well in view of the two trucks. He kept the Browning automatic in his raincoat pocket, wrapped the Smith & Wesson in a cloth and put it under the driver's seat. He got out and locked the car, put the car keys under a stone and went into the toilets by the door marked *FEMMES*.

He opened the door of the first cubicle, stood on the toilet seat and felt behind the rusty water cistern. Nothing. He looked around outside by the grimy washbasins: the liquid soap in the soap dispenser had frozen, a waxlike trickle hung from the spout. Nothing. He went in the second cubicle. Nothing there either, behind the cistern. He was in the middle of nowhere, in a filthy toilet, on a frozen World War I battlefield with no instructions about where to go next, what to do. He tried the men's toilet, felt behind the water cistern. No message there either.

He returned to the Renault, switched on the motor, defrosted his hands in the demister's hot air flow, and waited.

A minute went by and another and another. Five minutes. Then he saw in his side mirror a big dented Citroën CX pull into the crescent and park behind the trucks. A woman got out and went towards the women's toilets. She was wearing a thick padded ski anorak and was very muffled up about the neck and face. He couldn't see her face at all. After a couple of minutes she came out and went back to her car but did not drive off.

Heller returned to the women's toilets. He opened the door of the first stall, got up on the seat, felt behind. His fingers touched an envelope: it was scotch-taped to the cistern. He put the envelope in his pocket and got down.

The woman in the ski anorak was at the washbasin, pounding the soap dispenser to no avail. He couldn't see her face. Another woman came out of the second stall. She was also wearing a ski anorak, hers was blue and very bulky, and it had an acrylic fur collar which was zipped up to stand beyond her chin and reach to her earlobes. She had the build of a bear, this second one. The parts of her face that he glimpsed between the collar and the scarf were beaten red by the wind. She held a long thin smoked salmon knife in her hand, held it low down her body. She was motioning him to get inside the cubicle. The woman at the washbasin had turned around and was pointing a gun at him, her eyelids twitching.

He recognised them. The furies. He wondered if the whole complicated arrangement was to get him to this desolate lay-by on a World War I battlefield, in the middle of nowhere, for them to put a bullet through his head.

The bear told him to turn around and put his arms up against the wall, legs apart. She ran her hands over him roughly, searching him for weapons, while the other one kept him covered with the gun. She found the Browning automatic and after that the search intensified, her hands moving in pincer-like fashion over his body. Her fingers pinched his arms, his armpits, his groin.

He said:

—*C'est loin d'ici? Il faut encore aller loin?*

—*Tu as l'argent?* she demanded. He noted the familiar 'tu'. He said yes, he had the money. She demanded the car key. When he made no move to hand it over, she tried to find it on him. Not finding it, she became furious.

He said that wasn't the arrangement. The arrangement was that they got the money when Bill Gibson was handed over, not before.

The two women exchanged looks. The bear nodded to the other one with the gun.

He said that the big trucks had CB radios. He said he had told those truck drivers to watch out for him.

The two women looked at each other. Then they left.

He followed them out. The Lancia was also pulled up now, behind the Citroën CX. There was a man at the wheel, a second man next to him, another in the back.

The Citroën, driven by the bear, pulled out. The Lancia waited. Seemed he was going to be escorted.

He ripped open the envelope and read his new instructions:

PROCEED TOWARDS BAPAUME.

LEAVE AUTOROUTE AT ROYE/ RE-ENTER AT SAME.

TAKE DIRECTION LILLE.

PASS EXIT 14 (EXIT FOR BAPAUME).

AT 1000 METRES BEYOND EXIT 14 PULL UP IN EMERGENCY LANE.

TAKE OUT BAG CONTAINING MONEY AND CROSS AUTOROUTE ON FOOT. WAIT.

CAR WILL APPROACH TRAVELLING DIRECTION PARIS AND WILL FLASH ONE LONG/ONE SHORT, ONE SHORT/ONE LONG.

UPON THIS SIGNAL PUT BAG WITH MONEY ON GROUND.

APPROACHING CAR WILL PASS YOU SLOWLY. YOU WILL SEE GIBSON. THIS IS YOUR PROOF OF LIFE. THIS CAR WILL STOP IN EMERGENCY LANE 100 METRES ON.

A SECOND CAR WILL APPROACH AND MAKE SAME SIGNAL ONE LONG/ONE SHORT, ONE SHORT/ONE LONG. GIVE MONEY BAG TO PERSON IN THIS CAR WHO WILL VERIFY CONTENT.

IF ALL SATISFACTORY GIBSON WILL THEN BE ALLOWED TO LEAVE FIRST CAR.

He wasn't happy about this storyline but since there wasn't any foolproof way to pay over a ransom and collect a hostage, he would either have to go along with the arrangement or else ignore it, drive out at Roye and not return. That would call off the deal. And result in Bill's immediate execution. They wouldn't wait for Heller's counter-proposal.

He drove out of the lay-by and proceeded in the direction of Lille, and was followed out by the Lancia.

He glimpsed the back of the Citroën ahead of him, then lost it in thickening fog. Visibility had dropped to not much more than thirty metres at best.

He was passing through the valley of the Somme, with its wide fields stretching into obscurity. At times he saw barns, isolated farmhouses, a line of trees. Other times he saw nothing. He was seeking to keep his bearings, to pinpoint where he was at any moment.

Sortie Bapaume 2,000m.

This was where he was.

He passed exit 14, and pushed the kilometre counter to zero. Fractions of a kilometre unspooled on the dial. The digits jumped. One hundred metres, 150 . . . 200 . . . 500 . . . 700 . . . 1000.

He pulled up. It was a job getting the door open. When he succeeded in doing so, the wind slashed his face. He had difficulty standing up straight. He couldn't see across to the other side of the motorway, to where his appointment was. Couldn't see vehicles approaching, only the pale glimmer of their headlamps through the snow. He didn't know where his escort was. The Citroën must have gone on ahead, the Lancia might be behind him or might have passed him in the blizzard.

He picked up the money case, took the Smith & Wesson from under the seat and shoved it in his raincoat pocket. He listened for some moments to the traffic passing, to get an idea of how noise levels and distance correlated under present conditions. The wind and the snowfall played tricks with sounds; some of the big trucks were virtually on top of you before you heard them, and head-lights could seem further away than they were.

He made the dash to the metal barrier, felt the air around him shudder with the close passage of a heavy vehicle that he had not seen. A second wild dash and he was on the other side.

He waited.

He put the money case down between his legs so that he could put his hands in his pockets while waiting. His hands were stiff and numb from the cold. He didn't know if he had enough movement left in his fingers to be able to use the gun, if he had to. A special adviser to the Secretary of State was supposed to have recourse to reasoning and persuasion and the tactics of negotiation, wherever possible. But here, by the side of a desolate stretch of *autoroute*, on a blind date with the furies, his faith in the power of reason was minimal. Every so often, there was the sound of something massive approaching through a heavy swell of road slush, tarpaulins flapping. The trucks were going pretty fast, for these conditions. He had to stand back from the road spray they threw up in wide arcs. And then he made out one long flash/one short, one short flash/one long, and a yellow glimmer approaching at a much slower speed than the other vehicles. The yellow glimmer was in the emergency lane. Must be it.

He stepped back further and his hand tightened on the gun.

Presently he was able to make out a high vehicle, higher than an ordinary car, with a range of headlights mounted on a bonnet grid. A four-wheel drive vehicle of the Range-Rover type, he guessed. The fog lights gave the signal, and then the other lights of the grid fastened on him.

The dazzle, a splurge of bright diffused light, was approaching slowly, at no more than 10 kph. He saw a series of intersecting saturn-rings with bright centres.

Then the dazzle was moving past, and some degree of vision was restored to him. Blinking hard to regain normal sight, he glimpsed Bill in the rear of the slowly passing vehicle, sitting stiffly upright, red as an old devil, with an expression of contempt for the entire human race on his face. And drunk, oh yes, drunk ... definitely drunk. They were shining a flashlight in his face, for purposes of identification, which added to his somewhat macabre appearance, and he was mouthing something through the closed window, something seemingly important that he was trying to mime with large slow lip movements, and Heller thought that what the purple lips were insistently saying was: DON'T LET 'EM FOOL YOU . . .

Whether this was meant to be a general philosophical exhortation or if it was a specific message related to the present situation, Heller couldn't tell. He watched the car drive a hundred metres past him and come to a stop.

Then the second car approached, flashing its lights in the agreed signal, and Heller reached down between his legs and picked up the money case.

The second car was the Lancia. It approached very slowly, and when it got to within a few metres of him, its lights were switched off and he heard the slush-slush of its tyres churning through road mire. It approached him in darkness. When it was parallel with him, a door opened and a hand reached out for the money case. Heller held back, gripping the gun in his raincoat pocket with stiff fingers, looking up the road towards the spot where the first car had stopped. He pointed towards it, indicating that he wanted to see Bill step out of the car before handing over the money. He kept his trigger finger moving to prevent its getting frozen.

The Lancia flashed its lights in a signal and moments later the rear door of the car ahead opened and Bill stumbled out, legs buckling, and it looked as though he would fall flat on his face, but he managed to regain his balance and began cumbersomely to walk towards Heller. Bill was trying to run, but there was the slippery state of the ground, and he was an old man who had been kept tied up in a confined space for many days, and his movements were stiff and awkward and unsure. And he was drunk, very drunk. He was coming into view through the blowing snow, then disappearing as the snowfall thickened around him.

From the Lancia the gloved hand was stretching out insistently, urgently. Heller handed over the money case: immediately the Lancia began to move away at a slow pace, without lights. Heller calculated: it'll take them a minute to break open the combination lock.

He had his gun drawn as he started running through the snow towards Bill, showing Bill to hurry. Hurry! Hurry!

The Lancia's headlights were switched on full and it was accelerating away. Bill was stumbling about, trying to run. His legs were not up to it, though. The Lancia's headlights picked him out in his undignified endeavour.

There was a shot, followed a moment later by a second, then a third, and Bill was spinning about, sliding with a wild flailing of arms, his limbs becoming entangled. He went over and heaved about for a moment. There was a fourth shot, and then he didn't move any more.

When Heller got to him he was an unstirring bulk, eyes open and staring with drunken indifference.

TWENTY-THREE

ISABELLE WAS WEARING her old flying jacket with the fur collar open at the neck. The extreme cold was beginning to let up a little. In the rue Monsieur le Prince the fine coating of hoar frost that covered the statue of Vulpian, the nineteenth-century professor of experimental pathology, was beginning to dissolve, exposing patches of political graffiti beneath.

Isabelle was taking the broad steps down to where she had left her car parked overnight. On the cornices of the medical school building the pigeons jostled each other sheltering from the cold. The rue Antoine Dubois, closed to traffic, was quiet.

As Isabelle approached her car, two scruffy types appeared from behind one of the other vehicles illegally parked in the cul-de-sac. They looked at her like 'street poets', the sort that hung around in these parts and tried to sell you Xeroxed sheets of their terrible poetry. They were coming towards her, and she was expecting the usual approach: Pardon me, are you a lover of poetry, madame? She was feeling in her pockets for a 10f. coin to give them. But as they got closer to her she realised that they were not street poets, and she turned violently around and started running back towards the steps, emitting sobbing gasps and big breath clouds as she ran. The bigger of the two women, a bear-like figure in an anorak and snow hood, caught up with Isabelle, grabbed her from behind and forced something over her face, and then started to drag her back to a dirty cream Citroën van. The other woman, a thinner, smaller

245

type, of a tense, nervous disposition, had pulled out a strange-looking weapon, a sort of minature submachine-gun that could be held in one hand, and was looking aggressively around in case anyone should come along and try to interfere. But no one came. The only witness of the kidnapping, Nathalie Vanhaecke, a twenty-year-old medical student, was on the steps by the statue of Vulpian, fixed to the spot with fear. Though highly distressed by what she saw, she noted the make of the van into which Isabelle was bundled, and that it had a Parisian '75' registration number. While she couldn't swear to it, she believed the number plate included an 8 and the letter Z. She had seen the van drive off at high speed and turn into the rue Ecole de Médecine, and had immediately run to a café and telephoned the police.

The *revendication* came three days later. It said that the second shock commando of ACE – Attaque Contre l'Etat – had taken captive Isabelle Decourten as a retaliatory measure against the American imperialists and their French cohorts.

Isabelle Decourten would be executed in three days' time unless the following demands were met:

1 The release of Marco Vougny and of eleven others on the list attached
2 The payment of 18,000,000f. as a contribution of indemnity to the Fund for the Liberation of the People
3 The immediate resignation of the Minister of National Safety, Charles Decourten, in recognition of his crimes.

The faces of the people standing about in the Minister's office were sombre. Chaillet spoke inaudibly to another policeman. Juvin was grave. He did not look towards Heller. It was as if they were all at a funeral.

At 11.05 Le Quineau and one of the ministry ushers wheeled in a trolley with a monitor screen and a video-recorder. At seven minutes past, the Minister entered. He entered greyly, stiffly, and stood behind his desk, bent forward slightly, holding in his hand a video cassette.

Looking around the room, he asked if everyone was present, and when Le Quineau said yes, told him to close the doors. The Minister said that a video-tape had been received which he believed they should all see.

He nodded to Le Quineau. The monitor and the video-recorder were connected to an electric point. Lights were lowered and the cassette was pressed into the slot. There was a tense silence filled only with the whirring sound of tape being rewound, with everybody waiting for the click that would indicate that the left bobbin was full.

When the click was heard there was a concerted release of breath in the room. Le Quineau worked the controls. At first the screen was a grainy black and white jumble with a rumbling on the soundtrack that was like the sound of the ocean. Then the jumbled lines and dots formed into the face of Isabelle. To Heller she looked as she had on the night when she was beset by stage fright: Antigone going to her death in the cave. The living death in the rocks.

A jerky downward movement showed her holding up a copy of the previous day's *Le Monde*.

The camera jerked up again to her face. It was out of focus, and it took the unskilled cameraman several moments to get the focus right.

She seemed to be waiting for a signal, and when she received it she looked down and then spoke quickly, mechanically, in a manner suggesting that she was reading from a script.

Heller could feel her terror rattling around inside him.

—Father, I have been told I must address myself to you, that you are the only one who can save me. My captors, the freedom fighters of action commando II, the military arm of Attaque Contre l'Etat, have decreed that I will be executed in three days' time unless their demands are met. They have told me that I must persuade you, Father, to carry out what they demand if you wish to see me alive. They have told me that I must give the

247

best performance I have ever given, that my life depends on it.

Isabelle was attempting to slightly shift her limbs, to find a less painfully cramped position. Heller saw the chain tighen around her neck and restrain her, and when she sought to rearrange her legs there was a wince of pain as other chains pulled on her ankles.

Heller could feel her claustrophobia: tiny fists beating inside her head, a child screaming to be let out. He could feel her anguish and her humiliation. He was there with her.

The camerman having got the focus right did not budge, did not waver.

It was obscene, this obsessive recourse to the camera. They had first of all filmed their potential victims leaving homes or hotels, going to restaurants, stepping in and out of automobiles or trains, walking in parks, all unaware of the camera following them around like some baleful eye of fate. Now the eye continued its dreadful watch. It wasn't only the squalid practicalities of extortion that disposed them to the use of the camera, first in the case of Bill Gibson and now with Isabelle. The camera was there to record a history lesson and to exult.

Heller looked at the others in the room, with their professional distance, their ability to disengage themselves from somebody else's suffering, and he thought: for them she has been depersonalised, has become 'the hostage', another case that has landed on their desk. They didn't have to feel for her, that was no part of their job. Chaillet-the-stone. Juvin, sitting on the spike of ice, eyelids barely even flickering ... The blonde at a stenotype machine, set up on a card table before the monitor screen, impassively taking down everything Isabelle said.

—Father, I will only get out of here alive if you can find a way to meet their terms, that is my only chance, because for them this is a war, and in a war prisoners are exchanged, it's a legitimate and honourable practice, and that is what they are asking for. If you love me, Father, you must do this to save me. I am your only child. I know you will say that you are not able to give in to them, but am I not worth more to you than your principles? Your ambitions ...

Her voice broke and then recovered and became bitter. It seemed to Heller that she was abandoning her script, and that ancient grievances were manifesting themselves. Her eyes had become small and hard and mad with the rush of accusations welling up in her. Heller knew this phenomenon well, the way the captive came to perceive his persecutors as being *outside*, in the government, in the police, among the individuals who refused to comply with the kidnappers' demands. Uncontainable rage was displaced outwards when you were dependent on your torturers for survival.

—Father, I know how hard and cruel you can be, and ruthless, I know your cruel and ruthless heart. I know that nothing matters to you except your own ambitions and your pleasures, and that you will sacrifice everybody who stands in your way. Will you sacrifice me too, the way you have sacrificed so many others? So that people can say about you, you stuck to your principles, even though it was your own daughter . . . you let her die because it was necessary for the good of the State.

She was performing for them, a performing dog on a chain. They were letting her have her head, since it was in the service of their cause that Charles Decourten should stand accused.

—You will be guilty of my murder, Father. Father, there can be no triumphant outcome for you in this. I know how you have always wanted to triumph. Over everyone. But you must give up your triumph, if you wish to see me alive. You must take the hard stony road. That is the road you must take to find me. The bumpy road. The nauseous road. You must take it if you want to see me alive. You must give them what they want. There is no other way, Father. In a storm the tree must bend with the wind or it breaks . . . By the margin of a flooded river, trees lie broken. The storm has broken them . . .

Her words were arrested by a spasm of retching, a chained hand rose in an instinctive motion of covering her mouth, but the weight of her chains made her hand drop and she had to fight back her nausea in full sight of the relentless camera eye.

She seemed to be getting herself mixed up with Antigone. This was like the overly realistic performance that had offended so many people: the actress spilling her guts out. The stuff about trees bending in the wind was from Haemon's speech to Creon, when the son pleads with his father for Antigone's life. She was invoking the same argument ... for her life to be put before *raisons d'Etat*.

In the play the trees were situated on the margin of a flooded river. And with the big thaw, the Seine had become swollen with melted ice. Could this be some sort of coded message? Could she be working in clues, telling them where she was? Did she possess enough coherence for that in her present state?

Heller was trying to picture where she was. A low narrow place, judging from her very restricted movements. From the sensitivity of her eyes to the brightness of the camera lights and from the way she kept screwing up her eyes he guessed that she was kept in darkness. Where was she? A windowless place at the end of a hard stony road, by the margin of a flooded river. Where trees have broken in the storm. This was too damned fanciful. She was surely in no state to work in clues about her whereabouts.

He told himself: this is a mystery in which the clues are inside people's heads.

One thing he knew: she was in the place of her nightmare. A closed attic.

—Father, I'm not being allowed any more time. Say goodbye to everyone ... I love you, Father. I have always loved you. You are my love. Don't abandon me, Papa ... Papa. Papa.

Lights were switched on and Charles Decourten rose from behind his desk, drawing himself up stiffly, without any flexibility of the torso, supporting his weight on the arms of the chair, an old old man. Keeping one hand on the desk for steadiness, he felt his way around it and came to the other side. He stumbled slightly and Le Quineau was quick to provide a discreet supporting hand.

Charles Decourten brushed it away and stood up straight and stiff, swaying against the ministerial desk.

He looked down and said he would hear their comments.

Chaillet spoke first. He said he considered that the kidnapping of Isabelle Decourten was an act of panic and desperation; all the evidence indicated that Attaque was in total disarray, with probably only two or three of the leaders left at liberty, without money and the other resources needed to make 'the pyramid' function.

Marco Vougny was the crucial link-man of the command structure, connecting the leadership with the rest of the pyramid. As a result of the arrest of Vougny and the other terrorists in the Lancia, following the murder of Bill Gibson on the *autoroute*, Gavaudan was cut off from his troops. They desperately needed money to rebuild their shattered organisation. The kidnapping of Isabelle was a last resort, undertaken in an endeavour to obtain funds and 'prestige' within the ranks of the world terrorist movement. The arrest of Marco Vougny and the others, and the retrieval of the ransom money, must have a devastating effect on Attaque. He had intelligence to the effect that within a few days its leadership would not have the money to pay for petrol, food, and the other routine costs of their existence, and would be driven to undertake bank hold-ups.

Charles Decourten stared at Chaillet with sombre eyes.

—The kidnapping of my daughter, then, is a direct consequence of your "actions" on the *autoroute*. And of your failure to protect her, Commissaire. I shall set up an immediate inquiry into this and those found to be responsible for the police's blunder will be held to full account.

He turned towards Juvin.

—I understand, Monsieur Juvin, that the entrapment of the terrorists on the *autoroute* was the result of certain illegal activities carried out by your department. I want a full and unequivocal statement from you.

—Naturally, Monsieur le Ministre.

—Proceed, Monsieur Juvin.

—Here? Now?

—Yes.

—I do not believe, Monsieur le Ministre, that it would be in the interests of State security for our methodology to be the subject of, uh, inter-departmental "debate". I will willingly brief the Minister in private.

—Damn it, Juvin. You broke the law ...

—I beg to correct you, Monsieur le Ministre. There was no breach of the law. My department had authorisation on the highest level. The scheme, I venture to say, was a brilliant one. Every time Mr Heller made use of his Visa card, whether it was to pay for the car hire, or to pay *autoroute* tolls, the time and location of the transaction was recorded not only in the Visa main computer, as is normal, but also in our own. I doubt that you would wish to know the technical details, Monsieur le Ministre. Suffice it to say it was done with the knowledge and consent, indeed the direct participation, of Mr Heller. I therefore cannot see where an illegality has occurred.

—Your brilliant scheme, Monsieur Juvin, may have resulted in the recovery of the ransom and the arrest of three of the terrorists, but it has also led directly to the kidnapping of my daughter and further even more extreme demands from them.

—Sad to say, there is a price attached to every success.

In the present situation, the strategy to be used was the classic one of delay, Juvin continued. They must force the kidnappers to make contact again and again: as the last of their money ran out they would either have to make concessions or resort to ever more desperate expedients – bank hold-ups and so on, thereby risking capture. He said that while it was of course very shocking for those close to a kidnap victim to have to see a loved one exposed to such terrible threats, the fact that they had posed Isabelle with a copy of yesterday's *Le Monde*, furnishing proof of life, indicated a readiness to follow the rules of such negotiations, and lent support to the view that they would not act irrationally or precipitately. They were out to obtain money and 'standing', and would negotiate. He believed that they were probably at their wits' end and ready to accept a counter-offer, a system of step-by-step ransom payments. A comparatively small sum could be paid to them in the first place, they could be told that this was 'on account', while further sums were raised and 'other details were worked out'. Since they desperately needed money, he believed they would clutch at any straw. The negotiations would in due course afford an opportunity for their capture.

Charles Decourten said that all this would take time, would it not?

—Yes, Juvin agreed, we must play for time.

The Minister spread his arms and let them drop.

—Can you not see, Monsieur Juvin? She cannot hold out. She is a claustrophobic, and they are holding her in a tiny confined space, without windows or light. She is highly emotional – you saw. She does not have the resources to live under such conditions, under such a threat. At any moment her poor mind will break.

His eyes went over the faces of the others assembled in the room, all of them professionals who knew the score. They provided the Minister with little comfort. This was how it was, this was the only way. A step-by-step process. His eyes returned to Juvin.

—The hope must be, said Juvin, that there will be a breakthrough sooner rather than later.

Juvin stayed behind when all the others had left. It seemed he had something further to say to the Minister.

Heller waited in the gallery. Three days. Three days left. He was supposed to be an expert on terrorism. But he hadn't really known what it was before. Had known its techniques and its tactics and its aims. But now he knew what it meant to be *terrorised*. To be put in a position of helplessness vis-à-vis someone you love.

In the rue de Varenne the old snow had turned to slush with the onset of the thaw. It was becoming a mire, brown and shiny and thick. Only close to walls and in the gutters did any white snow remain. The street itself had been swept and salted and sanded to facilitate the continuous passage of cars. The flow was heavy this morning and the *porte-cochère* of Matignon was being left open, suggesting that more ministers and officials were expected. It was evident that something important was going on. A large TF1 outside broadcast van was driving into the courtyard, which had been cleared by the Garde Républicaine of the official cars normally parked there. Other media vehicles were arriving. Bunches of electric cables were being connected up, camera dollies positioned for interviews on the steps of Matignon, microphones at the ends of long booms readied. Evidently some important announcement was due to be made after the meeting of ministers. Reporters with hand microphones were stamping about by the Matignon steps, pressing against velvet rope barriers. Government dispatch riders were entering and leaving. The small staff door alongside the main entrance of Matignon was also open and there were people going back and forth between the annexe and the seat of government. Heller observed Le Quineau cross the road, come back, and ten minutes later cross the road again. The bustle and flurry of power.

Juvin was emerging from the Minister's office, his face solemn with satisfaction.

'*Ca y est, c'est fait*. The Minister has resigned.'

'Charles has resigned? What will that achieve?'

'It is a first step,' Juvin said. 'It meets one of their conditions. It will be for them a sign that they are winning, and give us more time ...'

'Gaining time doesn't solve anything in itself.'

'In any case, it was ... required. It will stop all this clamour in the press. The wild speculation.'

He took Heller's arm and started to walk him along the oval gallery, by the full-length portraits of great French statesmen of previous centuries.

'How did you persuade him to go? Ed Riflin couldn't do it.'

'I showed him that it would be in Isabelle's interest if they did not have a pressure point in the government. And in his own interest that the hue and cry in the press should stop. Like this he can go with honour.'

'Beaucousin was right about one thing. In France you are none too keen to get to the bottom of things.'

Juvin had paused by the portrait of Talleyrand; thoughtfully he regarded the astute face of the eighteenth-century statesman. 'A great hero of Charles's,' he observed. 'Of mine, too. A very modern spirit, lucid, unprejudiced, without preconception or adherence to doctrine. A great pragmatist before it was popular to be that. People say he was without principles, somewhat excessively adaptable to successive regimes. Possibly so. But he achieved a great deal for France. Charles modelled himself on him; he possessed his "adaptability", but not the political sagacity. You remember Talleyrand's remark to Napoleon? "Sire, worse than a crime, a mistake!" Charles made a "mistake" . . . and now has had to pay for it.'

The doors of the Minister's office had opened, and Charles Decourten appeared. Seeing Juvin, he hesitated before speaking. 'Whenever you have finished, Fred . . . a minute of your time.' He made an uncertain gesture and went back into his office, leaving the door slightly ajar.

'What "mistake" did Charles make? Comparable to the murder of the duc d'Enghien in the ditches of Vincennes?'

'Fred, I don't believe that it is in the interests of France that a man as eminent as Charles Decourten, enjoying so much public confidence and respect, should be harried and driven from office because of some mistake that he once made. His resignation solves the problem as far as I am concerned. You better go in and see him. He will tell you himself.'

Some mysterious change had taken place in the gorgeous office, depriving it of the electric atmosphere it had possessed until a few minutes ago. The power had gone from it. The banks of special telephones looked like so many instruments on a shop counter. They did not flash or ring. You sensed that the lines were dead.

'I expect Juvin told you about my resignation,' Charles said as Heller entered.

'Yes.'

Charles made a gesture that this was of no real importance any longer. His hands lacked their habitual verve, were heavy with sorrow and tiredness, and the gesture was a curtailed one.

'My career, I gladly would exchange it all if thereby . . . if Isabelle . . . But you know that. You must know that, if you know me at all.'

Heller made a noncommiital gesture. 'I wonder if I do know you, Charles.'

Charles Decourten walked slowly to the side window and looked down at the television and radio and press people assembling in the courtyard.

'I must go down to give my statement. Why I have resigned.' He laughed shrilly, and Heller could feel the painfulness of the laugh. 'What do you mean, you wonder if you do know me? You have known me for twenty years.'

'Have I?'

'Do you imply . . .?'

'Hardly matters now, Charles,' Heller interrupted him.

'It matters to me, Fred.'

'Charles, let's not pursue this . . . it's not the moment. You need to think about what you're going to say to the press.'

'A formula has been devised. I have resigned to . . . to give the government greater freedom of action. I am told it is best for the government, best for my Isabelle, if she is no longer a pawn in this ghastly business. A brief statement . . . Juvin thinks that they will not press me under the circumstances. And that they will stop their libellous insinuations about gold and currency dealings. It's the Bokassa diamonds all over again. What do you think? He says it will be held that I have chosen an honourable way out of a difficult situation.'

All the lightness had left Charles. His movements were devoid now of the swift grace that had always been his. He lumbered about the grand office aimlessly, clumsily, as if unsure of his own dimensions.

'You have an ironic look on your face, Fred.'

'I'm not too worried about your honour, Charles. It seems to be a pretty resilient commodity.'

Charles had become very pale, his head vibrated with the tenseness of the neck.

'Fred. Whatever Bill may have said – or implied – he was *made* to say. They put a script in front of him, the way they put a script in front of Isabelle. For a drink Bill would have said anything they wanted. Apart from which, as you must know, in his latter years Bill couldn't remember what the truth was. Came to believe his own lies. What with all his drinking and bitterness. His own scenarios blew back in his face.'

The polished marble of Charles's hair had gone dull white. His true age, which he had eluded for so long, had caught up with him.

Heller laughed. 'You were always pretty good at dodging between raindrops, Charles . . . I see you haven't lost that skill.'

Charles's eyes flashed with an upsurge of anger. 'I have lived in the real world,' he said. 'As we all have to.'

'Yuh. Only Isabelle couldn't take your "real world", she opted out.'

From the courtyard below the noise of the press and television crews assembling for the ministerial statement had risen to a restive note, and Charles, looking down, shook his head.

He made a wide gesture of supreme worldliness. Some things had to remain forever unsaid, the gesture indicated.

'I have to go to them now,' he said. 'They want my statement for the one o'clock news, and even in making one's exit one cannot be uncooperative towards the media.'

TWENTY-FOUR

CHAILLET AND BOSCH were returning to the quai des Or-fèvres, which could be reached through a series of narrow stairs and twisting passageways from the Palais de Justice, by those who knew these secret back ways. Heller walked with them to a junction of main corridors. He proposed a coffee.

There was a stale smell of cigarette ash and of chlorine-washed floors as the vending machine coffee plopped into paper cups. The wainscoting of the corridors was a dingy beige-brown.

Heller said:

—Look: I've been answering a lot of questions. Can you answer something for me now?

Chaillet glared at him with his chronically suspicious eyes, head nodding. Heller was beyond the Commissaire's comprehension. Heller didn't fit in any of his ready-made categories, and that deeply bewildered Chaillet. What he did not understand made him angry. In Heller's presence he felt left out of some rarefied game – the game of the 'specials' – that was conducted in a language he did not speak, for ends he could not conceive of. He said toughly:

—All right, you're out of there for the moment, but don't count on that being permanent. You don't have the Minister of National Safety to intercede on your behalf now, Eller. People say that your CIA have a free hand on French soil, can operate here with impunity. Funny thing is, nobody told me that. Maybe Juvin forgot to tell me. But since I haven't been told, I don't know, and what I don't know, I can't act on, can I? So I do my job … the way I think it should be done, that's what I do. And whoever you are Eller, in your shadowy life, if you run foul of our laws, I don't play the complaisant husband … You get me?

Heller said:

—I said I wanted to ask you a question, I didn't say I wanted to hear your marital problems.

—Ask Inspector Bosch. I'm busy.

Chaillet finished his coffee, crumpled up the paper cup and threw it down. Then he was off through the secret corridors.

—What you want to know? Bosch demanded.

Heller took a breath.

—There's only three days left, Bosch.

—We're all aware of that.

—Listen, Bosch. Listen to me. Maybe for Chaillet-the-stone it's all in a day's work. A young woman disappears, is kidnapped, violated, murdered, whatever. Happens all the time. You learn to live with the bad taste. Or let it out on the Americans. Or the Algerians … But I don't think it's as simple as that for you. One, because you're at least partly to blame, the protection she was supposed to get was your responsibility, and if she dies you are not going to stop hearing about the way she was kidnapped from under the noses of the French police, the crack anti-terrorist brigade, trained to storm airplanes, climb up sheer cliffs … free-fall from towers. But can't protect one girl in the centre of Paris. And second … secondly, Bosch, I think that … you have some feelings for her. I may be wrong about that but …

He thought Bosch, his long hard frame strung tight, was going to strike out at him.

—What d'you expect me to do, Heller? I can't do miracles.

—Help me.

—Help you! What can you do?

—Bosch, I'm ready to bend some rules, mine, yours, the American government's, anybody's.

—What d'you want from me?

259

—There are things I can't do on my own. I want you to go along with me.

—Where d'you want to go?

—The Goutte d'Or, Heller said.

Bosch drove in his usual style, contemptuous of other road users, whether in vehicles or on foot, throwing the unmarked police car into wild curves and sudden jumps.

Round the corner from the apartment that Marie-Ann Thurillet had rented for the terrorists, Heller told Bosch to stop.

—Wouldn't bet on finding them in! Bosch said with self-satisfied sourness.

Heller got out of the car and went looking around the streets, in doorways, up dim stairs that seemed on the point of collapse, in dark interiors.

—What you going to do, sniff out where they are? Bosch demanded.

Heller seemed to be looking for somebody in these streets of overflowing trash cans and rotting shutters. He looked in the Afro-Antillais beauty salon, in the Café Hotel du Nord, around the derelict Hotel d'Avenir, a squat barely held up by massive wooden buttresses. Blacks in flowing long robes, blacks in jeans. Lighter-skinned Tunisians, Moroccans, Algerians. Iranians. Yugo-slavs. Italians. Greeks. Turks. Heller peered through grimy net curtains at old men in fezzes gloomily huddled at a zinc bar; he stared into Tunisian take-aways, with their piles of beignets, tagines, bastela, couscous, exotic salads. He put his head into little supermarkets redolent of the spices of north Africa.

The person he was looking for wasn't in any of these places.

—Let's go in here, he proposed to Bosch, indicating the café on the corner.

Bosch followed him in. The place was in keeping with the overall seediness of the surroundings, metro and Loto tickets forming a rich mix with the sawdust on the floor. Mirror mosaics missing from walls and pillars. The Wurlitzer Lasergraph,

260

though, was spanking new; the current selection, Johnny Halli-day. Aggressive French rock.

Heller ordered *un Père* at the bar, and for Bosch a pastis.

—Somebody told me to come here, he said to the old guy in a fez behind the bar.

—Ah!

—Said I'd find him here. You know who I mean.

—I don't know him. I don't know this person at all. I haven't any knowledge of him.

—You know him. The one with the bangles. The tall black man. With the ivory bangles. And the necklaces. Goes click-click-click. Like a billiard table. You know the one. Who's got the stuff.

—The stuff? I don't know about that. Excuse me, I have to serve my customers, I don't . . .

—I'm a client, Heller said, low-voiced behind his hand. Has he been in today? Click-Click? When can I find him?

—I don't know who this is that you mean, I don't know any such person but you better try in an hour. Yes. Try in an hour.

They went out into the street again.

Bosch said:

—You know how many of these street dealers there are in Paris? We've gone through a couple of hundred . . .

—You haven't gone through this one, Heller said.

—So we left one out. What makes you think this one's the one.

—I know, Heller said.

—You know? How d'you *know*?

—Listen: I saw him around here, weeks ago, when Juvin first brought me here. I saw him shimmy down the road, bangles clicking and I had a feeling about him. You recognise the type, and there was something about the way he looked up towards the apartment that made me think he knows the people who lived there.

—It's late in the day for a long shot, Bosch said.

—It isn't a long shot.

—What is it then?

—I tried to find him. For weeks. He'd disappeared from the area. Too much police interest. That makes sense, wouldn't you say? OK. Three nights ago I found him. In this café. He was back. I approached him. I said I wanted Sensimilla. He didn't say No, didn't say Yes. Just stood there jangling. I said I wanted crack, and he laughed. He smelled a rat. I walked down the road with him, and we stopped outside the apartment, their apartment, and I looked up and I said: *they* sent me. And he jangled some more and finally he said he could get me some. Named a fancy price, to which I agreed. Give him two or three days, he said.

—He hasn't showed up, Bosch pointed out.

—He sold me a line that crack was hard to get in France. If he's true to type he'll show up. It's not that hard to get. It's just cocaine and bicarbonate of soda and water, all of which I do believe you have got in France. The delay is to justify the fancy price.

Why be a pessimist when for the same price you can be an optimist?

They hung around for an hour, and then they went back to the café. Johnny Halliday had been succeeded by Eddy Mitchell on the Wurlitzer. More aggressive French rock.

The dealer was not there.

They sat down, ordered coffees and waited, closely watching every person who came in through the door.

An old white-haired man with a small black dog.

—*Bonjour chef, ça va?*

—*Ça va, ça va . . . Il fait froid.* He blew in his hands.

—*Alors – un petit cognac pour vous rechauffer?*

A burly boy in a butcher's apron. Ordered a beer at the counter.

A man in a beret.

People came in to buy cigarettes, Loto tickets.

Five minutes. Ten minutes, twenty. No sign of the dealer.

Heller went up to the bar, and asked again:

—Have you seen him?

—What d'you want? I'm too busy. I'm too busy to see anybody.

He reached for a Ricard bottle on the glass shelf, seeing nobody,

262

nothing, and the young thin-faced *Maghrébin* boy with the long eyelashes, who served at table, said confidentially:

—There ... there he is. He comes now.

They heard the click-click of ivory at wrist and neck, and then they saw the tall, lithe black man with dreadlocks, wearing a flowing scarlet and blue and brown burnous and mules on his feet.

He looked around, saw Heller, saw Bosch, and his eyes went right past both, unrecognising, and he turned around and went out again.

—*Merde!* He saw you. Recognises a *flic* when he sees one.

They went after him. He had got a headstart, and he was fast, lithe-limbed, sliding smoothly through the crowd. They glimpsed his multi-coloured form as it disappeared into the teeming throng of the boulevard Barbès, where there were others in the same sort of bright apparel, same hairstyle. In the fading light Heller lost him.

They stood looking around helplessly, and it was a good minute or two before Heller caught sight of a distant fast-weaving form that looked like the dealer, from the speed he was going. A long way down the boulevard.

Heller said to Bosch:

—I'll keep after him while you get the car. Pick me up.

When Bosch drew alongside in the car, Heller jumped in and pointed ahead to where he thought he had seen the brightly robed figure, and Bosch went after him, hurling the little car in ferocious pursuit, through the crowds and the traffic.

They caught sight of the dealer going into a street market and were unable to follow in the car. He was making his way between stalls, past yellow-green mounds of bananas from Martinique, pyramids of pineapples from the Côte d'Ivoire.

—Keep after him, Bosch said, letting Heller out.

Heller shouldered his way through the fruit market, while Bosch made a wide, screaming loop.

A hundred metres along, the fruit market became a fish market, and the dealer was coming into the rue des Poissoniers, looking over his shoulder the whole time, and he didn't even see the small dangerously driven car that was coming straight at him and pulled up with the bumpers slapping his shins. He was big, the dealer, but Bosch quickly spun him around, got his hands twisted up behind his back and handcuffed them, and then kicked his legs wide, and pushed his head in through the open car window. With the next quick movement the gaudy burnous was hoisted unceremoniously up, from behind, exposing a polished nude form hung about with trusses to which substances in plastic bags were attached.

Heller reached the car and got in, and Bosch wound the window up on his side, until the dealer's neck was tightly held in a vice, the sparse flesh under his chin squeezed up into his jaw.

—We haven't got a lot of time, Bosch told the dealer, switching on the ignition of the car and putting it in first. He put his foot on the accelerator and moved the car forward in a sudden jerk which gave a wrench to the dealer's neck held in the vice. The car moved forward slowly and the dealer side-stepped smartly to keep pace and avoid getting his neck broken.

The dealer did not have much to say in the position in which he found himself; the best he could do was splutter and choke and gasp. And sweat. He was sweating profusely and his legs were scissoring at increasing speed to keep up with the gradually increasing speed of the car.

—You have a choice. About where you want to talk. Like this. Or you want to be more comfortable? What'll it be?

When there was no instant answer, Bosch stepped on the accelerator, jerking the car forward and then braked. Saliva was dribbling from the dealer's mouth and he was gagging. His face was contorted and his eyes bulged. Bosch wound up the window a couple of notches tighter.

—Well, what'll it be?

He put his foot on the brake and the sudden stop gave another wrench to the dealer's neck.

—Let me explain to you. You're in a lot of trouble, my black friend. The stuff you have got on you will put you away for between five and ten. Now on the other hand it could happen when I search you thoroughly, all I find is some *shit*, and you tell me it's for your own consumption, you're a consumer, not a trader. Different situation entirely. Want to sit in the back and talk? But don't waste time. If I wind down this window and I have to wind it up again, I'm going to wind it up so tight your Adam's apple is going to pop out of your neck so you look like a castrato. Understood?

He wound down the window very slightly, sufficiently to enable the dealer to breathe and give his answer. After spluttering and gagging for a minute, he decided he would sit in the back of the car. The rear door was opened for him.

Bosch fixed his driving mirror on him.

—Name, he rapped out.

—Inkumsah.

—That your given name or your family name?

—Family.

—What's your given name?

—Krobo.

—All right Krobo. As I said, I'm in a hurry. So I want fast accurate answers. I'm interested in those people who live round the corner from the café. Clients of yours, isn't that so? What's their fix? They like to smoke Sensimilla?

—Yes.

—What else? What other habits have they got? Coke?

—Yes, coke.

—And crack, are they on to crack?

—They tried it.

—I'm told, try it once and you got to have it again and again.

—Yes.

—When was the last time you supplied them?

Bosch could see Inkumsah shaking his head in the mirror.

—Crack's new in France ... not easy to get.

—You got them hooked on crack, and when they wanted more, you told them you couldn't get it. To put up the price. Charming, charming ... Krobo? You have a way of contacting them?

265

—There's a phone number. I leave a message.

—What's the number?

Inkumsah gave a number which was the number of Le Forum in Les Halles.

—That's where you do some of your dealing, isn't it? Heller said. I've seen you there. Are they still picking up the messages for Elvire?

—I don't know. Haven't tried.

—All right, here is what you do, Krobo, Bosch said.

Down by the river bank there was a sense of being removed from the flux and fury of the city, even the noise level was lower here, and on a day like this, cold and foggy and faintly drizzling, Heller and Juvin had the riverside promenade entirely to themselves. The Seine, with its broken back of rushing ice floes, was slime green, and with the texture of alligator scales.

Juvin had brought no encouraging news. The terrorists had made it known that the time of Isabelle's execution remained unchanged. The resignation of the Minister had not been enough to stop the clock from ticking.

'There was a phone call from them. It lasted thirty seconds. When our man did not immediately convey a willingness to comply with all their conditions, the phone was put down.'

Nor had Juvin's network of informants come up with any clues as to where the terrorists might be holding Isabelle.

'The pyramid has been broken. The head is no longer connected with the body. As a result my informants on different levels of the pyramid have no communication with other parts.'

'If they are so desperate, why isn't Gavaudan negotiating?'

'He assumes we are even more desperate, with only twenty-four hours to go. At any rate that is his bluff.'

'You going to call his bluff?'

'We have no alternative. The government cannot be seen to abandon its stance because the person whose life is at stake happens to be the daughter of an ex-minister. The Italian government

266

found itself in a similar situation in the case of Moro. If we give way, then no member of any minister's family is safe.'

'So you're going to let her die?'

'We are doing everything to find her.'

'Without success.'

'So far, that is so, alas!'

'Why her? Why her?'

'They strike at Charles Decourten through his daughter.'

'He's no longer the Minister of National Safety. So why is he a target?'

Juvin stood staring out at the rushing currents swirling and eddying around the prow of the Ile de la Cité, and Heller noted that his eyes were blinking at a more rapid rate than normal.

'You remember the German papers I once told you about, Fred, with their records of things that transpired during the occupation I think I told you that we decided not to open these papers, and I still believe that was the right decision.' He shook his head sombrely. 'Digging up the past is a dangerous business. You saw what happened to Beaucousin. More harm has been done by those who would rectify ancient injustices than by the original injustices. Turns into Greek drama. And there, you know, the fates invariably work out their final twist on the next generation.'

'You did open the German papers'

'I have taken a little peek, from time to time. For purposes of background information. Information that I may say I have never acted upon directly.'

'At the Ministry ... you didn't say what Charles's "mistake" was. You were in a hurry.'

'I am now concerned with more recent "mistakes", Fred.' A delicate frown ruffled his brow, and a pernickety note entered his voice. 'In recent days fixed parameters have been transgressed, ground rules have been broken. There have been "mistakes" committed that we cannot countenance ... You must make them understand in Washington, Fred, that this is France, not El Salvador.'

Heller nodded slowly, full of understanding. 'I couldn't agree with you more, Claude. As you must know, the "mistake" was not mine.'

'Yes, I do know that.'

'I will give them your message. I will make it clear that you have shown enormous forbearance in the cause of Franco-American relations but that those relations will be severely strained should there be further "mistakes" committed. Over-drawn as we may already be, Claude, given our past contributions . . .'

'I have not forgotten.'

'It was Charles who betrayed his brother, wasn't it?'

Juvin's head nodded in the direction of Notre-Dame, Châtelet, then swung back towards the Louvre.

'At Bill Gibson's behest. Bill was the instigator. The political reasoning was sound. A grave misjudgment to characterise Charles as a lightweight. He has always been a man of inordinate ambitions and desires. And at that time what he desired most was Annette du Breuil-Hélion de La Quéronnière.'

'I had come to that conclusion. All right. Tell me the final twist, Claude. The Greek drama.'

The swollen river was virtually up to their feet. The broken branches of trees had fallen before them. River refuse had been washed up and lay across the cobbled walk. A few metres further on, the embankment was impassable due to flooding. There was no way to continue along here, and Juvin, eyes blinking rapidly, turned back.

He said, 'I must return to see if there have been developments.'

'The final twist,' Heller demanded.

Juvin spoke with a kind of grandiose peevishness. 'There were things that I was not told. And you know that I do not like not to know. For example, that Charles Decourten has been for thirty years a CIA asset. That Bill owned him.' He made a tut-tutting sound with his mouth. 'That is no way to behave between friends. The final twist? In due course, you will discover it. Or not, as the case may be. It makes no difference to the practicalities of the situation. It relates only to strands of motivation.'

268

That was all he was willing to say. Claude Juvin's sense of quid pro quo was exquisitely exact.

Krobo Inkumsah sat at the copper bar of Le Forum, drinking a Schweppes. He was less colourful today, wearing a fur-lined lumber-jacket and jeans. Bosch and Heller sat at a small table, partly concealed by a coat stand overloaded with wet coats that dripped onto the floor, making a puddle. There was the smell of synthetic materials drying out in an enclosed, poorly ventilated space.

The final day. So far the bait hadn't been taken. Perhaps they were not that hooked, after all. Glimpsing himself in the mould-speckled Pilsner mirror running the length of the bar, Heller saw a man he scarcely recognised. He was unshaven, his eyes were red-rimmed. From time to time he fingered the heavy Smith & Wesson in the voluminous pocket of his trench coat.

They went to all the bars on Inkumsah's circuit. They went from one to the other, and then came back to the first again. And there was no relief, nothing to hold out hope as the hours that were left ticked away. If they kept to the timetable, the execution would take place at 19.00. When it was dark.

The day had begun with fog and cold rain and the pollution from densely jammed traffic lying heavy in the air. The sort of a day when it was best not to breath. The first round of the dealer's circuit had been done in a mood of growing desperation, and now they were back again at square one. In the long narrow bar in Les Halles, where there was hardly room to sit. Heller was exercising a desperate sort of calm. Keep thinking, keep thinking. This wasn't the moment to give up.

He said to Bosch:

—They had a personal animosity against Gibson. The United States. Maybe they had to kill the bugbear, to settle old scores. I understand that psychology. But what kind of man would pick on an innocent girl, because she's the daughter of Charles Decourten? There isn't even the element of putting pressure on the government, now.

Bosch's manner was muted with Isabelle's death getting closer every minute. That got to him, redirected his habitual anger, inflicted on him wounds of pain and guilt and loss that he couldn't comprehend. God knows what weird emotion he felt for her, but he felt something. Heller was digging around inside the despair, trying to draw understanding and solutions from thin air.

—Did you ever go into Gavaudan's background? What his origins were?

—The centre of France. Ordinary. Nothing at all special. Father ran a small hardware store, with a line in fishing tackle.

—Alive still?

—No, parents both dead. Mother when he was a child, father when he was fourteen or fifteen. His own family he abandoned in seventy-seven. And has not been in contact with them since. His other "family" is the group. And one of that "family", he killed. Marie-Ann Thurillet.

—What makes this man feel something? What does he love? Anything? History? The implacable unfolding of history? What made him become a history teacher? What's the history lesson he wants to teach us?

Heller wasn't really asking Bosch these questions; he was talking to himself: a conversation of last recourse.

—He wants to teach us, Heller said, speculatively answering his own question, that his view of history is the right one. He wants to be right. Being wrong is too painful ... Identifies with Ahab, and the quest for the white whale. He lives a fantasy. Perhaps the whole period of clandestinity is fantasy. What was his real life? What was it before? He's in his early forties, born ...?

—Forty-four. November forty-four.

—After the Liberation. Most of France was free, the occupation was over. Was it a family business, the hardware store in Nevers?

—No. They'd come from a small town near Vichy. Before that they were someplace else. They'd moved around in his early childhood. Lived in different places before settling in Nevers.

270

People were moving about a good deal after the war. Establishing themselves in new places.

—OK, a lonely solitary childhood. Not many friends. Perhaps none at all. And he was an only child. And then the mother dies when he's still small.

—Yes. He was brought up by the father. Father never re-married. He was "political", a hardline Communist. People say there was quite a closeness between father and son. And they do say that the father had a mania about the Americans. They were his bugbear too. Used to go around saying Hitler was a tool of American business. Big business needed the war to get America out of the Depression.

—Any record of involvements with military far-Left groups? The father, I mean.

—No, no, nothing we turned up. Looked after the shop. Subscribed to *L'Humanité*. Went to meetings. Voted for the Communists. Like millions of others. Belonged to some Franco-Soviet friendships associations. Took the boy on a trip to Moscow once, strictly the tourists. That's all. We turned up nothing sinister. The only thing . . . the only unexplained thing about him was he changed his name, the father. But then lots of people do that.

—Gavaudan wasn't his real name?

—*Our* man was born with that name. But the father was called something else on the marriage certificate. It was a wartime marriage. She was pregnant. You know how it used to be, in small villages. She was in her late teens. Barely out of school. He wasn't much older. Kids.

—You say they lived in a small village? What was the name on the marriage certificate?

—Gaudin. Something like that—Godin. Yes, Godin.

—Godin? The village was in the Morvan?

—Yes.

—Was it called Courteny?

—That was the place. Mean something to you?

Oh yes, it meant something all right. It meant the final twist.

The Greek drama. It meant that vengeance leaps across generations, and that village tales become myth, and that myth enters
the psyche and becomes the matrix of the man, it meant ...

He saw a large figure come in in a black leather one-piece
motor-cyclist's outfit with traverse zips slashing the torso and
abdomen, wearing a crash helmet. The crash helmet was removed
and Heller put his hand on the revolver inside his raincoat pocket;
he pulled Bosch back further behind the dripping coat stand.

The black leather one-piece was glistening wet from the rain
and there was the smell of dankness coming from her as she
lumbered across the room, a big bear of a woman. When she saw
the dealer, her eyes fixed on him for a moment. She gave a faint
signal, and then she went up to the counter and ordered a Ricard.

She was watching in the mirror, and when she observed the
dealer go down to the toilets she paid for the Ricard, drank it and
followed him down the stairs.

Two minutes later she came up, walking fast, putting on her
crash helmet.

Heller and Bosch followed her out and saw her get astride a big
black Yamaha. She started it with a booted foot. Bosch ran for his
car, with Heller behind him.

Almost immediately they lost her as the Yamaha darted and
dodged through the thick traffic on the boulevard de Sébastopol.
A red light held her long enough to enable them to catch up. She
did not go through the light, they noted. She was not taking the
risk of being pulled up by traffic cops.

Over the bridge and past the Palais de Justice, with the rain
turning to sleet and car bonnets steaming; they kept seeing her
surge ahead of them and disappear, and Bosch found her again
only by shooting red lights and running the gauntlet of the
slingshot traffic unloosed against him at junctions. Across to the
Left Bank. The place St Michel. Evening looming.

They lost her again, and guessed she would have turned into the
boulevard St Germain because that was the route the kidnap
vehicle had been seen to take. Some hard driving and shooting
of lights brought them another glimpse of the Yamaha's high

fleeting tail-light, and Bosch kept after it with maniacal determination, criss-crossing traffic lanes, wildly cutting across other cars, hurtling through narrowing spaces, while he worked accelerator and brake in frantic go-stop rhythm. On the long one-way boulevard the solid lanes of traffic afforded obstacles to the car that Gisèle Chenu on the motor cycle was able to get around.

At the Pont Sully, daylight fading fast, time running out, Heller held onto a twisting red point in a hodgepodge of lights that blurred into multi-coloured smears and smudges and streaks and saturn-rings.

—She took the quai, Heller called out.

Along the Seine the traffic became two-way – wipers not clearing the windscreen fast enough, yellow dazzle from on-coming traffic. They were following a single twisting tail-light. Past the university buildings of the Faculté des Sciences, through the prismatic rain and into the disordered ominous dusk. In the pointillist pattern of impending night it was becoming increasingly difficult to hang on to the Yamaha, with the glare of headlights dazzling the eye and the dense jumble of reds and yellows confusing the picture.

The roundabout of the pont d'Austerlitz was police-controlled this time of evening when the traffic was at its peak. One hundred metres ahead of them, Gisèle Chenu on the Yamaha had had to stop, with the rest of the vehicles in her lane, and Bosch used this stop to gain a few more metres.

With the go signal the Yamaha leapt forward becoming a blur rushing towards the vanishing point. Heller held on to it, held on to it, held on to it, while Bosch forced his way through the dense traffic sludge, and then in the complex tangle at the bridge Heller no longer saw the twisting light.

—We lost her! Heller yelled.

They were in the full flow of the traffic flood, with lanes splitting for the alternative turns, and a decision had to be made instantly.

A train rumbled across the railway bridge spanning the river to the Gare d'Austerlitz. The bridge's cast-iron columns shook. The Seine was green, flecked with sleet.

Left over the bridge. To Bercy . The Omnisports Centre. The Gare de Lyon. Bastille. The Right Bank. Right, to the *autoroute*, to Lyon. Metz/Nancy. Straight on for the railway station, the long dark cobbled quays stretching all the way to the eastern docks and Ivry. Warehouses. Railway goods yards. Sand dumps. Cement companies. Scrap-metal merchants. Wharves. Coal barges. To the periphery.

—Keep straight on, Heller yelled.

Even if you did not know which way to go, a direction had to be taken. One had to follow the thread, even the faintest of threads traced in the mind. *Father, you must take the stony road, the bumpy road*, and this was a bumpy road of cobblestones, this *quai*. And she'd said, *Father, in a storm the tree must bend with the wind*, and here on the margins of the flooded river, trees had bent and broken. ... *you must take the bumpy road, Father, the nauseous road* ...

Heller felt the nausea in her stomach, the flip-flop of the tyres going over cobbles, the terror in her airless confined space, chained up like a dog, tiles blowing off the roof, trees bending, breaking along the river bank in the high winds, the perpetual passage of trucks, their cargoes rattling and clanking at every bump, bottles vibrating. He entrusted himself to sympathetic magic. Keep going straight. The stony road. The bumpy road. The nausea. Follow the thread. The thread of nausea.

Past Austerlitz it was no more the city of light, the brilliance petered out abruptly. In the rapidly darkening sky the ancient smoke stacks and the level-luffing cranes and the grab cranes were disappearing like rubbed-out pencil drawings.

On the left was the river, dark between bridges, with the occasional minuscule light of a slow-moving coal barge. On the right the rotting quayside, warehouses, garages, goods yards, one or two dingy bars and cafés, derelict tenements with broken window-panes, disintegrating shutters, roofs open to the sky. Dark and empty. The Pearl of Asia restaurant was windowless, bricked up to keep squatters out. But the occasional naked light bulb in an upper storey was an indication that a few people still lived in these abandoned buildings.

The traffic was continuous, unrelenting. Two lanes of on-coming yellow lights, two lanes of red tail-lights, and as Bosch perilously pushed through the sludge, Heller glimpsed again, far ahead, a single light, a darting rectangular dot that twisted and turned with a particular degree of hurry.

Any moment now it was going to be night. The sky was turning from a patchy dark blue to deep mauve, and the black tinge was spreading.

Then the weaving dot had vanished.

Heller said to pull up. The bumpy road, the stony road. The margin of the river. The nausea in his stomach.

The thread, the faint thread which was all he had to go by, stopped here.

They were out of time. It was night.

Heller stepped from the car, peered over gates into junk-littered backyards, bent low to look under half-lowered iron shutters, peaked his hands to squint into ill-lit bars frequented by truck drivers and dock workers.

There was the occasional light. A young mother passed across a window, breast-feeding her baby; a man leaned out to pull dilapidated shutters closed. You could look through the gaping window spaces of buildings to unlit warehouses and scrap-metal yards on the other side.

A white brightness lasting seconds, followed by dark, and then the white brightness again, and then again the dark. He watched intently. It was a couple of hundred metres in the direction of Ivry. The light was at ground level, coming from within a yard, diffusing upwards, laying down a pattern of shadows across the fast-moving traffic.

Shadows in wrong places.

—Come on! he said to Bosch, running towards where he had seen the brightness and the shadows.

It was a low decaying building, in an advanced stage of collapse, supported by wooden buttresses. Ground and first storey windows were bricked up. On the two upper floors, light leaking from around the edges of closed shutters. The shutters were rotten, gaps must have been stuffed with paper and rags to keep the light minimal.

The people living there didn't want to be noticed.

The yard was closed off by a solid high wooden gate. Heller peered through a crack in the gate and made out a segment of a motor-cycle wheel.

He turned to Bosch.

—We've got to get in there. Into the yard. Come on.

The house next door also had a yard, with a rusty iron gate, two metres high, padlocked, topped by spikes.

Bosch, fingers interwoven, formed a step for Heller, and Heller climbed onto the top bar of the gate. As he leapt down there was again the flare of white light from the adjoining yard, lasting some seconds. Bosch came over the gate unaided, and got out his pistol.

The barrier separating the two yards was a wooden paling fence with many boards missing. There was a large enough space between gate post and house for a man to squeeze past.

They looked into the next yard and in the flare of a hand-held halogen floodlight witnessed the final preparations for the execution. It was going to be recorded for history. He was a historian after all, Gavaudan, and a historic revenge is nothing without a record, the record is part of it. So that the world will know. And understand. And learn its history lesson.

The yard was cluttered with junk. A former garage. Worn-bare tyres, rusty piles of car components, engine parts, rust-consumed exhausts, mangled wings, a deeply dented car door, a water reservoir, disintegrating rubber hoses, oil canisters. Mattresses displaying their rusty innards, a big heap of rotting polyurethane foam cushions, broken window-panes . . .

A lean-to of corrugated plastic roofing covered three quarters of the yard.

Isabelle, her mouth sealed with a wide band of black sealing-tape wound tightly around her lower face, was breathing by noisily snorting air through her nose. She had been stood up against the loading bay of the van, and someone inside it was attaching the chains of her hands to cargo grips, tightening the chains so that she was confined within the space of the open rear doors. Half her face muzzled by the black tape, all her terror was in her eyes, her enormous spilling-over eyes.

When the yard was dark again Heller pushed through the gap between fence and wall, Bosch following close behind. They saw ferocious, bearish Gisèle come out of the van; it was she who had attached Isabelle's chains and she had clearly relished her task. Gavaudan, very still and white, face lit up in the glow of the squat clay pipe in his mouth, was waiting with heavily lowered eyelids. There were four or five others, dimly seen, carrying pistols, submachine-guns, rifles. The 'foot-soldiers', the base of the pyramid. Hoarse low voices, urgent and tense, overlapping; words indistinct, but with a taunting note in the woman's voice, and the import was she would do it for him. If he wanted her to. Whoever was going to do it, it had to be done now.

The burning paste glowed around Gavaudan's face more rapidly, and the woman's voice was harsh and driving, impatient with this overlong preparation for the act. *I will do it*, Heller heard her offer again insistently, and when the halogen lamp flared once more she was standing with her gun at Isabelle's neck, ready. Heller, flat on the ground behind a pile of tyres, had the 357 in his hand, and Bosch had his pistol aimed. Heller sighted along the barrel, without hope, you had to live without hope, that was the only way, and even if there was no real chance of a successful outcome, the odds being too great, two against six or seven, maybe more inside the building, the attempt had to be made, that was what it was all about. He looked towards Bosch and nodded to him grimly, and was glad to see that the sour-faced policeman was ready to go too, without hope, without anything, because that was how it had to be.

Some muffled words from the man, from Gavaudan to 'intel-lectual Annie', scribe and think-tank, poisonous philosopher of violence, helper and bedmate of the Chief: perhaps at the last minute she would shrink back, feel some particle of womanly squeamishness. Gavaudan was in need of her 'moral support' for this ceremonial murder. He gave an instruction and the lights went off. He was the Chief, he was in command. Nobody else. He wasn't going to be hurried in his *mise-en-scène*, poised on the edge of history. In the dark he and Annie consulted out of earshot of impatient Gisèle, who wanted to get it over with, not so much fuss, kill the little cunt and be done.

Heller took a handkerchief from his pocket. Using his teeth, he tore a narrow strip down one side and then reached out to dip the rest of the handkerchief in a shimmering mauve puddle between cobblestones, and when the handkerchief was thoroughly soaked he crawled on his elbows and knees towards the pile of foam cushions. He did not know how many seconds of darkness he had left. When the floods came on again, that'd be the signal. It was going to be done before the eye of history.

Heller put the soaked handkerchief between two rotting foam cushions in the pile, and he pulled out the dry strip, away from the cushions. Working his way backwards he put himself behind the pile and lit the end of the strip inside his cupped hands. He watched the flame catch and climb and when it reached the soaked handkerchief become a fire flash. It ignited the foam, and in an uprush of thick noxious smoke the flames spread, reaching up to the plastic roofing of the lean-to.

Smoke enclosed the core of flame, keeping the yard dark. Harsh lung-straining sounds of coughing and choking came from all around. Heller was lying as flat as he could, breathing shallowly, close to the ground, limiting his intake of the poisonous air as much as possible.

He heard shouts to get water; saw part of the dense darkness thin out; saw someone climb a ladder. Somebody else was shouting about a hose. Was there a pail? Flame broke through the thick black smoke, orange-bright and yellow and pink, spreading through the cluttered junk, igniting everything inflammable, and finally reaching up to the corrugated plastic roofing. The fumes from the burning plastic became dense and dimmed the outshoots of flame. Too late. He and Bosch had been seen and marked, and from the dark came bursts of gunfire. Heller held his gun in his two hands, crawling on elbows and knees, holding his fire, until the inner lining of flame stuck out yellow-tongued, and then he fired in double action mode into the white glimmer at the edge of the smoke and Bosch was firing as well, crouched low, handkerchief over his nose and mouth, firing as he moved in sudden dashes and zigzags. The burning plastic was producing an impenetrable black pall, from which brief flashes of flame shot out before being doused again by even denser smoke. Heller waited for the flame to stick out its tongue, and when it did, fired at a flickering form and saw a man go down, dropping a Kalashnikov. Some of the other 'foot-soldiers' were spraying the whole area with semi-automatic fire from heavy police riot guns, and old tyres and engine parts and metal canisters were being sent scooting and spinning around the yard with the concentrated force of these fusilades. In the moments of brightness Heller sought to fix everybody's position in his mind: Gavaudan, Gisèle the bear, Annie, 'the foot-soldiers'. He couldn't see Isabelle. Where was she? Had the smoke overcome her? *They* could afford to fire off rounds in wild sweeping bursts, but he and Bosch had to respond with single shots fired at clearly defined targets, because Isabelle was in there somewhere, in all this thick choking smoke, maybe being used as a human shield, maybe already dead, executed by the Big Bear. Flat on the ground Heller breathed the last of the good air and waited for flashes of light to pick off targets when he could. He saw someone with a Skorpion go down, but it wasn't Gavaudan and it wasn't Gisèle and it wasn't Annie, and they were the principal danger to Isabelle, they were the ones who would execute her even in the thick of all this, just so it was done, for the record, for history. For the Idea. He saw Bosch make a weaving dash towards the van. Isabelle had to be in there. She was chained to the cargo grips. Had to be. Where else? Out of the interior of the van came bursts of automatic fire. One of the fuckers was in there with a Skorpion. Shit! The fucker was using Isabelle as a shield. Where? Where? More bursts from inside the van, shit! shit!

Heller couldn't return the fire because of Isabelle being in there. Where else could she be? He had a glimpse of Bosch making a dash up to the front of the van, saw him stick his head in through the driver's window and fire several times into the back of the vehicle and immediately the gunfire from inside stopped. Then one of the other bastards got Bosch in the neck, and so it was just Heller now. In the next flare-up he caught sight of Gavaudan and Gavaudan caught sight of him, and for a moment they took each other in, face to face, and both fired simultaneously, Gavaudan a burst from the Skorpion that sent rusty oil drums spinning across the yard. Heller's single shot, more accurate, got Gavaudan in the chest and he went down shouting to Gisèle, giving her the command now at which he had balked before. Shotgun in hand, she was going to the back of the van, the open loading-bay, to carry out the order. Heller was trying to get a fix on her that would not risk Isabelle inside, but he couldn't get the she-swine in his sights, with the smoke and everything, and it was looking hopeless, and then from inside the van there came a burst of automatic fire and he saw the Gorgon-head burst like a ripped-open sack. There were more shots, some of which he must have fired as he was blacking out and hearing the different sirens of the *pompiers* and the police and the SAMU ambulances.

TWENTY-FIVE

THEY KEPT ISABELLE in the clinic for one night only, let her leave the next morning. Heller went with her to the Palais de Justice to make their deposition before the *juge d'instruction*.

The office was small and poky and cluttered; dossiers tied up with ribbons were piled in stacks on desk and side tables and floor, and submerged under years of dust all along the tops of metal cabinets, right up to the ceiling.

A woman at a stenotype machine took down their answers to the judge's questions concerning the shoot-out. Without emotion Isabelle told how Bosch had shot the man in the van and how she had taken the dead man's Skorpion and with it shot Gisèle Chenu, who was coming to kill her. 'I saw her head burst,' she told the judge, 'and knew I had killed her, and I was glad.'

Heller took Isabelle back to the rue Monsieur le Prince. There was no food in the apartment and they went to the *place* and ate an omelette in the brasserie opposite the Jardin Luxembourg.

Afterwards, they walked in the park under the dripping plane trees; the thaw was continuing. He thought she was astonishingly well, considering what she had been through. The doctors at the clinic had said the same. No indication of post-traumatic stress syndrome. Some people made surprisingly quick and effective recoveries from this sort of ordeal, while others went under. People sometimes discovered amazing capacities within themselves, when it was a question of survival; there was the story of a music-lover who had survived Auschwitz by playing Mozart's operas in his head.

'You really are amazing,' Heller said to her, 'the way you've recovered. I'm proud of you. You're really over it.'

'It's because I'm such an actor,' she said with a sly kind of self-knowledge.

'Well, that was some "performance" you gave on the video!'

'They told me I must give a performance to save my life.'

'Did you consciously put in the clues? About the stony road, the broken trees by the river bank?'

'I don't know, Fred. It was happening to someone else. It wasn't real to me. Have you never felt that?'

'Yes; I have felt it.'

It was a sparkling fresh day, clear and bright, and he had never seen her eyes so unclouded, so free of portents.

'You look good,' he told her, 'you look amazingly good. Something has changed, hasn't it?'

'I've come through the nightmare,' she said.

'Yes, I can see that.'

'It's lovely, this park,' she said, looking around as if she had never been there. 'I never noticed the children before. I suppose I was always rehearsing something.'

He took her hand, and they walked like lovers of long standing, and he felt a new stillness in her, an abatement of something, a sort of return to normality after all the frenzies of the recent past. When she looked at him with her clear bright eyes he understood that the nightmare was indeed over. And from the strange becalmed state that seemed to have sprung up between them, he had a premonition that so was their uneasy love.